ENTER THE EX~~~~~~~~~~~~~~~D
OF *BL~~~~~~*

*Kate Richmond.* Be~~~~ ~~~~~~, and brilliant, she's come back to China to practice the surgery she'd studied in America. A missionary's daughter, she's ill-equipped to handle passion.

*Thomas Blake.* His desire for Kate is almost equal to the hatred he feels for a powerful entrepreneurial family. An adventurer and businessman, he is torn between his profits and his soul.

*Shen Sun Lung.* A charismatic Communist leader, he'd learned the toils of the land and its peasants the hard way. Ready to give his life to his cause, he is not prepared to fall in love with Kate.

*Ling Ling.* She's an exquisite concubine for the Nationalists, but inside, her heart beats for the Communists—and her idealistic brother, Shen Sun Lung.

*Yang Ho.* A Nationalist general, his sadistic nature flourishes in the Revolution, whether it be in capturing Communists or in humiliating women.

PLEASE TURN THE PAGE FOR SOME OF
THE RAVE REVIEWS OF
*BLOOD RED ROSE*

"Intrigue, adventure, and romance are mixed in equal parts in this readable saga of life and love in revolutionary China. Grant is a skilled storyteller. . . ."

*Chattanooga Times*

# BLOOD RED ROSE

"A vivid account of revolutionary China and the ordinary people involved."

*Library Journal*

"Provides superb entertainment, continuous action, and a unique view of the Red insurgency. Grant writes with both panoramic sweep and a keen eye for the fascinating detail. This is an exciting, crisply paced tale, a watershed event of the twentieth century from an unexpected viewpoint."

*St. Louis Post-Dispatch*

# A SWEEPING EPIC OF CHINA

"His description of the poor, peasant childhood of Shen is as moving as anything ever written by Pearl Buck, and the reader sees and smells rural China as it was on the eve of revolution."

*Rave Reviews*

# BLOOD RED ROSE

## MAXWELL GRANT

FAWCETT CREST • NEW YORK

A Fawcett Crest Book
Published by Ballantine Books
Copyright © 1986 by Maxwell Grant

Library of Congress Catalog Card Number: 85-23810

ISBN 0-449-21289-0

This edition published by arrangement with Macmillan Publishing Company, a division of Macmillan, Inc.

Manufactured in the United States of America

First Ballantine Books Edition: June 1987

*For Britt*

# Contents

# List of Principal Characters

KATE RICHMOND — American doctor. Daughter of American missionary parents, born in China and friend of communist leader, Shen.

THOMAS BLAKE — American businessman turned gunrunner, soldier-of-fortune. Born in Shanghai.

SHEN SUN LUNG — Communist leader; close friend of Kate Richmond. Born in the "Village of Wild Grass."

JANEY EDWARDS — Daughter of rich Far East English trading family. Also China-born. Kate's closest female friend.

CLEM RICHMOND — Kate's missionary doctor father.

BETTE RICHMOND — Kate's missionary doctor mother.

SIR NIGEL EDWARDS — Janey's father and head of the Edwards's Far East empire.

SHEN FU — Father of Shen Lung; a farmer and sometime coolie.

LIN TAN — Shen's mother.

SHEN LING LING — Shen's voluptuous older sister. Concubine of Ma Yao and subsequently, Ma Yen. Shanghai courtesan.

LIN HUA — Shen's uncle. A cruel grain merchant.

| | |
|---|---|
| LIN PAR-GAI | Lin Hua's wife; Shen's kindly aunt. |
| YANG HO | Nationalist (Kuomintang) Army chief for southern region. Sadistic general and Shen's hated enemy. |
| MA YAO | Shen's first "scholar master" (teacher) and an important Nationalist Government figure. |
| MA YEN | Ma Yao's father. A mandarin of Shanghai. |
| HSING-TAO | Gateman to Ma Yen and Ling Ling. |
| WANG LEE | Shen's chameleon cousin (although not of Lin Hua's family); a roguish spy for the Communists; in charge of their southern-area intelligence. Bears a strong resemblance to Shen. |
| HWANG | Railway engine driver, Communist, and close friend of Shen. |
| YU-MA | Towering railway engine fireman; deaf mute. Shen's "bodyguard." |
| WU ZHAO | Former Kuomintang officer turned Communist. Intellectual and teacher. |
| LU CHIEN | Close friend of Kate; graceful elegant wife of Wu. |
| SONG WEI | Female communist guerilla fighter; Kate Richmond's assistant. |
| PO | Communist guerilla fighter; close friend of Song Wei. |
| JOHN CARPENTER | American wire service correspondent; friend of Kate. |

China, oh China,
Land of my dreams,
China, oh China
And all that seems
So full of the grandeur
Of mountains and streams
So full of the people
Who make you so loved.

China, oh China,
Where will your life go
If the red in the river
Now starts to flow?
—CHINA THE LOVED,
Tuan-ho Hsu (English
translation, c. 1925)


An' the dawn comes up like thunder
outer China 'crost the Bay!
—MANDALAY,
Rudyard Kipling

# BOOK I
# Homecoming

1926

# 1

*The coast of China rose like a dragon from sleep as the sun* came up and Kate saw its tumultuous beauty on the horizon. She had known it would be this beautiful. She stood very still a long time before moving on.

Then she saw the Chinese youth, although she did not at first pay him any attention. She saw him out of the corner of her eye, scurrying along, hurrying, intent on something. But there was no reason to suppose he was looking for her. She supposed, if she stopped mentally to suppose at all, that he was on some errand; that he had been sent to fetch something from the aft deck behind her. All sorts of things were stored there, between the deck chairs and the life rafts. It was the point at which the ship rose, pitched, and fell its utmost; so it was not much frequented by passengers. But Kate went there. It was high above where the great brass screws drove the ship through the water like a soaring horse. She loved to stand there alone and feel the salt spray on her face.

She had, in fact, been out strolling since before dawn, knowing the stillness that comes then, waiting out the precious early moments of that absolute easy peace of the first hours of the sun. She liked to rise early but today had been special. She had wanted that first glimpse of the coast of China—and she had not been disappointed.

Then she realized the steward had stopped. She was aware of someone standing near her. She turned to see this small and obviously agitated young man. Kate looked questioningly at him, which was his cue to speak. He was quite breathless.

"Excuse me, Doctor Richmond," he blurted out in English, but with such speed it surprised Kate. "The ship's surgeon is busy operating and there is another case requiring urgent medical attention. The captain sends his compliments and asks will you help?"

"Of course," Kate answered promptly, "I'll be only too happy to—but I will need my bag."

"This was anticipated and it has been sent for . . . if you will just follow me . . . ?"

Kate nodded and the young man took off. She had to follow briskly to keep up.

As they strode hurriedly back along the deck, Kate collected her thoughts. She supposed the steward to be about nineteen. But even with all her experience it was still hard to tell. They were such an ageless race. He was dressed in a white cabin steward's jacket and black cotton trousers, and his trousers were short and showed bare ankles above his black Chinese work slippers. His hair was very black and shiny but stood up bristly around the part. It occurred to Kate that he had almost certainly used English to impress her. Most on the ship knew she spoke both the Cantonese and Mandarin dialects fluently. But his English had been faultless and way above that of the typical cabin steward.

After following for what seemed like some minutes, Kate realized they were now quite deep in the ship and, she suspected, heading for the crew's quarters. The space was more confined. There were more and thicker pipes overhead. And the smells of engine oil and Chinese cooking were strong and unmistakable.

Presently the steward turned a sharp left down a short passage and halted in front of a door. He took a key from his pocket and opened it, and then stood back to allow Kate to enter.

Inside it was very dark. The steward switched on the light and closed the door. Kate saw her bag on the floor beside the bunk. Then she saw a man in oiled and dirty seaman's clothes lying on the bunk. She knew immediately he was dead. But she carefully undid his shirt and listened to his chest.

"What happened to this man?" she said eventually, replacing her stethoscope in her bag.

"He fell from a derrick, Doctor."

Kate looked at the young steward again. He was not stupid, and she had not lived all her early life in China without gaining a rudimentary understanding of their ways.

"How are you called?" she asked in a kindly way, in Mandarin, judging him, from his fine high cheekbones, to be from the North.

"Wang Lee," he said.

"Now then, Wang," Kate said, pronouncing it in the Chinese way of "Wong" instead of the Westernized "Wang," and using his family name, which comes first in China, to observe the correct formalities, "you and I both know it is unlikely this man fell from a derrick. Shall we examine him together?"

The young man looked at Kate and wondered if he had bee. right to trust her; and indeed, if he should trust her further.

"If you wish it," he said finally.

Together they examined the man, gently turning his dead body first this way and then that. He was very old. All the cuts and contusions were consistent with a prolonged fight. His right fist had something in it. It was closed very tightly—so tight that Kate could not open it. He would go to his grave with it closed now, for rigor mortis was beginning to set in. Kate looked closer. The old man's fist held a very crumpled piece of plain red, cheap Chinese paper. It was a simple thing, and he was dead and long past caring. But for all the ignominy of his death below the waterline, in the dirty and cramped quarters so far removed from the grand life of the passenger liner above, Kate could not help thinking that that clenched fist, with the forearm bent half upward in its final grasp, had a certain triumphant look to it.

However, there were practical things to attend to. They covered him with a thin cotton sheet and Kate turned again to Wang Lee.

"Did you know he was dead?"

"He was not when I left him, Doctor. I hoped we might save him. I came as soon as I could."

"But how did it happen?"

"In a fight, as you supposed, Doctor."

"You were not there?"

"No, Doctor."

"Tell me, then, for I must have something for the death certificate."

The young man looked at her and began slowly: "Some of the Chinese supervisors fell upon him, Doctor. He was working in the engine room shoveling coal. But the sweatband around his head became loose and the piece of paper fell from it. One of the supervisors saw it, though the old one clutched it tightly to him and still holds it as you see."

"But why did they hit him so?"

The young man looked at Kate long and hard again and then answered slowly once more:

"Because, Doctor, they had asked him to tell where he got the piece of paper . . ."

"And—?"

The young man seemed reluctant to go on. Kate said it for him:

"And he had sworn an oath not to tell . . . ?"

"Yes, Doctor."

She paused then, looking at the young Wang Lee in an exasperated manner. The Chinese and their secret societies! Did she have to come up against them again so soon—these societies and their never-ending wars of contrition and brother against brother in the most populous nation on earth? And *this* society of all secret societies! The one she had heard was growing so quietly and stealthily! The one her father had written her about, the one he even allowed to meet secretly in the clinic! The one whose members treasured these tiny square pieces of cheap red New Year's paper! The one they called the Poor People's Secret Society!

The young man was staring back very levelly at Kate. He appeared to make a conscious decision to speak some more.

"There is a further thing I must ask you," he said hesitantly.

Kate raised one eyebrow and looked at him.

"It would not go well for me, Doctor," he began slowly, "if the British officers knew that I had brought you to the old one. I lied when I said they sent me. This I did myself, knowing that you spoke our language and hoping that you might understand how it is with we poor coolies who cannot get treatment because officer-doctors are too busy drinking whiskey sodas. Yet it was dangerous to ask you and dangerous to bring you and it is only good fortune we were not seen because the Chinese supervisors are all busy with the tugs alongside."

Kate looked at him again and shrugged. She believed the

young man's story. She did not believe he had had a hand in the old one's death.

"I must tell the captain something and fill in a death certificate," she said after a time, "but if the captain asks who you were, I will act like a stupid *yang-kwei*—a stupid 'foreign devil' —who does not know one Chinese from another and did not think to ask the steward's name. Of what happened in the boiler room, I can say nothing, for I was not there. But I must say that in my opinion the elder born one here who has now gone to be with his ancestors was killed in a terrible fight of some sort. Is this agreeable?"

"You create a debt of obligation that I shall one day honor."

"No, my friend, I do what is practical in the circumstances, as all who would practice medicine in China must do."

After asking the name of the dead man for her records, Kate said goodbye to the young Chinese steward and went to find the captain. The captain was very preoccupied with the pilot coming on board and the tugs looping their giant rope hawsers on to the liner to take her into Hong Kong Harbor, now they had passed the early part of the coast of China. So he thanked Kate, seemed relieved that that was one other thing he did not have to worry about, and passed her on to the First Officer. The First Officer appeared as little concerned as the Captain. Deaths among the Chinese crew were not uncommon, nor were fights among sailors. And the man had been old. Kate had stated her estimate of his age as seventy.

So after the forms had been filled in, the First Officer thanked her and she put her bag back in her cabin and walked out on deck again.

It was 1926. Sun Yat-sen—the founder of modern China, the leader of the first Chinese Revolution of 1911, and beloved of his people—was dead. A new young military leader, called Chiang Kai-shek, was in power. Kate, who had been born right after the turn of the century in 1903, wondered what difference this would make as she strolled along the deck.

It had, of course, occurred to her not to return to China. She had finished second in her class at Johns Hopkins Medical School. And some of her professors—the less prejudiced ones— believed that if she had not been a woman, she would have graduated top of her class. They had arranged for her to be offered, in turn, an academic post, with a scholarship to begin specializing immediately; a first-class hospital appointment, also with immediate specialization in her best subject—surgery; and a position in one of New York's finest private practices.

Of all, the last seemed at first to appeal to her the most and to be the hardest to refuse. Given the Faith Clinic, which her parents ran in China—meaning they were totally dependent on freewill gifts without solicitation—Kate never could remember a time when money was not short. She had no real ambition to be rich, but it would be good not to have to worry so much. It had taken all her parents' savings to fund her university course—scholarships for undergraduates were scarce enough without being a woman—and she'd still had to wash dishes and wait tables in the refectory to supplement her meager allowance.

She was anxious to pay her parents back as soon as possible. But it was not the money which attracted her so much as the freedom, the independence of having her own private medical practice.

If she went back to China, she knew she would be equal to any top surgeon Shanghai had to offer. In Peking there might be one or two better. But by keeping in touch with her professors, by subscribing to the British and American medical journals, and by getting lots of practice, she knew she could become the top cutter in both these cities. That, secretly, if she were honest, was her goal—to become such a good surgeon they would send patients to her from Peking.

"Be the best cutter in the whole damned country," her old professor of surgery, Jonas Elms, used to say to her. "A good cutter must always aim to be the best in the whole damned world and believe he—or she—is just that. No good going on to that operating table with a sharp scalpel and a doubtful hand. Whether you practice Stateside or in that heathen country you seem to love so much, and which I guess we'll lose you to eventually, be the best in the whole damned land. Nothing like it, you know, healing. We're the necessary 10 percent, we surgeons. Nature does the 90 percent healing. But we get nature started."

He was old and craggy and gray, always smoking his pipe because he said the fumes killed off the smell of death which was always around him. Death was the old arch enemy, to be fought every minute of the day, the way the greatest barrier to a good doctor was always the body's own desire to throw off anything good that was done to help it, like an operation. Good doctors, he said, had to learn how to coax out the cooperative part of the body and keep the self-destructive part at bay.

Katie had loved him like a father and missed him terribly. There had not been one bigoted, prejudiced bone in his body. He was for science and healing and said it was irrelevant to him what the sex was of anyone who wished to help him in this task. And, because he knew that Kate would always be near a hospital of some sort, because he was convinced surgery was her first love, he saw nothing wrong in her wanting the trappings of a private practice, too. "Hell, no, Katie," he used to say, when she confided to him once about her guilt, "that's all for the bigots. It would be an awful waste not to see that body of yours adorned for the beauty of the man you're going to marry. You're going to do that, aren't you? None of this sacrificing-yourself-for-medicine nonsense. Be a better surgeon because of your man and the warmth of a marriage and children. And I know of no law that says a poor doctor stitches up a better wound than a rich one—provided the rich one knows when to donate his or her services for free."

And so Katie had settled it in her mind's eye—or so she thought—settled it in the heart of the imagination where one's realistic dreams and aspirations lie; settled it that she would return to China and be the best of cutters and live a good life as well.

But the closer the final exams came, the more she wavered. Professor Elms, who had offered her a teaching grant in America, now seemed to be supporting her return to China. And although it did occur to her that the wiley old professor might be using reverse psychology, the more he argued the advantages of her returning to China, the more she leaned towards staying in America. She agonized over it. Where would she be needed most? That was really what a doctor wanted. Where could she do the most good? On Fifth Avenue? At Harvard or Princeton, provided the men accepted her? In the big, well-equipped American hospitals? She thought of the money she might send her parents. She could buy them a hospital—quite literally. Buy them a hospital and finance it in China from her earnings in America. But in the end, one day—for no real additional reason but perhaps because of an accumulation of all the reasons—one day she just knew.

The positions in America would always be there. Jonas Elms would always find her something. But in the meantime she must satisfy herself about the strange mystic call the Orient exerts on its children—natural and adopted. She laughed at herself—there was nothing strange and mystic about it, and that was simply a romantic way of describing the compulsion which everyone feels at some time or other to return to the scenes of childhood and growing up. And yet she knew there really was something beyond that. Perhaps it was the feeling that China and its people were a mystery, and if you had once been exposed to it, then you needed to go on delving into it, trying to find a complete understanding, to accept everything, and to be accepted. Yes, it was that. And there was also her father—his letters of late had been worrying her.

So one morning she got up and walked from the dormitory to the teaching hospital and along the corridor to Jonas Elms' office. She knocked on the door to find him there early, as he always was, lighting his first pipe of the day with his first cup of hot, freshly brewed coffee, and she said, "Well, I've decided . . ."

And he looked up at her and said, after taking her in, "Yes, I think you have . . ."

"I'm going home," Kate said, "I'm going back to China. There's going to be a war and I'll be needed."

Two weeks later she had left.


# 2


K*ate stopped now by the rail and sniffed at the early morning* breeze. She stared alternately down at the gray-green ocean and up at the quay in the distance. This was where the ship would dock. She strained to see if someone was waiting there. But the distance was still too great.

She looked instead at the junks crowding the harbor. Then she sniffed again, in delight this time, like one doing deep-breathing exercises. The smell of the Orient came off the water towards her, the land smells of Hong Kong and the ocean smells of the boat people.

On an impulse, she reached up and pulled her pearl hatpin out, taking off her wide-brimmed, cream straw hat with the ribbon, and letting her long blonde hair fall loose. She let her hat dangle down from her hand. She had long thin fingers, straight and thin as they held the hat. Her fingers did her work for her. Her fingers and her head.

She was of medium height and her body was slender, almost boyish, with just a touch of fullness. Her face was pretty and she had a small mouth and lips which were round and full and warmly moist. The new, fresh sun came off her eyes like reflection from the water, with a sense of life and vitality and shining full of promise.

God it was good to be home. She could feel it all and smell it all and see it all again now. She smiled. Others were starting to stroll along the promenade deck and she could feel them looking at her. She knew it was poor form to take her hat off. Oh well, who cared? She was back. She had done what she had gone for and now she was back.

Behind Kate, in the shadow of the rising sun cast against the white bulkhead of the ship, by the thin brass rail running around the super-structure, stood Yang Han Ho. He had, in fact, been watching her for some time, ready to turn away quickly lest she should look in his direction.

He was dressed this day in his full military uniform and stood, despite his wish for anonymity, with his hands behind his back, flexing his legs, immaculate in the jodhpurs and jacket of a Kuomintang officer of field rank.

He looked again at Kate.

So she was home! After all these years she was back! She had grown prettier. That little extra fullness and ripeness that a woman being in her twenties brought, though he was only three years older himself. She was the last person he had supposed to see this morning, though he could have known she was on the ship, or any ship for that matter, if he'd had a mind to. He had stopped having her movements noted, and thought he was over her. But now?

For the present he must concentrate on what had brought him on board with the pilot in the darkness just before dawn.

All known instances of people carrying those little red paper flags had to be reported to him personally, whatever the time of day or night. When he'd heard an engine room coolie had been found with one, he had hurried to reach the ship before it berthed.

Of course the sightings of the red flags were becoming more frequent now. But he was sure this was due to the carelessness of the stupid peasant-coolie types being recruited. He was sure it was not due to increased numbers joining. It would be a flash in the pan, this new movement against the government. There had been others. Why even this present government—the Kuomintang, or Nationalists—which he represented, had started as a revolution. But the ruling class had got hold of it in the end and would be equal to this so-called new threat too. Still, it was wise to be cautious. One red flag on this ship was one too many, given its cargo. Yet even as he thought this, Yang Ho knew he had not traveled all this distance to be here personally just because of the cargo and the red flag, though certainly they were important enough to command his attention.

The fact was, he hoped that someone might be here or close by; or at least the beginning of a trail that would lead to him. More and more the communist struggle, the stupid, ignorant communist struggle, centered around Shen Sun Lung. More and more, Yang Ho saw Shen as the only one standing between him and his ultimate ambition. It was Shen who had brought the poor people into the struggle. Before that it had been a handful of intellectuals and disgruntled Nationalists. These they could handle. Why they had even governed in coalition with them. But Shen was intent on numbers; and stealth; and the sort of revolution Yang Ho dared not think about. He had to be stopped, and that was final.

Yang Ho unconsciously flicked at the pocket of his jodhpurs again with his hand. If only they hadn't killed the old coolie! He might have told them something. He might have known who Shen Sun Lung was. Now all Yang Ho had was a dead body.

Still, it was true the Communists who had been tortured had stood up very well. But they were so hard to find! They kept their leadership secret very effectively. And some of the ruling politicians of Yang's government were not much help. They still refused to believe the Communists could become a threat. Anyway, they had asked, had Yang not heard of the danger of making people martyrs to a cause? Perhaps there was some logic in that. But the danger of letting them grow unchecked was greater.

If Yang Ho had his way, he would outlaw them. He would issue a proclamation outlawing them one day, and wipe them out the next. Or perhaps he would not worry about the proclamation until later. It could be done in a day with careful planning. But first he had to find the leadership. And Shen Sun Lung was the key to that. Find him and you found them. Once Yang Ho knew who Shen was, he could be watched and followed until Yang had them all together in a meeting. All the ones who counted. They'd be meeting all right. In some warehouse or home lent by sympathizers. Somewhere in Shanghai, the cosmopolitan city, always the home of political ferment as well as vice and corruption. But first Shen had to be found. And if the old one could no longer tell him, perhaps there were others on board who might.

Yang knew all about their stupid cargo, had known about it since it left New York. What worried him more was whether they knew about his! Was the old one who had died just a fanatic with a piece of red paper, or a carefully placed spy?

Yang Ho turned to go. Then he stopped and looked at Kate one more time. Strange how she still affected him. And he wasn't really sure she would recognize him after all these years. Quietly, unobserved, he slipped inside the bulkhead doorway and up the gangplank towards the bridge. He must tell the captain what he wanted done when the ship docked.

Two hours later Kate prepared to leave the ship. An immigration official had come on board and sat at a desk right at the point where the passengers stood in line to disembark. Kate handed him her passport.

They were closer to the quay now, and there was an English Marine brass band, in their fine white pith helmets and red jackets and black trousers, playing welcoming marches. The quay, both at upper and lower levels, was crowded with waiting relatives and friends and lovers, four deep along the top, like an army division ready to land.

Below was the hustle and bustle of the wharf where the Chinese coolies—with their black skull caps or conical straw sunshades; their ubiquitous blue and black jackets and rolled-up trousers; and their cane baskets and rickshaws standing ready among the stacked cargo crates and derricks—managed to give the impression once again that all the world was here, all of bustling, thirsting humanity.

Kate kept searching the crowd with her eyes. Now where was Janey? She had so much to tell her. Janey was her best friend—they had grown up together in Shanghai. Would she have changed? Would they both be different? Would their friendship still be strong? Oh, it would be like a sister dying if it wasn't. Worse. They were closer than sisters. Where was she? How was one supposed to see in a crowd like this? She should have told her to wave a white handkerchief or bring her parasol. The sun was quite strong closer to the quay and away from the wind on the bay.

The ship was only about fifty yards out now, coming in sideways, pulling itself closer and closer along the giant rope hawsers fastened earlier by the tugs.

The official was British and seemed to take as long as all civil servants everywhere. He kept turning Kate's passport over and over. He was a fat, pompous, overflowing man, red and florid-faced with untidy muttonchop whiskers and pudgy, dirty hands. When he spoke, it was in that patronizing tone of voice which Kate had long since realized a certain breed of insecure Englishmen used towards Americans in general, and American women in particular.

"Please state the purpose of your visit to Hong Kong, Miss Richmond," he said in a manner which seemed designed to remove an unpleasant smell from under his nose.

"In transit to China. And it's Doctor Richmond, thank you," Kate said sharply.

The speech of the man at the desk now became even more patronizing. "Ah . . . ? Really . . . ?" he answered slowly in as off-hand a way as Kate had ever heard. "I would have thought most young girls preferred to be called Miss . . ."

"Is there some reason I'm being detained?" Kate cut in icily.

"If so, I'd like to know why. But in any case I wish to see the American Consul. I want you to record that fact now."

At this, the man's eyes, which had so far avoided direct contact, flicked warily, the way those of an animal will when it senses danger.

"There's no need to take it so seriously, Miss Richmond," he continued, still determined not to give her her official title. "It's just a routine matter of the death certificate which I have been asked to discuss with you. We have an obligation to inform the Chinese authorities when one of their nationals is killed on a British ship."

"Inform them then. Send them the certificate which I have duly signed and executed."

"I'm afraid it doesn't say a great deal. We really need a little more information as to how this happened. Who told you about the dead man? Who brought you to him?"

Kate glared at him and said, "Are you a doctor?" She saw his face turn even redder than his normal color.

"Well—?" she continued when he did not answer. "Are you?"

"No," he said at last, breathing heavily.

"Then don't presume to tell me what should or should not be part of a death certificate. I am quite happy to discuss the matter with any relevant Chinese or British health authorities. But I am certainly not going to waste my time with some minor desk functionary such as yourself."

The man's face started to contort. Kate thought he was going to explode.

"Don't do it," Kate said. "Don't even think it. Don't say another word or I'll have every American authority from here to New York and back demanding your removal from contact with passengers."

And with that she scooped up her passport and brushed past him towards the gangplank.

But it still took another thirty minutes for the ship to dock and the gangplank to be lowered. When it finally was, Kate was one of the first off. She searched everywhere on the upper promenade of the dock, her high heels clicking on the wood and asphalt as she looked for Janey. But the crowds kept blocking her view.

She kept searching and searching but she knew Janey was not there. She had not come—not Janey, nor her parents, nor anyone.

She had arranged for her luggage to be forwarded onto the train. So after a few more minutes of staring around dejectedly she walked down from the upper concourse to the lower level.

Just as she stepped forward towards the rickshaw rank, she thought she heard her name being called—from far away and over the noise of the crowd so that she could not tell if the voice really was calling her or even if it was a man or a woman.

She turned but could see no one. Then she heard her name again. She was sure this time. It was a man's voice, a Chinese calling, "Doctol Lichmond, Doctol Lichmond." The sound tugged at her heart. Another thing to remind her that she was home. The language without any "r's"—none at all.

She turned and saw an aged rickshaw-puller running towards her. Obviously late for an important assignment, he had had to pass the long line of waiting rickshaw drivers, who spat and swore at him. This was one fare they would not get.

Eventually he arrived, pulling up beside her, panting heavily.

"You have come from Mumma San?" Kate asked in Chinese, lest his English only extended to the rehearsed words he had uttered.

The man nodded. Kate wanted to say perhaps they should wait for a moment while he regained his breath. But she knew this would never do. The other drivers were watching him and he would lose much face.

"Then take me to her," Kate said, "but be careful to travel slowly, for I am unused to the heavy traffic, having been away some time."

The man nodded, well pleased that the *yang kwei* spoke his language and understood the nuances of Chinese politeness. He knew she spoke this way out of concern for his breathlessness. She must be a very unusual foreign devil indeed. Very few understood the many levels of subtlety of Chinese courtesy.

Kate thought she knew what the old man was thinking and smiled at him as he picked up his rickshaw shafts and jerked her forward into motion.

But even so, she noticed the poor old coolie shaking his head as he ran and she knew what that meant, too. He would have been stopped in the street, outside a particular establishment;

given Kate's name and a brief description of her; and told to pick her up and bring her to that address. Since the address was that of the most notorious mumma san in Hong Kong, the old man was shaking his head to himself as if to say nothing was the same any more, nothing, when a white foreign devil such as this went straight to a mumma san on her arrival back in the Orient.

Many twists and turns and much breathless, spirited rickshaw-pulling later, they were at The White Body Bar. The driver helped Kate down and she went inside.

No sooner had she entered than there was a shout, a loud screeching cackle of enormous vitality and strength. "White slave, white slave, another white slave . . . come in lady, we pay well for good honest work."

There was more, loud prolonged cackling as an aging Chinese lady, perhaps fifty, perhaps more, of huge and billowing proportions, waddled out from behind the bar where she had been standing. She was all rolls of tanned fat and smiles. It seemed impossible that she had ever been anything other than fat and happy, although Kate knew full well that she had. From all accounts she had once been one of Hong Kong's prettiest, most sought-after bar girls. Her hair was still good. Though a little gray, it fell down to her shoulders loose, in good honest tresses.

"Tea, tea!" she shouted. "Bring the good gin tea, the good English gin tea for my favorite round-eye."

Kate ran towards her and hugged her, with Mumma San's shrill clear cackle still dominating everything else as she shouted for all the world to hear:

"My God, Katie, you doctor now and come do checkup every month my girls free for old Mumma San, hey, hey, ha, ha, ha, ha?"

They laughed again, and then Mumma San took a good, deep breath—her first—to indicate she was out of breath. So Kate walked her over to her special table near the door and they sat down and soon the gin came—in small, delicate Chinese tea cups without handles.

"You very good for trade," Mumma laughed. "Two men look in already after you get out of rickshaw although we not even open yet. The White Body Bar very short white bodies at present except for couple of Swedes and those White Russian refugees. Still plenty White Russian housewives not wanting to starve. But no English or American. You sure you not change your mind after all these years?" She cackled again.

It was part of their ritual of friendship every time they met. It had been so since they had first encountered each other when Kate and Janey, as schoolgirls on holidays in Hong Kong, had skipped away from their parents for a couple of hours. In their early and restricted adolescence they had been determined to see a real house of ill repute in Hong Kong.

With some help from a Chinese rickshaw boy, the two girls, still in school uniform, had stolen a look into Mumma San's establishment. She had beckoned them in and offered them a job with great glee. Then she had given them a lecture and a cup of proper Chinese tea before sending them back to their parents in her own rickshaw. After that they had visited her whenever they came to Hong Kong, pouring out their teenage troubles and regaling her with their exploits. There was, perhaps, an earthy happiness and warmth of nature about her that their reserved parents did not possess. Since their mid-teens she had allowed them a drink or two if they wished, and would never take anything from them, although the exchange of Chinese New Year gifts had been an established pattern for years now.

"So, my Katie, what you do now? You work at the mission with your parents?"

"I don't know, Mumma San. I don't know. Daddy has Mummy to help him, of course, although there is no doubt a third doctor would be useful. And they will expect me to work there—especially after all the sacrifices they have made to pay for my tuition. But I really should be attached to a big hospital for at least part of the time if I'm to further my career."

"You work it out Katie. It be all right. . . . Your health is good?"

"Thank you, yes. And yours, Mumma San?"

The old woman nodded courteously.

"I don't suppose you've heard from Janey?" Kate said when the ritual of Chinese polite talk was over. "I hope she's not ill."

"She not ill unless it from one too many parties," Mumma San said sarcastically.

Just then the horn of the Star Ferry sounded in the distance. Day and night, Mumma San ran her life from the sound of the ferry.

"Lunch!" she shouted, cackling with delight again. "Lunch. I hurry and change so you not be late for train." As she finished speaking she got up from the table and hobbled off towards a big Chinese screen in the rear.

When she reappeared she looked, despite her size, like any elegant Hong Kong lady.

"Now I take my favorite white daughter to lunch," she said. And with that, Katie got up and walked Mumma San out of The White Body Bar and into the sun, hearing the sound of the Star Ferry again in the distance and sniffing the heated smells coming up from the cobbled alleyway as they headed for Nathan Road and their favorite restaurant.

## 3

*At the border station, where travelers from British Hong Kong* must change trains for China, a young American nervously watched the movement of cargo. Normally Thomas Blake was not nervous. But this time he was. He tried not to let it show as he stood against the long wooden building, lighting a midday cigar. He pulled his white straw hat down a little more over his eyes. As he watched for his cargo to be unloaded, he wondered where Wang Lee was.

The boat train from Hong Kong Harbor had arrived a few minutes earlier and already the crew was beginning to unload the cargo. Soon they would come to his. He drew deeply on his cigar and looked at the passengers so as not to appear to be watching too closely. Those taking the China train began to walk past him. He saw a young blonde woman, followed by a steward carrying an old black metal trunk. The trunk had "Dr. K. Richmond" painted on it in white.

Damn it! Where was Wang Lee? It was *his* job, after all.

Blake only supplied the cargo. It was Wang Lee's job to get it to its destination. Blake had come along only because it was his first shipment for them and he wished to see they did not handle it carelessly. They would want other shipments, he knew. But if they did not handle them properly, Blake would not supply them. Already he was regretting his decision. Still, it was business. Their money was as good as anyone else's. It was a big order. And there would be others.

But he did not like it. Wang Lee was supposed to be in the crowd, quietly supervising the moving of the cargo from the Hong Kong train to the Shanghai train. Still, he might be there and I would not know it, thought Blake. He could be any coolie face, really. And he *is* under instructions not to speak to me or even recognize me unless he is absolutely positive it is safe. Blake was grateful for this. The Nationalist Army, under Yang Ho, was getting very determined.

At thirty-five, Blake was at the top of Shanghai's second rung of businessmen. But to make the jump into the first rung was almost impossible. Those at that level were huge traders, with generations of family money behind them. He had only his own money. He had started in business just nine years ago—when the war had ended. Although born in Shanghai, he was of American parents and had signed up to fight for the American Expeditionary Forces in Europe.

His father had been a sailor on one of the American gunboats which had helped keep the peace along the Yangtze. It was the job of such gunboats and their crews to protect American nationals and American trading concessions. Chinese feelings towards these concessions had run high for years. Sometimes there was a skirmish—Blake's father had been killed in just such a fight. Blake had then been in his teens.

His mother had been a secretary in the American legation. She had married his father when he was on shore leave. But as he grew older, Blake discovered that his father was very much a "liberty" sailor. He was given to wild, drunken, and happy but totally irresponsible behavior when he was on liberty, usually leaving his wife and one child totally without funds by the time the leave was over. His mother had had to give up her work at the legation after giving birth to Blake. The position could not be kept open.

For a while the mother and the boy made do on what the errant sailor father sent home. But eventually his mother had to find work—which was not easy for a white woman in Shanghai. Finally, one of the English *tai-pans*—the name given to giant European businessmen in the Orient—hired her as his secretary. His name was Edwards and he had some of the biggest *godowns*— warehouses—in Shanghai.

When Blake grew older he heard gossip that his mother was her employer's mistress. He was then twelve. He had already been subject to a cavalier upbringing by his father's financial neglect—not to mention the neglect of warmth and love. He had been prey to his mother's consequent insecurity and depressed moodiness. In the cramped Shanghai apartment they called home, she sat silently embittered for long hours; her New England pride preventing her from returning home to America because she had married a sailor—even if she or her parents could have afforded passage for her and the boy, which neither could.

All of this had conspired to turn Blake into a particular sort of individual. Fathers might come and go. Mothers might be unable to cope with the ebb and flow of life. But Blake believed he could see one type of security in life: money. Money was what his mother's employer had had and what his father had lacked. Blake believed, moreover, that the lack of money had caused his mother's unhappiness.

At Sunday school, where Blake was sent each week even though his mother herself never went to church, he was taught that the love of money was the root of all evil. But he and his Chinese playmates observed no such creed. They roamed the streets after day-school and by stealing and stealth and cunning in tricking tourists, were working at becoming Chinese merchants. And Blake noticed that those he saw at church on Sundays worshiping God, worshiped another thing much more during the week. The head elder of the church, then as now, was his mother's employer, Nigel Edwards.

Blake never knew why he had hated Edwards from the start. Certainly, at first, he should have had every reason to worship the ground the man walked on. Edwards had given his mother work when no one else would. But as the years dragged on, Blake came to hate Edwards even more—and began to act on that hate.

Perhaps Blake's hate had to do initially with the fact that his mother, when home, seemed so unhappy. Perhaps it had to do with her spending less and less time at home. Often an *amah*, a Chinese woman who helped at the Edwards & Co. orphanage for children of coolies crushed on the wharves, had to be sent to look after young Blake. Or perhaps it had to do finally with that terrible twelfth birthday.

His mother was late coming home from work although she had promised to be early. This time two *amahs* had come, arriving in their employer's limousine in great glee as Blake watched from his bedroom window. He supposed they did not realize his Chinese was as good as it was. Or perhaps they did not realize how sound carried up the hollow-sounding stone staircase to the apartment.

But as he ran to the apartment door to greet them, not so much out of joy but to ask urgently when his mother would be home, he heard them talking. He barely knew then what a mistress was. But he knew the Chinese words for concubine and for prostitute; and they used both about his mother as they climbed the stairs, complaining about having to sit with him—"that one"—while she was with the master so they were not able to get home to their own families.

It was years later before Blake began to understand about guilt and his mother's unhappiness. But he came to hate Edwards more and more, Nigel Edwards, the third generation of the famous English trading company. And his hate was directed at this one rich man, not all rich men. It was a specific hate which gave strength to his dream, his purpose in life: to become a rich man, whatever the price.

It was a strange dream in one sense, for a boy to form while passing into the first of his teens; and not so strange in another sense, given his young feelings. And if he ever needed any further justification in his own mind for what he set out to do from his earliest years, it came with the war.

When he was twenty-three and America was entering the war, he enlisted with the American Forces despite all his mother's protestations. He was never sure why he had done this. But later he believed it had to do with establishing his own identity as an American, that it had to do with being part of that country to which he felt such a strong tie, although he had never seen it. He had been away barely a year when he received word that his mother had died of consumption. It was not until he returned home that he learned she had died alone in the small apartment, without help or medical attention. Her employer had terminated his relationship with her some six months earlier, although he had kept her on in his firm for the same money, albeit in a lower position. She had fallen ill and had refused to send for him.

Blake blamed himself for being away when she had needed him. But he blamed Edwards more. And if, as a child of thirteen, he had sworn that one day he would be rich and powerful enough to avenge the things Edwards had done to his mother, he swore this doubly when he returned from the war.

Since leaving school he had chosen positions deliberately to learn the importing business, working in various jobs but mostly as a shipping clerk-overseer because he was good with the coolies and kept the cargo moving quickly.

Now, after the war, with his accumulated army pay and a little money from his mother's insurance policy, he started a business of his own with a large purchase of American Army surplus bicycles. Bicycles were a prized form of transport in China, and possession of one gave the owner much "face," although few coolies could afford them. Blake rented a small warehouse and promised coolies who had worked for him while he was an overseer a bicycle each if they helped him repaint them at night. The repainting, in bright colors, was done in record time, and Blake made a huge profit. He undersold his nearest competitor by more than fifty percent.

Cheap bicycles and paying coolies piece rates to moonlight a second shift became the backbone of his business. When the army bikes ran out, he imported second-hand ones, repairing as well as repainting them.

Over the nine years to the present he had moved steadily forward. He eventually bought the small warehouse; then a larger one; and then others. Everything was mortgaged the moment it could be to help finance further expansion and to pay for his withering round of social engagements. These were more than idle pleasure, although he found he had a great capacity for enjoyment as his confidence in himself and his business ability increased. But he saw early the enormous business advantages of good social contacts. And yet, however much he expanded, it was still not enough to get him into that absolute first rank of giant trading houses which were backed by generations of old money. He realized he needed a massive amount of ready cash—cash the banks could not get their hands on to reduce his mortgages—if he was ever to match the biggest Shanghai firms.

Of course, as the years progressed, there was no love lost between Blake, an American, and the big established English companies such as Edwards & Co. Whereas before there had been an element of polite cordiality towards a competitor, now Edwards barely spoke to Blake when they met at social functions. Part of the reason for the growing animosity was something more than Blake's continued success. It had to do with the manner of his success. While he had been a small, and younger, businessman, some of the big merchants had tended to look on his price-cutting as inconsequential. But now they saw him as a threat because he challenged their established methods of doing business. In addition to his price-cutting, he started to pay his coolies more than the others.

Indeed it had been one of his coolies—Wang Lee's uncle—who had come to him with the proposition of supplying arms to the Communists. Wang Lee's uncle had said it was important that they had someone who could travel freely without suspicion. Moreover, they noted that Blake did not side with the other big merchants so they did not believe he would betray them. And they respected the way he paid his coolies more than the other merchants did.

To this Blake had bluntly replied, "Yes, but that is business. I want the best coolies. I have no communist sympathies. I am a capitalist and will do it only for the money."

Wang Lee's uncle, who was a very quiet, wise old Chinese, had simply smiled and said, "Then it is agreed."

But now Blake was not so sure. Where *was* Wang Lee? Just then he looked at the boxes being unloaded and recognized one of the markings.

He stared, as nonchalantly as he could, while the unloading continued.

Blake had never really thought of gunrunning himself, until Wang Lee's uncle suggested it. Then he realized there were really only three ways he could make the money he needed—

opium dealing, child prostitution, or gunrunning. Gunrunning seemed the most logical.

It took Blake only two weeks with his business contacts in Hong Kong before he had the names of possible suppliers in England, France, and America. He visited all three countries and used a false name after establishing credit through the Bank of China in Hong Kong. He was sure the false name was unnecessary. Indiscreet suppliers of illegal arms would soon be out of business. But he still took the precaution. He also made it clear from the start that no arms shipments must ever be delivered to his warehouse. The goods were to be sent in the normal way, as commercial freight by sea, watched over by Wang Lee. This meant the shippers would be unaware of what they carried, and therefore could inform no one. The warehouses in which the goods rested temporarily in Shanghai would be the normal transit warehouses for goods on their way to the countryside. And special markings were to be used to ensure that the goods could not be traced to Blake.

He looked at these markings now, which he had designed, and thought how hopelessly inadequate they were. Chinese characters stenciled on the wood in black, and below them the translation in English: "Agricultural Plan." He looked at the two coolies carrying the boxes with growing apprehension. The coolies wore cone-shaped straw hats and black cotton work jackets and trousers, and had bare feet. They were hauling heavily between them one box from the back of the boat train.

Was the box really that heavy? Why did they take so long? Surely the soldiers—standing nearby and smoking—would notice? Surely that was why they were there—to inspect the overseas cargo being shipped to China?

The coolies were closer now. The cargo should have been packed in more boxes, that was obvious. More boxes and less weight. He must fix that next time. If there was a next time! Where was that damn Wang Lee? This was his job. Blake was too well known. He should not have been within a mile of the same train as this cargo. He had been stupid. Silly and stupid. But he was a good businessman; and that was why he was here. Things like knowing to use more boxes next time were important. But the heaviness of the boxes shouldn't matter. The customs officials and soldiers would expect them to be heavy. That's why

Blake had used those markings—so they would think the boxes were farm machinery and parts. And there *was* such a thing as an agricultural plan—a small, token plan which the government had instituted.

Perhaps he was being too apprehensive. Yet even as he thought this he saw the two soldiers suddenly snap to attention, their cigarettes going down and their rifles coming up in one movement. Blake instantly knew why they had been so slovenly. Their officer, a lieutenant, had been off somewhere. But now he was back. And with him a very high-ranking Kuomintang officer. Blake could not see the senior officer's face. But he knew by his uniform that he was of field rank. Blake's heart sank. The two soldiers, having obviously been reprimanded by their lieutenant, were now bending to Blake's box, shouting at the two coolies to bring tools to open it. Damn! It was just his luck! A few seconds more and he would have been clear!

Then he heard the senior officer give an order. Blake was just able to hear the words. "Let the Agricultural Plan Box pass."

Blake could hardly believe his good fortune. So his ruse had worked! The officer had thought the box was part of the government's agricultural plan. Now the other boxes would pass without inspection too, he was sure.

But just then the officer turned sideways. And Blake, seeing who it was, turned instantly away himself to avoid being seen. Yang Ho! In person! At this train, of all trains! Still, he didn't know what was in the boxes, so why should it matter if he saw Blake was on the train? It shouldn't, but it did. Blake found it disconcerting. Whatever people thought of Yang Ho—and Blake certainly had a sneaking admiration for him—no one doubted how smart he was. He was young, tough, quick as a whip, and battle-hardened, with plenty of experience in the field. Some said there was a sadistic streak to him, and perhaps they were right. The saber scar on his right cheek seemed to fit that description. But cruel or not—and some might have argued cruelty was a necessary part of an officer's equipment—Yang Ho had a record as a brilliant young military tactician.

Somehow it worried Blake that those crates had not been inspected. He was being stupid, he knew. But he couldn't shake the feeling that one as smart as Yang Ho would not have stopped the inspection.

Blake had his back to them now. He would not look again and he would do his best to avoid Yang Ho on the train. Of course Yang Ho might not board it. But Blake rather thought he would. And in any case he could not take the risk of looking to see. Damn it, where *was* Wang Lee?

There was still no sign of him. Blake stamped out his cigar and turned towards the train. He stopped at the point where the movable steel stoop led up to the main part of the carriages. His luggage was already on board. He would wait just a few minutes more—until the train was about to leave. Perhaps Wang Lee would make a last-minute dash.

# 4

Kate sat back in the train and watched again the interminable peasant plains of China. She had hoped someone might have been at the ship to meet her. It took more than two hours to travel from Hong Kong to the Lo Wu bridge at the Shum Chun border station, out of the New Territories and into China itself. But after the formalities had been completed, her baggage placed safely aboard and all the porters tipped, she sat back in the luxurious carriage of high-backed, laundered, beige cotton-covered seats, with starched lace headrests, and large roomy aisles with low tables in between. On these tables porters were forever placing scalding hot green tea in large magnolia white China cups the size of mugs, with delicate scenes hand-painted on the sides and little China lids on them, like teapots without pouring stems. Other porters, in crisp white starched jackets, dispensed pears and bananas and lychees, fresh lychees from Canton—all the wonderful fresh and steaming good things of Chinese life Kate remembered from her childhood.

It was then that Kate saw the first peasants in the fields beside the train. It was so good to be home. She felt such a continuity of life here. The green rice shoots, and the families in the field, generation after generation of them. She waved, and some waved back. One young girl waved and when Kate waved back straight at her, the young girl ran after the train, waving and waving until it was out of sight.

There were the clay brown and white hills in the distance; the green flooded fields and the good black earth cut out in parts between; and a fresh clear sky and a fine high strong sun with the peasants tanned a good honest brown over their yellow skin.

Kate thought for a moment how much she would love a country clinic. But what of her love for cities—for parties and balls? There were these, too. She had had so little of them. And Shanghai was the partying capital of the world. She would drink that cup first. Then perhaps she could think of the country. But how would she finance a country clinic? The clinics in the countryside were almost exclusively mission-run. And she never could see herself in the business of saving souls. Bodies, yes. But that mightn't be enough for a mission hospital or clinic. You were expected to say, "Well now, thank the Good Lord for providing the good doctor to lance your bad boil." No one thought of the natural consequence of that line of reasoning, that if the Good Lord provided a cure for the boil perhaps He provided the boil, too, or the malnutrition that caused it. "If the Good Lord provides the good doctor to lance the boil, would it not be easier for Him to prevent all boils in the first place?" a Chinese scholar had once said to her with a smile when she was a young girl helping in her father's clinic.

She had actually heard some Europeans say that such an answer was "just their Chinese logic." Yet it *was* logical, and Kate was never sure you could really qualify something you had admitted was logical.

She must have dozed for a moment. Then suddenly there was the sound of someone knocking on the door of her compartment. She looked up, half-dazed, and saw it was a porter. There was a man with him. What a nuisance! Having been overjoyed to find she had a compartment to herself, Kate now was annoyed that it seemed she must share it. And she was doubly annoyed at having her homecoming thoughts interrupted. Yet there was nothing to do but nod and allow them to enter.

The porter slid the door open and waited while the passenger walked past him. A second porter soon followed and started to stow the man's two black leather suitcases in the overhead wire-basket racks. The man tipped him, nodded to the more senior porter, and waited until both had gone and closed the door. Then he turned to Kate.

"I'm sorry for the intrusion," he said in a tone which she felt did not really indicate he was. "I'm Thomas Blake."

"Katherine Richmond," she said quietly and evenly.

"Ah, so *you* are the doctor," he said, gesturing with his hand towards her labeled trunk, which was wedged against the seat in the corner farthest from them.

"Yes," Kate said flatly, her voice showing the slightest touch of annoyance. Although she was well used to the automatic assumption that "Dr. K. Richmond" would be a man, and had arrived at the ship to find herself designated to share a cabin with a male surveyor traveling to the East, some annoyance always seemed to show however hard she tried. She knew for convenience she should have all her labeling changed from K. to Katherine. She also knew that her stubbornness would prevent her doing this.

She was aware who Blake was, of course, but made no effort to indicate that she recognized him. He must surely have expected some sort of recognition. His face was certainly well known in Shanghai. Even after her six-year absence Kate knew him instantly. When she was growing up, his photograph had often been in the social pages of the English-language daily. And Janey, who followed these things, used to point him out to her in the street when they were teenagers.

There were so few eligible bachelors of European origin that the matrons of Shanghai society were prepared to acknowledge even an American as at least part-European, particularly if he was wealthy. Kate could hear the matrons talking now. They used to come to her parents' clinic to talk to her mother. For although her mother was far removed from their society, she always encouraged such women to drop in for a cup of tea, hoping, she once explained to Kate, that her Christian witness might help to convert them. Perhaps this was so. The truth was, however, they were gossips, and so was her mother; and Kate might only be in her mid-twenties but she was old enough to know that such people have a habit of finding each other.

She looked again at the man opposite her and wondered what he was really like. He was tall and dark and thick-set, with blue eyes and a moustache and a look of living about him. There was an urbanity which created a certain warmth—and the lines of wear had not completely taken away the shine of boyishness— but his eyes looked cold and hard and determined. Kate found herself feeling sorry for him. He looked very tired.

Just then he glanced up and smiled at her. She wondered if he had known she was taking him in. She attempted a polite smile back but felt herself blushing. Then, out of the corner of her eye, she saw him close his eyes.

Across the aisle, Blake, resting with his head back, wondered if the girl knew he had chosen this compartment deliberately. After finishing with the cargo, the prospect of a beautiful young doctor's wife traveling alone had seemed too good to pass up. He had noted the name, and it had been a small matter, as a few *yuan* changed hands, to ask to look at the conductor's list. But now he was not so sure he had made the right decision in choosing her carriage. This was no doctor's wife. This was a lady doctor—a single lady doctor. Single women at her age could be difficult—and wish to marry. Then, being a doctor, she might be an intellectual. And he had a decided prejudice against intellectual women. They never seemed quite able to enjoy life like the others.

He decided, on balance, that it would have been better had she been a doctor's wife. Then she would have been used to traveling alone back to America or England to see her family. She would have had enough savoir faire to engage in a discreet affair without expecting too much.

Still, why look a gift horse in the mouth? A lady doctor was better than traveling alone. And that's what he had been facing before he saw her.

An hour passed and Blake awoke to realize he had dropped off. He opened his eyes and stretched and looked at his watch. Then he glanced across towards Kate.

"Would you like to join me in a drink?" he said, rising to ring for a steward.

"No thank you," Kate said, shaking her head, although she would have dearly loved one.

Presently a steward entered and walked towards Blake. Kate stared at the steward. He seemed about to talk to Blake when Kate suddenly realized who it was and caught her breath.

"Why Wang Lee," she said in genuine surprise, "what are you doing here?"

At first the youth had not noticed her. Or pretended not to. But as he heard his name he turned towards her, smiling awkwardly.

"Forgive the discourtesy, good doctor," he said hurriedly.

Then he turned quickly back towards Blake.

"Excuse me, sir," he said, giving no indication whether he knew Blake or not. "A European gentleman stopped me in the passage and pointed you out and asked me to give you this." He took a small piece of folded white notepaper from his jacket pocket. "You *are* Captain Blake?"

Blake nodded. Kate was staring at both of them. Wang Lee was obviously anxious to be gone. He kept glancing towards the outside corridor as he talked. And although he acted as if he did not know Blake, and Blake was responding in like manner, Kate was sure they had met before.

Just then she heard the sound of voices in the corridor. Wang Lee turned sharply and took off through the compartment door. The next moment Kate saw Kuomintang soldiers flash by her. She heard hurried talking but it was not loud enough to understand. Then she heard one shout, "There he is . . . stop him . . . stop him!"

As Kate watched, Wang Lee jumped from the train. He rolled over, hit the grass embankment, appeared to go down, and then was up and running again. She looked back, straining, as the train sped on. Then she heard shots. And then the train lurched. Someone must have pulled the emergency cord. She jumped up and ran to the window. She did not know what Wang Lee had done, but she hoped they would not catch him. She had thought him a quiet, serious young man, and it seemed incongruous he should be the same person out there running for his life.

There were soldiers everywhere now—and dogs. Was this standard procedure on trains these days? She had been away a long time. And even if it were standard, what could one so young as Wang Lee have done to make them so anxious to catch him?

Kate walked back to her seat. Blake had not moved.

"They've set the dogs onto him," she said.

"Oh. Who?"

"The Chinese steward—or whoever he was," Kate said.

"Oh yes, of course. You knew him, didn't you?"

Just then the drink steward arrived. Blake ordered a gin and tonic and was about to dismiss him when he turned to Kate and said:

"I think you may have just had a nasty little shock. Won't you change your mind and join me in a drink? I think you could probably use one."

Kate hesitated. Of course she would like a drink. She had wanted one earlier. But it was not this which made her change her mind. Her university years in America had cast her in what she saw as the suffragette mold of an independently-minded woman, and she was well able to do without a drink if it meant not giving in to some insufferable male attitude.

But the fact was, *his* attitude had changed. It was now conciliatory and polite. Indeed, as she accepted his offer of a drink, and ordered a gin and tonic as well as some cigarettes, she realized it had gone even beyond that. He had seemed concerned, genuinely concerned.

"What do you think he's done?" she asked.

"Who? That steward? I've no idea. And in case you're wondering about the note, it's from a business colleague in Shanghai who knew I'd be on this train."

There was nothing in his manner to warrant such a suspicion, but something told Kate that he was lying. "Why should Wang Lee be running messages on a train? He was a steward on the boat I was on."

"It's wiser not to concern yourself, Miss Richmond. It's all part of the inscrutable Orient."

"You don't need to patronize me, Mr. Blake. I've lived in China for most of my life."

He was not disconcerted by the annoyance in her voice. "Sorry." He grinned. "So you're coming home, are you?"

"Yes," she said wistfully, "home to Shanghai. I was born there."

"So was I."

"Really? Strange we never met. But then . . ."

Kate stopped and realized she was blushing. She had been about to say, "I wasn't allowed to go to many parties." But she stopped herself—she didn't want this man to think she wasn't worldly.

"But then we probably grew up in different parts of town," he said, finishing it graciously for her and then adding, "and you were probably still in short pants when I was a teenage street urchin, although I do wish we had met then."

Kate felt the beginnings of another blush at the base of her neck and hoped it didn't show all the way up. With great concentration she stopped the blush before it got full up to her face—though she had no doubt he was experienced enough to read a blush on the top of a woman's collarbone—and managed to think of what she hoped was a smart response:

"I expect, Captain Blake, there are many women in Shanghai who would take that as a compliment."

He laughed out loud. "Oh dear," he said, "I fear my reputation has preceded me, as they say. I didn't bargain for the company of an intelligent, as well as pretty, woman on this train journey."

"Do you usually prefer one without the other?" Kate said, a little more jocular and relaxed herself now.

He laughed again. "Sometimes," he said, "yes, sometimes."

Kate smiled broadly. There was an honesty about him which she liked—an honesty about himself.

And suddenly they were chatting—about her parents and the clinic and her plans. And with each sentence, Kate found herself thinking there might be a lot more to this man than she had at first realized. He was not just greed and skirt, as they said in the town. And not only cold eyes, either.

He had that gift of asking questions and listening to the responses as though you were the only person in the world. And there was a kind of quiet dynamism and power about him. Kate was strangely attracted. Perhaps she would meet him again in Shanghai—their paths might easily cross. It was more than likely, and she was already looking forward to it.

# 5

*It took days to reach Shanghai. As the train finally steamed into* the station Kate was alone almost for the first time since she had met Blake.

Blake had gone to see to his luggage. He said he had some urgent business and must be away from the station as soon as possible. He had offered to see to Kate's luggage, too, but she had refused. Perhaps it was silly. It would have been nice not having to worry about it. And she was probably the only woman on the train, the only woman in male-dominated Shanghai, if it came to that, who would have refused. It was, in a sense, almost more impolite to refuse than to accept.

But she did not wish to be obligated. She felt that to accept such a thing carried with it a subtle idea of dependence: a dependence which implied an even subtler sense of obligation. Perhaps she was wrong. Perhaps having to fight to be a female doctor among so many men had made her too self-reliant. Perhaps being continually discriminated against by the all-male lecturing staff in so many ways—some of whom had made it quite clear they felt it was all right for women to be nurses but not doctors—had made her too sensitive. But she had refused.

Besides, she was sick of Blake offering to do things for her. It was as if he'd taken up her independence as a challenge, determined to turn it into a humorous contest. He had kept wanting to buy her drinks, or dinner, or little Chinese artifacts as welcome-home presents at the stations where they stopped, asking all the time with a big smile on his face as if he expected her to refuse. When he had offered her his sleeper, Kate had been infuriated.

She had not booked a sleeping compartment for the simple reason that she could not afford it. When Blake heard she did not have one he insisted she use his. He had, in fact, this time offered without his usual jocularity. But she could not in all conscience accept it and told him so as politely as she could. Somehow on this occasion it got a little out of control.

"It is something, Miss Richmond, that I would really like to do," he said. "You've made what I expected to be a dull journey enjoyable, and I'd really like to show my gratitude. If you won't take mine, won't you let me see if another's available? I'm sure there'll be a spare, and this way you won't feel you're depriving me, although I assure you I am used to sleeping in much harsher conditions than these,"—he pointed to the train seats—"when I go into the countryside on business."

"I'm sorry," Kate said, "but I can't have you spending your money on me, nor can I take your sleeping compartment. I'll be all right here, really."

"If you don't use it, it'll be wasted," he said.

"What do you mean?"

"If you sleep here in the compartment, so will I."

"What in God's name for?"

Blake noted, and recorded as the first indication that there was more than a missionary's daughter under the dress, this use of blasphemy. He suppressed a smile, and said:

"Why to keep you company, Miss Richmond, and show you just how infuriating stubbornness can be."

Despite all Kate's protestations, he had then rung for the steward, ordering blankets and pillows and a bottle of champagne. He explained to Kate that they would both surely need something to help them sleep. And in the end she took some champagne with him, eventually snuggling down after he had lifted the arm rest for her. So they had both slept stretched out opposite each other on the compartment seats. And Kate, despite all her outward show, had enjoyed being looked after and having a man close by who was watching over her while she slept. It was this which had infuriated her more than anything else.

Blake now returned after seeing to his luggage. The train was just pulling in.

"Well goodbye," he said, suddenly very formal again. Kate realized this was how he would be if ever they met socially.

"Goodbye," she said.

And with that he touched his hat, pulling it down over his eyes—which Kate had noticed was his one nervous mannerism—and was gone.

As she sat in the train, still staring out the window, Kate was somewhat confused in her feelings about the past two days, about what they had meant and what she had felt. She thought it was important, as a doctor, to be aware of her feelings. But even as she began to try to sort them out, an emotion of another sort took over. She began searching the platform for her parents.

It was so often assumed, Kate thought, that relationships with parents were all of a piece: that one loved or hated one's parents uniformly, and if one did the former, one could not do the latter, or vice versa. But the truth was, Kate had both loved and hated hers at times. She hated them less now. The time away had at least done that. In her teens she had felt very frustrated. Her parents had been so concerned about what they saw as the great temptations of Shanghai that she had been allowed out on only the most carefully chaperoned occasions. Drinking and smoking had been forbidden to her and on some occasions, dancing.

But now she looked through the window for her parents and saw them standing on the platform—two lonely, gray, and erect old people—and she felt suddenly very guilty for her anger towards them. They had loved her. They did love her, and she loved them. They were strict, but they were warm and kindly. Her mother was grayer. Bette Richmond adjusted a strand of straying hair that had slipped out of her bun at the back of her neck. Then she fingered her steel-rimmed spectacles as she searched the train compartment windows for her daughter, her Kate; the apple of her eye and heart; her one and only child, though she had hundreds in her Sunday school; the daughter she still prayed for and hoped might one day follow in her footsteps. And there was Kate's father, Daddy Richmond, the Doctor-Preacher, fencepost straight and tall and thin and bristling, always bristling with his salt-and-pepper crewcut hair, receding far back but still cut short and military. He had a kind face and wore rimless glasses.

Kate often wondered how such a kind face in which even his rimless spectacles seemed gentle, and such an intelligent mind, could hold God, Satan, and Hell as things so self-evident.

Perhaps it was his Southern Baptist origins. Both Kate's parents were Southerners. They had been born and raised in Georgia, attended medical school together, and felt called to China as medical missionaries at the same time. They had left straight after their marriage and had not returned except for one furlough. Kate, their only child, had been born to them soon after they arrived in Shanghai. There they had founded a non-denominational medical clinic for the poor.

Of the two parents, Clem Richmond was perhaps the less strict. She was his Katie girl, his friend as well as his daughter, and although he knew he was losing her from his beloved religion, and perhaps even his God, his love was as warm as ever. Bette Richmond found it harder. There was the competition that always occurs between two women in the same household; and because Kate realized it and her mother didn't, it was Kate who made the allowances. It was hard, and she didn't always succeed. But she tried for her father's sake. She knew he watched her silently and admiringly, and realized that if there might be difficulty for her swallowing God whole, some of the love and forbearance had rubbed off. She could feel her father's silent, happy pride. To tell him she did not want to work with him would be hard; even harder because he would understand. But her mother would not. Her mother would pray for her and alienate her further by so doing.

Yet as she saw them both on the platform, standing together, they were old folk now. She had not been born to them early. They were stooped and a little sad, searching the windows with those uncertain eyes which aging folk have when they are no longer sure of their vision or perception of things; when the certainty of youth has gone and the assurance of middle age is waning, and doubt as to one's faculties is creeping in.

But then *they* saw her, Bette with her lilac dress and old comfortable black shoes, and Clem in his gray trousers and faded black silk jacket and fawn shirt and brown tie. Bette and Clem. When would she ever get him to worry about his clothes?

Bette and Clem, together on the platform, smiling now, the sad look gone. It was so good to be home! Her mother would have cooked a Thanksgiving dinner, she knew that. One had to keep one's strength up to do the work of the Lord. Gluttony was a favored sin among Christians, Janey and Katie had joked to themselves. That and sex, although the latter wasn't so much a favored as an allowed sin, provided you employed the missionary position; only did it once a week and never on Sundays, and always had the lights out.

Yet for all the childish fun she sometimes made of her parents, she loved them very dearly—for all they had done for her and for all they could not do but would have wished to. And as the train pulled in she was off and running; down the platform towards them and then into their arms. All three stood hugging each other, with her mother sniffing and sobbing just a little. Her father was watery eyed, too, as they finally came apart. Then he said, "Well, and let me look at you," but he said it gently, and kindly, and with meaning, forcing himself to use an everyday phrase and not to say something religious like her mother did; Bette, smiling below her glasses which had slipped a short distance down her nose, said, "We prayed the Lord would watch over you and bring you back safely to us."

Kate never could resist the temptation to answer her mother back just a little when she said such things, however goodnaturedly she might have meant them.

"The Lord and the shipping company, Mumma," she said.

They all looked at each other then for a moment in awkward silence, for it was Kate establishing her independence again, so quickly, so soon after she had come home.

Her father smiled quietly and said, "Oh well, I suppose that's right, when you think of it, Mother—God and the shipping company. I suppose that's right . . ." And then they all laughed, glad for the opportunity of having something to laugh at to bring them together again without the distance starting already.

"Let's get your luggage," her father said, carefully maneuvering himself so that Kate walked between the two of them. "I suspect they'll have it ready by now. And by the by, darlin', you did swell on your exams. You did us proud, Katie—you did us proud."

Kate felt her mother take hold of her arm at last and hug it warmly. "You did so well. We're very grateful you're usin' your fine talents in the service of the Lord. My little girl, my Katie, a doctor. Fancy that. Fancy that! It'll be so good to have another hand in the clinic."

"Let's not talk of that now, Mother," Clem said, as they found Kate's luggage and he beckoned for a porter.

"Do we need a porter, Clem?" Bette asked. "Couldn't we leave it here and have one of the boys from the mission come and get it?"

For a boy to come with a rickshaw, rather than pay a station porter, was cheaper and normal practice. But Clem simply smiled and nodded to the porter to pick up his daughter's bags. A few minutes later they were in Clem's car and on their way to the Mission and the waiting dinner of roast turkey and cranberry sauce and pumpkin pie and angel food cake.

# 6

*Just as they were finishing their meal, a note arrived. It was* from Janey. She apologized for not having been able to meet Kate. Her mother was out of town. So Janey had had to stay home to oversee the household for her father. But could Katie come for coffee? Janey was dying to see her. Kate could come with the chauffeur and Janey would drive her home later.

Kate looked at her parents as she finished explaining what was in the note. "Would you mind awfully?" she said.

Her mother adjusted another strand of straying hair and unconsciously moved her spectacles tighter on the bridge of her nose.

"Go and have a good time," her father said. "We'll talk in the morning—whenever."

Kate looked at him with the accumulated warmth of a lifetime. Then she looked at her mother, not needing her approval but wishing it might come spontaneously. Her mother nodded resignedly.

"It was a wonderful meal and a wonderful homecoming," Kate said cheerily to ease the slight that still hung in the air.

Then she picked up her hat and purse and ran outside to the waiting car.

In some ways, Kate thought, the friendship between Janey and herself was the most unequal of friendships. Janey was so many things Kate was not. Janey was rich, very rich. Her father, Nigel Edwards—or, more properly now, Sir Nigel Edwards—was one of the most important businessmen in Shanghai and president of the famous Shanghai Club. Of course it was family money, inherited from his father, but he had increased rather than wasted the family fortune.

Although English, the Edwards family had lived in Shanghai for generations. Theirs was one of the biggest trading empires in the East. When newcomers foolishly asked what the Edwards family traded in, old established Shanghaiese just laughed. There was very little the Edwards group did not trade in. Like the powerful house of Jardines in Hong Kong, if you looked at the bottle of Scotch on your table, it was likely to have been imported from Scotland by the Edwards company. Cheese, butter, bicycles, Scottish smoked salmon and Bradford tweed and worsteds, Sheffield steel and Irish linen—all came through Edwards' warehouses. In short, everything from the home country for which an Englishman overseas might yearn. Edwards & Co. imported and sold goods from many other nations, too. Their latest move had been into farm machines and automobiles. They owned enormous pieces of Shanghai, and the buildings on them, and the Edwards home was the most famous in the city.

There was no son. So Janey, as the only child, was heir to all this. But she did not work in the business. It was not a thing women did. And her father, for all his love for her, was adamant about that. He would not employ her even as a secretary, he had said when she had expressed interest in the business while still in her teens. Her father had explained that he employed good group managers, many of whom had sons who would later enter the business and be loyal to the family. By the time he himself was ready to go, the succession would be clearly defined and all Janey would have to do was sit back and enjoy her fortune. Her father would word his will so that anyone Janey married would not be able to get more than ten thousand pounds out of the business in any one year. And in the event of the marriage breaking up, and there being a divorce, the husband would get nothing. Janey's father was against divorce, believing it better to stay married and have mistresses—of which he had many, including a permanent Eurasian beauty whom all knew about, even Janey's mother. Janey and Katie had once secretly spied on this mistress when they were children, having found Janey's father's address book lying around in his study.

Many called Janey frivolous. Some said she was flighty. Yet Kate had found her the staunchest of friends. Perhaps each envied in the other what each lacked. Perhaps Kate, if she were honest, envied Janey's rich life-style just a little, though she was free to share it as much as she would. Janey had wanted to pay Kate's way through college and Kate had had to think hard and long about it, knowing what a burden her college expenses would be on her parents. But in the end she had said no. Perhaps Janey, too, envied Kate her somewhat simpler, more stable background and her intellectual accomplishments.

The car turned into Janey's drive. Janey was waiting on the steps. The house had a long row of white columns and inside it was brightly lit.

Chinese lanterns were hanging in the garden. There was a smell of jasmine in the air.

The two girls hugged in silence for a few minutes and then walked inside with their arms around each other.

"Sorry about this," Janey said. "Another of Daddy's business parties. And you know what a stickler he is for having a hostess in attendance. As I said in my letter, Mummy's away."

"Home in London again?"

"Oftener and oftener," said Janey. "Can't say that I blame her."

"It must have been lonely for you."

"As bloody hell," said Janey, with a deep sigh, "as bloody hell. Still, that's over now. You're back. Why don't you go on up to my room and ring for a drink. You won't want to say hullo to this lot—there's no one interesting—and in any case they're already into the no-ladies-brandy-port-cigars-routine. I'm just going to excuse myself, say goodnight, and I'll be right with you. All right?"

"Of course."

They were standing a few feet apart by this stage. Janey suddenly came over to Kate and hugged her again tightly.

Kate could sense the choked-back emotion as Janey said, "Oh darling, it's so good to have you home."

"See you in a minute and we'll have a nice long chat," Kate said softly as they separated and she started up the long, wide staircase.

When Kate reached Janey's room she kicked off her shoes, fell into a chair as she had done so many times before, lit a cigarette, and rang for a drink. Presently a waiter arrived, took her order, and was soon back with it, held aloft on a silver tray.

Before long Janey came in and sat down beside her. Janey had long hazel hair and brown eyes. She wore a black jersey dress with string shoulder straps and a simple strand of pearls.

Kate took a small box from her purse and handed it to her. It was gift-wrapped and packed with tissue paper. But eventually Janey took out a tiny gold bell on a thin gold chain. She smiled a silent thanks and got up and walked in her stockinged feet to the dressing table, where she took off the pearls and put on the bell. Then she took a small blue and gold leather box from her dresser and returned to her seat. "Graduation present," she said quietly as she handed it to Kate. "Congratulations, Doctor."

Kate opened it and was quite overcome. Inside was a gold watch. She took it out and put it on. "It's beautiful," she said, "I'll treasure it always . . . Thank you."

"My pleasure," Janey said. "And thanks for the bell."

"It has a meaning," Kate said.

Janey smiled. "I think I know you well enough to know that. Doesn't everything with you? Let me see now . . . It is the Liberty Bell . . . not any old bell . . . and you have given it to me, your closest female friend. Does it signify liberty for us as women, perhaps? Does it represent our female emancipation, do you think?"

Kate was smiling. She had missed Janey's teasing sense of humor. But behind the teasing was a serious intent. The girls, ever since their teens and their meeting with Mamma San, had worked at freeing themselves from some of the strictures of their environment—Kate from her sometimes strict parents, and Janey from her often stuffy establishment background. Each had set about being as independent as the times allowed. Kate had chosen a tiny gold charm replica of the Liberty Bell as a present for Janey to represent this independence each had always sought. And Kate had not been disappointed—Janey had understood the symbolism of the present.

# 7

*Some distance across town from Kate, in the poorest part of* the city which he had come to know as a boy, Blake sat in a cramped teahouse off a cobblestone Shanghai backstreet. A youth who looked young enough to be his son sat opposite him. Blake was explaining what had been in the note Wang Lee had handed to him on the train.

The young man sat in front of a square fretwork pattern of latticed wood. The wood had been painted red once and then lacquered, but now it was chipped.

Behind the wood, in the shadows, sat the man they called Shen Sun Lung. He had arrived early in order to observe but not to be observed. He had had many such meetings and would have many more. He no longer trusted the government. Since Yang Ho had taken over the Southern Command any possibility of Communists and Nationalists working together was gone. If Yang Ho knew where to find Shen, he would have him killed and explain it away as an accident.

Shen looked at Blake through the fretwork and wondered again if they were right to trust him. They had little choice. It was too soon to come out into the open—too many lives would be lost. But would Blake's ambition and hatred be equal to their task? Soon they would know. Shen Sun Lung settled back to listen as Blake said, "The main thing the note said was that Wang Lee's uncle was dead," Blake began. The young man nodded, showing no emotion. Blake hated that. He never had gotten used to it. And the Communists were worse. They were actually trained to show no emotion, at least in business dealings. Blake, for his part, was furious that his first major arms deal had fallen through. He'd had his suspicions when he had seen Yang Ho at the Lo Wu bridge at the border. When Wang Lee had burst into Blake's carriage on the train and hurriedly shoved a scribbled note at him—little doubt Blake knew something must have gone wrong. The fact that Wang Lee had had to flee the Kuomintang soldiers was further evidence. And, of course, the bitter confirmation had come when Blake had read the note later that day while Kate Richmond was temporarily absent from the compartment. Yet he had been careful not to show her his disappointment and annoyance. And he would not show it to this arrogant young Communist either. To do so would be to lose face. The Chinese showed little respect for Westerners who had no grasp of the need for Oriental inscrutability. Besides, Blake had trained himself to be poker-faced in business.

Blake was also annoyed because they had allowed one as old as Wang Lee's uncle to sign on as an engine room coolie. Blake had liked the old man and had been angry when he'd read the note. "He was beaten to death after a piece of red Chinese New Year's paper was found on him," Blake continued. "The crew members who beat him were government supporters. They told the Kuomintang soldiers at the wharf about the paper and also that the old man had appeared friendly with a steward called Wang Lee. But Wang Lee escaped and hid in the customs shed to watch the cargo. He saw soldiers search the crates and discover the ones containing arms. He saw them take the arms out and substitute metal weights . . . Then the crates were sent on their way . . ."

Blake stopped and looked at the young man opposite him. He did not even know his name. But they always knew him. A luggage porter had bumped into him when he had arrived at the station and told him to be at this address at this time. When he had arrived the young man had greeted him and shown him to the table, saying he was a representative of Shen Sun Lung, the man reputed to be the leader of the Communists for the whole of Southern China. And Shen was not yet twenty-one! Wang Lee was also said to be highly placed and about the same age. It seemed incredible. But the middle rung of the Communist Party of China, which was comprised largely of the intellectuals, was reportedly very good at maneuvering young men into strategic positions for the future. They had earlier accepted the election of aging, not-so-bright party hacks to the top leadership as the price they had had to pay in the interim. Now the day of the young men was here.

The young man had been listening very attentively. But the moment Blake paused he simply nodded and said, "All that is past history which we must now forget. But I have a new piece of information which may interest you."

"Why should your information interest me?" said Blake.

"That is for you to judge. But Shen Lung believes it is information you will want to have."

"I know too much about your people already. I don't wish more information."

"You will want this information," said the young man, firmly. There was something in his tone, the Chinese confidence of knowing what another wants to hear, that persuaded Blake to listen.

"Go on, then," he said at last.

"You will know," the young man said slowly, "that we are not the only ones in the market for arms. The government must itself also buy arms on the black market. It does this because it does not wish the foreign powers such as America, Britain, France, Germany, and Japan—all of whom have huge trading interests here—to know the full extent of its arms capacity. This is one thing the goverment and we Communists have in common—we both wish the foreigners out, although the government certainly does not wish to let the foreigners know how strong it is becoming by buying all its arms from them directly. If the foreigners knew this they might act as they have in the past and precipitate a war to *k'ow t'ow* the government again. So the government pretends to be friendly while it builds up arms on the black market."

He paused and smiled. Then he added, balancing the tips of his fingers against each other in a delicate in-and-out movement:

"It has recently come to our attention that a very large shipment of arms for the government will arrive by train in three weeks time. It came from America on the very same ship as your confiscated weapons but was held in Hong Kong for safety after

Wang Lee's uncle was found with a red paper flag. It is a huge shipment, perhaps the biggest yet.''

Blake felt like exploding. He could not believe his good fortune! Another shipment—an even bigger, better one—to replace the one he had lost!

But he kept his face expressionless, listening even more intently as the young man continued:

''It is necessary for me to say only two more things. Firstly, we will pay you the going rate for arms whenever and wherever you are able to procure them for us. We will not ask their source. We are in desperate need of weapons as quickly as possible, more desperate than when Wang Lee's uncle first approached you. Secondly, you will, of course, be aware that in the same way as we use you as a middleman to prevent the government from becoming suspicious, the government in its turn must also use a middleman to prevent the foreign powers becoming suspicious.''

Blake nodded and the young man smiled knowingly and continued:

''It has recently come to our attention,'' he said, ''that the main middleman and supplier of arms to the government is a company called Edwards and Company. This is a firm, I think, of which you have some knowledge.''

For once Blake's breath was taken away. He had not known. He had not had the faintest idea. And the Communists had known that. The young man's phrasing had been masterly Chinese understatement. He had wanted something of Blake and he had dug the knife in at exactly the right spot to get it.

How strange the fortunes of war were! His old enemy, Edwards, had been gunrunning, too—and on the very same ship as Blake. The prospect of relieving him of this second and huge shipment was something for Blake to savor.

But Blake was also annoyed. And this time he let his annoyance show. The young man had been arrogant and truculent and one must not appear weak with the Communists. Besides, Blake must test the water with questions. He must be sure it was not a trap.

''Why should you pay me so much money for something you might so easily do for yourselves?'' he said irritably.

''Ah, that is just the point, Captain Blake. No Communist

must be seen to be connected with this in any way. We know the day will come when the government will outlaw our party, when to be a member will be punishable by death. Before this happens we must be armed. Should we attempt this thing ourselves and be caught, the government would surely outlaw us immediately. It would be proof positive of plotted insurrection. But if an American gunrunner and his hired Chinese coolies should be caught, what matter? Even if he said the Communists had put him up to it, that would be hard to prove. But if *we* did it and were caught and outlawed, our key people would soon be in prison or dead and we would never get the chance to arm. No, we must arm first before we openly risk being caught in such an operation."

"This is a heavy financial price to pay."

"Not if you believe as we believe."

"Where will you get the money?"

"This is no concern of yours. But as evidence of our good faith, I am empowered to tell you. We will get it from our friends in Russia. They will lend us the money."

"I do not like the idea of the train," Blake said. "Will the goods go to the Edwards and Company warehouse?"

"Yes, they will be stored in their *godown*, of this we are certain."

"Good. The warehouse is better. The train is too open and warehouse coolies are paid less. They are easier to bribe. But I must think on it. I would be paid in full at once?"

"The moment the arms reach us. You know men you can trust to recruit those you will need?"

"Yes. Some of the Chinese friends I grew up with."

The young man nodded. "Good. A letter of credit will be drawn on the Bank of China in Hong Kong under the name you now use with us. We will meet again in one week's time when all the preliminary arrangements are completed. Is this agreeable to you?"

"It is agreeable."

"Good, then we shall drink tea on it."

Blake nodded and sat back. He lit a cigar to kill the taste as the steaming tea came in with ceremony, despite the poorness of the surroundings. He never had gotten used to the taste of their tea. He wished for some American coffee. But he drank the tea with smiles. In China politeness was everything.

Behind the fretwork screen, in the dark, Shen Lung smiled. Blake had risen to the bait handsomely. The noose was tightening. Once they had these arms the Communists could make their move.

Unknown to either Blake or Shen Sun Lung, Wang Lee, the other partner in their chain of intrigue, was entering Shanghai at that very moment.

But he was entering slowly, carefully, by a very circuitous route. The Kuomintang had no photograph of him. But it was best to be careful. So he entered by the open sewers. The soldiers who had chased him when he jumped off the train had long since given up. But he had no doubt they would have telegraphed every major city along the route to look out for a fugitive—any fugitive or anyone looking like one. No one had ever seen him up close when he'd been a fugitive. And he'd been that many times. They'd seen him up close in his other roles. But that didn't matter as long as he remained undetected. He had to be doubly careful for another reason. His likeness to the Shanghai Communist leader Shen Sun Lung was uncanny. It was one of the reasons the central leadership, particularly Comrade Mao, had chosen him for this important assignment.

Wang Lee and Shen Lung might have been brothers, they looked so much alike. In fact, they were related, though distantly. It had been natural to discuss their family backgrounds when Wang and Shen had first stood face-to-face. They had discovered, by tracing family trees, that Wang Lee was the son of one of Shen's father's cousins who had fled to Hong Kong before the last revolution. Although that revolution had been led by the kindly doctor Sun Yat-sen, Wang Lee's father had been too closely identified with the last of the Manchus. He had been a poor merchant who had become involved in Imperial politics for a price. Because his trading sometimes took him to Hong Kong, the Manchus had employed him as a go-between with the foreign powers there to try to prop up their ailing dynasty.

When the dynasty had fallen, Wang Lee's father was still in Hong Kong. Not only was he unable to receive payment for his assignment, he was unable to get his meager savings out of China. It was some time before even his wife and family could join him.

In fact, the strain of poverty in Hong Kong proved too much for him. He died less than a year later, just after his family, including Wang Lee, had moved into the steamy port city. Wang Lee, being the eldest, immediately went to work—at twelve years of age. Yet even at this age, there was something about Wang Lee that drew people and opportunity to him. His mother reconciled herself to being separated from her children, including Lee, by allowing them to be taken to the orphan settlement at Rennies Mill. At least they would eat. But Wang Lee said such orphan disgrace would not do. He would find work.

They all laughed at him. The compradore system of hiring relatives and friends was as tight in Hong Kong as anywhere else in China. But within two days Wang Lee had work—work on the Star Ferry. And not as an engine-room coolie, either. He was a conductor's boy up top, where one could make a little extra money in addition to one's wage by cheating the rich. Wang Lee never told anyone, not even Shen when they later became friends and joked about compradores, how he had gotten the job, although his charm had certainly failed to work on the compradore the first time. After that he had watched the ferry coming and going all day and who did what. Then, when the day shift changed, in the descending Hong Kong dusk, he had followed one of the conductor's boys home through the backstreets and beaten him up.

The next morning he had arrived in the boy's uniform and hat, and with his money bag, reporting for duty as if he had been working there forever. When the compradore gruffly stopped him, Wang Lee looked at him quietly and said:

"This matter had been decided by the *Ching-pang*. I am to take the other's place."

The *Ching-pang* controlled gambling, vice, murder, and prostitution. All Chinese lived in fear of it.

"The boy is my nephew," the compradore said. "What have you done to him?"

"I? Nothing. I was just given his uniform by my superior and told to report to you. Shall I tell him otherwise?"

The ferry was getting up a full head of steam. The man was also frightened, Wang Lee could see. He was frightened what might happen if he disbelieved Wang's story and it turned out to be true—which was what Wang Lee was counting on. Wang's father had often wailed in his last months that he should have accepted the protection of the *Ching-pang* when it was offered.

"Welcome aboard," the head conductor said finally, as two more whistle blasts came from the bridge of the ferry.

Wang Lee boarded with a smile. He felt no guilt about what he had done. The compradore system was evil. If men wished to cheat their masters and employ only relatives and friends who paid them secret commissions in turn, they must be prepared to take the consequences. Besides, he had not even knocked the boy out. The boy would have had much worse beatings from his father many times. And many wives were made to bend over naked on their wedding night to be beaten to promote a long and harmonious marriage. He had hit the boy only once with a glancing blow with his fist before demanding his uniform. Of course he had also threatened him, warning that if he or his father said a word, it would reach the *Ching-pang*. "You use the influence of your family, I use the influence of mine," Wang Lee had said. His family, in fact, had no connections with the *Ching-pang* at all, although perhaps the boy within the man still wished for some powerful protector in place of his father; in any case he would use this supposed connection many times to great effect.

He would use it on the stupid Kuomintang soldiers if any tried to stop him this night, he thought, as he entered Shanghai. But they would not. That was why he was coming in by the open sewers. Even the most conscientious Kuomintang patrols swung wide around them. Once closer to the city, nearer the inner city, it would be more dangerous. For everyone had to carry a pass and he had only his pass as a steward from the train. Although it was a forgery, he was sure it was impeccably done. Forgery came under one of his areas of responsibility and he had recruited the best Hong Kong had to offer. Not all agreed with his methods of paying, however outrageously, to get the best.

It was a wonder they had let him into the party at all, really, with his background and methods. The truth was, Wang Lee smiled to himself as he picked his way among the filth and the rats, they had not known his background or his methods before he joined. Nor had he known much of theirs. It was only later they had found out that for Wang Lee, the swashbuckling chief conductor of the Star Ferry line, the ends invariably justified the means. And despite his good job and happy times, the boy had lived for only one thing since the day his father had died: to return to his beloved homeland of China. The pull of home for an estranged Chinese is as strong as for Jews of the Diaspora. And Wang Lee believed in communism. The nationalist government was rotten to the core, as bad as the Imperial court—particularly after the death of its founder Dr. Sun Yat-sen and the failure of his dreams to materialize.

So Wang Lee, too, had joined the Communists, although at a different time and in a different place from his second cousin Shen. A relative of Mao's had befriended Wang Lee on the wharves and had quietly drawn him into the fold. When they slipped him back into China he was introduced to the young man who, with Shen, was said to be one of the rising Red stars. Mao, an intellectual, immediately saw how Wang Lee's chameleon-like, freewheeling way of doing things could be of great value to the party. Even in its infancy the party was in danger of burying itself in bureaucracy. Wang Lee cut through the red tape and got things done. He was also discreet, as well as smooth and urbane. Mao and the others in the central area of control groomed him. By the time he was twenty-one he was Chief of Intelligence for the whole Southern Region. The only person senior to him in that area was Shen himself.

As he thought again of Shen, Wang Lee's mind turned to Ling Ling. He knew her only by reputation. But, like so many other Shanghaiese, he knew what she looked like, sitting in her open sedan chair with her breasts and knees pushed out into the sun at her favorite spot on the Bund. And that image of her was enough to stir his loins as he ran. He had often coveted her; wondered how he might meet her. He wondered now if he had even, without realizing it, been a little shoddy in his work so that just this might happen. They had never gotten close enough to him to chase him before, never seen him jump and run from a train or anything like that. But he had a standing arrangement with Shen,

instituted by Shen himself. If ever there was an emergency he
was not to go to any of their known places. He was to go directly
to Shen's sister, Ling Ling. He would need only to tell her, or
have a message sent to her, that a friend of the owner of the
blanket was there, and she would understand and know what to
do.

"I did not know she was one of us," Wang Lee had said.
Shen had laughed out loud when he had heard this. "My sister—?
No . . . she is not one of us. She will do this for the sake of
family and because she honors me . . ."

Wang Lee looked at him aghast.

"What is wrong?" Shen said, still smiling. "You think me old-
fashioned? Too much part of the traditional China? It is a criticism often leveled at me. Perhaps you will be the one to enlighten
my sister. Perhaps you will recruit her to the party so she may
act from higher motives. Until then, however, you may have to
rely on her family honor, and her love and understanding and
compassion as a person."

Wang Lee nodded. He was beginning to see why Shen was so
highly thought of.

"I shall do my best to bring your sister into the fold," he
countered, with his street urchin smile.

"Do not underestimate her," Shen said quietly. "It is a
mistake many men have made."


Wang Lee was closer to the center of the city now, keeping
within the shadows of the walls. He saw a road blockade ahead
and swung quickly to the side. That one was new. They kept
changing the positions of the barriers all the time now. If he had
had a current Shanghai pass, he would have felt no hesitation in
walking straight up to the barrier. After all, if the Head of
Intelligence cannot trust his own forger, who can he trust?

But the person for whom the troops would be looking this
night was a steward from the Hong Kong train. He was sure that
was all the information they had. But that was exactly what the
pass he carried said. It was enough to get him arrested on the
spot on the basis of his occupation alone. And on the slightest
suspicion the Kuomintang knocked you down and beat you, and

then threw you into jail and asked questions later—if they ever bothered to ask any question at all.

So each time he saw a road barricade Wang Lee swung wide around it. And each time he made a swing he watched carefully to see if he was being followed. This was the hardest thing of all to teach his young recruits. They got overconfident when they thought they had outwitted the Kuomintang by avoiding a blockade, not knowing that the local area garrison also had troops hidden in the nearby streets, along the approaches to the wooden barricades. When people appeared deliberately to avoid stopping to have their passes checked, the soldiers followed them quietly and automatically arrested them—but not before they had noted who they were and what their destination was and reported all to the Blue Shirts, the secret police.

Wang Lee had lost two of his best men this way. They had never been heard of again. He had himself been followed twice. But not for long.

He worked his way around, painstakingly, street blockade after street blockade, knowing he was tired and fearful lest he was not alert enough to determine whether anyone was following him. For not all soldiers wore uniforms. And not all were men. Some of the specially-trained women were the most expert. He could be followed by someone who looked like a businessman, or a prostitute, or a street boy; or even a mandarin or a wealthy lady. The only safe rule was to make sure that no one—no one at all—was following you—even from a great distance. And on this night of all nights, he had to be doubly careful. It would not do to involve Ling Ling. Besides, he needed to sleep without fear tonight, without fear of being roused only to have to flee again. He was tired. More tired than he could ever remember. He desperately needed a safe spot to sleep.

He reached her street. It was long and wide, a graceful boulevard lined with plane trees, properly guttered at the edges and spotlessly clean. There was a half moon. Wang Lee entered the street cautiously, using first the cover of the shadows of the houses and then the trees.

At the farthest edge, the street ended abruptly in a square. Right across one side of this square, blocking the street completely so it became, in effect, a forecourt, was the house of Ma Yen the Mandarin, sitting imposingly in the moonlight in all its

red-pagoda glory. Halfway along the street Wang Lee paused
and looked behind him.

He waited five minutes but nothing moved. He slipped out
from the cover of one tree and onto the next. He waited another
five minutes. Still nothing. Was he being overcautious? Because
of Ling Ling? Soon he would have to think about Ma Yen's
gateman and walk openly towards the house so as not to arouse
suspicion.

He had not seen one single, solitary person following him
since the last barricade. And yet his sixth sense, the sense he had
learned invariably to trust, told him there was someone. Someone there as faceless as he; someone in the shadows, somewhere.
Someone who might not even have turned the corner yet. His
whole body ached with tiredness now. He wished only to sit in a
hot bath. To see Ling Ling. To eat and drink. To sleep. He had
not rested in two days. He had not eaten since noon the previous
day. The Kuomintang had people everywhere and it was better to
go hungry than to trust someone you were not sure of. One of his
men had been missing from his food stall yesterday and he had
passed by on the other side when he had seen another manning
the stall.

He knew, really, that there was only one thing to do, however
tired he might be.

Summoning the last of his inner resources, he grasped the tree
trunk by which he stood and, locking his arms around it, began
to seesaw himself upwards with his bare feet splayed around the
trunk. He pushed himself up by his haunches and then on up
higher with each frog-like lift of the body by hands and feet. He
reached the lowest branch and drew himself up into the cover of
the tree. Quietly he positioned himself so he had an almost
uninterrupted view of the street below. Then he waited.

An hour passed. Still nothing. Twice he had to stop himself
from falling asleep. Surely an hour was enough? Not if the other
were as clever as he. Perhaps the person had poked his—or
her—head around the corner when Wang Lee was not looking.

But Wang Lee also knew that human nature was strange. In
some ways he had based his adult life on the weaknesses of
others. And he knew that what most men might endure for one
hour, they would not endure for two. Sooner or later, if he were
right, the other one, if indeed there was another one, would want

to look again. Would want to be sure which house Wang Lee had gone into. Would want to see if it were safe to take up a position in the actual street where it would be easier to observe but not be observed.

Wang Lee waited for what seemed like another hour. Then, when he was sure he must have been imagining things and was about to drop down from his hiding place and walk openly towards Ma Yen's house, he saw a head appear quickly around the left-hand corner of the street. It was visible for only an instant and then darted back. Wang waited a few minutes more. Then he saw a dark figure slip silently around the corner and behind the first tree so swiftly that Wang Lee had to admire the professional technique of whoever was following him. Wang took his knife from its leather sheaf inside his black trouser band and clenched it in his teeth, edging around to the left-hand side of the branch on which he sat. He saw the dark figure below darting from tree to tree. He could see now it was a man and he was working his way up the street. Did he know Wang Lee was there? Wang doubted it but he could not be sure. And if the man were a soldier in plain clothes, of which Wang Lee had little doubt, there was bound to be a German mauser pistol poked into his trouser band. They all used the square-chambered German mausers, these Kuomintang. They were German-trained and German-equipped. Chiang Kai-shek had German officers from the Great War everywhere. German and Japanese, teaching Chinese to fight Chinese.

Wang knew he could not rule out that the man might know, or at least suspect, which tree he was in. Wang would have to jump first, before the man had time to draw his gun.

Quietly Wang positioned himself again on the branch. The man was getting very close now. He was very agile. One more tree. As he comes out from the next one . . . now!

With all his force, Wang leaped—far out and to the side so he was down behind the man, landing on all fours with his hand going up to take the knife from his teeth in the same movement as he saw the man, expertly-trained, go for his trouser-band as the man's whole body began to pivot around towards the source of danger in a reflex action.

But Wang's opponent was too late. Wang's blade thrust deep into his middle back, coming out in one clean, beautifully timed

withdrawal; and as the man's face saw Wang and showed first
agony and then despair, Wang drove his blade in for the second
time, striking with all his remaining energy right for the heart.

As the blade came out again, the man slumped dead at his
feet. Activated now with adrenalin, Wang looked quickly about
him and saw the street was still deserted. He was about to leave
the body where it lay, walking openly out onto the road and
straight for the house at the end, when he suddenly saw the
man's face.

He let out a gasp. There was no mistaking who this was. This
man was too well known. It was Ma Yen's son, Ma Yao; Ling
Ling was his concubine.

So he was a member of the infamous Blue Shirts too! How
long had he been following him? Just from the last barricade?
What would one so senior be doing at the barricades? Wang
knew that someone as highborn as Ma Yao would be very senior
indeed. Had he been expecting Wang? If so, how many others
had he told? And how much did they know?

But these questions would have to wait.

There was nothing for Wang to do now but to leave him there
and go on. There would be all hell to pay. But the important
thing was not to be seen. He looked around once more, confident
now that the street was empty. Slowly, he began to pick his way
along towards the house at the end. He stayed in the shadows for
some time until he had to come out into the open and walk
towards the gate set in the wall which would let him into Ma
Yen's courtyard.

It was past midnight—a late hour for a caller. The gateman
was technically supposed to stay awake all night. But many
slept. This meant one had to risk noise to wake them. Yet even if
he were fully awake, would he admit Wang Lee? Would he even
carry the message to his mistress?

Wang Lee knocked quietly at the red lacquered gate in the red
cement wall. There was a stout oak door behind the red lacquered one, and presently Wang Lee heard the bolts creak; a tall,
burly Chinese gateman appeared. He came fully outside the door
with his bare arms crossed, confident of his own strength.

"What is it you wish?" he barked.

"That you tell your mistress Ling Ling a friend of the one
with the blanket is here."

Wang Lee had been wary of delivering such a message but Shen had assured him it would be all right.

"You expect me to wake my mistress at this hour with such a message? Be off with you, you running dog. I would not give my mistress such a message even in the broad light of day."

"Better to give her a message she wishes to hear than receive a beating as a bad servant," Wang said, standing his ground.

At this, Wang thought the big man's expression softened just a fraction.

"My mistress does not have her servants beaten," the gate- man retorted. "But perhaps you know my mistress? Prove to me that you know her and I will carry the message."

"I do not know your mistress. I am sent only to deliver the message and wait on her."

"Perhaps you would know some friend or acquaintance of hers then? Tell me who it is who has sent you."

Wang was now suspicious. He began to think again about the dagger hidden in his trouser band.

But just as he was doing so, the big man broke into a broad smile.

"I would not think about risking a fight with me, Comrade Wang," he said. "Despite the high esteem in which you are held, I have this position here because of my strength and ability in hand-to-hand combat. Step inside now and excuse my rough arrogance, but I had to be sure it was you."

"But you have no description of me," Wang Lee said.

"No. But my comrade leader Shen said I would know you by your manner," the big man laughed. "He said you would not be intimidated by my questions and you would refuse to give any information other than the simple sentence you had been told to say."

Wang smiled through his weariness, his first smile in nearly three days.

"I am Hsing-tao," the big man said, extending his hand and then, noticing the other's tiredness, added, "Sit here in my gatehouse and take tea while I go for my mistress. There is steaming water in the thermos and green leaves in the brown paper packet. I shall return presently . . ."

But Wang was shaking his head. Despite his tiredness, he knew there was a matter more urgent now than anything else.

And he had decided to trust this man, rather than risk further delay in getting a message to Shen.

"There is a favor I must ask you, Comrade," Wang said slowly.

"Of course. There was trouble . . . ?"

Wang smiled to himself. His admiration for Shen was increasing all the time. This was no simple hunk of muscle he had entrusted with the task of guarding his sister. This was an alert, intelligent, highly trained party member.

"There was trouble . . ." Wang nodded. "There is a body nearby. There was a danger he might have known where I was going. He saw me enter this street . . ."

"I understand. My mistress and I are grateful for your concern to protect us. I will take care of the body. It is not far away?"

Wang Lee shook his head, gratefully. It was death for the man to be found away from his post. He might move around inside to deliver messages and the like. But never outside. "It is not far," Wang Lee replied, "just halfway along the street on the left."

The gateman became serious and nodded. "You will wait here and guard the gate and open only to my voice . . . ?"

Wang Lee nodded. But he put his hand on the big man's arm as he was about to move off.

"The face is a face you may not wish to see dead," Wang Lee said simply.

"Is it the face of a Blue Shirt?"

"I believe it to be so," Wang Lee said.

The big man spat on the ground at the confirmation of the hated Secret Police.

"Then it is a face I wish to see dead."

"Good. Where will you take him?"

"To the mulch heap in the garden over by the west wall. The earth is soft there and smells of decay from the rotting vegetable cuttings. There are many from a Great House such as this. I will dig deep tonight and by morning none will know what lies at the bottom of the pit."

"It is fitting," Wang Lee said simply. "The body is a son of this house."

"It was only a matter of time, Comrade," Hsing said. "He was always scheming and plotting. You will not tell my mistress?"

"No. I shall ask Comrade Shen to tell her only that he has

heard Ma Yao died in the countryside. It is better this thing tonight not be connected with you or me in any way.''

The big man nodded.

"What will happen to your mistress now?" Wang asked.

"Who knows?" Hsing said.

Wang nodded. "Let us clear away the evidence quickly, then.''

Without another word Hsing slipped quietly out through the gate. Wang had barely had time to pour himself tea before he heard the big man's quiet rap on the lacquered wood door and his whisper that he was alone and that Wang should open the door. When Wang did, he gratefully saw how easily the big man carried Ma Yao over his shoulder. Wang closed the gate and together he and Hsing made their way to the vegetable patch. Then they dug quietly together in the far corner of the garden under the moon, sharing a cup of tea and hoping no one was watching.

But even so, it was nearly 2 A.M. before the big man was rousing one of Ling Ling's maidens-in-waiting and sending her for her mistress while Wang Lee waited in the antechamber. Then he saw her coming, a long thin gown thrown quickly about her and her hair long and tousled from sleep. Her deep almond eyes seemed barely awake but they were nevertheless alive and smiling—the kindest, softest, most welcoming eyes he had ever seen in his life.

She stood little on ceremony. She thanked Hsing for bringing Wang to her and delivering the message. When he had gone, she turned to Wang Lee.

"My brother has sent you?" she said softly.

"Yes.''

"How does my brother?"

"You have no doubt seen him more recently than I. It is many days since I was last in Shanghai.''

"This is true. It was a test question. Forgive me. But even with the trusted Hsing at the gate it is wise to be prudent. These are difficult times.''

Wang Lee smiled. Communist or not, she had Shen's mental agility and caution.

They were still standing in Ling Ling's outer chamber, looking at each other, the maidens-in-waiting having departed. Ling

Ling now walked over to Wang Lee and took his hand easily and began to lead him inside.

"Come," she said, "for I can see that you are tired and would like to bathe. I shall have my maidens prepare a bath, which I think you will enjoy, and there is cold duck and fresh lychees which we may bring you from our private larder without sending to the kitchen, which would arouse suspicion. Is this agreeable?"

Wang Lee nodded and forced a smile through his tiredness.

"Bathe first and then the food?"

He nodded again.

"Good."

"It is safe with your maidens?" he asked carefully.

"They are loyal to me. Besides, they are used to men coming and going. My master is away on government business a great deal and the Old One, his father, allows me some freedom so that my friend, the general Yang Ho, and others may visit me."

She saw Wang Lee's face stiffen, though he tried to hide it.

"Why does the Old One allow this?" he said.

"Because he is kind and knows that his son, of whom I shall not speak disrespectfully, has different ways from his father. Besides, it gives the Old Lord much face for the general Yang Ho, whom all say will one day be second only to Chiang Kai-shek, to honor his house with such visits. And I am sure that however much of an idealist the young communist spy Wang Lee is, he knows that a poor country girl like myself must make her way in the world as best she is able, even if this means accepting favors of gentlemen friends. What if something should happen to my lord and I was without other friends to help? I would starve in the streets like so many others."

At the mention of his name in the same sentence as Yang Ho, Wang Lee had winced. Hsing was a member of the party, with loyalty sworn to the death to protect the names of all members known to him. But this girl! What of her? And did she know already of her young master's death in the street? Had Hsing told her when he went to have her maidens arouse her before he brought Wang Lee to her? Hsing had agreed not to tell. To let Shen contact her, without any mention of Wang Lee or Hsing's part.

But perhaps, Wang thought, she was just imagining a possible situation. It was, after all, what a Chinese woman in her situation would think. And she was charming. Charming and disarming, for all her direct speech. And he was so tired. He had not liked the reference to himself as a spy, either. They had said she had a very open nature. But he had not known how far this extended.

"You presume to know a lot about me," he said, overcoming his tiredness once more to keep his wits about him.

"As you know about me. Did you think my brother would not tell me when he asked me to risk my life by hiding someone in my bedchamber who was on the run from the government and the Secret Police? What we know, we know about each other. You might just as easily betray me by a slip, an indiscretion, as I you. And so, I think we must trust each other and be friends . . . ?"

Her words had an implied "Should we not?" as she finished talking on an upward intonation. There was a slightly cheeky tone and the trace of impish laughter in her voice. It was almost as if she were saying, "Why take this so seriously? Why not enjoy the delights of the house in which it has been your good fortune to find yourself?" Could one say all this by intonation and smile? It was certainly what he felt. He relaxed, noticeably.

"Good," she said. "I see we trust each other. Come. I shall have the bath prepared and I shall bathe you myself and tend to you and afterwards you will feel better and we shall sup."

She said it as naturally and unselfconsciously as one friend greeting another in the street. And Wang Lee found himself following. Was this not, after all, what he had dreamed of? And yet, even he knew that to be bathed was one thing. This was a courtesy she might extend to any traveler who was a friend of her family. She might bathe him fully robed. Or she might unrobe. No matter. It might mean little more than pouring tea, especially to a professional concubine. What came after the bath and the meal was what mattered. And he had no way of knowing how she would receive his advances. But he must try. He had desired her secretly, longingly, passionately in his dreams from the day he had first seen her sitting on the Bund with her wares displayed for all the world to see.

The bath was a luxury such as one born poor never expects to have in his lifetime.

While the maidens prepared it, Ling Ling, still in her loose night robe, brought tea and fortune cookies. Then, when the head maiden, a girl barely in her late teens herself, brought word that the bath was ready, and after she and her companions departed, Ling Ling rose and took Wang Lee's hand once more and led him into an inner chamber.

It was a large room, with ornate hangings and tapestries and a large, square marble bath in the center. The bath took up most of the floor except for broad walkways around the edges. The most exquisite Persian rugs covered these surroundings, from the wall to the bath's edge. At the edge the marble was built up six inches all around to keep the water from splashing out. But Wang Lee was sure this was not to save any expense of damage to the carpet. It was simply to avoid the discomfort of having to step out of a bath onto a wet rug.

As he looked and stared in amazement, thick clouds of steam rose from the water with wafting smells—the sweetest fragrance of perfumed oil that he had ever smelled. Ling Ling now stood discreetly behind him. He heard her ask softly, "Ready?" Slowly, he turned to nod, and as he did so her loose gown fell about her and she stood still, unmoving, letting his full gaze rest upon her.

He was transfixed. He had never seen a naked woman before and his heart leapt. Could anything be this beautiful? Her breasts were full and her waist narrowed before it rode out into the rounded firmness of her hips. The cavern above her legs and thighs was edged by the thinnest of dark black hair.

"Oh Ling Ling," he gasped, and never knew the words were inside him or where they had come from.

She smiled an appreciative smile, as one who likes her beauty to be admired, and then said, ever so softly again, "And now you."

And something within him, something her voice reached, began his fingers moving, without embarrassment, though it was the first time he had ever undressed before a woman. His jacket and pants came away effortlessly to the floor. Ling Ling stood and looked at him for a moment and smiled a gentle, warm smile and then walked over and took him by the hand. Bending only momentarily to pick up a huge cake of scented soap, she led him down the marble steps into the bath.

\* \* \*

It was inevitable they should become lovers. Wang Lee had the Hong Kong streets within him—which Ling Ling found exciting. His was a cavalier, swashbuckling nature that would put him at variance with the communist leadership. But underneath, Wang Lee was a peasant, too. And Ling Ling found herself responding to this as well. In the bedchamber Wang Lee was a simple country boy of her own kind, whom she could feel close to and at ease with in a way she could not with her masters and generals.

So on that first night, after they had bathed together, and eaten, she took him straight to her bed. They lay side by side, both of them naked together, the thin white wisps of the mosquito net all around them and their bodies front up under the gentle stirring breeze of the camphorwood fan.

Wang Lee fell asleep immediately, but Ling Ling lay awake thinking. Although on this occasion it was not the type of insomnia that sometimes came to her in the middle of the night after she had been with a man she hated, so that the dragons of the deep came up to haunt her until she cried herself back to sleep again. On this night she lay awake because of the easy pleasure she had found in Wang Lee's company. They had laughed and jumped and played in the bath like two country children naked in a pond. They had sat together easily at table afterwards and talked of the past, times they could barely remember and yet times they felt they knew and longed for, times before Wang Lee and Shen and Ling Ling moved away from the Village of Wild Grass to the depths of the city.

But what if she came to like him more and more?

She fell asleep herself then and when the first light stirred, Wang Lee rolled restlessly awake. He was not used to sleeping safely for more than a few hours at a time. This morning, as he moved beside Ling Ling, she stretched and slid her leg across his thigh so that he felt the soft-rough rub of her maiden hair; and soon his hands were on her tiny buttocks, pushing and turning her in the peasant intensity she had expected, taking her and taking her quickly, yet not roughly, and whispering sweet things to her, surprisingly sweet and gentle things, as he mounted her and rode her in on the clouds where the Seven White Dragons roam in the land of longing, ecstasy, and fulfillment.

He stayed with her several days, on the orders of Shen, her brother. Shen came to visit on the second day and to tell her of the news that her master, Ma Yao, had been taken by bandits and executed on an important government misson in the countryside. Shen had arranged for Ma Yao's father, Ma Yen the Mandarin, to receive the same news through a reliable source. The old mandarin immediately made arrangements for Ling Ling to stay in her same quarters but as one of *his* concubines, though there was much wailing and arguing in the house. Ma Yen's Number One Wife, whose son Ma Yao had been, felt it indecent for such an old one as her husband to take such a young and pretty concubine of her son's. But all knew Ma Yen would have his own way in his own house.

Whether Shen knew that Wang Lee had slept with his sister, Wang was unable to tell. In any case, Wang had to stay for at least a week. They all knew that.

For once it was known Ma Yao had been following him, urgent inquiries had had to be initiated with a whole range of informants inside the government to find out how much was known.

Of course the name did not matter. Wang Lee's real name was Shen Lee. Wang Lee was the name he had used while working on the Star Ferry in Hong Kong to avoid any trouble for his family—in case anything ever went wrong with his *Ching-pang* story. Wang Lee was the name the party had put on his forged identity card when they had first smuggled him back into China. It was now known that the Kuomintang had discovered "Wang Lee" was the name of the head of Communist intelligence. How they found out did not matter. It had enabled them to connect the person who had made the run from the train with the man who, next to Shen himself, was the one they most wanted to question. But identifying the name had, of course, also given them the briefest of descriptions. For a few remembered the white-jacketed steward on the train, and many had seen him as he jumped from the train and ran.

The late Ma Yao, the bureaucrat deputy head of the Secret Police, known as the Blue Shirts, had studied the reports carefully. He was also shrewd enough to know how poorly patrolled the open sewers were. So far as Shen knew, Ma Yao had gone there alone to wait and had been rewarded by seeing Wang Lee slip quietly into the city at dusk on the second day.

As expert himself at following as Wang Lee was at evading, Ma Yao had gotten very close to tracking the communist tiger to his lair without being seen. It was only Wang Lee's sixth sense that had defeated him. The sense of someone following. Ma Yao had remained invisible until the slightest lapse had made him poke his head around the corner.

Now Ma Yao was dead, buried under his own vegetable patch. But would it end there? How many others had he told? Just how good was their description of Wang Lee? Had Ma Yao, ambitious to be head of the Secret Police, told no one so that he alone would get the credit if his plan was successful? Or had he told others? If not his superior, then maybe a trusted lieutenant?

Either way, one thing was certain. Wang Lee would have to be doubly careful in the future. They all would. And in the meantime, until another safe place and a means of getting him there undetected were found, Wang must stay where he was.

Shen apologized to his sister, who smiled and said only that she was honored to have their cousin stay in her humble court. She said it was unusual for any to call unannounced and she was sure that if any problem arose, Hsing and her handmaidens would find a way of hiding Wang Lee until the danger was past.

The week passed swiftly. The lovers talked a great deal, discovering each other, learning of each other's family, attitudes, hopes, and political beliefs. They found that they shared the same sense of humor, and they laughed a lot and teased each other; often their minds would meet so that they began to know what the other was thinking before the words were spoken. And because their origins were so similar, they had the same tastes in food and the same way of eating and the same type of politeness. Wang Lee admired the quickness of Ling Ling's intelligence and was bewitched by her beauty and the delicate porcelain of her body, while she discovered in him not only strength and vitality, but tenderness too. They made love often, and what had begun as little more than lust gradually became much much more.

By the end of the week Ling Ling and Wang Lee were so much in love they could hardly bear to be parted from one another. When the time came for Wang to be smuggled out, lying beneath Ling's feet in her sedan chair as she went on one of her outings to sit in the sun on the Bund, neither wanted to leave.

And even when the sedan chair stopped by the river, and they said their goodbyes while some comrades crowded around and Wang Lee slipped quietly into a waiting junk, Ling Ling knew that she would see him again whatever the cost, and that he would risk all to see her. But more than that, she knew too that she would be unable to avoid passing him pieces of information, things the generals told her which would limit the risk for this man who took so many risks and whom she now so desperately wanted to keep alive and safe from harm.

Thomas Blake sat in his suite atop the Cathay Hotel overlooking the Shanghai waterfront. There was a brandy balloon, half full of Five Star Courvoisier, and a silver, methylated-spirit brandy warmer on a table beside him. He sat on a red leather Chesterfield, with his feet up, smoking a Romeo and Juliet Havana cigar.

He did his best thinking this way and today was a day for thinking.

He loved the cut and thrust of business, the excitement—and his venture in "arms dealing" was certainly providing that. He smiled at his own use of the term "arms dealing"—the euphemism of polite society for gun-running. He had laughed out loud to himself when he had arrived home after his meeting in the backstreet teashop with the arrogant young Communist. His old enemy Edwards in gun-running! Blake should have realized it for himself. It had taken the Communists to tell him.

And yet their scheme provided the perfect vehicle for Blake to deal a body blow to Edwards.

What a strange week it had been! Skulking in the shadows at the border to oversee the shipment of contraband guns; then the surprise appearance of Wang Lee in his train compartment; the note Wang Lee had given him, bringing the bitter disappointment of the failure of Blake's first arms deal. When Blake had actually been watching his "arms shipment," disguised as agricultural machinery, the boxes already contained lead weights. They had been substituted for the guns after Yang Ho had uncovered the contraband. The trail had led from the onboard death of a known Communist—the old coolie, Wang Lee's uncle—to a search for communist contraband. What a chain of events the piece of red communist paper falling from the coolie's headband had created.

And yet it all served Blake's purpose. For after his disappointment had come the excitement that a second batch of arms—quite different from his own and much larger in size—had also been on board the ocean liner. This shipment of arms, organized by Edwards, had official government approval. There was no chance of them being confiscated—except by Blake! And who better to "confiscate" them from than Edwards. If the government hadn't paid Edwards for them—if it was cash on delivery—Edwards would be ruined.

Blake made his plans. He had sent his old Chinese friend, Shan Li, to recruit some labor for the midnight assault, and inspected the Edwards warehouse where the guns would be stored. Now all he had to do was wait.

# 8

$K$*ate had been dreading the moment when she would have to* tell her parents that she wanted to go into private practice. She felt herself blushing as she tried to explain her reasons, because of her guilt at not saying she would join them in the clinic and perhaps eventually take it over. They were both clearly disappointed—especially her mother. But it was typical of her father that he simply asked if she was sure. When she replied yes, he said, "Well then, we'd better make certain you work with someone good."

After that he telephoned the most respected surgeon in Shanghai, who had a successful private practice as well as his work at the hospital. Clem Richmond, because of his great warmth and tranquillity—and because he did not convey any feeling of judgment for a way of life different from his own—was very well liked. Besides, truth to tell, the surgeon knew that Clem was as good a surgeon as he, if not better, and there was great respect and friendship between the two colleagues. And the surgeon immediately said yes, knowing that Clem's daughter was likely to be a fine doctor.

But if this was a hard decision for Bette to accept, it was even harder when Kate told her she was moving out into an apartment with Janey. Kate knew her mother disapproved. Her mother's saintly silence confirmed that. At times the unspoken murmurings of her mother were almost more than Kate could bear.

Again her father came to the rescue. Janey had found an absolutely luxurious apartment on the Bund. Kate felt that even her share was too expensive and insisted they find something else. But her father asked to see the Bund apartment. When he did he said, "Why not take it, Katie? I can see you like it, and I think it's important for you to discover your true likes and dislikes at this time. They may be very different from ours, you know. There's no guarantee children will want the same things as their parents—nor should they be expected to, nor should one be regarded as better than another. Take the apartment and enjoy it. You can afford it. Your salary will soon increase. And in any case it'll only make a couple of months' difference at the end in terms of paying us back."

"Oh Daddy," she said, leaning up and kissing him, "oh Daddy . . ."

Then she went to sign the lease with Janey. It would be two weeks before they could move in, as the lease provided for repainting. But they were so excited they got the key and went there that night.

They sat on the floor drinking a bottle of champagne Janey had brought. Janey's "flight from the nest," as she called it, had not been without incident, either. Her father had shouted that he needed Janey to run the household while her mother was away. Janey had shouted back, "Call in one of your bloody mistresses, then!" and walked out, slamming the door behind her. She was telling Kate about it now and they were both laughing.

"I hope he doesn't stop your allowance," Kate said, "or we mightn't be able to afford the apartment."

"He'll cool down," Janey said. "He always does. And if he doesn't, Mummy'll threaten to expose his mistress and sue for divorce unless he increases her allowance. Then she'll send me the extra money from London." They both laughed again. Then they talked some more about inconsequential matters.

After a while, Kate turned to Janey and, trying to sound as casual as possible, said, "I don't suppose you're planning to go to the Shanghai Club ball in a couple of weeks, are you?"

"Yes, of course I am, darling. Mummy's not likely to be back in time and I can't see Daddy taking one of his concubines. So I suppose I'll have to do the dutiful darling daughter bit for at least part of the night." Janey put her hand to her mouth and feigned a yawn. "You surely don't want to come, do you? I mean it's never been your cup of tea at all."

"Would it be awfully hard to arrange?" Kate said very slowly.

"Not a bit of it, darling. You know me, fix it in a trice, if that's what you want. Mind you, you might have to put up with being escorted by one of Daddy's bright but very dull young men. But that should be no problem. You could certainly jettison that cargo the moment you got there. And then I'd see to it that your card got filled up very quickly with the names of those who at least had some claim to not having completely empty heads. Would you like me to arrange it?"

"Yes, please, I rather think I would," Kate said quietly.

"Good. Consider it done, then," Janey said. She got up and poured them each another glass of champagne. As she was about to sit down again she added: "Anyone in particular?"

Kate shook her head. Janey looked at her.

"Just someone I met on the train," Kate said.

Kate's appointment at the hospital—where she would work part-time with the surgeon, Ballantine, as well as join his private practice—was not due to start for three weeks. She had been disappointed at first, for she was anxious to start and she needed the money. But when she heard the apartment would not be ready for two weeks, she saw the other delay could be used to some advantage.

Her parents had wanted to take a holiday for some time but found it impossible to get away.

Kate now insisted. She knew her father, particularly, wanted to take a trip into the North. He had often spoken of it in his

letters. Besides, she would be glad of the practical experience in
the clinic. Running it alone—even with Nurse Dwyer's help—
would be a heavy work load but one she would enjoy. She would
also feel that she had been of some immediate help to her
parents.

Her father accepted her offer right away. Her mother felt she
should stop and help Kate. But Clem Richmond told his wife she
needed a holiday too, although not with him. Traveling in the
North could be uncomfortable and even a little dangerous, he
said. Bette said that if he was going, so was she. But in the end
Clem persuaded her to spend three weeks visiting her closest
friend—a lady missionary Bette had trained with and who now
lived in Peking. He said he would return in two weeks and help
Katie in the clinic until her mother got back.


Some wonderful days and nights followed for Kate. She was
determined not to call on the other missions for help if she could
possibly avoid it. So she worked extra shifts, staying open late
and starting very early so people could come before work. Word
soon got around. She loved the feeling of being responsible for
all these people and their lives, and of being in charge of the
clinic.

The clinic was hopelessly out-of-date with equipment, of course.
But she kept turning a blind eye to this and thinking she might
even stay after all and work in the clinic with her parents. She
loved the people so and she knew she would deal with a very
different style of person—rich Chinese and Europeans—if she
went into private practice.

And perhaps she might even have stayed at the clinic if a
seemingly simple incident had not occurred on that day four
weeks after she had arrived home.

During *xiuxi,* the Chinese siesta time, when it was unusual for
anyone to come at all, Kate had sent Nurse Dwyer off to lunch.
She was just sitting down to have her first cigarette since breakfast when there was a knock on the door.

She put her cigarettes back in her purse and went to open the
door. A fat young mother shuffled in with her son. Kate supposed the boy to be about six or seven.

When Kate indicated that the mother and boy should sit, the

mother shook her head. They were of peasant stock and it was unthinkable they should sit while one of Kate's position stood. So Kate walked over to her desk and beckoned for them to follow. Once there, she immediately sat down, indicating two chairs in front of the desk for the mother and son. They sat down a little uncertainly. Kate then produced a jar of candy. The boy took a piece, while the mother began to explain things. She said, a little shamefully, that she had come during *xiuxi* so that her husband would not know. He was at home nearby, sleeping. The boy had had trouble with his hearing since birth and all sorts of herbal medicines had failed to cure him.

Kate carefully gave the child a complete physical. Then she proceeded to examine his ears, looking first in one and then the other with an aperture tool and light.

"It is only the right ear, Child's Mother?" Kate asked kindly as she got up to search for another instrument.

The woman made no sound but Kate looked over her shoulder to see that she was nodding, stupefied, as if this were some rare knowledge that one might know so quickly—which was the troublesome ear.

Kate was searching for the audiophone. But she couldn't find it. She took her keys from the pocket of her white coat and went into the equipment room to look for it. Still nothing.

The audiophone, which was old and outdated but had been there before she left for America, would allow her to test the boy's full hearing range. Designated levels of sound on a wire recorder were played to patients through earphones, and their responses measured. Kate now proceeded to try to do this herself by speaking in ever-reducing levels—first into one ear and then the other. She had already told the child in his good ear that he should nod when he could hear and shake his head when he could not.

She finished the examination. Now she was 90 percent sure.

"Will you let me give your son something so he feels no pain and then let me put something in his ear?" she asked the mother.

The woman agreed.

Kate gave the boy a local anesthetic and laid him down on the examination couch, putting a kidney dish under his ear to collect any fluid that would come out. Then she asked the mother to hold his head still. Next she swabbed herself, sterilized a long

thin scalpel, and put a headband light on her forehead. She bent
down beside the table so as to be level with the boy's head and
slipped the scalpel into his ear, moving it slowly towards the
position she had memorized from her examination. She gave a
couple of pinprick jabs, withdrawing almost in the same motion.
She saw the tell-tale fluid start to run out and breathed a sigh of
relief. The boy had an abscess.

"Do you hear better now, little one?" she whispered in the
boy's ear at a level both she and the mother knew he had not
previously responded to. They looked at each other when they
saw the boy nod his head in wide-eyed agreement. Kate thought
the mother was going to cry. Then she thought she herself might.

One of Kate's professors had always warned her that identifying too much with her patients would probably be her greatest
problem as a doctor. Still, for just one day, why not? A simple
abscess which the baby had developed after birth and which had
been reinfected and reinfected—how many times? She dared not
think. But she breathed one secret sigh of relief—that the continual infection and inflammation had not damaged the eardrum.

"I will give you something with which to rinse the ear out, to
be used for a few days," said Kate. "After that I'm sure his
hearing will be completely restored."

"It is better now, Doctor."

"Yes. It is at least good enough to save you from a beating for
sneaking out while your husband slept," smiled Kate. "But it
will get even better in the next few days. You must come and
visit me and tell me how it is."

She helped the little boy down, patting him on the head and
giving him an extra caramel. Then she showed them both to the
door.

When they had gone she sat down with a cigarette and a cup
of coffee. She was glad she was alone. She had the feeling that
wherever the practice of medicine took her, there would be few
days she would enjoy as much as this one. She would remember
the look on the little boy's face for a long time.

Kate believed later that at that moment she was about to
decide in favor of working at her parents' clinic.

But when Nurse Dwyer came back, Kate asked where the
audiophone was.

"Broke down and couldn't be fixed," was all she said.

The nurse, Rhoda Dwyer, who was also American, was abrupt and of few words. She and Kate had never got on.

"How long ago was that?"

"Just after you left."

"Why in goodness name wasn't it replaced?"

"Your parents said it was something they could do without."

"Yes, but for the sake of a few dollars . . ." Kate said, and then suddenly stopped.

"Yes," she heard the nurse say sharply.

Kate knew then that she had to go into private practice after all. She had to earn the money that would allow the audiophone to be replaced, to give her parents all the other equipment they needed so desperately if their healing work was to continue unhindered. And for herself, too, she needed to be able to afford all the best aids of modern medicine.

# 9

*N*igel Edwards was an irascible, red-faced Englishman, fattish and florid, with beefy hands, who looked every inch what he was: a managing director of one of the great British trading houses of the Colonial East, a giant of a *tai-pan* who ran his business and his life for pleasure and profit. He was one of the class who, so it seemed to many who knew them, decided the future of men and their cargoes over stout whiskey sodas in the long bar of the exclusive Shanghai Club.

But if Edwards was fond of whiskey sodas at the club, and all the things that went with the high life in Shanghai, including a massive array of women, Kate knew that none of these things diminished his business capacity. The fact was, these other matters were occasional diversions from the rough and tumble of the business world which was his life. He was a multimillionaire in pounds sterling, yet he would cut and thrust like a buccaneer, or a poor Chinese street urchin, to save a half-penny in a business deal. It was not the money, he would say, but the principle of not paying more than one ought.

Kate, admittedly, had found some of Edwards' business philosophy a little difficult to digest when confronted with it over the years by Janey or by Edwards himself. She found much of it, as she grew older, a rich man's rationalization. Coolies in Shanghai were still paid starvation wages. And Kate, perhaps in her simplicity, she sometimes thought, believed that men like Edwards had it in their power to alter such things by a wave of their hands. If they led, others would follow. Yet she liked Sir Nigel well enough. For all his bullying, business ways, there was a warm streak to him. It had shown itself when Janey had told him Kate wished to come to the ball. Janey relayed the message.

"Daddy says you're to go with him," she said. "I'm to accompany one of his young managers."

"That's nice," Kate said. "Tell your father I'm very grateful."

"He says we'll be free to leave our escorts when we get over the introductions, provided we keep them a dance each," said Janey.

"Seems like he's thought of everything," Kate said.

"He *can* be awfully kind and thoughtful sometimes." There was a tone of far-off reflection in Janey's voice.

"He wants to give me a lot of *face* by arriving with him because I'm not known in society," Kate said, simply and directly.

Janey looked at her friend Katie in a kind and warm way. Then she said slowly:

"Yes, darling, you're so right, although I didn't see it at first. But then I've never bothered to become half-Chinese like you and Daddy."

The two weeks they had to wait while the apartment was being painted seemed like an eternity. But eventually the apartment was ready and they moved in. It was Monday and the ball would take place on Wednesday.

Kate had been hoping for some respite from her work at the clinic to give her time to make last-minute preparations for the

ball when her father returned. But by Monday evening—the day
he had been due to return—her father had still not come back.
Kate was a little anxious. But not unduly so. Her father had been
traveling in regions where, away from the main railhead, trans-
portation was largely by mule or horse and where it was very
easy to miss a train connection. A week either way in China in
those days was no great cause for concern and she had known this
when she'd agreed to work at the clinic. As much as anything it
was a minor inconvenience in relation to the ball. She would
have to hurry on Wednesday to get her shift at the clinic finished
in time to get home and dressed.

The night of the ball the Edwards party forgathered with the
committee in the club's main bar—the one night of the year
ladies were allowed in—before going on to the British Legation
where the ball would be held.

They had just arrived and Nigel Edwards was taking their
drink orders as a waiter hovered by. Edwards was at his ebullient
best. "Now come, ladies, come, what will you have? Let's get
the order in quickly. We've a night of heavy drinking before us
and we don't want to waste any time. A sherry, perhaps? We
have a new consignment that is absolutely superb. But order
what you will, it makes no difference—Edwards and Company
imports it all." He gave a little laugh, or what he would have
called a laugh. But it was in fact a bull roar, which was heard
along the entire bar. Yet no one minded. He was, after all, their
captain, and this was their ship, and on board the captain may do
as he likes.

"I think I'd like a bourbon, if I may, seeing how it's a special
night." Kate was the first to speak up.

"What an excellent idea," said Edwards. "A bourbon indeed,
waiter. And I think I'll join you, my dear. Though I must say we
don't have any branch water. Will you have plain water or
soda?"

"Plain, thank you."

"Quite right. Now Janey dear, what is your particular pleasure
this particular night?"

"Glenfiddich, thank you, Father, with soda,"

Edwards nodded approvingly. He felt it fitting his daughter

should nominate an excellent scotch. It would be very plebeian not to specify one at all. Of course he had known she would order scotch, and would have been disappointed had she not, although he was mannered enough always to ask her. Scotch was Janey's invariable drink, and Kate could not help wondering once more, as she saw father and daughter together again after all these years, if it was much of a strain for Janey to be son as well as daughter to her father. There was not a hint of tomboy in her sweet hazel beauty. Yet in her there was her father's ardor, sometimes his explosiveness, and certainly his drive, for which Janey found it so hard to find an outlet. It occurred to Kate that there might be something to be said for letting Janey have a part in the business, however small, to provide just such an outlet, instead of her endless round of social engagements which Kate knew left Janey feeling frustrated and useless.

Perhaps a husband and family and a household of her own was what Janey needed. Perhaps it was what Kate needed too. But in the meantime Kate could not help feeling, as a doctor, that she would prescribe a healthy involvement in the Edwards family business. Then Janey might not feel so bad, secretly, about not being a son, and Nigel Edwards himself might not feel so bad about not having fathered one. Although Janey, when she had talked about it as a teenager, had said that her father had only been able to have one try. After Janey's birth it had been discovered that there was something not quite right with her mother's womb and that it would be highly dangerous for her to attempt another labor.

In a fit of pique at having to fulfill so much of her father's friendship needs, since her mother was away so often, Janey had once said she couldn't understand why her father didn't get his bloody Chinese mistress pregnant and have a son that way. But then Janey had said she knew why: Her father wanted a son all right, but he didn't want one so badly that he was prepared to let a half-Chinese bastard be heir to the Edwards millions. Besides, there'd be no guarantee he'd drink bloody whiskey sodas with him all the time. He'd probably order a *mao tai* if he ever got into their damned self-righteous club, which of course he never would.

Looking at her friend and reminiscing to herself, Kate believed Janey had gotten over most of it—except perhaps wanting to be part of the business.

Edwards was now asking Janey's escort what he would drink. He ordered the same as Janey. He was a quiet young man for a manager, although Kate realized he was only one of several managers.

"My God, did you hear it—?" Janey was saying as she took Kate half to one side, allowing the young manager, whose name was Fox, to start the invariable round of business talk with her father, which was really why they were there.

"What do you mean?" asked Kate.

"His accent, dear, his accent. It's North Country! He's North Country! It's well disguised, but the more whiskey he drinks, unless he can hold it very well, the more it will sound as clear as the day he was born."

"You're an awful snob, you know. I wouldn't even know what a North Country accent was if we hadn't had this stupid conversation once before with some other poor unfortunate."

"Yes dear, I know, but isn't it fun? I mean, what else is one to do at parties?"

Kate looked at her, exasperated but smiling. "You mean his speech lacks the gentility of the South?" she said with a wicked twinkle in her eye, mimicking the Georgia accent of her parents.

Janey looked at her and they both burst out laughing. But by this time almost everyone was on their second or third drink and no one really noticed. They drank for another half hour before the special rickshaws arrived to take them the short distance to where the ball would be held. The weather was cold and they had to wear wraps.

When they arrived at the British Legation, Kate began to realize she was a little nervous. She felt the perspiration forming under her arms. She would have to stand to the left of Nigel Edwards, in the receiving line. For as president of the club he was host to all the guests and had to greet them as they arrived. She wondered how he would greet Blake. And, indeed, how she would. But her concern over this was soon absorbed in another nervousness. It had not occurred to her how much she would be eyed by the now rapidly invading hordes of guests.

And if she were concerned with this, it was nothing to what she felt some three-quarters of an hour later, Blake still un-

sighted, when the line was over and the president and his committee were about to make their grand entrance down the stairs
of the ballroom. In those days the opulence of Shanghai society
was unmatched practically anywhere in the world.

Kate had worn a ball gown of pale blue silk, bought not in the
Street of One Thousand Nights, where the wealthy of Shanghai
shopped, but in a backstreet she knew from her schooldays. The
old lady who ran the shop sold her off-cuts from rolls of good
Chinese silk and made them up for a reasonable price. The gown
was not extravagant, nor were her simple black slippers, and
purse, made of the same fabric as the dress.

But if Kate was totally unaware of the presence she created,
Janey and others were not. For in the simple dress, with her
slender but tight figure, with her fresh, clear complexion and her
blonde hair, Kate wore the freshness of youth. And as she
arrived at the top steps of the ballroom, to be announced with her
escort, the effect on those gathered below was immediate. If they
had not previously noticed her in the receiving line, they certainly did now. Despite their secret conversations and loud guf-
faws and polite stomach rumbling for another night of glorious
champagned dyspepsia, the white-tie-and-tails and silk-and-satin
assemblage turned, head over shoulders, to look as the president
entered. Then there were second looks taken and, if not a buzz
of conversation rising above normal level, certainly an increased
animation as everyone asked who she was. A doctor? Oh really?
A lady doctor? Clem Richmond's daughter? Clem *who*? Oh, the
missionary doctor with the clinic down by the docks, behind the
silk company's warehouse, its *godown?* Oh well, that explains
it. How would anyone have heard of her? Wily old Nigel. Yes,
that explains it all right. Must be his new mistress. And thus
satisfied for the time that this newcomer posed no threat to their
ranks, that she was not there in her own right but merely with
Nigel, they all breathed a sigh of relief.

The music now started for the first dance, and Kate soon
found herself engaged in the fervor of Nigel Edwards' version of
the waltz. It was a hectic pace but as they twirled and twirled and
she felt the blood rushing to her cheeks, she felt wonderfully and
joyously alive and warm all over, and realized that with the

alcohol and the exuberance of the company and the occasion, she was secretly hoping Blake would see her and like her and want to spend the whole evening with her.

But when the music stopped and Edwards, true to his word, took Fox off and told the girls to enjoy themselves, Blake was still nowhere to be seen.

It was strange that he should not have come to such an occasion as this, and she wondered what could have kept him away. Surely he would want to be seen here, to indicate by his mere presence that he was not unwilling to confront Edwards socially as well as in business? She was surprised at the depth of disappointment she felt. It was in fact infuriating, especially after the embarrassment of having to plead for an invitation.

Just then Kate saw Lu Chien coming towards them. The three girls greeted each other warmly. They had been friends since schooldays at the America-China school, the main educational institution in Shanghai for Europeans and wealthy Chinese who wished their children to have Western educations.

A group of Kuomintang and German officers stood close by, resplendent in their full-dress uniforms. Kate noticed that one of them was Yang Ho. She had heard that he was now a general, the youngest in the Chinese army, in charge of the entire Shanghai region and its surrounding provinces. She thought he might not recognize her. But when their eyes met briefly he smiled back warmly.

"Hullo," she mouthed softly over the crowd, and saw him make the same silent motions for lip-reading to her. Then he went back to talking to the German officers.

Since the end of the Great War in 1918, German officers had acted as military advisers to the Kuomintang army. One German and two Chinese officers had also smiled broadly at Lu Chien as the girls had greeted each other. Kate now turned to Lu Chien and said:

"It's so good to see you again. Forgive me for not visiting sooner."

"The sin is mine. I heard you were back," said Lu Chien with the Chinese formality typical of her upbringing and her graceful and elegant nature.

"It is wise to leave a friend who has returned from a long journey a little time to be with herself and her family before visiting," said Kate, returning the appropriate quotient of Oriental righteousness.

"Lu Chien, you look beautiful as always," said Janey, "but I wonder if you will excuse me. I know you two will want to talk and there is someone I wish to see."

"Of course." Lu Chien gave a polite courtesy bow. Janey smiled fondly at them both and left.

Lu Chien was the daughter of one of the city's oldest and most prestigious families. She was very beautiful. She had skin like satin, and her oval face was delicately featured, with expressive sloe-eyes and lips which were perfectly shaped. She seemed always calm, gracious, and happy, and full of sweet Oriental virtue. She was engaged to a man much older than she, who had been an officer in the Kuomintang before he had resigned his commission. It was rumored he was now a radical. His name was Wu Zhao and he was a handsome man in his thirties with a thin brush moustache; he still dressed very much in the Western manner, as was the mode with young officers. He was from a family background similar to Lu Chien's, but it was also rumored that he and his father no longer spoke or exchanged courtesies.

"Oh Kate," Lu Chien said suddenly, breaking her normal reserve. "I had so wanted to come and see you—" She broke off as if lost for words and ashamed of her extreme lack of formality. Yet it had always been part of their friendship that with Kate she could be rather less formal than her standards of Oriental upbringing demanded, rather more honest about her feelings.

"Why, Lu Chien," Kate said with deep feeling, "then why didn't you come? You know you are always welcome."

Lu Chien, close to tears, nodded.

It was the only time Kate had ever seen her friend lose her composure, and even as Kate looked she saw the emotional outburst which had flowed up in Lu Chien subside, so that with her grace and ease coming back like a sweet mask, Lu Chien replied quietly and with dignity in a voice almost a whisper, "We will talk on it another time. We will talk on it."

"And Wu—?" inquired Kate.

Lu Chien smiled that particular Chinese smile which was polite but said nothing.

"So you are still *betrothed?*" asked Kate.

"Only in our own eyes, though you are a good friend to suggest it," said Lu Chien. "Here is the conflict and why we do not marry. We are still old-fashioned enough, Wu and I, to wish our parents' consent. And they will not give it, neither my father nor Wu's, while Wu holds such anti-government views. Yet to marry against their wishes would be a dishonor and would mean to be disowned for all time. This is a heavy burden to place on one's parents, especially my mother."

Kate nodded. "Forgive me for not asking. She does well?"

"As well as may be expected, thank you friend."

"Give her and your father my regards."

"And mine to your good parents."

"Surely. My apartment is on the Bund near the Silk Road *godown*. When will you visit?"

"Soon. I will visit soon."

Kate and Lu Chien gave each other courtesy smiles and Lu Chien returned to her friends.

Janey arrived back almost immediately. "Sorry to have left you, dear, but she's always been more your friend. Finds me a little *fast*, I think. Anyway dear, I've had a good look around, and there's no one terribly interesting—not yet, anyway. Any sign of your young man?"

"No, not yet," Kate said, becoming apprehensive. She realized she could not even be sure that Blake would ask her for a dance.

A waiter came by with drinks. They were just beginning to sip them when Kate noticed an orderly in Kuomintang uniform approaching Yang Ho. She was never sure what made her look in Yang's direction. There was certainly one of those lulls in conversation, which one may have even with friends, when one relaxes to sip a drink and survey the scene. It was also true that Kate was fascinated by Yang Ho's rapid rise to power and kept glancing at him, as one will do with successful people, as if by glancing one will be able to discover their secret. But whatever the reason which caused her to look in Yang Ho's direction at this precise point of time, she caught her breath as she did so. The orderly in Kuomintang uniform was Wang Lee! He saw her at almost the same moment as she saw him. But he showed no sign of recognition. What was it this young man did? Who was he and how could he be chased by the Kuomintang one minute and wear their uniform the next?

Kate had a moment of sudden anxiety about the ease with which she had helped him. She realized she was staring again and looked away. When she looked back he had gone.

The dancing commenced again and as Kate and Janey's partners came over, Kate tried to put Wang Lee out of her mind. But as she stepped onto the dance floor she noticed something else. If Kate had shown surprise at Wang Lee's approaching Yang Ho, this was nothing to the audible "My God!" she uttered— which caused Janey and the others to start—as Kate saw Wang Lee stop on his way out and talk earnestly and animatedly to Lu Chien. He was obviously more than a steward—perhaps, she thought, he was a spy. Lu Chien's friend Wu was said to be a communist sympathizer, and perhaps he had infected her with his views. And if Wang Lee should talk so freely to her, did that mean she was involved in his nefarious activities?

# 10

*The following evening Kate was sitting at home alone. Shanghai had always had occasional snowfalls. And the first chill winds of winter had brought one in from the mountains this night.*

Kate lit a log fire in the big open fireplace.

The apartment was on the twelfth floor of one of Shanghai's most famous apartment buildings, known as Broadway Mansions, at 20 Suzhou Road North. The twenty-two-story building had a facade of red, brown, and black bricks. They were set in variegated patterns, giving it, from the front, the look of colored street paving. But there were also octagonal and rectangular towers, capped in pink-brown circles and squares, above the metal window frames.

The apartment was spacious, and Janey had furnished it in the latest style and without thought of expense. There were thick carpets and comfortable chairs, and settees upholstered in white leather and tables of glass and chrome. Several paintings hung on the walls—abstracts, which Kate found somewhat disturbing, though anything more conventional would have seemed out of place in a room which was almost aggressively up to date. She would, of course, have preferred ancient Chinese wall hangings, such as the famous rampant horse and willow-pond patterns. And she would have opted for round camphor-wood tables with brass or marble tops. As it was, she had to settle for the small inlaid camphor-wood chest she had in her bedroom.

Janey had gone to Hong Kong for a few days with her father to sign some papers. Nigel Edwards had, for some reason which mystified Janey, recently appointed an attorney in Hong Kong as well as in Shanghai.

Kate had stopped at the street market on the way home to buy fresh vegetables, which she had made into a broth. She now sat sipping the broth with crisp French bread and butter. She had turned the light off so she could look out through the window. She could see Garden Bridge, over Soochow Creek, and the great curving "S" bends of the Bund—the famous Shanghai water-front boulevard which ran beside the Yangtze. The Bund was a focal point of Shanghai life not just because of its scenic beauty or even its strategic importance on the waterfront. It was also famous because of the buildings that stood along it—buildings like the British and American consulates, the Cathay Hotel, the American Club, and the Shanghai Club. Kate also took in the great trading houses of the East—the Glen Line Building, Jardine Matheson and Company, the Yangtze Insurance Building, the Yokohama Specie Bank, and the Bank of China. This was the city's financial heart, controlling the huge trading enterprises.

Kate looked now at the wind driving the snow across the Bund. There were huddling, hurrying Chinese on foot; and rickshaws; and cars pushing through the early evening traffic, their orange lights standing out like lamps on miners' helmets. It was warm and welcoming to see all that humanity padded against the cold; to see the people and the lights and the river and the junks beyond—yet to be sitting by one's own fire with a bowl of soup. It was like sitting in the middle of the world, like seeing all of history—past and present—passing by one's own fireside.

Just as Kate was reflecting on this, the porter phoned to say Lu Chien was downstairs. Kate excitedly said to send her up. It was a perfect time for Lu Chien to visit. She was such a dear friend; yet so reserved, so cautious. But with Janey away and Kate on her own it was an ideal time and a good night for old friends to sit by the fire and chat.

A few moments later the bell rang and Kate opened the door. Lu Chien stood there looking very serious.

"Come in, come in out of the cold," Kate said warmly.

Lu Chien hesitated.

Kate looked at her: "What is it, Lu Chien, what is it?"

"I am sorry but I have someone with me downstairs who needs a doctor."

"Is it Wu?"

Lu Chien shook her head. "It is a friend of Wu's," she said.

Kate looked at her with genuine concern.

"You know I'd treat any friend of yours who needed help," she said. "But wouldn't it be better for your friend to see me at the hospital where I have better facilities?"

"It is not possible."

"I see." By this time Kate was beginning to believe that perhaps Lu Chien had a friend who was pregnant. Perhaps she wished to ask about an abortion and this explained her embarrassment.

"Well we'd better at least see her and decide what is to be done, Lu Chien. Shall we bring her up? Or do you wish me to come down and talk to her?"

Lu Chien took a deep breath. Then in one sentence, with a speed of conversation unusual for her, she said:

"It is a man and he has been shot. We would prefer a back staircase if that is possible—?"

Kate gasped. "My God! I don't know if I can help with that. How serious is it? Is he bleeding badly?"

"He was, but we have packed the wound."

Kate looked very levelly back at her friend of so many years, the mild-mannered and graciously elegant Lu Chien, and wondered how she came to be on her doorstep involved in such things this night.

"It is certainly true that he should not be moved more than necessary, Lu Chien, you know that . . . so he should really be taken straight to the hospital rather than brought upstairs . . . and there is the matter that it is illegal for me to help him . . ."

Lu Chien now returned Kate's gaze. "This is why I was so reluctant to come to you. But Wu insisted we should ask you. We place the man's life in jeopardy if he goes to hospital—and so many of our other friends who might help him are being watched . . ."

Kate was now certain that Lu Chien and Wu were at least communist sympathizers. It would be a very serious offense indeed for her to help this man if he had been involved in any anti-government activity. And it was an offense not to report a shooting wound.

She hesitated. Could she afford not to help Lu Chien? What would happen to her friend if she took the man to the hospital? She would be arrested. And if the man did not go to a hospital—or get urgent medical attention—he would no doubt die.

Slowly Kate nodded her head.

"All right then, around the back," she said reluctantly. "We don't want him bleeding to death. I will meet you at the bottom of the back stairs."

Lu Chien looked at her in gratitude and Kate thought her deep almond eyes were finally about to lose their reserve and spill over and cry. They stood in silence for a frozen split-second of time, and then Lu Chien hurried out to the elevator while Kate looked at the instruments she had in her medical bag. She took them out, one by one, and laid them on a towel. Then she walked to the elevator herself. It was already on the ground floor and she had to wait for it to come back. When she finally reached her destination she could see Lu Chien and Wu waiting, crouched in the shadows through the near glass door, a man on the ground between them. As Kate beckoned them in she felt herself weaken at the knees. It was Blake!

He was very pale. Although he appeared unconscious—held slumped between Lu Chien and Wu with his head on his chest—he was just conscious enough to gasp, so faintly that Kate could barely hear it, "I'm cold, so very cold. I'm so damned cold."

Kate leaned down towards him, taking his wrist as she did so, to feel his pulse. It was frighteningly weak. She stiffened herself with all the admonitions of her training so he would not see her fear.

"Do you know me?" she said softly and kindly. "It's Kate, Kate Richmond, and I'm going to look after you. You mustn't worry. We're going to have you feeling warmer and better in no time. But first we must get you upstairs. Do you think you can manage it . . . ?"

His head did not rise off his chest. But it moved. It moved almost imperceptibly. But Kate was sure it had moved. My God! This was serious. She must move fast. Nodding her head to indicate they should start, they dragged Blake up the first small flight of stairs to the back of the apartment building lobby.

Kate knew immediately that this would not do. Even with the three of them it was like dragging dead weight. It would take too long to get him up the back stairs, to her twelfth-floor apartment. They must take the elevator. But she did not want the porter to know.

"I will talk to the porter while you use the elevator," she said evenly. "The door to my apartment is unlocked. Take him straight in and place him on the couch and start boiling water. I will follow immediately in the next elevator."

They nodded and she pushed the elevator call button as she made her way to the front part of the lobby.

Near the front door was a desk where the porter sat. He was a chubby little balding Chinese who had his pillbox hat off. He reached for it as he saw Kate coming. It did not matter to her whether he wore his hat or not. But she never told him this for that would mean she would lose face in his eyes. To him, indeed to all Chinese, despite the fact that she had been born in Shanghai, Kate was still a *yang kwei*. He would feel that foreign devils should care about whether he wore a hat or not, because not to wear a hat was not to give full service for his wages when it was part of his uniform, and if one did not care about this, one might be taken advantage of in other ways, too.

"Are you sure there were no letters for me today, Ying Tai?" Kate said as she came up to him. She had, in fact, asked about her mail earlier. But she needed an excuse to talk to him.

"No mail, Missy Doctor. No mail. I tell earlier. I tell earlier."

Ying Tai's English was much better than this. But like many Chinese who had lived all their lives in an international city, he felt it added to the flavor of the place and that it was almost expected of him to add a certain ingredient of pidgin to his speech.

"Yes, I know I asked," Kate said, "but I was expecting a special letter and I just wanted to be certain I hadn't missed anything."

"Ying Tai no miss, Ying Tai no miss. I tell if letter there all right, Missy Doctor."

"Of course. It was just a thought. How is the family?"

"Rice bowl full, missy. Rice bowl full." This was standard jargon, too. Indeed, compared with many Shanghai workers, Ying Tai's bowl would be more than full. There were always opportunities to earn extra money in a position such as his. There were one or two higher echelon prostitutes operating in the building; and there would be several mistresses of wealthy businessmen. Ying would be paid to note who came and went. A little spying on one's mistress did no harm. It kept her honest. And besides, there were others to spy for in Shanghai. More every day now. Kate felt a chill run through her. Ying's question did little to dispel that fear.

"Your friend find apartment OK, Missy Doctor?"

"Yes, yes, she did," Kate answered, trying to sound as unconcerned as possible. "I've left her up there. I was expecting some news from America which I wanted to give her and that's why I wanted to be certain about the letter."

Kate heard the elevator go up. Thank God! The wait had been interminable. Had Ying Tai heard it? Of course. But his expression had not changed. And tenants did sometimes use the back entrance.

"Perhaps letter come tomorrow, Missy Doctor. Only bad news travel fast," he said, smiling.

"Isn't that the truth?" Kate said, managing a smile at the typical Chinese platitude and its accuracy. But her mind was on Blake in the elevator and whether he had dripped blood on the floor. "Well thank you, Ying Tai," she said finally as she turned to go trying to look as casual as possible, "I'll just have to wait until tomorrow's mail . . . goodnight for now . . ."

"Goodnight Missy Doctor . . ."

She felt his eyes on her as she walked to the elevator. Was she imagining it? And if he was staring, so what? It didn't mean he knew anything! He couldn't have seen anything! He couldn't have! But presently the elevator arrived and her attention was diverted. For when Kate reached her apartment and saw Blake on the livingroom couch, she knew she must go in immediately. She must find the bullet, remove it, and get him stitched up as quickly as possible or he would die. It was as simple as that.

She hurriedly sterilized her instruments and looked at the wound. The pieces of a shirt they had stuffed in to stop the bleeding made her grimace. She was already worried about septicemia and he would certainly need a transfusion.

"Do you know anyone at the hospital who could get some blood?" she asked urgently of Wu. He shook his head.

"We must have some," she said. She paused for a brief moment. Then she reached for her purse and took out a set of keys to her parents' clinic.

"I will need three pints—and a bottle of saline. We must hope he is O positive, for if he is not I might kill him and there is no time to check."

Wu nodded and left.

As she had been talking, Kate had quickly scrubbed in anti-septic solution from her bag. She soaked a cotton swab with chloroform and held it over Blake's nose. "A little of *my* champagne, this time," she said gently, coaxing him to inhale the anesthetic. She was already uncapping a jar of tincture of iodine. And now, as she pulled the temporary packing out of the wound and the blood flowed again, she heard him gasp in pain and saw his body wince.

"Sorry," she whispered, "but you'll be under in about three more seconds . . ." She counted to three. "And I need every second I've got," she added to herself under her breath, "before the chloroform wears off. I wasn't exactly prepared for a major operation tonight and I've just used the last of it."

She threw the bandages into the hands of a horrified Lu Chien, quickly sprinkled on the iodine, and, taking a scalpel carefully in her hand, went looking for the bullet.

It had entered from the right-hand side just under the armpit. It would be up near the lung. He was lucky it was on the right-hand side. If it had been on the left near his heart he would already be dead. She dug away. Blood spattered everywhere. The couch and the rug would be ruined. No matter. Out to the side a little more . . . in deeper . . . more . . . pressure . . . deeper still . . . God, where was it? She was already two inches in.

She'd switched all the lights on when she came back. But she still needed more. She shouted to Lu Chien to bring a lamp. Yet she knew light wouldn't get in where she wanted to go; light was no good that far in . . . It was pure feel; feel and luck the whole way.

Where was it? Where the hell was it? Then she thought she struck something. What was that? Something hard? She was in past the rib cavity now—dangerously close to the lung. So the hard thing she felt could not be the rib cage. She edged a little closer . . . Then she felt some flesh give way . . . She pushed down harder . . . More flesh gave away . . . Dare she go farther or should she try to pry it out now . . . ?

She remembered Jonas Elms through the haze. ''Be the best cutter, Katie.'' She knew what that meant. Courage. Courage to cut hard. She could feel the beads of perspiration all over her. But she had to go in farther; harder. She pursed her lips as she firmed the pressure on her blade. ''Deeper now . . . deeper . . . careful . . . easy now . . .'' and then the dull click. That wasn't flesh any more, nor was it bone. It was the foreign element! Her quarry! She had found it! Gently, ever so gently now, she pried, levering it up and out. She breathed a sigh of relief. But there was no time to congratulate herself. She was ripping at the gauze she had laid nearby—ripping, dabbing, stemming the flow of blood. Then more dousing with iodine and more gauze.

She pressed the gauze down tightly with her fingers as she turned to Lu Chien and said, ''Here. Give me your hand. No! Don't touch it! Rinse in the antiseptic first! That's it. Now press. More. Press down hard. That's it . . .''

The cultured mandarin's daughter had obviously been removed from the realities of life and death. As Kate hurriedly threaded up for suturing, it crossed her mind that Lu Chien might see a lot more of death before she was through.

Now Kate was ready. She stood with the needle and thread poised.

''Let me get around into position first before you let go,'' she said, gently now. "Then, when I say 'go,' lift the gauze quickly and get another lot ready. OK?"

Lu Chien nodded.

"Ready?"

Lu Chien nodded again.

"OK, then—go!"

As Lu Chien's hand came away Kate stepped forward. In one movement she had the skin pulled together and her first stitch in. She pushed, pulled, and pushed again and again until the tattoo-like marks were made and the wound sutured. Then she cut ends off the cat gut sutures and sprinkled more iodine.

Now the gauze and a bandage.

Just as she was finishing up, there was a knock at the door. Kate beckoned with her head for Lu Chien to open it.

Suddenly she heard a strange voice and wheeled around without moving her hands to see a small but incredibly strong-looking young Chinese with a military haircut. Despite his young age he had a great presence of authority even in her fleeting glance at him. But it was not this which left her wide-eyed and speechless, with the last of the suturing thread in her hand, as she still bent over Blake, her head turned towards the door.

She heard the words "I have brought three pints of blood and saline and drip as ordered and a stand which was not ordered and will place them here," and still she did not believe it as she stared at the one who uttered them. It was Wang Lee! At least it looked like Wang Lee! But the voice was different. And this one used a tone of command more forceful than any she had ever heard.

"I am Shen Sun Lung," he said simply.

Kate might have only been home a few weeks, but that was long enough to know what that name meant in Shanghai.

She bent to her final stitch while Shen set up the stand and drip beside her. It was immediately obvious that he was very good at it.

"We have people at the hospital who teach us," he said, reading Kate's thoughts. "The time will come when we will have need of such things."

Kate wished every nurse she had ever had might have been as efficient as Shen. There was a confidence and competence verging on arrogance in this young man. This was what Communists were said to be like. It was very untypically Chinese. Even in the Nationalist Army, among the government Kuomintang forces which Yang Ho commanded, there was still said to be the ancient Chinese sense of timelessness and appropriateness of moment, of waiting out the battle. Kate did not sense any such approach from the man next to her. And, as if to underscore her thoughts, Shen Lung added, "I was waiting outside, to supervise, so that when Wu came out with your order for blood I left him to watch and drove straight to the clinic."

Kate nodded. Shen Lung finished getting the saline and blood ready and then beckoned for Lu Chien to come and stand in his place while he disappeared into the kitchen. By the time Kate had hooked the blood up and inserted a tube in Blake's arm, Shen Lung had returned. He was carrying a tray of Oolong tea.

"You must rest now, Doctor," he said, placing the tray near her, "and I shall watch the patient while you take tea."

Kate was still not sure she liked him giving orders when she was in charge, but it was obvious he was not going to stop. Besides, his action in making the tea would cause her to forgive him a multitude of sins. What he had done was unheard of. He was the first Chinese man she had ever seen make tea. In the old China—the China Yang Ho and the Nationalists represented—making tea involved carrying water and serving. This was woman's work. No Chinese man would be caught dead doing it. But the Communist leader did it effortlessly. She looked at him and saw him smiling. She bowed gratefully, in the traditional Chinese way, and took the tea, drinking the first of it standing.

Shen Lung smiled again. "A cigarette, perhaps?" he said, offering a packet. Kate took one of the Virginia-leaf Chunghwas from the red ten-pack and inhaled deeply. He indicated a chair and Kate took it. While she was sitting down, Shen poured tea for Lu Chien. Then he sat by Blake while Kate and Lu Chien rested.

After a time Lu Chien rose and said to Kate with a short bow:

"You have honored me and my friends and this is a kindness I will not forget. Do you please now excuse me and keep our friend Blake safe for us until we can arrange to have him moved?"

"Of course, Lu Chien. You honor me to ask these favors of me as a friend."

"I will stay and take care of all matters so the doctor may sleep," Shen Lung said in his commanding way as he said goodbye to Lu Chien.

Kate checked that her patient was resting well and then sat down again near the window, opposite Shen Lung. She took another offered cigarette.

"With this one you now begin to relax," he said warmly. Kate smiled. Communist or not, he was hard not to like.

"The patient really should go to hospital," she said, tiredness showing in her voice. "But I suppose if that had been possible Wu would not have insisted on bringing him here in the first place."

"Wu—?" the young man said.

"Yes. Was it not Wu?" Kate asked. She was sure that was what Lu Chien had said.

"It was not Wu, my good doctor," Shen said emphatically, "it was I. Wu said what he did to Lu Chien on my orders. Although you are not a Communist, I knew you would not refuse us and that our friend Blake would be safe here. You do not remember me, do you?"

"Well I thought I did. From the ship—and the train and the ball. You look so like Wang Lee. But you are not Wang Lee, are you?"

"Oh no, my good doctor," he said, laughing, "I am not Wang Lee, nor would I have presumed to trust you on so brief an acquaintance. It was many, many years ago, before any of these things, that I first encountered you and your family."

Kate shook her head in disbelief and looked closer in the glow of the fire. The lamp stand was still over by Blake.

The young man opposite her smiled and, passing the cigarettes over again, lit another for each of them and said, "Well, it *was* a long time ago," and then proceeded to tell his story.

# BOOK II
# The Seeds of
# Revolution

*1906–1926*

## 11

*The boy had been born just after the turn of the century, in* 1906 in Feudal China.

Today was his twelfth birthday. He awoke early and went outside the mud hut and scratched himself in the sun. In the distance he heard the neighbor's chickens awake. Soon the rest of his family would be up. He filled the big old stone jar with water and carried it indoors to the iron cauldron over the dry grass and dung fire which his mother, Lin Tan, was now bending at. She rubbed her long fine gray hair, which still had strands of black in it, as she built up the fire under the pot to set it alight.

She nodded a friendly smile of thanks, more friendly than a woman ought, for it was woman's work and her son was twelve today. Twelve already, she thought as she bent, feeling the pain in her back above her left hip from her last girl baby as she did so—twelve, her middle one, her man, was twelve already. But ah, that was something! She had borne a son. He had been in the fields helping his father since he could walk, this one. And he was kind, too, with things like the water for the pot.

After smiling her friendly smile she half unbent from her expert handling of the forage fuel and doing her hair with her hands all at once. She feigned a proper deference to her son, lowering her eyes and her head, lowering and turning her head half down to the chin, in a very demure and effacing way to indicate she was not worthy of so great an honor as a man carrying the kitchen water for her.

Her son giggled, his wonderfully healthy, good rice teeth showing wide across his brown face. His face and body were brown—tanned darker beyond the pale yellow of gentlemen. His hair stood short and full, black and hard as iron. His mother giggled a little as she ended her charade and moved towards him to smooth his hair. He recoiled in a reflex action as she did so, so quick he surprised himself as much as her. Both stood momentarily still then, with nothing to fill the empty space between them. Eventually the woman turned and bent heavily, feeling the pain in her hip sharper this time but showing nothing.

The boy stood silent, still scratching the sleep from his body, and then said, at last, "Good morning, my mother," as if this were the first contact for the day and nothing else had happened. It was the Chinese male practice of denial, which she knew only too well and questioned mentally only on occasions as rare as this one. He was small to be a man, this one; tiny like her and shorter even than her husband.

"Good morning, my son," she said warmly, to show there was no anger which would last on this most important of days. She said it warmly and loudly and lit the fire and muttered on to herself as he went in to dress, "Good morning, my little one, my boy, my son, my man."

Then she remembered they had nothing for his birthday, nothing at all, and wondered if he knew.

She looked out of the square hole cut in the wall of the hut. Everything was scorched and brown. The drought had been a long one. She wished they had sacrificed more in earlier years to the gods of the earth. But it was easy to forget to be grateful when stomachs were full and there was even enough money for rice cakes at the New Year's festival. She had always blamed her son's shortness on insufficient incense before his birth. She had felt so good about the baby growing inside her, better than about her first baby, the girl, her eldest; for she was sure the second baby would be a boy, that she had been a lazy woman and not saved hard enough in the kitchen to put a little aside for more than a couple of sticks of incense just before the baby was born. The fact that she had conceived in the Year of the Monkey should have told her something.

But she had been wicked, she knew that. For she'd had two pence spare at the end of one moon of good harvest but she had spent them on the old woman fortune-teller in the town, the old one with the withered face and yellow eyes which saw into the future. She had spent the two pence to be told that her baby would be a son and a leader of his people, which was what the old one had been telling every mother since Lin Tan herself had been a child and even before that. She did not believe the prophecy had anything to do with her son being born a man child, but she did believe it had something to do with him being born small, for if there had been no fortune-telling the money would have gone on incense to placate the gods. This would have given him a better chance of growing into a great one, although of course she did not believe any of it.

So after all that money was spent on the fortune-telling, Lin Tan still did not know what her son was supposed to be, and because she did not know this, she could not guide his course. She kept thinking that the old one had said he would grow tall. Well, there was a stupidity. Anyone could see the boy would be short forever now, shorter even than his father. She kept asking the old one what she meant, but she would say no more except to cackle that more good fortune cost more money.

Lin Tan filled an old China cup with water and took it to her husband. He would be up now and looking for his tea before he and the boy went off to the fields. The crops were long since gone, but they foraged for fuel and scratched at the furrows, so rock hard their implements made no impression. And they looked at the sky and hoped it would rain soon, before the little flour they had left, to make a few more noodles, ran out. If it rained, perhaps her husband and the boy could hire out to wealthier farmers until they were able to buy seed to sow their own land again.

When Lin Tan reached her husband's room, for thus it was called although it was theirs, he was already awake, sitting with his legs hanging over the edge of their *k'ang*. This was the brick bed on which they placed their mat and under which in winter, if there was fuel, they built a fire in the square hole to keep warm. Often in the bitter cold of mid-winter all the family would sleep on the *k'ang*—she and her husband and the three children and the two surviving old ones. In the Chinese manner of caring for the old, her mother and her husband's father had honored places.

"Good morning, my husband," Lin Tan said, placing the tea on the hard-worn earth floor beside his feet, which did not quite reach the ground.

She stepped back and busied herself, appearing to clean up the room, though it was not cleaning day and there was little enough to clear away. There was no furniture except her mother's trunk, an old wooden thing, hooped with a little common metal, but a wedding gift nevertheless and their one possession which might give them some status above dirt peasant poverty in the eyes of their fellows.

But she did not clean; she pretended rather to clean as women will when they are wont to watch their husbands out of spite or concern.

She watched, deeply concerned, too respectful of her husband's position as head of the household to make him lose face by commenting on what she knew to be upsetting him. Her husband had said nothing. Perhaps he had kept hoping that some good fortune would befall them before the day arrived. Now it was the day and nothing had come and her husband was sad. He loved the boy. Although he treated him firmly sometimes, it was a firmness of the times, for a boy must be a man as soon as he is born in such a society. And the boy knew how much his father loved him. The father had a continued, loving pride in his son, for not all had sons, and families were too poor to be large; and even those who had sons—even the rich who had the large families China became known for—could not boast sons as his son, as dutiful, loving, and hard-working.

Lin Tan looked at her husband Shen Fu. She looked at his legs as they hung over the side, too short to reach the ground—his tired legs, his old legs, his boat people's legs, his coolie's legs, and now his calloused and water-creased paddy field legs, rice legs when they could afford to plant rice. His legs were spotted white around the bottom parts of his brown ankles, spotted with callouses and wrinkled with water around the lighter foot soles which, with the callouses, stood out so on the dark legs, suntanned and burnt and shrunk with work and age. They were short and very bandy—she had noticed that the first time they had met after their betrothal—bandy from the boats and the basket-carrying on poles which he had done as a coolie after his father had been dispossessed from his farm.

Shen Fu had sworn to get back to the land one day, but he had not returned to the security of his peasant's existence, however poor, before his legs had been permanently bowed by the crippling loads of those enormous cane baskets, hung at either end of the rod of yoke which the coolie passes across his back. Shen Fu was corded there with muscles and callouses like twisted strands of bamboo which would now never go away.

Indeed, as he sat there and pondered, conscious that the woman was watching him and knowing his misery, he wondered if he would even want them to go away. There was no dignity in coolie work, and there was no joy in bringing up a family in the cities where all the foreigners were, by which he meant Chinese unfamiliar to him and his country ways. But the work had been steady. In a good year he could make more in his fields, but in the city there was always something to carry, even when the crops failed, for the rich people still found goods to buy somewhere and trade went on.

He was not a clever man but he had a certain logic characteristic of his race and he knew as he bent, looking so tired and old in the half-light that his wife caught her breath, that he had three choices. Either he must cut his queue, his traditional tail of hair, and sell it for a wig in the town; or he must return to the city and take hated work as a coolie again; or he must ask help of his wife's brother. All touched painfully on his pride. But of the three, the last was the most painful to think upon.

When some good fortune which one always hopes the gods might cause to come to pass did not happen by this morning of his son's birthday, he felt it was a bad omen. He felt that things could only get worse. Part of him felt that although some young men now wore no tails of hair, he would increase his misfortune and fail to honor his ancestors if he were to have his shorn. But he would do it to have a present this day for his son and it had to be considered.

Of all the solutions he felt that returning to the city perhaps would be best. They would get nothing for their land, even if a buyer could be found in these bad times, so he would not sell it. Then, if perchance he worked very hard as a coolie, he and his son together, perhaps they could return. Yet he doubted they ever would. He was only fifty but he was too old and tired to work much longer as a coolie, and he knew it would only be a matter of time before his son would have to support them all.

There were other ways to make money in those days. His youngest daughter was pretty and those who worked at the Great House over by the town had already cast longing looks at her.

She was only seven, but had a moon face and rice skin and eyes like deep dark almonds.

One had even offered money already on behalf of his master. Shen Fu hated himself for even letting this thought come into his head, although in those days it was a thing often done and no shame was attached to it. Many a man saved the lives of others in his family by selling a daughter or two to the rich. If his daughter had been ugly it would have been easier to think upon. An ugly daughter could be sold as a kitchen slave and her ugliness would ensure she was not taken to the bedrooms of her masters. Still, his Lotus Blossom, which was a common pet name he called her in the manner of so many fathers, was not for sale, not his one with the delicate skin and gentle nature and almond eyes.

He did not, however, think of his other daughter on this day, although she was just thirteen—a good age for such things—and prettier than her father imagined her to be, as is often the case when a man has a younger who is his favorite.

The weak green tea was nearly cold now and Shen Fu bent to it again to use it all up, to drink every last drop. He believed later, when his mind wandered back to it as it often did when he got older, that he had already decided to sell his hair; to have it cut off that very morning, quickly, with the silver straight into his palm so that he might return with a little pork and perhaps a small fish and a sweet delicacy or two for his son's birthday. This would be something, this would be seen as a present and would be a thing of honor to do. His son would not expect money to be frittered on something idle, but a little good food once or twice a year for the family—that was honorable and a fine gift, for then the young man of the household could share his gift with the family. Perhaps, if Shen Fu could do this, all would be well. Perhaps, too, this could be good fortune and things might change. He felt better now and turned to his wife and said, "Good morning my wife, and how does our son this day?"

"He does well," she smiled, relieved to see her husband less anguished. "He does well."

But just then there was the sound of loud banging at the front door.

It was barely the start of the first hour of the sun but in the peasant farming community people were up by this time so no undue heed was paid to the knocking. In fact, if it had not been for the drought and so little to do, the man and the boy would have been in the fields by now, rising in the dark and walking to the fields, some distance away, to get the most out of the day.

But in times of drought it was stupid to expend useless energy. Still, Shen Fu pulled his faded blue smock on, and wound and tied his black waist cloth quickly and expertly, with one end tied up and under his legs so he appeared to have an enormous baggy loin cloth on. He would not seem a lazy man who was not about his business, even in hard times when there was little to do.

He nodded for his wife to go and open the door, which was in the middle room of their three rooms. He and his wife had one room; the middle one was for cooking and eating and all other things, and the third room was shared by the old ones and the children.

Just as he nodded to his wife, he heard the door open and his son greet his wife's brother. Shen Fu motioned with his hand and made as if to batter himself with it on his forehead and then let out the low guttural exclamation, *ai-ee,* just loud enough for his wife to hear. It was a thing between them, Shen Fu and this brother of hers, not because of the brother's success but because of the way he tried to impose the benefits of that success on others. Of course, to look after family was one's duty, and a relative in need of help could call on one such as a brother, or a wife's brother, and there was an obligation to feed and clothe if the other had any to spare. But a respectful asking was one thing. Making a show of one's generosity was another. There were little gifts, little kindnesses, that might have been taken when offered, if his wife's brother had offered them in a humble way, in the true old-fashioned Chinese way of discounting the gift and finding virtue in the other. His wife's brother could have said, ''You have treated my sister well from the day she came to your house and you took our mother in when I was a poor wretched youth and you are a good husband and father who would honor us by dining with us at the New Year's festival.'' Such a statement would have shown honor and respect.

But this one, the grain merchant, there was none of that in him! And to come on this day. *Ai-ee!* He knew it was the boy's birthday. A good uncle would know that. But a good uncle would wait to be asked to the home for supper and a special dish or two. If he were not asked he would know the family could not afford it and would stay away as a courtesy.

Yet if Shen Fu *hated* his wife's brother, this was not a word he would ever use to her. And in all the time he had had to deal with the man he had never been other than polite to him as befits a husband's attitude towards his wife's brother.

When Shen Fu felt he had waited long enough to be dignified before greeting his wife's brother, he cleared his throat long and hard, which he did not really need to do but it was a sound a man may make in the morning in his own household.

Then he hurried into the middle of the room.

"Good morning my wife's brother." It was for Shen Fu, the householder, to greet first.

"Good morning my sister's husband," Lin Hua replied dutifully, and with a big laugh, for he was a happy enough fellow within himself, who cared not how others saw him.

"You and your family are well?" Shen Fu asked.

"For a poor man who lives in the town, I and my family are well."

The way Wife's Brother conducted himself in exercising the Chinese virtue of humility never sat well with Shen Fu. It was good that a man should be humble, for not only was this a virtue in itself which enabled others to say, "Ah well, and is not so-and-so a fine and wise man, the way he does not puff himself up but always speaks less well of himself than is really the case," but it also prevented evil spirits from knowing one's true status. Only a fool walks around saying he is good at this and that, or has had a good crop of wheat or rice that year. Any of the evil spirits passing in the air might hear such things and immediately set about to undo the good that has befallen one. It is better to say, "Oh, I planted just a little corn this year," or some such thing, for your neighbors will know the truth and respect not only your humility but your wisdom in not tempting the evil spirits. Shen Fu secretly hoped that Wife's Brother might one day be caught this way. Still, the man did try to respect the traditions of their way of life. But Shen Fu felt it to be a very dishonest humility.

"And your family on this special day—?" Wife's Brother continued the ritualized form of greeting.

"We are well for poor farmers."

That was the end of the formal greeting and Shen Fu knew his wife would have offered tea had she had it. It was no dishonor among his neighbors to be without tea in a bad year, yet he felt awkward about not having it.

"You will sit awhile, my wife's brother?" Shen Fu now asked, indicating a seat, a small bench of rough wood at the small table.

"It is a nice day for walking," Wife's Brother said.

At this Shen Fu brightened a little. Now this was as it should be. This was doing a man proper honor and saving his embarrassment at having no tea. This is what a neighbor might do who understood. Did Wife's Brother understand after all? Shen Fu felt a moment of sympathy for the man, and shame at himself for thinking so poorly of him.

"It is indeed a nice day for walking. Although it is dry, the sun is not yet hot."

The two men walked out the door together and for some time chatted as friends might, about this and that, before the merchant, Lin Hua, felt free to discuss what was on his mind.

"It has been a bad season," he said at last.

"The gods of the earth have not been kind."

"And last season was bad also."

"Only a fool would say otherwise."

"And the year before that, so that now there have been three bad years together."

"For a man of the town my wife's brother keeps himself well informed of the fortunes of poor farmers."

There was no malice in Shen Fu's reply. There were still forms to be observed, particularly now that the important part of the conversation was coming. So this thing he said was not something said at the other's expense, something akin to "How would you know about farmers?" but rather a compliment, as befits conversation with a near relative.

"Well, and is it not my business, also, since I must buy what grain there is?" Wife's Brother replied.

"This is so," Shen Fu said in polite agreement. It was true that his wife's brother, by his business, was also linked to the land. But it was no life or death link such as farmers have. Wife's Brother was successful enough to be able to keep stores of grain available, to be used in famine years. Even now he was selling at huge profits to those who could afford his prices. Those at the Great House always could. And, in addition, in times of such scarcity, Lin Hua brought goods from the city by train engine to the nearest stop, and then by mules to the town. The people at the Great House paid what he asked to have some variety in their diet—a cabbage or two which the city in the south with its better rainfall could provide.

*Ai-ee*, a cabbage, Shen Fu thought to himself as they walked. Think of it, a cabbage! It was a long time since his family had had a vegetable of any sort. It was nearly three years. When he had been a boy they had eaten grass in a time of famine. Soon it would come to this again. Unless they moved.

Shen Fu believed Wife's Brother was about to offer him grain—his own good grain no doubt, stored from times past—as he had once before during hard times. At first he had offered it free, then at a discount when he saw Shen Fu's anger rising, and then as a loan against future harvest.

But Lin Hua did not this time make any of these offers, although he would have liked to. He was not a stupid man and whatever others thought of him he was as much a part of traditional China as they. Had not the Chinese merchant been a thing of fame for centuries? All knew of the caravan routes and spices and the great silk road. He could not read or write but he had learned to count, on the abacus at first and now he could do sums in his head. And he knew himself for what he was—a successful merchant with a desire to help his sister's husband who was such a foolish, pig-headed fellow he would let none help him. So, aware of this, Lin Hua trod carefully as he began to broach the subject he had come to talk about.

"There is something I would speak on touching my wife's husband's family, if I have his permission," Lin Hua said very carefully.

"Speak on then, and let us see what you shall say," Shen Fu replied, but not with ease.

"You know I am a poor fellow," Lin Hua went on, using *poor* in the correct way in which it may have many meanings other than not wealthy, such as he used it now, word and tone denoting that he was not a worthy fellow and making Shen Fu think again that perhaps there was a little more genuine humility to Lin Hua than he had thought.

Whether this was so or not, Lin Hua was choosing his words very carefully, as a businessman might when, skilled in the ways of dealing with people, he wants to create an exact impression of being the sort of person one would want to do business with in this particular circumstance.

"You know I am a poor fellow," Lin Hua said again, "who has only three worthless daughters and no sons. And soon my wife will be past childbearing—"

Shen Fu stopped and looked at his wife's brother and there was a silence.

They had stopped by the hardened furrows of the land in the broad heat of early morning.

The plains in the distance were wide and white and led up to the hills. There were no clouds. It was very dry. Both men wished they might be somewhere else.

Shen Fu stared again at his wife's brother and looked pained. So he had come for his son. It was strange that this was a thing Shen Fu had never considered. No, not ever. Not even in arguments with his wife over her brother had this ever been mentioned. Not even in anger.

"Speak on, Wife's Brother," Shen Fu said at last, his voice thin and his spirit heavy. He was not smart, as were other men, he knew that. No, and not stupid, either, as some thought poor farmers were. He was like a good loyal old ox that pulls the plow through the field, day after day and year after year, and asks little more than his food and sleep and occasional contentment. But he knew enough to know that sometimes one does not think upon things which have lain there hidden because one knows that although they are the last things one would want to do, they are the only practical things to do in bad times.

He was hardly hearing the words as his wife's brother spoke on. He knew the terms would be fair. He even knew that the boy was too bright to stay in the fields all his life. But they had been such a team, the boy and he, and the boy loved the open air so.

"It would be one less mouth to feed," Lin Hua was saying, "and above his food and clothing and shelter at my house, there would be a small wage, a very small wage—"

Shen Fu turned on the man and glared angrily at him. It was his one defiant gesture.

"It is normal, it is normal," Lin Hua added hurriedly. "It is not charity."

"The boy will honor his father but he must be asked," Shen Fu said determinedly.

Well now, here was a thing! Here was his sister's husband who in everything was a man of such Oriental virtue and pride, here was his sister's husband saying the son must be asked.

But Lin Hua had gotten what he had come for and was too good a businessman to spoil a bargain with idle chatter, so he said nothing.

Shen Fu, as if sensing what the other man thought, said again, "The boy is now a man and he must be asked. He has worked with me in the fields these many years and broken his young back to help feed the family and honor his parents and now his parents will honor him by asking."

Lin Hua nodded and then both men turned and walked back, Shen Fu kicking at a furrow here and there with his bare feet.

When they reached the house Shen Fu took his son aside and explained everything to him, and the boy said:

"And what does my father wish?"

"Whatever you wish, my son."

"This cannot be, my father. I would always obey my father in such matters."

The father took the boy to him then, and had to turn his face away as he said, "I know this to be so, but yet you love the land, the thick rich black earth when the seasons are good and even the dry earth when they are bad and I fear lest you shrivel in the town and become as some others."

He phrased it this way, so as to avoid an impolite reference to a relative, though the boy knew well what he meant, for he was quick and agile and bright as a young fresh button and his uncle had certainly seen this in him.

"I will take the position in the town for a season, if my father wishes, since there is little work to do here and perhaps I may provide a little food for my sisters while my father works for my mother and the old ones. Would this honor my father and his house?"

The man turned right away now and pressed his head into his son's neck, and they held each other for a time.

"Let it be done then, for a season or two as you say," the father said when he was able to look at his son again.

Then he went out of the room and walked into the town, to the street of barbers, and had his queue quickly cut off; and took the money and bought his son a new long robe as befits a man of the town, but more like a scholar would wear than a merchant.

For Shen Fu had decided one thing. If his son must leave the land, it would be to become a scholar, not a merchant. So on the way home he stopped at Lin Hua's house and told Wife's Brother that the lad would go with him, but that he must have one lesson a week, in his free time, from the scholar in the town, and that he, Shen Fu, would pay for these lessons for a year from what was left of the money for his hair.

Lin Hua did not like it, for a scholar was above a merchant and he was annoyed with Shen Fu for giving himself and the lad airs. But he gave in. In the town they would know and laugh to themselves and say, "Well, what is this farmer's boy doing acting like a scholar? Is he not apprenticed to the grain merchant? And how will one lesson a week and a long robe make someone a scholar?"

By the time Shen Fu reached home it was evening. So the family sat down to a meal of noodles and a little bit of spiced pork which he had extravagantly bought for the boy's birthday; and the lad sat in his new robe and they joked about what a fine man he was now; and no one mentioned that Shen Fu sat at table in his hat, as if his hair were curled up under it, and they all laughed a little, the young ones their wide bright rice smiles, and the old ones their toothless straying gray hair grins, and all were happy, despite their misfortune.

The next day the boy left early for the town.

# 12

*The following six months were desperately unhappy ones for* Shen Lung.

Although a relative, he soon began to realize he was little better than a servant.

Previously, he had known his uncle only as his mother's rich brother who visited them. And although always giving himself airs, which Shen knew his father detested, his uncle had never really been unkind to him.

But from his first day of apprenticeship Shen began to realize what a stern taskmaster his uncle was.

He gave Shen a makeshift bed in the coal shed, away from the main house. As the winter drew on the boy began to feel the cold desperately. At home he had always slept inside in winter, where the warmth from the *k'ang* was enough to penetrate to the other rooms. But in the very depth of winter—or if they were out of fuel because they could not afford it—they all slept close up together in the one room.

Shen had assumed this was how it would be in his mother's brother's house—that he would be treated as one of the family.

Then he realized that he was being silly. His uncle would not be so unkind. It was certainly true that he had refused Shen oil for the stone lamp which stood on a box beside his bed. But oil was expensive and an unnecessary luxury to see by at night. And his uncle was very careful about money, which, as a poor boy, Shen Lung fully understood. Even the rich were careful about money. But everyone used a little coal in winter, even the poorest of families. In the bitter cold of central and northern China it was a necessity, not a luxury. He was sure his uncle had intended him to use a little coal. Was there not an old iron brazier in the corner? Of course Shen intended to ask his uncle first, but on one particularly cold night, when he awoke shivering and knew the others to be asleep, he made a small fire in the brazier and placed it beside his bed, soon dropping off again in the comforting warmth beside him.

He dreamt of sweet things and home until he was rudely awakened by his uncle shaking him and shouting:

"Wake up, thief . . . Wake up thief! Who steals my coal and starts a fire to burn us all down . . . ?"

Shen was still half asleep, trying to focus his attention as his uncle continued:

"What if this brazier were to be knocked over and it then set the other coals alight . . . ?"

"But Uncle . . . " Shen began to say, "it was so very cold and the brazier is firm and strong. What am I to do for heat in the middle of winter if I do not light a few coals . . . ?"

"Heat . . . ! Winter . . . ! It is not the employer's responsibility to provide other than a bed. There is your bed. Besides, you have your own quilt."

Now it was true that Shen had an old quilt of sorts, which he had brought from his home. But it was only a cheap cotton one, no thicker than a jacket, worn old with use and passed down from his father. It was of use only while one slept inside with the heat from the *k'ang* or when one slept up close to others.

But he knew it was useless to argue with his uncle in this mood and his uncle's next words confirmed his worst thoughts:

"If I ever see one more puff of smoke coming from this shed, or find one piece of coal missing, I will beat you within an inch of your life."

Shen Lung, even at twelve, knew this was no idle threat. He had seen the bruises on the arms and legs of his mother's brother's wife and her three daughters.

But if those first six months of his apprenticeship were desperately unhappy for Shen, they were also brightened by two new friendships.

The first was with the one they called Guard Boy, who was really an indentured slave and watched over Lin Hua's precious stock in the granary opposite the house. Shen Fu had always warned his son about making friends too easily, particularly with strangers from other parts of the country. But Guard Boy was so warm and friendly that Shen was sure it was all right. And the slightly older boy was, after all, his uncle's slave.

Shen's second new friend was the one they called Weng Feng, the old tailor of the town.

One day, soon after his argument with his uncle over the coal, Shen went looking for something to keep him warm. He had to wait until he finished work, so it was almost dusk by the time he found himself near the tailor's shop. The old man was still at his bench, behind his shop window, working by the light of a single oil lamp and peering down over his spectacles at the cloth which lay before him.

Shen tapped on the window with his fingers. The tailor looked up and smiled, beckoning the boy in.

"What is it . . . what is it . . . ?" the old man said in a kindly way as Shen entered.

"Excuse me, Elder Born, but there is something I wish . . ." the boy said timidly.

"Of course, Little One, of course. But how are you called, so I may know to whom I speak, for you must surely know that I am Weng Feng the tailor?"

"Oh yes, sir, I certainly know that. Everyone knows the tailor's name. As for me, I am just Shen Lung, poor grain apprentice . . ."

"Then sit here, Shen Lung," the old man said warmly, indicating a chair and putting down his needle and thread, "sit here and tell me what it is you wish."

"Please sir," Shen began awkwardly, "I wondered if you might need a boy to help clean your shop late at night."

Weng Feng looked at him kindly over his spectacles.

"It is not a large shop, as you see," he said gently. "What would you wish in return?"

"Oh no money, sir," Shen said quickly, "just a few odd pieces of cloth that I might sew together into a rug."

"You are the one apprenticed to Lin Hua?" Weng Feng said simply.

"Yes sir."

"The son of Shen Fu the farmer?"

"Yes sir."

"And in what year were you born?"

"The Year of the Monkey, sir."

"So I hear."

"Excuse me, sir?"

"Oh, no matter. The old one at the end of the street with the creased opium face who tells fortunes keeps track of such things."

Shen nodded out of politeness.

"So you need something to keep warm, Little One, do you?" the tailor said, stretching himself and walking back towards a cloth partition at the rear of the shop.

"Yes, sir, I do. But I am willing to work."

"Of course you are, of course you are," the tailor said shuffling back to Shen, carrying under his arm the most wonderful-looking red rug Shen had ever seen.

"Here," said the tailor, tossing it into Shen's lap, "here, take this as a gift."

As Shen's hands grabbed instinctively at it and felt how soft it was, softer and warmer than any material he had ever felt, he did not know what to say and his eyes began to fill with tears.

Again and again he protested and gave the rug back to the tiny, wizened old man. And again and again the tailor pushed it back towards him and said he would take nothing for it. He said also he would not have Shen work for him, for the boy was breaking his back already with his uncle. But if perchance, when Shen had a moment to spare, he would come and talk to the old man, that would be payment enough.

Shen said he would be happy to come and talk but he must still find a way to pay for the gift. At this the old man moved over closer to him and whispered:

"Accept it from an old man who senses his time is near. It is a rug fit for a soldier and, who knows, one day you may have need of it."

"I wish only to return to the land, sir."

"Of course. But one day you might have to fight for your land to stop the landlords from taking it from you."

Shen nodded. He knew little of such things.

"You can keep a secret?" the old man said suddenly, his eyes immediately alight and more intense.

Shen nodded.

The old man leaned under his table and from some secret place drew out a small piece of crumpled red New Year's paper.

"Tell no one you saw me with this," the old tailor whispered, "but if any with such a piece of paper ever ask a favor of you, be kind to them for my sake."

"I will honor them as I honor you for this fine gift," Shen said.

"Good. So you will take it?"

"Yes," the boy said, not knowing why he had suddenly decided to. "Yes," he said, "I will take it gratefully."

"And you will come and see me and keep our secret?"

"Of course, sir."

"Good. Good."

And with that Weng Feng opened the door and showed Shen out into the night.

They saw each other several times after that.

Then one day Nationalist soldiers came to the town and rounded up the townspeople. Several were made to kneel in the main street—or k'ow t'ow as it was called—while the others watched. Then the officer-in-charge beheaded each in turn with a big, curved execution sword, thicker at one end than the other.

All—including Shen—had to watch.

They kept Weng Feng until last, but they did not execute him by beheading. Instead, they chained him to a tree, with arms and legs outstretched. Then they tore off his clothes so he was naked. Next, with several men working on him all at once with thinner, sharper swords, and the officer counting out loud all the time, they began to make razorlike incisions all over his body. Shen watched dumbfounded. This was the oldest and most painful death of them all—the Chinese ritual torture, the Death of One Thousand Cuts.

In this torture, a man or a woman is slowly cut into one thousand pieces, peeled like a peach with the skin pulled off the flesh while he or she is chained or tightly held. All the private parts are cut, too—a woman's nipples and vagina and a man's penis and testicles—while feeling is still at its greatest and the cries the most agonizing. This is done for torture; to make an example of the victim; and to make sure the relatives and ancestors are not presented with an intact corpse. A dismembered body of so many pieces, incapable of being reassembled, will find no place in any celestial heaven. It is the final and most terrible torture; the complete eradication of identity.

The threat is real. Many peasants believe that a soul is all they ever own on the terrible treadmill of existence from cradle to grave. They believe that even beyond the physical pain, the Death of One Thousand Cuts so destroys a man or woman that even their souls cannot be found in the afterlife and therefore must wander without rest forever.

On this day the officer-in-charge made clear one very important thing. Those beheaded had been suspected of being members of, or collaborating with, a secret society which carried little pieces of common red New Year's paper as an emblem or badge. Weng Feng the tailor had been discovered to be the local leader and found in possession of one such piece of paper.

It was only with great difficulty, after that, that Shen was able to use Weng Feng's blanket at all. He was also careful not to put it on his bed until very late at night. And always, in the morning, before he left for work, he hid it under a sack at the bottom of a pile of coal.

# 13

China, *in those years of the First World War of 1914–1918*, still had slaves. There were many levels of slavery in China. A daughter could be sold as a slave to a great house, such as had entered Shen Fu's mind on his day of desperation. A girl might also be sold as a concubine to a rich merchant or mandarin. She might even be sold as a bride if she were pretty enough. These transactions often took place when the girls were only eight or nine and they were expected to begin sexual relations from the start.

A boy child could also be sold as labor. Because the male sex was more highly prized, this was not as frequent but it was still quite common in bad times. Slavery could be for life or for a specified period—perhaps five or ten years. This was called indentured labor.

Five years ago Lin Hua had bought himself from the impoverished North a healthy strong male child with good teeth. The boy, who was his indentured slave for ten years to do with as he would—to feed well, or starve if he misbehaved, or beat if he were slow to learn—was now the guard of his granary. At fifteen he was ox-strong and bullocky, with the broad head and hard, high cheekbones of the people of the North. He had been innocent and open of nature once. But five years of brutalizing work had changed him. He was laborer as well as guard and had been beaten on his bare buttocks with bamboo many times until he bled. So now he was sly and evil. With his cunning went the most disarming of smiles for any who could influence his master on his behalf.

Shen Lung, the new boy, master's poor sister's child, got the obsequious No. 1 smile from their first meeting—despite the fact that Guard Boy instantly hated him.

What a terrible mismatch this was: an innocent twelve-year-old boy and a fifteen-year-old youth who had all the cunning and whip-smart deceit that only years of abusive child labor could give.

He was so smart this one, saying in such a friendly way, "young master this," or "young master that," that he completely disarmed Shen Lung, who believed Guard Boy to be his ultimate friend and protector. Since Shen Lung sat at table with the family, which was the one privilege accorded him, and Guard Boy did not, but ate his miserable food in the granary, Shen took to smuggling little delicacies from his own food out to the barn. He slipped them off his plate and under his coat when his mother's brother and his family were not looking.

Once Shen thought that his mother's brother's wife, Lin Pargai, had seen him. But she was a kindly soul, despite being so pock-marked and ugly. She said very little, like so many wives of angry men, and Shen Lung soon discovered that the whole household—of mother and three daughters—lived in fear of his uncle's temper. Shen also knew he must not get caught smuggling food, even if it was his own food. His uncle would see that as an act of disobedience. It was for the master to decide what his slave would eat. And if there were no difference between what master and slave ate, why then what was the difference between master and slave and what hope would there be for a country where everyone ate as everyone else?

Yet Shen kept taking the morsels to his friend in the granary and enjoyed what he believed to be the comradeship of the older boy.

Although Shen did not know it, it was Guard Boy who had deviously contrived to get the food, leading Shen subtly little by little to ask questions about his diet. In this manner he could reply, without disrespect, that he was very well taken care of by his honorable master, but he did not want to be a poor one all his life; and he had only heard of some of the delicacies they had in rich houses and did not know what they looked like and if in later life he were to become a little more successful, why then what a silly fellow he would look if he did not know what some foods were. Everyone would then know him for one who had always been poor.

Because this touched on a thing Shen Lung himself felt sometimes, in common with all the poor the world over, as if the indignity of having been poor would always show like soiled pants even if one might some day cease being poor, because of this, and in his innocence of wanting to help a friend, Shen Lung had started bringing a little food to Guard Boy.

Guard Boy was all sweetness and light and kept thanking the "young master" for his Oriental righteousness in doing such a thing.

Then, one day, Shen's uncle was sitting at his high desk near the door to the granary. He was teaching Shen Lung how to count on the abacus. Lin Hua was talking freely about this and that, which one more cynical than Shen Lung might have interpreted as talking loudly so that even those who passed by the door in the street might hear what a great and busy man he was. Suddenly Lin Hua took a piece of paper from his desk and almost shouted, "Well now, and here is a thing! I have a special order for delicacies from the city which must be picked up by mule cart from the train and here I am such a busy merchant I can hardly spare time to go myself.''

In fact Lin Hua always went himself, for he would trust none other to count the order to see that nothing had been stolen before the goods were handed over and the money paid.

But this day, just as he said it, Guard Boy was passing by the desk, carrying heavily two huge, square-laced reed baskets of grain.

He knew his master's moods well enough and so as he passed by he risked the words which came out with labored breath. They were as fawning as only he could make them:

"Well, and is not my master the busiest and wealthiest merchant in the town, and why should he be bothered to do such a task when he now has an assistant?"

He went on with his work, for it was a beating to stop without being told. But every word had been carefully rehearsed with all his sly skill for just such an opportunity, and presently Lin Hua called, "Come here my slave for your master would have words with you.''

The boy placed his load down carefully. To spill grain meant beatings for a week. When his load was safely down he walked over to his master's desk and stood with eyes lowered until spoken to.

Now the guard boy had no wish that Shen Lung should be sent to bring the goods. He hoped only to make his master think upon it. For, although a slave, the guard boy knew the story of how his master had married his own master's ugliest daughter. So the boy had it in his mind for some time now that when he was twenty, and his term of indenture was over, if he worked hard and avoided too many beatings and made himself indispensable as his master grew older, then perhaps with good fortune he might find such a place for himself in his master's household. There was one ugly daughter for whom his master would have trouble finding a husband.

But of course the coming of Shen Lung, a relative, changed all that, particularly when it was known that Lin Hua would train him up in the trading side of the business. To have any chance at all, Guard Boy knew he must rise above the status of laborer. He was no better than a common peasant. He was worse. He was a slave. Shen Lung now stood in his way.

So he had hated Shen Lung from the start, and that was why he had been so nice to him—as part of his plan.

Lin Hua now turned to Guard Boy and asked, "How can this be, another going in my stead to collect the goods from the iron road?"

"My master has taught his young nephew a little of his own great knowledge so perhaps my master could send his nephew . . . ?" Guard Boy replied stealthily.

"Is the boy not too young?" Lin Hua replied.

"Well, then, if this be so, my master's unworthy slave might go while the young nephew"—he was careful not to call him "young master" in the presence of the true master—"stands guard."

The servant had judged the master's mood correctly. Of late Mother's Brother had been becoming very full of himself. With the protection of the local warlord as long as he paid his levy, he saw himself as invincible.

Indeed, Lin Hua told himself, he *should* be able to order one here and another there. He would gain face in the eyes of the villagers and townsfolk if his slave were to go and collect the goods, more so even than his young relative.

The townsfolk would say, however begrudgingly, "Well, here is a thing, this Lin Hua is now so powerful that none will dare cheat him, not even the merchants from the city so that he lets his slave pick up the goods they send to him."

And so it was arranged that Guard Boy would go with the mule cart to bring back the goods from the train. But he would be away overnight. Nephew Shen Lung would have to guard the grain store in his absence.

Guard Boy left the next day after showing Shen Lung how to shut the bolts correctly. The security of the granary was that the guard locked himself in each night, sliding the big bolts on the door shut after he entered. There were no windows. The thatch was strong. It would show if anyone tried to break in. Shen Lung was so excited with his responsibility that he hardly slept all night. If he heard a noise here, or a rustle there, he was up with his lantern and peering into the darkness to see that all was safe. He had, after all, only to ring the giant bell of the granary, the rope for which hung inside, and his uncle and half the town would come running.

But the night passed uneventfully and the boy proudly looked forward to his uncle's coming to check the stock as he did every morning.

When his uncle did arrive, and after the lad had opened the door to him, he checked the stock slowly and carefully. To the left of the entrance, near the office, there was a stack of special grain—neat little packages done up in brown paper and tied with red string. This was the very best quality grain, for sale only to the Great House or to the warlord and his concubines.

When Lin Hua had finished his count, he found that one parcel was missing

"Where is my grain?" he shouted as his temper began to rise to a screech.

"I do not know, my uncle," the child said in his innocence. "I have not touched it and no one has been here."

"Where have you hidden it? Who have you given it to? Tell me!"

The screaming went on, but the lad could say nothing, for he knew nothing. And in his innocence he did not even stop to think that his trusted friend might have betrayed him, indeed set up a complicated plan to trap him and slipped the small package of grain under his shirt just before he left while Shen Lung bent at the locks under his friend's instruction.

Lin Hua continued his screaming and screeching as he strode into his small office, his long robe flowing, and returned with his bamboo rod.

He lifted it as if to beat the boy and then held it aloft, his hand and rod quivering.

Then slowly he lowered it and a stranger, more frightening look replaced the look of overt anger which had been there a few moments earlier.

"To beat you now would be an easy thing, soon over, so get you to the grain baskets and fetch and carry until all is stacked neatly like my trusted slave does and know that if you stop or even falter with running with these loads, taking two at a time, I will beat you until you start again and work like the peasant coolie you are. But also know and fear that any beating I give you today will be as nothing compared with what I will give you tonight. Tonight I will beat you not only as a thief but as one who dishonors his family.''

At this, the boy, who was only twelve-and-a-half and missed his family terribly because he had been unable to visit, began to weep. He had done nothing to dishonor his family, nor would he, and he still did not know how the grain had become lost.

At the boy's tears, Lin Hua became violently angry again. He lashed out with his rod and caught young Shen Lung across the back.

Whether through instinct, or fear, or both, Shen Lung swung out of the way before another blow could land. He ran, trying to inhale his sobs as he did so. He reached the spot where the bulk grain was kept and began hurriedly scooping it into the first of two baskets.

"And do not think to escape me!" his uncle cried. "Do not think to escape me, or run away. For if you try I will give you to Warlord Yang Hung, or set his men on to catching you so that you will be punished as a grain thief with the Death of One Thousand Cuts.''

To say this to a grown man would have caused fright enough. To say it to a boy, and one who, despite the harsh years of poverty he had survived, had been surrounded by the love and peace and contentment such as only those who live as peasants the world over may provide, savoring the goodness of the land and its crops despite all the bad seasons, to say it to such a one, such a small one, who had seen his friend Weng Feng executed so, was to cut to the very marrow of his bones with a fear and brutality he would never forget.

Shen Lung was strong enough, for he had worked these many years in the fields with his father. But his strength was for the hoe and bending, and not for lifting heavy loads. Yet he had determination, the determination of long hours in the sun. And although he faltered once or twice during the long afternoon, only to feel the scourge of the bamboo rod across his back again, for his uncle kept walking out of his office and striding beside him, cursing, yet the boy kept going. However many times he fell, he kept going until the sun set and he heard the sound of Guard Boy coming along the street with the mule cart.

He heard his uncle and Guard Boy talking quietly for a time and then his uncle came back inside and shouted loudly:

"Now here is a fine thing, my slave goes all that distance and comes back quicker than I myself and everything is accounted for and correct but I cannot trust my own nephew. Get you into the house now you dog of a peasant family, you dirt farmer's son, and get ready for your punishment."

Shen Lung finished what he was doing and walked slowly out of the barn back to the house, his eyes looking at the ground the whole time, except once when he glanced up and saw Guard Boy grinning at him.

Presently Lin Hua followed. His eyes still bore the look of the deeper anger which had replaced the earlier overt anger.

Now this deep anger had no reason. It seethed with all Lin Hua's old hatred of his sister's husband whom he had always felt was unworthy, forgetting as rich men do so easily that he and his sister had once both been as poor as Shen Fu. So his anger which had no reason did not stop to think that the boy he had chosen to work for him was an honest boy and might have been telling the truth.

There was no way he might suspect the real culprit, for the slave boy had always had such a spotless record. He believed none of the villagers would dare steal from him. And there was the matter of the door. The place had not been broken into and it could only be opened from the inside. So Lin Hua could see no farther than that his sister's child must have bad blood in him, bad blood from his father's side, from the poor side of the family, which had now shown itself once the boy had been faced with temptation, and this blood must be thrashed out of him.

So Lin Hua strode into the house, still clutching his long, heavy bamboo cane. When he saw his wife and three daughters comforting the boy, he silenced their mutterings with a look. They had become attached to the young man since his coming and this Lin Hua secretly resented. All the women had known the swift strike of his bamboo cane, and none wished to feel it again this day, despite the fact that they liked the boy.

And today the women knew that Lin Hua believed he had just cause, and would not spare them should they become involved.

So they scattered like a flock of pigeons at his stare and ran towards their bedrooms until he called them back:

"Stay and watch this punishment," Lin Hua shouted, "so you will know what I do with thieves and those who oppose me in my own household, and so that the boy who thinks he is a man and can steal from his uncle will know the shame of women watching him."

In the China of the time, this was a great shame.

So the women stayed, trying to avert their eyes, but knowing they must watch when the punishment started, for they had never seen him in such an angry mood, no, not ever. And they feared for themselves even more now, lest whatever they did, he would punish them too.

They heard the man order the boy to take off his loose cotton smock, which he wore without a shirt of any kind.

They looked momentarily, and the man's wife, the ugly one with the pockmarks who knew so much about beatings, could not suppress a gasp as she saw the red marks already across the boy's back.

Her husband heard her gasp and turned on her as he pushed the boy forward and over the table:

"Will you now join him or will you be quiet—?" he shouted.

The woman shook her head in fear and the man turned angrily back to the boy, grasping at his pants. They were loose and baggy, for the boy's mother had made them for him to grow into and they came away easily in Lin Hua's harsh tearing rip of anger. Now, as the women looked, they saw the boy's completely bare body and how really small it was. He still had his peasant sandals on his feet and with the rest of his body so bare and slumped and shivering in cold and fear, he looked doubly pitiful. The second smallest girl, who was about the boy's own age, began to cry.

But the cane had already started to swish through the air with a merciless intensity. Lin Hua struck the boy first on the buttocks and then on the back. And then again and again Lin Hua vented his sadistic anger on the boy's buttocks and legs until the child was sobbing uncontrollably. The boy felt something damp and thought he had wet himself and did not know it was blood. But still the blows kept coming. They kept coming and coming for a long time and then suddenly everything went black.

# 14

*S*hen Lung, *when he awoke, was terrified that the beating* would continue.

He awoke to find the woman and three girls standing over him, all still as terrified as he.

"Where is that one—?" he stammered out. His aunt noted that the tone level, which is everything in Chinese, was equivalent to a very derogatory reference for a relative, suggesting that however terrified the boy was, there was a defiance of survival, too.

The old ugly one put her finger to her mouth to quiet him. She cursed again under her breath the day her father had let Lin Hua in under their roof.

"He has gone to the teahouse," she said now to the boy, "and will drink more than tea before he returns. If fortune smiles on us he will fall asleep with the drink as soon as he comes home. But he will not beat you again this night, that I promise you."

She was not sure how much the boy was hearing. He was starting to writhe in pain now. The unconsciousness of the shock which had caused him to faint was wearing off.

But at her words he turned his head slightly and smiled. They had placed him face down on a bed in the kitchen.

Lin Par-gai did not believe she herself could take another beating. But she knew the boy certainly could not. She had loved him like the son she did not have from the moment he had come to her house. And her daughters loved him too, particularly the youngest. He was a kind boy and she would not see him beaten again this night—or ever—even if it meant she must come between him and her husband.

But she did not believe it would come to that. And already she had a plan for the little one which would, she believed, anger her husband more than he had ever been angered. But if she were careful it might work.

She said little, this old ugly one with the pockmarks, but she was the heart of China. She was bowed down with the weight of her shuffling years so that her age and sadness showed in curvature of the spine as she bent to the boy's bed. Yet she still had fight in her peasant face, and movement in her clodding unbound shuffling peasant feet, as she moved heavily around the room now, ordering this daughter to feed more dry grass under the fire and get the water warm but not hot, ordering another to bring salt and the good oil to rub on after, and sending the third, the little one, with the bright eyes and the skip walk and two tiny queues of hair which sat awkwardly out at the top of her ears where the red ribbon bound them, sending her to the old one at the end of the street, to the ancient one who smoked pipes and told fortunes and mixed herbs, to tell her that her mother had need of the mixture for pain again.

The little girl stopped and looked at her mother with her wide almond eyes, forming them into a silent question. For although she was the prettiest of them all, and nothing like her mother in any way to look at, in this she was like her mother, that she spoke little.

"Go, go, my small one," the mother said, knowing what the child's look meant. "The old one will understand what I want." The old one would understand, all right, the mother thought, and spat on the ground. The old one made more from her potions for healing than from fortunetelling. And of all her potions, the three she sold for beatings were her main business. The mother had the special salt and the special oil, but she had used the last of the pain potion the previous time she herself had been beaten. She dared not put salt and water on the boy's wounds to cleanse them before she gave him a draught of the old one's mixture. Some said she ground opium into it. Well, what if she did? The boy was fortunate to have fainted. Only the one welt had bled and then only slightly. The ones that didn't bleed and could be hit over and over again were the ones that would stay and take a long time to heal and could hide broken or burst things inside the body and leave scars like she had. The boy would have some too. Some. Not many. Three or four. Not as many as she.

She knew she must get him out of the house that night. But it must be done after her husband returned. The boy would not be strong enough before then. It must also appear that he had left on his own, without the knowledge of the women, else they would all be beaten too. But first she must fix his wounds as best she could and risk her husband's return.

While her daughters were busy she bent down beside the boy and whispered to him again. It was hard for her to talk, but she knew it was necessary and she labored with the words to get them right.

"Listen, my little one, listen—you must leave tonight. We will help. But husband must never know—"

The boy had turned in pain at the mention of leaving and his eyes stood wide in terror.

"What of the Death of One Thousand Cuts?" he sobbed. But she interrupted him quickly.

"Oh no, that is his trick. *Zao-gao*"—she uttered the Chinese curse and then added—"the coward. He would never report you or anyone to the warlord for the Death of One Thousand Cuts. For like as not the warlord would peel his hide for allowing anything to be taken. And my husband would never bear the shame in the village of doing this to a relative, to his sister's son . . . never. You will be safe from that. But when he has beaten someone once . . ." She stopped and threw up her hands, though the boy could not see them. "It is better that you go . . . You will work no more for that one." She used the derogatory tone Shen Lung had used before. "There are those in Shanghai who are good. They will help you and you are not afraid to work. I will tell your good parents that someone has tricked you and there is no dishonor, though perhaps there will be some for them in the village for a time until the real culprit is found and he will not be easy to catch out, that one."

She heard the boy straining again to talk and she beckoned to her eldest to bring water for him to drink for she could not hear. When he had sipped from a gourd, she held him up a little so that he was able to say, "Who, my mother, who—?"

At this the woman nearly cried. The boy had not made a mistake in his pain and fuzziness. He was very old-fashioned this one, she thought, fighting back the tears. He had given her the honorary title of "mother," as one might do to someone to whom one owes a great debt—a debt as great as the one owed to the one who has brought you into the world.

She noticed something else, too. As well as the kindness of tone which had brought the words he spoke about her forth, there was now a chill in his eyes which had replaced the terror.

For a moment she wondered if she were right to name the one she believed to be the culprit. But the boy deserved to be told. And he would have no chance to do anything before he left.

"The culprit will be Guard Boy," she said simply, and Shen remembered the way Guard Boy had grinned at him. "He is an evil one who would have one of my daughters and become part of this house by cheating his way into my husband's good graces . . ." She paused, and wanted to go on to say, "like he did when he came to this house." But despite the hate, she was a Chinese woman of her generation. She had said more than she should have already. It was not good to dishonor her husband in front of a relative. So she left the sentence unfinished and put Shen Lung's head gently back on the bed and made ready to tend his cuts. Fear had gripped her again. The time drew near when her husband might return. She hoped when the time came she would have the courage to help the boy escape.

Her little one had come back and was standing in the door holding a small blue medicine bottle.

"Come, come. So there was no difficulty—?" the mother panted heavily.

The little one shook her head. Then the woman remembered that she had forgotten to give her money. Oh well, the old one had trusted her before. She would know it was an emergency.

"She did not ask about the money?" the woman said as she took the bottle from the child, unstoppered it, and held the boy's head up again to help him drink from the bottle.

The child shook her head but instinctively the mother knew there was something else, something the old woman had said.

"What—what is it, my little one? What is it that she said?"

The child inhaled to make sure she had enough breath to get all the words out at once, like one getting ready to blow out a candle:

"She said to tell my good mother that there is no charge for one who helps the Monkey Warrior."

The child said it with a skip and a laugh, proud of herself for remembering and getting it all out.

Her mother frowned and then smiled. "She is a strange one, that old opium face. Whoever knows what she will say next?"

When she was sure the opiate had taken effect, the woman bathed the boy's wounds and then rubbed soothing oil on them, and helped him back into his clothes while she talked softly to him. She had mended his trousers while he dozed and his long robe she had rolled into a bundle.

"Listen well, my little one," she said, "or there may not be time to tell you later. When my husband comes home and is asleep so that I am sure he will not wake again this night, I will come and help you out on to the road which leads to the steam engine. You know of this?"

He nodded.

"The road is a long one and you will not reach it before night and you must not hurry for your wounds will still be sore for many days. But there are plenty of good travelers on this road of whom you may ask directions." She paused, breathing deeply with the exertion of all this thinking and talking. "It would be better," she went on, "not to ask of anyone whom you recognize from this village. But if you must, it cannot be helped— only look for a friendly face. But whatever the face, say only that you wish the steam engine for Shanghai. Tell no one where in Shanghai you intend to go."

The child went to speak but because the woman was concerned that time was short she silenced him and continued:

"I will tell you in a moment those you must seek when you reach the city," she said.

As she talked, she shuffled across to where she kept her cooking pots. Then she knelt on her hands and knees and with her fingers pried loose a mud brick from the floor.

From under the brick she took a piece of folded red New Year's paper covered with dirt. She looked at it fondly all the while as she walked back to the boy's bed. Then she dusted the dirt off the paper and carefully unfolded it to see that the silver was still there. Reassured of this, she quietly folded the silver into the paper again and slipped both of them into the child's pocket.

On seeing the red paper the boy was excited and again went to speak. But again she silenced him, this time with a finger placed on his lips.

"By the wharves in Shanghai," she said, "is what is called a white man's mission. Here there is a *yang kwei,* a white doctor who will be good to you and tend your wounds and tell you where you may find work. Tell him all your story for he will not betray you. Remember—the white doctor and his wife who live by the wharves. The wharves are easy to find. Anyone will show you. And at the wharves all know the white doctor and his wife. They are foreign devils, of course. But they are not false foreign devils. As to the piece of New Year's paper, show it to no one until you see another with just such a piece of common red paper. But if you see his piece of paper, then show him yours, for he is a friend."

She was tired now but she had said it all. Now there was only to wait.

The child looked at her, this woman who had shown him so much kindness. He wondered how she might know such people. Real foreign devils. Not just people of the town, not just people of the city—who were foreigners enough for country folk such as he—but real foreign devils. And how she came to have the same piece of common red paper as Weng Feng the tailor.

He looked at her kind face again and said, as best he was able:

"But my mother, if I should take your money how will I repay such a sum?"

She looked at him and said almost harshly:

"Do not be such a foolish one. Everything is not Oriental righteousness and virtue. Sometimes they are poor weapons against a beating such as you have taken. You will not dishonor your parents for I will tell them. It is a gift. A gift! You will need it for the steam engine." She used the kindest tone for the words now, to cover the earlier harshness.

The boy, despite his youth and half-shocked state, had the feeling he was being given what had taken a lifetime to save. That this money the woman had meant to be her own passport to freedom.

"It is a fine gift," he said now.

The woman smiled but did not speak. She wiped his forehead again with a piece of cloth dipped in the fresh water in the gourd.

The child fell asleep then, asleep into a deep and restful opium sleep, and dreamt of good times in the fields rich with green before the harvest was ripe; of times knee-deep in mud with the whole family out in the sun, even the youngest on her mother's back as they worked; and the good meals at home after the sun was down and the harvest in.

When he awoke the chill of the early morning was upon him.

He felt a hand shaking him. It was the woman.

She beckoned, and then bent to help him, holding him until she saw that his young legs, however sore, would take the weight. She knew the medicine would last at least two more hours.

Together, in the dark, the old one and the young one groped their way out of the house into more darkness. Quietly, ever so quietly, they passed down by the granary, and then out along the main street of the town.

The boy moved slowly enough, yet the old one panted and sniffed back phlegm, as if each next move would be her last. But she kept moving. And the boy limped with her, the two of them hand in hand so that another would hardly have been able to tell who was leading whom or whether either should have been out walking at all.

They passed the thatched village which called itself a town because of the few stone buildings, and because of the Great House at its edge which was soon slipping back into the darkness behind them.

The boy was more awake now, and suddenly afraid. Perhaps the old one, who trundled beside him like the faithful old animal she was, sensed it. For presently she said:

"It is a hard thing to do, to leave one's parents. But you are nearly thirteen now, and a man—and strong despite your size. We have a saying that it is not the dog in the fight but the fight in the dog that matters. You would not be the first to make good his way in a city. And if the gods of the earth will it, you will see your parents again."

She had stopped at the roadside now, panting with the exertion of her words and the walking. She seemed to have spoken more this night than in the past year. But secretly, under the shyness and the self-effacement which had been beaten into her over the years, she was proud of herself. She had used the money with which she might have bought her own freedom—once her daughters were settled with husbands—to free this little one.

The boy had stopped now, too. She gave him a package she had been carrying. It contained some cold rice and the last of the medicine.

"Make it last until Shanghai, my little one—until the white doctor."

He nodded. He was trying not to cry, but was very close to tears. He looked up at her large flat face with its marks, and her dull straight hair, square around her head, and her big bulky frame, and he hugged her tightly until eventually she had to withdraw and turned to go.

## 15

*There are many ways of being alone and feeling alone and the* boy felt them all that morning.

As the shuffling Lin Par-gai moved off, the boy turned his face up the road. But after he had gone a few steps he faltered and turned back. The old woman kept moving, however, without looking behind. The boy kept staring down the long distance of the white dusty road between them. In the half dark he watched her go until he could see her no more.

He could not move on at first. He was sore all over; and stiff; and hurting with burning pains such as he had never felt before. The knowledge that pain such as this existed—and could be inflicted by someone he had trusted—hurt almost as much as the pain itself.

He stood there a long time. And now, alone, he wept.

When he had dried his tears to a whimper, he turned and looked forward again.

He forced himself to move a few paces. He had this dreadful feeling that he would never see his parents again. A dozen times as he edged forward, he nearly turned and ran back, ran back despite the pain, in the direction of that sure, safe haven which would be there for him on the farm, if not to stay then at least to see and hug them all just one last time: his father, his mother, his baby sister and his elder sister, Ling Ling.

Yet even his young mind knew he must not turn back. To do so would be to miss the engine which would take him south; to do so would be to place his father in a jeopardy of honor, for he would be duty bound to return his son to his wife's brother, particularly without any evidence of his son's innocence and however much the father knew the boy to be telling the truth. And the farm, that small plot of impoverished earth less than one acre in size, there and at their little cottage, half a *li* away, would be the first place his uncle would look.

So, with his small strength, he started down the road.

But as he walked, he looked back just one more time. He looked out to the side, to where the hills ran up to the mountains. He walked and looked and remembered, fearing that he would never see his beloved countryside again. He thought that this farmland, so rich and black in good season and so brown and dry in bad; he thought that these hills, which became green when they reached the mountains; he thought that even this light brown and clay white dust of the roads which seemed to smear everything with a film in the driest of dry weather; he thought that all these things which he loved so and took with him as a remembrance were unique in all the world to his village. He could not believe—because he had never been anywhere else and never been shown pictures—that the deep green overhang of pine-layered leaves and stilted trees which sprung out from the sheer shale cliffs, standing like uneasy ghosts of the sky in the last mists of the night, that these mountain strongholds of trees and rocks and caves and brave men were China.

The boy walked on, tired and sore, but committed now in his young mind to his goal of reaching the engine.

Long after the sun was up and close to the forenoon he passed through another village and after that there were more people on the road. His way had led straight through the village, so he was reasonably sure he was still on the right road. But he thought he should ask and now began to heed Lin Par-gai's warning to search for a friendly face. The boy looked around. None appeared to be of his village. And, indeed, since he had been traveling slowly and no one had passed him, this seemed likely enough. Few ever traveled on the engine, save those wealthy enough to do business. It never occurred to the lad that some might even afford it for pleasure.

As he looked around he saw too many austere faces. There were men in long black robes and black, pointed cloth hats, with thin beards and hands crossed in sleeves. They reminded him of his uncle. He would have none of them! In his child's mind, which thought in terms of black and white, a lesson had been seared for all time: merchants were not to be trusted. Somehow, in his childish way, he had gotten the idea that greed had caused his trouble and that greed was a part of a merchant's stock-in-trade. He had no way of knowing that what he had discovered intuitively, others had seen before him and even now were making into a religion. But it was a very atheistic religion; a religion which said power flowed from the barrel of a gun.

In this mood he trusted no one. As for the men in the long robes, they did not give him a second look. He followed, certain they would lead him to the engine if only he could keep up.

At dusk, trailing a long way behind the others, he finally saw the engine in the distance.

His aunt, Lin Par-gai, had described it to him so that he would not be too frightened when it hissed and steamed like boiling water. She had also told him not to give more than one piece of silver for his fare; and to tell no one that he had the second piece.

Shen Lung hurried now, in the descending dark, for the engine was already steaming and he feared it might leave without him. He desperately wanted to be on it and to fall asleep while it carried him to safety.

As he got closer he saw a cheeky lad, little older than himself, hanging on to the outside of the engine, shouting over and over that soon the engine would leave.

Shen Lung waved and the boy saw him. When Shen Lung

finally reached the engine—which had two big wooden wagons attached to it—he was out of breath.

"What is it that you wish?" said the boy whom Shen Lung now saw wore a cap.

"To travel to Shanghai, in the south."

"You have the money?"

"I have the money."

"Let me see how much you have."

Shen Lung looked at the boy and their eyes met. Even without the warning of his aunt, Shen had the care of money that only poverty teaches.

"Are you in charge then of this train that you give orders to those who would pay? Tell me quickly where is the great man with the wisdom to drive these two big wagons and I will talk to him."

It was the sort of thing he had heard his father say, when as a smaller boy he had accompanied him to the town where tradesmen invariably tried to cheat the peasants.

The boy had learned many lessons in the past forty-eight hours, of which he was only dimly becoming aware. But the lesson he now learned was immediate and gave him great glee.

His directness was obviously so unexpected that it took the cheeky conductor's boy aback. Into the silence came a voice from the engine, chuckling, and then a face—round and happy with a set of huge teeth under a peaked cloth hat.

"So here is one who recognizes the importance of the driver and is not frightened by some cheeky conductor's servant," said the man with a huge smile and laugh. "Step up young man and take tea in my humble dwelling. The night will be cold but we keep a good fire here, and who would want a good honest farm boy like yourself to spend the night with the merchant riff-raff in the carriages?"

Shen Lung did not quite understand the word for carriages, but knew what the man meant. And, in any case, while he pondered, the man, who was huge, now that he had fully emerged from his cabin, leaned down with one giant hand and offered it to Shen Lung so that almost automatically the boy held his out and felt himself being scooped up through mid-air on to the metal floor of the engine driver's cabin.

"Be off now, you laughing jackass," the driver shouted to the conductor's boy, "be off and do your duty. This one is more than a match for you and tonight he rides with me."

Another huge man was also in the cabin, stripped to the waist and sweating heavily, like men do in the fields in summer, as he shoveled coal into the big oven.

"Now my young man," the driver said, "I am Hwang, a man of one name only, and this poor fool of mine who has been my fireman these many years is a deaf and dumb one who has no need of a name. But smile and shake hands with him if you will, for he likes that."

And having said this, Hwang tapped the other man who was as big as he on the shoulder, and Shen Lung gave a very big smile and held out his hand so that the fireman took it and pumped it very vigorously until Hwang tapped him on the shoulder again to let go. Then the man returned to his shoveling and Hwang pointed to a couple of wooden stools with pieces of sooty jute bag on them.

"Sit here, my young friend!" he shouted. Shen Lung was to discover that the man shouted all the time, even when the engine was stopped. "Sit here and we will have some tea. You will get a little dirty, but it is not something that will not wash off, and it will be warm and friendly here and better for you than back there. You do not mind?"

Mind? Shen Lung shook his head vigorously and then said:

"I am very honored, sir, but I must ask you how I may pay my fare."

"You must, eh, little one? Yes, I believe you must. Give me a farm boy every time, that's what I say, don't I?" he shouted, stamping his big heavy boot with nails in it on the metal floor.

At this the mute stopped his shoveling again for a moment and turned around and smiled; Hwang nodded.

The boy smiled, too.

Seeing that the boy had been smart enough to understand that somehow the poor fool could feel the vibration on the metal floor as a signal that his friend was talking to him, and respond with a smile as an answer though he had not understood a word said, Hwang patted the lad on the knee vigorously.

"He's not so silly, is he, my fool?" the driver said in a tone that required no answer. "Now, let us rest and have tea as befits all Chinese gentlemen, for there is a moment before we must depart. As for the fare, my young man, if you will talk to me while you are awake about crops and the land and good and bad seasons, this will be payment enough. For it seems not so long ago that I was in the fields myself and the fine thing about this employment of mine is that it allows me to ride a fiery horse through the fields.'' He snortled at his own joke. Then he was off with his shouting conversation again:

"Now watch this and see how well we speak, my poor fool and I,'' he said, as he stamped his foot on the floor three times.

At this the mute fireman stopped shoveling immediately, took from beside him a large burnished and almost black copper kettle with a bamboo-wound handle, pulled a lever which released water and a deafening whistle—so that Shen Lung jumped and Hwang laughed—and then placed the kettle, with the dried green tea leaves now thrown on top of the water, between them both.

When the tea had steeped a little, Hwang took three large white but soot-stained China cups from behind him, poured, and made room on his stool for his fireman friend while they all sat and drank.

This for Shen was a great luxury. These men obviously had tea in their water all the time. *Ai-ee*, there was something to tell.

He sat back and drank gratefully, hardly feeling his wounds in this wonderful little cabin of new-found friendship, and totally unaware what this meeting would lead to.

They talked well into the night, he and Hwang, with Shen sitting on a stool beside the driver and the cold of the night kept out by the fireman's periodic shoveling. When they made a stop, Shen took a little more of his medicine, the second for the day, while the others were busy on what they called the platform. Then he lay down on a pile of coal bags Hwang had put aside for him, and before his friends returned to the cabin was fast asleep.

When the boy shook himself awake it was light. He walked over to where his companions stood by the furnace, Hwang holding a lever and looking out at the track and the mute one leaning on his shovel.

Hwang noticed that the boy moved stiffly but said nothing.

"Ah, my little one, so you are awake—and in good time. Soon we will see Shanghai. You will smell it first—a good smell

I think—and then you will see a sight such as will never leave you.''

The boy smiled and stretched himself very gently.

"Enough of this talk!" shouted the big man, who talked most of the time. "Enough of this talk—it is time for breakfast now that you are awake." Hwang had the ability always to make the boy feel part of the conversation, as if he were important and things revolved around him.

Smiling broadly again, with his smile that was almost a silent laugh, Hwang jumped three times on the metal-cleated floor with both feet. As the double clang of his hobnails sounded on the floor, the mute fireman jumped forward like a dog running to a morsel. In an instant he had the door of the furnace open and his shovel in, but to the side, extracting something from a ledge above the fire. Then out came a burned black metal cooking pot, steaming with the warmth of good food. Shen Lung looked and saw and smelled beautiful hot noodles sitting in the pot held out the length of the shovel.

With a quick and easy flick the fireman set the pot down on the floor. Then he went into his tea routine.

"Right foot for tea, left foot for food," Hwang laughed as he saw the boy's fascination and tapped the shoulder of his mute friend. This was obviously another signal. The fireman immediately honked energetically on the engine whistle with great glee.

They ate standing up, for as driver Hwang would not leave his post. Shen Lung felt particularly important when, because of this, he was asked to pour the tea and pass it around. This was an honor he had not yet been given, even in his father's house.

The engine—which by now Hwang had explained to the boy was just the front part which pulled the wagons and the whole was called a train—rattled on into the fresh morning air.

Presently Hwang shouted, "Now!" and the boy looked and could see nothing except the low country they were passing through. Then suddenly he smelled it. The most delicious of smells he had ever smelled.

The boy had never seen an ocean, nor a great river for that matter, and did not know the open country smells they gave, the smells of size they gave, quite different from the smells of small farms.

Now coming at him with the speed of wind, as he stood beside

Hwang, was the smell of eight centuries of delta mud and ocean and all that Shanghai had ever been and done and now was.

As they approached the Huangpu River, where the great city stood some ten miles above the junction with the Yangtze, the smells of a new world came to Shen Lung. It was that slimy, mud-salt, freshening breeze of the Yangtze, the smell of the Yellow Sea to the North and the Bay of Hangzhou to the South; the lingering smell of the old century and the exciting smell of the new; the smell of nearly one million people bustling themselves awake in backstreets and on the Bund; the smell of silk and spice and human degradation and success and profit and death in the canals where unwanted babies were thrown; the smell of every nation on earth that had footholds leased out to them in Shanghai, little countries with their own laws within a Chinese city in these places they called concessions; the smell of rickshaw sweat and coolie feet, of French perfume and Russian fish roe, of Japanese saki and English roast beef.

The boy knew nothing of the recipe of the smell, but he sensed it to be a world-opening and beckoning smell, something exciting and alive set against the plodding past of China.

There was present and future in this city, as well as past. And if the boy felt something exciting and alive in the smell, this was nothing compared with what some men, the men with the secret oaths and little red paper flags, were now planning for this city.

Whatever miseries might lie behind the facade of the city, the boy had felt in the breeze that day the smell of freedom, of opportunity. So something in his tiny frame stirred to tell him, as the tall buildings which swept along the river were visible now, that in a city such as this perhaps even a small one, with hard work, might grow great and wise enough to deal with unjust men such as his uncle.

Before he knew it they were at the railway station, pulling into the platform, with his friend the driver busy with much shunting and whistle-blowing and shouting and steaming. From the platform Shen could see the whole station. It was alive with such people—*ai-ee*, it made him tremble to think how many evil spirits might be around in the air this day. There were so many foreign devils—truly foreign devils—with strange hats and coats and such pale skins and beards, and women with bird feathers in their hats and animal fur over their shoulders and dresses of silk of such quality that he gasped. And soldiers! Everywhere there were soldiers. And conductors. And boys like himself but in flat, round, box-like hats and uniforms to match. And coolies—everywhere coolies pulling great carts loaded with huge boxes made of straw and leather.

His friend the driver looked at his adopted charge and saw his eyes wide with wonder.

With his engine now safely installed at the platform, he turned to Shen Lung and said:

"And so, my little friend, you see it all and yet it is only the beginning. Your new life starts today, and that is not such a bad thing, for the cities have much to teach—much good and much bad. I and my poor fool here will see you into the city and we will all sit together and have tea one more time, and perhaps an apple pear or two, such as is a favorite from your region when the seasons are good."

At this the boy's eyes lit up. Yet something was troubling him which he wished not to mention. He was grateful above everything that this big man had asked nothing of his past and why he was running away—a thing a boy his age traveling alone such a distance would be almost certain to be doing. And he believed above all else on this day that he could trust this stranger as no other. He wished, therefore, to tell Hwang of his destination so that perhaps he might guide him there. There was, too, a secret wish that the good Hwang, if he knew where to find the boy, might come and visit him from time to time.

But the boy felt he must heed his aunt's warning to trust no one and therefore not tell the man his destination, especially as Hwang knew where he had got on the train. If his uncle ever came looking, or got his aunt to confess under beating, which worried the boy, then his uncle would have only to ask of the engine driver. "Did you see such a one?" and the driver could reply, "Not only saw but can take you to him for such and such a sum of silver."

The boy was ashamed of himself for even thinking this of his new friend. Yet his whole upbringing had taught him caution with strangers, even apart from his aunt's warning.

So Shen Lung mustered all his strength and said with great civility and formality:

"Sir, you would honor me if you and your friend would take

tea with me for I am in your debt and would ask one more thing.''

''What is that little one?''

''That perhaps you might use your wisdom and influence so that if any come seeking me at the place where I got on, the conductor's boy will not tell he saw me—no, not even should he be offered silver.''

It was a very Chinese thing the boy had said and done, a very old-fashioned Chinese thing, yet one for which Hwang was full of admiration in one so young. The lad had asked Hwang and his friend not to betray him, not even for money. But he had done it indirectly, by talking about the conductor's boy and enlisting Hwang's help there to silence him as well.

''Not even for silver, little one, will that one betray you. And none shall hear from us.'' He was talking quietly now for the first time. ''But what if someone who is a friend or relative might wish to find you? What then? For surely such an honorable one as you would wish his family to know . . .''

At the mention of his family the boy broke down. He told Hwang all, then, although a sixth sense still made him withhold the name of his village and the address he would go to in Shanghai.

When the boy had finished the big man Hwang looked very serious indeed and spat on the platform where they now stood.

''Zao-gao,'' he said, ''we bring it on ourselves by doing nothing.''

The boy did not understand this but he understood that the man was angry.

Shen Lung watched while Hwang turned to his mute friend. Away from the confined space and often dim light of the cabin, where their hands were busy with tasks, the two men had quite a range of signs for talking and the boy realized Hwang was telling the mute fireman what had happened. He saw the mute one go serious and then look very angry.

''Well, little one, here is what we will do,'' Hwang said at last. ''I will show you the room below the signal box where all we drivers go before and after our journeys. If anyone comes to ask of you at my engine, when I return to Shanghai, I will leave a message for you at the signal box. There is an old one there who sits on duty. Inquire of him when my next train arrives and then

I will describe to you the one who asks for you. I will tell whoever asks that I have not seen you but I will ask of other drivers. I will say to return in a week to see if there is any news. This way we will know who asks for you and why, and you can decide if you want them to know where to find you."

The boy smiled in appreciation.

"And now," said Hwang, his shouting laugh back again as he put one hand around the boy and the other around his mute friend, and began to walk with them along the platform as if he owned it and all the others as well, and was talking as if his mute friend had perfect hearing, "now we are to enjoy the hospitality of our young friend here and take tea. Did I not say, 'Give me a farm lad every time?' "

# 16

*T*he year of 1918 passed into 1919. Back in the Village of Wild Grass, Ma Yao, Shen's scholar master, was paying a visit to the boy's parents. He wore his long black silk scholar's gown and his pointed open-flap black silk hat. He had his arms crossed and folded into his sleeves. He did this not as a protection against the cold but so that people might know he was the scholar master of the town.

He had not told Shen Lung's parents of his coming. He knew how formal they were, and how poor. And he wished, despite his pride, to spare them any expense.

The boy's disgrace was now known, although the villagers were not fools, and already angry whispers were being made against Lin Hua. For the people knew the boy to be of good peasant virtue and his uncle a fool. So far none spoke openly, for fear the evil spirits in the air might hear and do them harm.

At the rough wooden door to the thatched cottage, Ma Yao

paused. Despite the great virtue he knew himself to possess in that he sacrificed his good life in the city to come to this poor village, he found certain things difficult. Although he was the son of a rich mandarin, there was a touch of conscience about Ma Yao. It was very small. But it was enough to prevent him being the perfect idealist.

Ma Yao was a Nationalist. To be a Nationalist was not Communist. Nationalists were the people who would save China and bring her into the modern world. Everyone knew that. Even now the Nationalists were building their network with local warlords, offering them money and eventual high commissions in the army. This was essential, they said, if all the different Chinese areas and provinces—counties or states—were to be united. With nearly 600 million people already, spread out in an area which made Europe and America look small, this was how the Nationalists saw unification occurring. With the history of bandit warfare and tribal invaders, with the corruption and decay of the Imperial court, China had become all the little Chinas again. Bled more and more by the landlords and warlords into whose hands the weak rulers had given the country, this was the only way to unify the whole area, said the Nationalists. They must use the warlords. No one stopped to question the methods so many warlords and landlords were already using; or to ask if giving them military power as well might be an opiate too heady to resist.

Ma Yao had been sent to this village to act as liaison with the local warlord, Yang Hung, who was favorable to the Nationalists because the warlord's son, Yang Ho, was a rising Nationalist officer. So Ma Yao bothered little to inquire into what methods the warlord used. It was enough that he was favorable to their cause, although there were those who would say Ma Yao must have known—must have known and cared not to inquire further.

But it was not on such things that his conscience occasionally troubled him. His slight touch of conscience this day had to do with the real reason for his visit to Shen Lung's parents. He told himself that his visit was to assure them of his faith in his student. But in reality he knew he had come to meet their eldest daughter, Ling Ling.

Ma Yao had first seen her walking with her brother near the schoolroom. But they had not been formally introduced, for she had left as he came up. The scholar master had guessed from the likeness that she was Shen Lung's sister, and the boy had confirmed this and said that occasionally she came to town to deliver a message from his father.

But although Ma Yao had looked for the girl—and seen her once or twice again—he had still not formally met her. She seemed always to flee demurely, with eyes quickly averted, whenever he approached. And it would not have done for him to ask her brother to call her back so that he might meet her.

Indeed, because she did flee demurely like a maiden should, it made Ma Yao even more interested in her. He liked the old ways when it came to women, although he prided himself on being modern in his thinking.

She was fourteen and very pretty and had tiny feet. When she ran off it was with that delightful little duck-like shuffle which Ma Yao found so sensual. And once or twice, after running off, she had looked back as if to say goodbye to Shen Lung. Yet the way she placed her head on one side and dipped it in playful deference to her brother, the way a cultured Chinese woman would do to a man, gave Ma Yao the mandarin's son an even stronger feeling inside, and he knew he must have her to lie with. In a society such as he had grown up in, in a rich household with his father a great one, such a thought was normal. Anyone Ma Yao wanted was his for the asking and easily procurable by one of his servants. His father had at last count, besides his wife who was Ma Yao's mother, some forty-nine concubines.

Here in the country it was really no different. Many girls, Ma Yao knew, were sold into great houses of the town or sent to the city to support their parents in their old age.

But some farmers had more pride than others. And Ma Yao knew from the boy's behavior that he would have to be careful with his father, Shen Fu. But once he had met the girl formally, others might speak on his behalf. This would satisfy the old one's traditional ways.

Ma Yao took a deep breath before the weather-worn door and knocked.

\*     \*     \*

In Shanghai the boy and his companions bustled through the backstreets towards Hwang's favorite teahouse.

The boy had never seen so many people together all at once, but the exhilaration of the jostling crowds more than overcame his fear.

Eventually they reached the teahouse and had tea and fruit and cakes, although Hwang insisted on paying for the cakes. The boy paid for the apple pears and tea, producing one piece of silver. Hwang saw to it that he got his proper change, which was many coppers. Shen could now count to one hundred, and add and take away, but he had not wanted to act superior in front of his friends.

They started to walk back to the station then, by way of the waterfront, the boy having told them he must leave them there.

Eventually they came to the Bund, the big sweep of buildings and jetties on the tidal river. There were so many wharves. Shen wondered how he would ever find the white doctor and his wife. Here on the Bund half the world seemed to be foreign devils. *Ai-ee*, they were everywhere. Yet his quick ears had picked up at least one thing that would be helpful. Several of the round-eyes seemed to speak his language, or parts of it.

But it was time to say goodbye. And so, right on the Bund, in the heat now of early summer, on one of the great cosmopolitan boulevards of the world, Shen Lung shook hands with his friends and very formally thanked them. Then, on an impulse, he turned and ran off quickly. But as he ran he heard Hwang shout, *"Joy geen, joy geen,"* "Goodbye, goodbye, little comrade." Then he heard the big, heavy buck-toothed man's shout above all else, above all the traffic and crowd noise, "And keep in touch, keep in touch through the railway station, little comrade."

The boy stood for a moment in the sun then and thought about his friends as he watched them move off in the distance. He had never before heard the word *comrade* used quite like that as a form of address.

He looked around for someone to ask directions of, but all he could see, apart from foreign devils, were coolies. And even a stupid farm boy knows not to talk to coolies while they are running with swinging bamboo poles over their shoulders, loaded like scales, lest you block their way and interrupt the rhythm of their run, and make them unbearably angry.

Somehow he had understood from his aunt that the people he was to see helped the poor. So in the end the boy went and asked of the people down by the water who seemed poor and out of work.

He tried to pick one who looked like a peasant, and sure enough the first man he spoke to had a country accent like his and was friendly. He told the boy that if he would walk about half a *li* and then turn at a big *godown*, at a big warehouse which he described, he would find the doctor and his wife in the basement at the back.

Shen walked for some minutes until he came to the big timber *godown* and turned down the alley, suddenly dark away from the sun.

It was a long building and he seemed to walk for some time before he saw stairs leading down below street level.

There was a sign but he could not read it. He did not even know that the red cross meant hospital or clinic.

A little fearful now, away from his friends and the safety of the crowds on the Bund, he descended slowly.

He came to a door and knocked and waited. Presently a woman opened it, a real white foreign devil—so white the boy nearly fled in fright. He had, of course, never seen a white woman of any description before he had entered Shanghai on the train that very day.

He had seen one white man once, who had come to the village to visit those at the Great House and who his father had pointed out as an oddity when they were passing. To see now not only a white *yang kwei,* a white foreign devil, but a white woman foreign devil, and one dressed all in white, with even white head and white legs and white feet, *ai-ee,* there was something.

The nurse was dressed in her full starched uniform. It was something she insisted on.

"Well now, young man, what is it you wish?" she said.

"Please, lady, I wish the good doctor and his wife and am sent to ask for them."

"Who is it that sends you?"

The boy paused, uncertain whether he had the right woman or

not and not wishing to be impolite. But finally he said, without answering her question, "I am come to see the doctor."

"Are you indeed?" she said, standing aside and beckoning him in as she held open the door which was covered with a wire-like mosquito net. "You'd better come in and get in line then." She pointed to the end of a long bench where a dozen other miserable souls were sitting.

It occurred to the boy that he might make a run for it. She was like one of the warlord's soldiers, this one. No wonder they called them foreign devils. He dreaded what the doctor might be like if this was the woman in this strange house. But in the end he sat down timidly. He was smaller than the smallest child there, although some were younger than he. It was just that he was so small and he always felt it when with other children.

But he sat and waited, for there was nowhere to run to, although his alert mind had noticed during the day that cities were wonderful places to lose oneself in. He also believed he would find work. He had seen coolie boys, and hotel boys at the station, and teahouse boys. There were also places where people slept by the wharves. And because it was summer, although sometimes still cold at night, he knew he could survive here and get work and somehow send money to his parents. Hwang would tell him how. He would trust Hwang when it came to the sending of the money.

So although he sat, and with the childish ignorant peasant part of his mind, feared—for he knew nothing of the ways of the foreign devils—he kept his eye on the door and knew that if it came to it he could make a run for it and survive on his own in the city.

Already, away now from all that his peasant life had represented, away from the drudgery of the grain store and the humiliation of the beating, away even from the love of his aunt and his own family, changes were taking place. The lessons of his directness to the conductor's boy, the confidence stemming from the admiration which Hwang had shown for his polite cunning—already these lessons were at work in the boy to make another boy of him, adding an extra instinct, as it were, which street boys all over the world share.

Shen sat with his head down. To hold one's head thus was very Chinese. It was to *k'ow-t'ow*, to knock head, the deferential thing expected before one's father, or the lord of the Great House, or one's master. For one such as the all-white *yang kwei*, the foreign devil, Shen Lung had automatically taken up a half-bowed *k'ow-t'ow*.

But he did not like it. And the longer he sat, looking up from time to time as the line moved, the less he liked it.

He never really knew what took him. It might have been the cry of alarm from behind the big white piece of cotton where the doctor was obviously wrestling with evil spirits. It might have been that despite all his aunt's assurances, he did not wish to cast his lot with foreign devils.

He hoped it was not done out of childish fear.

But the next instant, as the all-white one went behind the white curtain where the doctor was, Shen Lung was suddenly up and running—out the door and up the stairs to the alley like some startled cat, bounding in little strides back towards the Bund and daylight.

He moved swiftly, despite some stiffness from the beating, but fast enough nevertheless so that as he propelled himself along with his head down, he did not see the figure come out from around the corner, halfway along the alley.

Indeed the sixteen-year-old girl, blonde and slender of frame, did not see him either. Or if she did, she saw him too late. For as she turned the corner, idly, not hurrying, daydreaming a little of things such as only sixteen-year-olds dream of, she was suddenly knocked flying. The young girl was completely winded. Shen, for his part, had gone down too, for the sudden blocking of his run by however flimsy an obstacle had put him off balance. So both had gone down together and lay sprawling. Yet the fear which had set Shen running was still active. No sooner had he gone down than he was up again almost immediately, instinctively knowing like any animal to keep moving out of the path of danger.

Yet something stopped him from running straight off. Just as he was about to, not knowing what he had hit but believing it to be something human because of the softness he had felt on his head, he risked a quick look. *Ai-ee!* He had knocked down a foreign devil—and a female foreign devil at that! Now there

would be all sorts of misfortune to pay. It was just his luck that
if someone had to come out of a side alley it had to be a female
foreign devil. Why could it not have been a coolie who would
have just sworn and spat at him and then paid him no heed?

And yet it was not just because he saw that the girl on the
ground was a female foreign devil that he did not take off. She
was holding her stomach and *ooing* and *owing* most fearfully. He
was worried that he had done her great harm. He could not leave
her like that. He stood in a quandary, unable to move.

Presently, with Shen still standing over her, the girl opened
her eyes. She hurt so much she was sure she must have been hit
by a car or a bicycle, at the very least by one of China's
ubiquitous cyclists who, at fast speeds, could be as deadly as any
motorcar. But she could see nothing except this small young
boy—this extremely worried-looking young boy.

"I am all right, Younger Born," she said in Mandarin, trying
to gauge whether he was from the North or the South and if she
should use Cantonese. She decided from his high cheekbones
that he was from the North and that Mandarin was correct.

For the boy, the fact that she spoke not only Chinese but the
correct dialect was a point in her favor and did much to alleviate
his anxiety. "I am all right," she repeated, "I'm just winded."

But she saw terror return to his eyes as she began to get up.
"No, don't go, please," she said hurriedly. "I won't hurt you.
I'm just winded. Please help me up."

Shen Lung looked at her and held out his hands. The girl
noticed how strong his grip was as she took hold. It was vice-
like the way he held her hands. She was amazed to find such
strength in one so small. But even as she thought this, she felt
the grip tighten even more and then suddenly she was wrenched
clear of the ground onto her feet.

The boy's actions, once he had been asked for help, had been
instinctive. But as he hauled her up bodily with both hands, the
muscles across his back tightening, he winced, involuntarily.
Despite her surprise at being lifted bodily, and despite a slight
ill-ease from being winded, the girl noticed the boy's momentary
look of pain.

She had lived so long in China that the language she spoke
and the customs of the people it sprang from had engraved their
centuries-old lessons upon her. The form of language she now

used, the order and tone in which she couched her words, found exactly the right response in the rather old-fashioned young man who stood before her:

"You are very strong, young cousin, to lift me so easily."

The boy hesitated and looked deeply at her. He must reply. It would be most dishonorable not to.

"My strength is less than it appears."

"You honor your family by being so modest but it is a considerable strength and I am now in your debt for helping me."

"This is not so for I am truly a stupid one not to look where I am going and knock down such a lady as yourself."

"It was an accident. I, too, was not looking where I was going. My head was in the clouds with my thoughts. So there is no more blame for one than for the other. But I see that in helping me perhaps you have pained a muscle in your back and I would be happy to have my father look at it if you would permit him, for he is the doctor at the clinic. Perhaps you know of it?"

At the mention of this the boy's face clouded over and he looked as if he might run off again. But instead he shook his head violently and managed to get out the words "Please do not trouble, please do not trouble. My back is healed, my back is healed."

Shen wondered later why he had used those words, for he did not intend that the girl should even know that he had a sore back. But somehow her Chinese courtesy speech had disarmed him. Kate herself did not know at this stage of her life that she was one of those people that other people told things to. But she smiled at the boy and said, "Oh well, and so your back is healed, but it will do no harm for my father to look at it, to see you have not hurt it again helping me, and afterwards we will take tea."

Again the boy shook his head and this time Kate frowned. She had helped at the clinic since she was small and she knew the ways of the people who came there. They were very proud, she knew that, proud in human dignity, especially the farmers, and this boy was certainly one. Then again they were shy. The fears of a clinic, and standing in line, and another knowing one's inner secrets were quite strong.

"There is a back way," she said suddenly, in a moment of

inspiration. "There is a back door I may knock on and which my father will open himself and where you may go in and not be seen by any other and speak only to my father."

"Without the all-white foreign devil?" the boy blurted out.

"Yes, yes indeed without her," said Kate, sensing now what the trouble was and suppressing a smile at the very apt description. She and Kate had never got on. Nurse Rhoda Dwyer was a sergeant major of a woman at the best of times, and had held just that rank in the nursing corps during the war. Having been converted in the closing stages, she had signed on as a medical missionary after her return to the States. They were overjoyed to have her, of course, but as Kate's father used to say, she was no Florence Nightingale. And in a land where civility and face and nuances of meaning were everything, she had about as much sensitivity as a steam engine.

What this poor little Chinese boy didn't know was that he'd been lucky enough to escape an instant Bible reading in Chinese so woeful that Kate had never known anyone to understand a word. They just stood there bemused, which made Nurse Dwyer think she had them spellbound, whereas in reality they were just too polite to tell her.

But at Kate's mention of the fact that Shen might indeed see her father without interference, the boy now spoke up, delivering in full, and for the first time, the message he had been given:

"You would do me a great service if you would arrange this, for my aunt has sent me to see your father because of his great wisdom."

"Has she now?" Kate said with interest and warmth, pondering again how profoundly simple is the manner of entry to the Chinese heart if one observes the age-old conventions of human dignity in conversation. "Well that is a fine compliment and my father would hate to miss hearing it. Perhaps you might give him some news of your aunt. Come along now and I will slip you in through the back door as soon as the next patient leaves. Then I will go around to the front and guard the curtain against the white dragon. And later, when I hear my father call for a new patient, I will know that you have left. So I will return to the back door to meet you and we shall go and have tea. Is all this agreeable to you?"

At the mention of the "white dragon," Shen had been unable

to avoid a chuckle. Here was a strange thing, one foreign devil making fun of another. He would not have thought it possible.

"It is well, it is well," he answered quickly with a smile when the girl had finished. "It is well."

"Good," she said. "Then that's settled. Come. I've got all my breath back now and I'm feeling fine." Truthfully, she was not fine. Her stomach was very sore but she did not wish to mention it. She started to move off. Shen followed slowly. But she was as good as her word and did all that she had said she would. Yet when she came around to the back door of the clinic, after the next patient had been called in, the alley was empty.

When she asked her father about it afterwards, as he bound her bruised ribs with tape, he said only, "You were right to guess it was a private matter, Katie, darlin', and I love you for treatin' him just right. I was all the help I could be and gave him some medicine. I told him to come back for more though I doubt we'll see him again. But I'll tell you one thing. He'll remember you. He'll remember your kindness, I could tell that. And in the long run that might be far more important than the medicine."

They looked at each other then, in great and deep love of daughter for father and father for daughter, and she leaned up and kissed him on the bristly undergrowth of his chin. Then they hugged tightly and presently, she being the last patient of the day, they switched off the single light without a shade which cast its glow wide, shut and locked the back door, and began to walk home, arm in arm.


They often walked home together like this. Kate had been helping in the clinic since she was old enough to roll bandages. By the time she was twelve she was as good as many trained nurses, and of course her command of the Chinese dialects was the best of any in the clinic. Nurse Dwyer had never really learned more than a few phrases. Her parents had become very fluent over the years. But this was nothing compared with a child—albeit an American one—born in China.

By the time Kate was fourteen her mother began taking a little time off when Kate was on duty with her father at the clinic. So she and her father often walked home together. But today the walk was special. It would be their last for some time. The next day Kate was leaving for America to begin her studies—first at college and later at medical school. She had always been a bright student and would enter college at sixteen. Her father was particularly proud—and grateful she had won a scholarship.

Often when they walked, they walked silently, hand in hand, each alone with their thoughts. Kate knew just how hard it would be for her parents to manage financially while she was away. It was hard enough when she was there. There had never been any surplus money. But she had never wanted for anything, although in considering her entire childhood she could never remember any other white children—except for those of missionaries like herself—who were as poor as she. Almost all the other white children were from wealthy homes—sons and daughters of *taipans* or at least from the homes of employees of these wealthy traders. Even the children of junior civil servants or ordinary sailors ("ORs"—"other ranks," as they were called, to distinguish them from officers) were rich compared with missionary children. Not that Kate minded. Well, not too much. She had thought at the time she hadn't minded. But she knew she had—just a little. That was why Janey's friendship had been so important, at least at the start.

Janey knew that Kate invariably went straight to the clinic from school and one day she asked if she might go too, to see what it was like and to escape from being alone with her *amah* at home. So Janey went to the mission clinic, where Kate often played with the Chinese children waiting for their parents. And afterwards, Kate's father, perceptive as always in these matters, phoned Janey's father and asked if Janey might stay for supper, saying he would drive her home afterwards. Nigel Edwards, with some pressure over the phone from his daughter, who even then was learning how to have her way with him, agreed. After a time Janey regularly visited Kate, who, in turn, stayed with Janey at the big home on the hill overlooking the harbor.

It was at a party at Janey's that she had first met Yang Ho, the son of a fabulously wealthy regional warlord with whom, it seemed, Nigel Edwards had some business.

But Kate was never able to be quite as social as Janey.

It was not just the clothes, because she knew Janey would always lend her some. And it was not just that her parents had reservations about dancing. It was more that it had always been assumed Kate would be a doctor. And this meant—however naturally bright she might be—long hours of study. For in addition to the strenuous standard curriculum, Kate needed to be the top in her class in biology and chemistry, as well as physics and math, if she were to have any hope at all of getting a scholarship to an American college. After that she would have to win another scholarship to medical school. All this had been made very clear to her from her earliest years. So every spare moment she had she delved into her father's and mother's medical books. For her fourteenth birthday her parents had even bought her a second-hand copy of *Gray's Anatomy*.

Kate and Janey used to lie on the bed in Janey's bedroom for hours, looking at the line drawings and joking about how good it was of Katie's parents to give them their own sex education book.

And yet, despite all this, Kate wondered again for the hundredth time whether she should go to America. She had always wanted to be a doctor. For as long as she could remember, she had wanted that. And it was not just her parents who wanted it for her. The Chinese who came to the clinic had even called her "the child doctor." They knew as well as she what pleasure she got from helping them with even a simple procedure—washing a wound, applying ointment, scraping a tropical ulcer. She had known how to set a broken leg since she was twelve. Of course there was no question of *not* going to America. And she did have a scholarship. But she knew what a financial burden it was going to be. And she was going to miss China—miss it terribly.

Yet the excitement of the trip was also already lifting her up and taking her with it, like a wind filling the sails of a ship, and as the day for her departure came she was suddenly caught up by it all—in being sixteen and making her first sea journey halfway around the world on an ocean liner to the country of her origins, America, a country she had never seen.

Within a few days, China seemed so very far away.

# 17

*T*hose same few days were occupied in a very different way by the young Chinese boy who had scampered down the lane away from the clinic instead of waiting for her.

The girl had been kind enough but Shen was still new to the ways of the round-eyes, of the foreign devils, and embarrassed to be near them. After seeing the white foreign devil doctor, he had suddenly wanted to lose himself in the streets, packed tightly like a sardine with his own kind.

So Shen lost himself in the crowds of Shanghai and in the days that followed, as Kate sailed farther and farther away to America, he looked for safety and anonymity in the already blighted urban streetscape so different from the free-moving fresh air and honest smells of newly turned earth which he had been forced to leave.

Probably at the back of his mind, too, was the thought that his uncle might get it out of his wife that she had sent him to the white round-eye doctor and his family; that he would be safer away from them lost in the crowds. But he soon learned that the crowds of a city were a mixed blessing.

Week after week for four months during the early part of 1919 the child wandered aimlessly in the backstreets and alleyways of Shanghai, looking for work in the daytime and absorbed into the darkness at night. He wandered past the collapsing driftwood houses which rose as if on stilts in the backstreets. Poles of gray washing jutted out from each—as though they were determined that light should never reach those who were so poor they lived below.

But Shen Lung soon discovered there were so many poor there were not even enough good places to sleep in the streets. He had to wait upon the sheltered spots to sleep in the streets from the middle of the afternoon, only to discover that others were there before him—others who had not moved from the previous night. And so, however hard you tried, you finished up in one of the hovel alleyways or backstreets, with a newspaper over you against the chill of the night if you were lucky, knowing that the stench, if not the noise of the body cart, would wake you as it passed, carrying away those who had died in such poverty that ceremonial burial was impossible.

Each day, each hour, since his time of running away from the American clinic, Shen thought to go back; or at least to try to find his friend Hwang.

But each time he believed he was about to do one or the other, something in his mind stopped him. Not fear—unless it was of rejection. He wanted to be self-reliant, independent. He spent the night of his thirteenth birthday in a back alley alone.

He had been working in the fields since he was five. The harsh exigencies of land and climate and poverty had built into his small mind a certain stamina of circumstance; a certain intuitive survival need.

As Shen moved around Shanghai he learned that, in those days, three kinds of people had money: Chinese of the mandarin or merchant classes; rich foreign devils; and rich Buddhist priests. But whereas some Chinese were rich and others were poor, and whereas some Buddhist priests were rich and others were poor, all of the foreign devils were rich.

The boy needed money to send to his parents, whom he felt he had let down. So he determined to work for a foreign devil. Perhaps if he did this he might become rich himself. But there was also another thought tugging at his mind about foreign devils. His scholar master, Ma Yao, had said that foreign devils spent more time at their lessons than most Chinese—and that this was why the foreign devils were so successful at many things at which the Chinese were backward.

So Shen had it in his mind to find out what things it was these foreign devils learned which made them so powerful. He was determined he would not be what so many peasants were—stupid and backward.

So on the fourth day Shen Lung set out to walk along the Bund and see if he might find a foreign devil who dealt in grain.

To such a one he would show that he could count a little, and that he knew coarse grain from fine, and where and how to stack it so it did not rot, and how to protect against rats and mice, and other things that might be useful to give him a worth above other Chinese boys.

He walked along the Bund towards the *godowns*, the warehouses, of the foreign devils.

*Zao-gao!* there was not one but many. He knew the Japanese were bad—all Chinese knew that, even the youngest. But how would he choose among the others?

He asked the Chinese sailors who were the most powerful foreign devils and they said, "the British, of course, because they are the Ocean devils." So he looked for British *godowns*.

But whenever he found one and stopped to ask, no one would let him see the foreign devil in charge. Always an angry Chinese came out and sent him away while the other Chinese workers laughed.

When Shen went back to his friends at the wharves that night and said there had been only Chinese there who had laughed at him when he asked to see the foreign devil, his friends at the wharves laughed too.

"Do you know so little of how things are in the city, you country bumpkin?" one burly sampan lad said. "The *tai-pans* always use a Chinese compradore, which is very helpful for all the compradore's relatives and friends and very helpful for the *tai-pans* in that they like to do as little work as possible, but it is not very helpful for country bumpkins looking for work."

The boy Shen Lung hated to be laughed at, but he had set his mind to do this thing and was not so easily put off.

"You must forgive my country ignorance, it is true," he said to the stout sampan fellow, "but I must ask you out of your abundant wisdom to explain to me what is a *compradore*."

The other lad puffed himself up then and said, "Why he is the Chinese middleman who does all the hiring for the foreign devils. All Chinese staff are his to do with as he would. And of course he gives all the jobs to his relatives and friends—all but a very few for whom he pays next to nothing and yet poor people still clamor for them, even though they know the compradore cheats them and pays them nothing compared with the money the stupid rich foreign devils give him. But it is an ancient system."

The fatalism of the last remark was not lost on Shen, for it was such that he had set his face against—this idea that all must be poor and starve like their fathers. But he sensed that the boat boy was a silly fellow who liked to hear himself speak and so he thanked him and moved on. *Ai-ee* it was not easy. Here was the uncle principle at work again—the greed that makes men starve, the greed that denies them even their just wage. His friend Hwang would know a way around this, he was sure. But he was determined not to ask. He must find an answer himself.

But there *was* no answer and the days soon stretched into two weeks.

Three weeks later he had seen every compradore at every *godown*. But they had all laughed at him when he asked for employment.

Slowly, sadly, swallowing his pride, Shen decided he must seek the help of his friend, Hwang. He began to make his way to the signal box where Hwang had said he could be found.

But when Shen finally arrived, Hwang was not there.

The boy waited all day. Then, just before dark, he heard a happy shouting voice in the distance. It was Hwang!

The boy ran out into the fresh air and saw his friend coming in the distance. When Hwang saw him he ran and scooped the boy up, and there was much shouting and laughter and merry dancing around as Hwang shook hands in an exaggerated way with Shen, and Shen with him, and then each of them with their mute friend, as if they were acting out a mime.

Then they had tea in the signalman's hut while Shen told them all that had happened to him. When he had finished Hwang clapped him on the knee and said: "Come now and stay with us, little one, for we are lucky enough to have part of a room to sleep in which is used for something else during the day. There will be space for one more bed beside my fool and me. And you will be safe there and may stay as long as you wish and we will ask our friend the professor for good advice concerning your future."

The boy said nothing but gave a happy little skip and smiled. A professor. He knew that to be higher than a scholar master. His father would surely approve of that. Here he was among good honest working men, like Hwang and the fireman, and they had a friend who was a professor as well. He did not ask, or even doubt, how this might be. For now he trusted his two new friends completely. So he walked on, happy to be among his own people again, rather than having to seek employment from the foreign devils, although there were plenty of foreign devils walking by on the boulevard.

It was not until later that he learned he was from too backward a part of the country to know how much the foreign devils prized Shanghai and had fought for it. If one lives in the countryside, and is an ignorant peasant who cannot read or write, how may one know of such things as the Opium Wars, in which Britain had beaten China and in 1842 got as her prize not only Hong Kong but the International Settlement of Shanghai as well? Shen Lung would not even have known of the Great War which had ended the previous year, 1918, if it had not been for his scholar master, Ma Yao. And even then, as he walked happily along in the sun on this day in 1919, he knew few details of the war, except that it concerned Japanese seizing German interests in China.

No one, not even his friends, of whom Hwang was better informed than one might suspect, knew of the events already taking place in Peking that day. It was May 4th, 1919.


In the countryside, in the place they called "the Village of Wild Grass," Shen Lung's family had been visited secretly by Lin Par-gai the same day the boy had escaped. The old and shuffling woman often foraged for dry grass fuel in the countryside, a habit from her childhood which her husband, if it meant saving a little on the fuel bill, let her and the girls do. But this day she left the girls to forage on their own and went to see the boy's parents. There was the usual wailing and weeping that takes place when one dies, or leaves home, and then much thanking, and the father saying how much he was in the woman's debt and the boy's mother cursing even her own brother, but softly, so the evil spirits would not hear.

The father thanked Wife's Brother's wife most profusely for helping the boy to escape. The woman had said openly to the family only that the boy was in a safe place. Shen Fu knew this was to avoid his knowing and subsequent dishonor as head of the house if he failed to tell Wife's Brother. He also knew the woman would tell his own wife, who would eventually tell him, but this was different and would not be dishonorable to withhold, for how might he betray a secret from his own wife?

So all this had been done and the old woman gone, and therefore it was with some fear on the next day that Shen Fu opened his door to find the scholar master Ma Yao.

But Shen Fu was courteous. And, as luck would have it, they had a little tea—just a little left from some that Lin Par-gai had smuggled out of her own house to bring as a gift the day before.

When Shen Fu saw how the young man looked at his eldest daughter as she helped her mother serve tea, he relaxed a little. The scholar master said only good things of his son, and comforted Shen Fu as much as was polite and proper, so Shen Fu was pleased that he looked favorably on his daughter, Ling Ling. The old man could not see past his youngest, and feared it would not be easy to arrange a marriage for his eldest. So he was encouraged by Ma Yao's interest. These were difficult times, and many men were being taken by the Nationalists for the army, even some as old as he. At fifty-one he did not think they would come for him, but one never knew. Some were already whispering that the Nationalists were as bad as the emperors, or worse, and were now aiding the warlords.

To see his eldest daughter settled with a man of some station, as the scholar master was, would guarantee that his wife and youngest would be looked after.

By sunset that night, the boy Shen Lung had not the slightest doubt that he had made the right decision in turning to Hwang. He was already installed among a whole group of new-found friends, sitting on the ping-pong table, where Hwang had put him to introduce saying, "Well, now, and here is another of us who although small has much fight for his size and no cause to love the landlords."

They had all clapped then, the people around him in this not very big room which looked even smaller because of the table, which had many papers on it as well as bats and a ball. Shen had never played this ping-pong game, but he knew of it. The room was crowded at the edges with rolled-up mats which would serve

as beds, and dishes and chopsticks and tea cups, and a small fuel
stove and kettle by the window.

Presently the crowd quieted down a little, and then Shen Lung
saw from his vantage point on the table that they were looking to
the door where a small, fat old lady who must have been nearly
sixty had entered. She wore common black pants, a gray cotton
coat like a man's, and cheap black slippers from a market. Her
hair was mostly gray, with only a little black, and it was cut very
square around her head. She wore steel-rimmed glasses.

"She's a professor," Hwang whispered to Shen. "But she's
one of us."

Everyone became very quiet and waited for her to speak as if
she were head of the family.

Before she began she looked around the room and smiled very
quietly. Then she spoke, trying to use as little emotion as
possible: "The students have held a demonstration in Peking,
because the League of Nations has refused China's request for
self-determination. Many have been arrested and jailed."

Shen Lung drew his breath in quickly. *Ai-ee, ai-yh*, what a
terrible thing, he thought. To be put in jail! What shame on one's
family. Then he realized everyone else in the room was cheering. What manner of people were these that his friend Hwang
had brought him to? Next he saw them all, en masse, produce
little pieces of common red New Year's paper and start waving
them.

After all the cheering and everyone wanting to talk to the
kind-looking old lady who was little taller than Shen, she eventually came over to the ping-pong table, where Shen sat swinging
his feet and playing with the ball he had picked up off the table.

She said only:

"Welcome, young one, to the First People's Commune of
Shanghai."

"Thank you, Elder Born," he said courteously, reaching into
his pocket and taking out the piece of red paper his aunt had
given him and placing it quietly on the table. When the old lady
saw this she began to cry.

# 18

*The days tumbled into weeks and months then, once his friend* Hwang had taken him under his arm. The three of them became inseparable—Hwang, Shen Lung, and the mute one—as they walked the highways and byways of Shanghai together.

Hwang seemed truly to know everyone. The first thing he did, the very first thing when he saw that "the little one Shen had decided to join us," was to get Shen a job shoveling coal at the railway station. Needless to say, Hwang knew the compradore.

"It is not much, little one, but it is a living and will leave a few pence to send to your parents," Hwang said seriously and then added with his large laugh, "and although the head shoveler is an old friend of mine, he was surprised to see how short you were so I had to say to him, 'and do you not need one to shovel at the bottom of the pile, as well as at the top?' "

Hwang and the mute one had made Shen a bed of empty coal sacks. Technically these were supposed to be refilled, said Hwang. But when they got old they had to be replaced, lest the coal fall out. So he and the fool washed them on their next train journey, when there was plenty of boiling water, and brought them home.

The boy thought of the backstreets; and the newspapers to keep warm; and the dead bodies. These sacks would be like heaven. He smiled his thanks and both the men knew what passed through his mind. They had seen their cold and hungry days, too. There were few Chinese who lived in this big city who had not.

Hwang, whom the boy came to trust more and more, had that sphere of influence which only men of certain dispositions in particular occupations enjoy. The hinterland of China was still largely primitive in terms of communications and accessible mainly by horse. To be able to send or receive something by train was a wonderful good fortune. One could not easily send by mail—even if one had the money—if one could not read or write. For then one must go to the professional letter writers who sat in their long black robes at their tall desks with brush and ink bottle. And one had to pay a pretty penny for their work and had to suffer many insults about one's ignorance and the words one used and what one said about one's family affairs.

But to his friends, which included many businessmen, Hwang was a network in himself. There was always a merchant slipping a package into the cabin with Hwang, or one to whom Hwang delivered a package on his return. Shen never saw Hwang charge for this service. But the merchants gave him gifts of tea or morsels of food so that the three of them and their commune friends never went short. Shen tried to pay Hwang for his share of the food but Hwang would not hear of it and would accept only a share of the rent for the room plus any food they might have to buy.

And apart from the merchants, there were always friends, or sometimes even strangers Hwang had never seen, coming with messages to be passed along the line. Hwang never turned anyone away and never wrote a message down, though he could write, for he had been to normal school in the country before his father fell poor in the great famine and had to come to Shanghai with his family.

Of course other drivers had such systems, too, so that what one could not deliver in one area, he might prevail on a friend to do in another. It was that particular sort of improvisation, that basic, clever, yet matter-of-fact peasant inventiveness which had always been born of necessity.

At such hand-to-hand and mouth-to-mouth communication, the great Hwang was an expert, and there were those who had already noticed this expertise and how valuable it might be.

To young Shen Lung it meant, at Hwang's suggestion, that he could finally contact his parents.

But even then it took some months. His village was a very small one and Hwang would not trust just anyone with the message. The big man had to wait until he found someone he knew who worked as an agent for a big merchant and was going to the town near the Village of Wild Grass on his twice-yearly visit to take silk orders. He was a friendly enough man, and when asked about the extra distance he must walk from the town to the farm said politely he would do it as a favor to Hwang, and so all was explained to him, and a little money sent, and Shen's address given.

When the man eventually returned, he said that Shen Fu, Shen Lung's father, had said to thank his son for sending money despite his bad fortune but that his sister had come upon good fortune which she was sharing with her family and indeed she was even now in Shanghai, and if Shen Lung wished to see her he should inquire at the house of Ma Yen the Mandarin.

# 19

*I*t was by now the New Year's festival of 1920, so as soon as Shen could get a day off he hurried to see his sister.

On the seventh day of the week Shen and his friends arrived at the address which the man had given.

Hwang spoke kindly to the gateman who sent a boy to find Ling Ling. Presently she came to the gate herself—which was a great honor—and she did her brother an even greater honor by asking him and his friends to tea.

Although her formal family name was Shen Ling, she was, in fact, always called Ling Ling by family and friends, or sometimes just Ling. Perhaps Shen Lung, her brother, but only two years her junior, had started this as a baby when he first began to pronounce her name. Or perhaps their mother had started it, demonstrating as she had by the ringing of a simple bell the sound "ling-ling—ting-a-ling-a-ling." But soon Ling Ling, or just Ling, was the only name used of her.

After they had exchanged the pleasantries one must, and had asked about each other's welfare, Ling Ling told her story.

When Ma Yao had first visited the farm to speak of his respect for Shen Lung, it had become apparent that he also favored Ling Ling. Ling Ling herself was grateful for the scholar master's attention, for she had feared that because she was then nearly fifteen, and not betrothed, her father might sell her to the Great House on the edge of the town to work in the kitchen.

After Ma Yao's first visit Shen Fu had sent for the old one, the ancient one who smoked the pipes and told fortunes and arranged all these things for a fee. He asked her to speak on his daughter's behalf. It was suggested Ling Ling would, if placed in a great house in the city where she might learn, make an excellent No. 1 concubine for a man such as Ma Yao. When all heard he was the son of the chief mandarin of a great city and when the old one brought papers to prove it, they knew no one would think ill of Ling Ling becoming a concubine, particularly one of such high rank. Besides, the old one said, there would be no need of a dowry for such an arrangement, whereas a wedding would cost a dowry which a poor family could not afford. And there would be money for the girl to spend on herself and also some to set aside to send to her parents at each full moon so that they might live as would be expected of those whose daughter lived in a great house in the city.

The girl Ling Ling now explained to Shen and his friends that she knew she was not the most favored in the family—as her own brother who loved her most knew. What might the future have held if she had not taken this good fortune? How would her family have eaten in the hard times?

So at the time of the next full moon, when Ma Yao returned to his birthplace of Shanghai, Ling Ling left with him, bringing only her mother's old wooden trunk with the hooped metal.

Ling Ling now showed Shen Lung and his friends the trunk in the corner of her room, where it stood under a silk covering. Shen Lung knew his sister loved the old trunk as he did, for it was the one real piece of value from their childhood and it had meaning even to rich Chinese in a house such as this. It meant that his sister's family would not have her come empty-handed to another's house, and even Ma Yen, Ma Yao's venerable father, when he had greeted the girl and saw the trunk had said, "It is well, it is well."

Thus Ling Ling came to Shanghai.

\*     \*     \*

Now it transpired that the coming of his sister Ling Ling was at first a great good fortune for Shen Lung. For a time they were happier than they had ever been.

Ling Ling had her own rooms in Ma Yao's inner court. Ma Yao lived in the house of his father, Ma Yen the Mandarin. Ling Ling had rooms second only to those a wife might have, and young Shen Lung was free to come and go as he would. Though they missed their parents, there was great pride in being free and able to send a little money home. Soon they heard that their parents' lot was greatly improved. There was tea all the time now; and rice, noodles and cabbage; and a few sweet delicacies at the time of the festivals.

So when Shen's nightshifts of coal-shoveling would allow, he and Ling Ling spent happy, joy-filled days, days they would later say were their best. Shanghai was such a place to be, in those days. No one could have foreseen what would happen.

Another year passed. Ling Ling now walked the boulevards openly with her brother and his two companions. It was a great honor for them and she also won much face in their eyes that she did not mind being seen with humble working men. Ma Yao laughed at it, but he did not forbid it. And sometimes he let her take a sedan chair, or a rickshaw. For with her beautiful, tiny feet—which Ling Ling had no doubt had helped her get to such an elevated position in a rich man's house—she could not walk idly by with others.

The sedan chair was a particular luxury, not only for the girl, but for her brother and his friends. This gave them great face in the eyes of those who passed by, to be seen with one who was from such a great house that she rode in a sedan chair. Of course people would assume those with her were her servants, sent to protect her. But no matter. They were high-ranking servants, for they walked and did not carry. There were others to do that, so the prestige was still there.

But all knew, too, that although the sedan chair gave great face, the best days were the days Ling Ling sat in the rickshaw. Then even the foreign devils stopped to stare.

Ling Ling was now sixteen. On this particular Shanghai day in 1921, strolling along the Bund in the sun, Hwang wondered if Shen Lung knew what a jewel his sister was in this city of exquisite treasures—and what might lie in store for her, or indeed both of them, because of what men would do to own such a jewel.

She wore a blue *cheongsam* and sat lightly on the edge of the padded rickshaw seat. A blue silk shawl had been thrown down before she had been helped up. It was hard not to look continuously at her knees tucked neatly together in front of her.

*Zao-gao*, Hwang thought. And what he saw would be nothing to the silk and satin underthings she would wear for her master's pleasure. She would shop well, this one, at the place they called "Pants Alley," off the Bubbling Well Road. And the fragrance of perfume he smelled now would be insignificant beside the oils and colognes her servants would bathe her in the night her master came to her court.

Yet there was something more to this girl which made Hwang like her above her beauty, which any Chinese knows after all is skin deep and will fade, and is this not why rich men have concubines in their season? No, Hwang had noticed, or perhaps felt—for not all these things did he think out one by one for himself but rather felt the effect inside him—that there was a ripeness of soul about her too.

She did not look out at poor working men such as Hwang or the fool as a rich one might. Even those on the wharves she looked upon with warm friendship, as if they were part of her, too. As if her ripeness of body, which made it so easy for her to slip quietly into this new life with Ma Yao, had a ripeness of soul also, in which all men were one. Being the child in the family who was loved routinely, and not specially like the mother loved the boy or the father loved the youngest girl, Ling Ling had to learn to love well in order to receive love, and this she freely gave to all, so that she might keep receiving it. So there was an open richness about her which was hard to deny, which made her attractive to all who met her, even the foreign devils. And although on this day she was barely sixteen, there was a promise of rich fulfillment in this girl. As she sat there and laughed there was the feeling that she had much to give beyond the delights men might find in her body.

Even after Ma Yao had taken his first wife, Ling's star continued to rise. And as the years passed, Hwang watched her as she became a known and popular figure, always exquisitely dressed, often to be seen at restaurants and banquets and grand balls, for in those days even a married man might take his concubine with him wherever he went.

Hwang himself did not change, but continued in his general role as everyone's strong and happy friend; and in his particular role of Shen's guide and protector, even though he was slipping more and more into the background as the training he had organized for his young protégé, through their friends in the Communist party, bore fruit.

# 20

*A*t the house where they lived there were students and scholars, like the aging lady professor. There were intellectual men like Wu Zhao, the former Kuomintang officer who was betrothed to the beautiful, young, and quiet of spirit, Lu Chien. They were happy to help poor working people like Hwang, the mute one, and Shen. So from 1922 through 1923 and 1924, they began classes so that Shen, although only a poor shoveler of coal, was able, when his shifts permitted, to study with good scholars, some of whom even lent him books such as foreign devils study. These books also told of modern methods of western warfare.

And they talked of politics, Shen listening avidly as the lady professor spoke of poverty and injustice; of the oppressive Kuomintang regime; of the brutality and corruption of the Blue Shirts, Chiang Kai-Shek's Secret Police, against whose activities there could never be any appeal. She spoke of the French Revolution and its stirring slogan—liberty, equality, fraternity—

and of Karl Marx and the more recent Russian Revolution. Only communism, she told them, with its basic creed "From each according to his abilities; to each according to his needs," could change the face of China and bring hope to its poor, starving, uneducated, slave-ridden masses.

"Look at the luxury in which our present leaders live," she said. "Yes, and the foreign devils too—luxury derived from exploitation of the work forces and the peasants and all whom they consider their inferiors. And look at the way the ordinary people spend their lives in misery and want. Do not look with envy in your hearts, but with thoughts of justice and freedom. These rulers must be overthrown. When the emperors were driven out, there was to be a new age, but the Kuomintang's system is as venal, as unjust, as terrible as anything we had before. And they rule by force, and must be overcome by force. I preach rebellion, my friends and comrades, the rebellion which will set our people free."

Shen listened and absorbed and learned, and sometimes he too would speak. And, despite his youth, the others would give him their serious attention. Then Hwang's heart would swell with pride as he saw his protégé growing in stature within the group. One day Shen's quick intelligence, his decisive mind, his power to stir his listeners, and the strength of his personality would make of him a leader, of that Hwang was sure.

By late in 1924, because of his learning, Shen was able to get regular day work as a junior clerk at the railway. Then, in 1925, he was made a ticket clerk, responsible for money. And finally, later that year, a senior clerk.

There were classes in other things, too. Physical fitness was prized highly. Although Shen was small, he was very strong. The years in the fields from the time he was five, and the carrying of grain, and the shoveling of coal, and the memory of the beating—which had turned into an inner strength—had made him very strong indeed. He and Hwang and the mute one wrestled and practiced *t'ai chi*, shadow boxing, daily. During the weekend there were horse-riding classes in the country. And all went to secret classes to learn about weapons.

The mute one, their loved and silent friend, was also finally given a name. For as the idea grew that all men must be free, truly free and equal and able to walk around their land with dignity, Shen said it was a part of the warlord and landlord mentality under which they had grown up that a mute person should have no name because he could not hear it. The injustice which Shen himself had suffered, and which had made him so receptive to the communist ideals, would never be cured until the revolution came, but here was a human indignity to be acted upon immediately. The mute one must have a name.

Not that any disagreed. And indeed it was all done with great good humor.

A big weekend conference was called to consider what name to give the mute one. And, even more importantly, how to tell him. For it was seen from the start that this would be no easy matter.

The meeting went on all of the first day. Shen Lung was later to remark that more than any other organization on earth, the Communist party could hold a ten-day congress in place of a ten-minute meeting in place of a ten-second decision. They just couldn't agree on a suitable name.

Hwang kept saying his friend should be called Horse, for he was strong and good and loyal. But when he said it for the twentieth time, Shen pointed out that *ma,* the word for "horse," was the name of his sister's master, Ma Yao, one of the Nationalist leaders, and who would wish to impose any similarity with that one on the poor mute?

"But why not Yu-Ma?" he suggested. *Yu-Ma* meant "Small Horse," which would distinguish him clearly from the other Ma.

And so it was finally agreed.


The naming of the mute, though the discussion had been long and was apparently taken seriously, had been at the same time a somewhat lighthearted occasion. Nevertheless, it had a profound effect on Shen Lung's future. For during it, without any formal appointment to the position, he had acted as chairman. It had seemed natural, since it had been his idea in the first place, to look to him for comment on their suggestions, and of course it was he who had finally broken the deadlock.

But it was more than that. There had been an inner strength in his voice and attitude, a sudden flowering of his authority, and from that time on he was the acknowledged leader of the group. His fame spread, and he became widely known as a rising star in the Communist movement.

# BOOK III
# The Rising flood

1926

# 21

$K$*ate had listened to Shen's story with fascination, not only for* its own interest, but because of what the manner of its telling had conveyed to her about him. He had spoken almost flatly, without self-pity, when describing the hardships of his early life, and without undue pride in his rise to leadership. She was filled with admiration for him.

"So you were the frightened boy in the alley," she said at last. "I often wondered what had happened to you. You were a grave disappointment to me. You were my first patient. I thought I had won your confidence. I'm sorry I didn't recognize you. But then we met so briefly, and of course I had to leave almost immediately to study."

Shen nodded, smiling, but said nothing. They had talked well into the night, Kate getting up intermittently to check on Blake's condition.

The rain had stopped, but the wind was still gusting across the Bund, giving the water and bright lights a shimmering, other-world dimension, a place in space and time removed from them by light years, despite the fact that it was only across the boulevard from the big picture window by which they sat.

Shen's story had enveloped Kate in China again in a way none of the rest of her homecoming had. She felt she had relived her childhood; had come in touch with the countryside in which they had lived when her parents had first come to China; the country-side and its people which she missed so. Shen's gentle telling of his story had done all this.

She looked across at him and wondered where friendship with him might lead. Was he such a rising star for his people, as they said? Was he truly their talisman? What was it that made her feel drawn to him in a sense of events happening to her which she could not avoid? Even if she wanted to? What was there in him which made her feel so suddenly again such an important part of China? Made her feel that perhaps she had a part to play in its future?

"Some more tea, perhaps?" she said. "It is surely my turn."

Shen nodded without moving, and Kate got up and quietly checked the drips connected to Blake, feeling his forehead to make sure he was not becoming feverish from infection from the wound. Then she busied herself in the kitchen for a time with the tea, finally returning to Shen with it and a fresh packet of cigarettes from the desk drawer. They had smoked all of Shen's.

There was much she wished to ask him about Blake and the previous night. What had really happened, and what was Shen's and Blake's relationship to the ubiquitous Wang Lee?

As she returned to her seat it was as if he had read her mind.

"Blake must tell you what he wishes of the events he has been involved in," he said slowly. "As for me, it is enough that you know who I am. I will tell you where to find me and will help to the utmost should you ever be in need. Wang Lee, who looks so much like me, is my cousin. Few know either of us, let alone both, as you do. This is a heavy responsibility. It seems fate has decreed that your path and that of communism should cross, Doctor."

Kate smiled and nodded.

"You appreciate I cannot guarantee what the outcome of your helping us tonight will be," Shen continued.

"I understood the risks," Kate said. "It was a debt of friendship I owed to Lu Chien."

"This is the best motive. And now both she and we owe that debt to you."

"And where *do* I find you?" Kate said. "Where does one look for the young will-o'-the-wisp communist leader?"

"At the signalman's hut at the railway station, of course," Shen laughed. "Go there and identify yourself and say only that you wish to see Hwang. The message will reach me."

"What of your family?" Kate asked. "Are they still in the countryside?"

Shen nodded, but his smile suddenly disappeared. "Except for Ling Ling, as I mentioned," he said noncommittally.

"Of course," Kate said, "I know her—or rather know of her. My friend Janey pointed her out at the ball. Everyone knows her . . ." Kate suddenly stopped.

"It's all right, Kate Doctor," Shen said quietly, unconsciously getting the English word order wrong, reversing it the way it is placed in Chinese and indicating to Kate again that this was a difficult topic for him. It was the first time she had noticed the slightest slip in his usual faultless English.

"I'm so terribly sorry," she said, "I just didn't think . . . It was stupid of me."

"It is quite all right, good doctor, I assure you," he said, recovering his composure. "She is, as you quite correctly say, known to everyone. She is the widely known courtesan, the one they say is of warm heart and easy virtue, the one they say the generals favor, particularly since the death of her former master, Ma Yao. She is now just twenty-two and was sold into slavery as a concubine on her fourteenth birthday. It is not surprising that the use of the female body for the pleasure of men is the only trade she knows."

"I'm sorry," Kate said again.

"There is no need. We accept what we must for the time. Perhaps you would like to meet her?"

"I'd like that very much indeed."

"Good," said Shen. "Good. Then we shall arrange it."

After they cleared the tea things away together, Shen turned and spoke quietly to Kate.

"And now you should rest," he said. "I will watch the patient, be assured of that. For although I cannot tell you what he does, no man in Shanghai is more important to us. And besides this, he is our friend."

Kate nodded. She was very tired. "I think I will sleep for a couple of hours. You should get some rest yourself after that. Wake me in two hours, otherwise you might get sleepy and doze off."

He smiled at her. "Thank you, but that is not necessary. I shall not fall asleep."

Kate smiled and nodded. Then she went to draw a bath so she

might soak in the tub and relax. As she ran the water, threw in some bath salts, got undressed, and climbed into the hot tub, which immediately began to ease her tired muscles, she thought about Shen's last remark. It was as if he were positing again that Communists were some special breed of men who could go without sleep. And, judging by his disciplined attitudes, she did not doubt it.

She soaped up and as her thoughts turned to Blake she felt warm and good. Before she had wanted Blake almost as an experiment, as an experienced man of the world who might help her to usher in a more mature womanhood. But tonight had changed all that. Suddenly he seemed a man of greater depth, of worth.

There was much she still did not know of the Chinese mind. But for a Westerner, having grown up with the Chinese, she knew as much as any man or woman. She knew that the way Shen had spoken of friendship, not single friendship but some sort of united and almost extended family friendship for Blake, made him a very special man of substance in their eyes. They did not use the word *friend* lightly, especially of foreign devils.

So here was this man who had appeared a slightly worn soldier-of-fortune, but who was now exciting and appealing beyond the surface. But more than this, he needed her surgical skill. And, as she lay in the tub, however much a part of her mind told her he might simply be using her and had wanted her only because she was a doctor in whom he believed he could trust, yet another part of her believed it was more than this. And the very vulnerable side of her, the side people might hurt because of its sensitivity, the side which at times craved for a strong man to protect her, was nevertheless the same side from which her loving came, and from which her need for dependency issued forth in a need to be needed. This, above all else, was the healer in her. And in Blake needing her, for whatever reason, and in her giving, in warm and spontaneous treatment, the first flow of true affection had begun—the first of those juices which, however they might start, once flowing, lead on to all those irrevocable thoughts and actions which the world describes as falling in love.

Having washed and dried herself, and still with that newly-washed-perfumed-soap smell about her, she put on her dressing gown, whispered a quiet goodnight to Shen, and a quieter one heard only by herself to Blake, and retired to her bedroom. Switching off the light, she was presently warmly tucked away and floating into that world that only a woman's dreams are made of.

# 22

*Yet she slept fitfully and awoke early. So the next morning,* while the frost was still on the ground and the coolies on the Bund were barely stirring, Kate got up and hurried around to her parents' clinic to try to fix what was troubling her. The wind was sharp and kept cutting at her as she walked with her head down.

When she reached the clinic there was no sign of Nurse Dwyer. Good! Kate started to search for the blood register. The clinic was not heated. She wished she had time to make some hot coffee. She also wished her father might have been there. She knew he would want her to put a record of the blood transfusion in the register. She was starting to get very concerned for him. What if he was not just late getting back but had been detained by the Nationalists? What if they were watching the clinic? Had she been right to take the blood? What if the Nationalists were watching even now? What if they already knew her father had sometimes allowed Communists to meet in the clinic? What if they at least suspected and asked to see the blood register?

She wished her father was back safe and sound so she might discuss it with him. But he was not. And so, with her teeth chattering, and her fingers almost frozen with the cold, Kate finally found the blood register, which was required to be kept by law, filled in the amount of blood used, and signed it, leaving blank the patient's name. Then she quickly put it away and ran from the clinic.

On the way back to her apartment she stopped to buy a newspaper. As she began to read it, her heart sank. All over the front page was a story about a raid on a government arsenal. It had taken place the night before. A huge shipment of arms had been stolen. One of the raiders had been shot, but he had still managed to get away. There was no detailed description, but it was thought he was a European.

Kate looked at the paper as she held it and saw she was trembling. Carefully, she placed the newspaper under her arm and began to walk slowly back along the Bund.

When she arrived back at her apartment, Shen had already left. Lu Chien was there in his place. She was sitting beside Blake. Kate thought he appeared to be stirring. The painkiller she had given him before she went to sleep was wearing off. She smiled at Lu Chien and sent her to the bathroom for hot water and towels. Then she sat down on the couch beside Blake and brushed the hair from his forehead. She saw him smile weakly. He was still very pale.

"I'll give you something more for the pain and to make you sleep soon," she said. "But first I'd like to get you cleaned up . . . All right for just a few minutes more . . . ?"

He nodded slowly.

"Good," she smiled. "Good. I didn't think we'd be sharing another compartment so soon, did you?"

He made a faint attempt at a smile and shook his head.

Kate was a great believer in warm, reassuring patient talk, though she had to fight desperately to keep her mind off the newspaper article. "I think it'll be best if I move you into my bedroom as soon as possible," she said. "It's not going to work if you stay out here. There are no facilities. It was really only until we got you patched up. You'll be more comfortable in a proper bed, and it'll be easier for all of us if you're closer to the bathroom. I'll be right there if your wound gives you trouble in the night. OK with you?"

Blake nodded weakly again—so weakly it worried Kate. She saw his eyes fill up.

"My poor dear," she said, touching his cheek tenderly with the back of her hand and dropping her professional tone. "You came very close to death last night, didn't you? Somehow the patient always knows. But it really is over now. OK? You can trust me. You're going to get better. You might feel like a herd of elephants hit you full on in the chest for some time yet. But you *are* going to get better. That I promise you. OK? You let me do the worrying. In a few weeks it will hardly be safe for me to be in the same room with you.''

He forced a proper smile now, his moment of vulnerability gone. ''Good,'' Kate said.''Good.'' But she was surprised with herself. She had wanted to overcome the hidden fear that always lurks—to make sure he knew he was going to get better. But her last remark about not being safe in the same room as him hadn't been part of the plan. It had worked, but she hadn't intended to say it. Or had she? Had that other part of her mind, the unconscious—which Freud always spoke of—intended it? Was that secretly how she hoped it would be in a few weeks' time— not safe to be in the same room with him? Yet she knew so little about him. So what if Chinese such as Shen placed much store by him! That could be a double-edged sword. For there seemed little doubt that the unidentified gunrunner mentioned in the newspaper was Blake. How else would he have gotten a gunshot wound he could not report?

Who was she getting involved with? A mercenary gunrunner? A would-be martyr to the communist cause? Or a little of both? And if she knew the real truth, would it matter? Had that pool of unconsciousness deep within her already made up its own mind? What if it were true as the Bible said that there was a time and season for everything under the sun? What if her appointment with human love was about to take place? It was certainly true that she saw human love as the ultimate expression of her emancipation as a woman; as the ultimate exercise of the dignity of decision; as the ultimate taking of individual responsibility for her own actions in a world so often at war with women doing just that.

But was all this just mental mumbo jumbo or did she really believe it? Would she be able to put it into action when the time came? If the time came! And what of the thing called *guilt?* Why should a woman losing her virginity have to face the accusations of the seven white dragons within, while a man was taught to see the exact same act as a *rite de passage,* as a very legitimate entry into society with which society found no fault? And indeed which it even encouraged him to perform before marriage and condoned afterwards?

Lu Chien came back with the hot water, soap, and towels. Kate turned her attention back to the more practical task of washing Blake. She must get him cleaned up. She must get rid of his dirty clothes and get the last of the dried blood off him.

But Kate soon realized it had obviously not occurred to the Chinese patrician's daughter, Lu Chien, that she was to help with the cleansing of a male body. When Kate indicated as much Lu Chien was horrified.

Kate was well aware that although Shanghai was one of the most promiscuous cities in the world, girls like Lu Chien would grow to womanhood without ever having seen a man's genitals. And it would be extremely unlikely she and Wu would have broken this old-fashioned code of repression while betrothed. Certainly Wu—if he became her husband—would be supposed to be the only man she ever saw naked.

Lu Chien looked now at Kate, her eyes pleading. Kate looked at her friend of so many years and smiled gently. It would be easier with her help. But it was still early. And Kate's first patient was not until 9 A.M. There was also the question of this being Lu Chien's decision as well as hers. Kate suspected it would take more than communism's avowed aims to free the women of China who had grown up like Lu Chien.

"You make us some tea," she said softly. "I'll cope on my own out here." Lu Chien nodded gratefully and disappeared in the direction of the kitchen.


Slowly, carefully, Kate washed Blake all over. She dried him tenderly with the softest towel she could find and then, taking the beautiful little cylindrical pink cardboard box with roses on it which she had bought duty-free on the ship, she dabbed him all over with the sweet-smelling talcum powder, using the powder puff from the box. When she had finished she eased him up off the old sheet they had thrown down on the couch the night before, slid a fresh sheet under him and another crisply ironed one on top, put a blanket over him, and stood up.

"Thanks," she heard him say weakly. "Thanks very much."

Kate could tell he was trying to force some energy back into his voice. She smiled back at him.

"Sssh," she said. "Sssh. Don't try too hard to talk. It'll come in time. By the way, I'm sorry about the lack of pajamas. I'll get you some today. Warm enough in the meantime? Just nod if you are. That's right. Good. I'll tell Lu Chien to keep the fire alight. There's plenty of wood. Then we'll move you into my room when Shen comes back. Now what about some breakfast? Feel like a boiled egg and toast?"

He nodded.

"Good. Then another injection and off to slumberland. All right?"

He nodded again—with his eyes this time—in warm and grateful thanks.

Eyes, thought Kate, as she went off to the kitchen. Eyes. They said everything. She hoped hers weren't saying too much.

Two hours later, after Kate had left for work, a flower truck pulled up outside the Broadway Mansions apartment building. Ying Tai, the doorman, was waiting. A Chinese youth in a bellboy's uniform got out, holding an exquisite bunch of five dozen, long-stemmed red roses.

"You know what to do?" Ying Tai said anxiously, as the youth entered the building.

"Of course," said the youth, with such a tone of firmness and ridicule that Ying Tai was taken aback.

The doorman nodded quickly and hurriedly showed the youth the way to the elevator.

At Kate's floor the youth got out and walked quietly to the door which had been described to him. He pressed the bell and presently Lu Chien came.

"The good doctor is in . . . ?" the youth inquired.

Lu Chien shook her head. The bellboy moved closer to the door.

"I have some flowers which must be delivered personally," he said.

"That is not possible," Lu Chien replied. "But I'll see the doctor gets them."

The bellboy seemed hesitant but then nodded and handed them over.

* * *

When Kate came home that evening the flowers were on the dining-room table. Lu Chien said only, "They arrived for you today. I put them in water, but there was no note."

"How strange," Kate said. "But what a lovely thought. They're gorgeous. Blake didn't ask you to send them, I suppose?"

Lu Chien shook her head.

"Oh well, perhaps a young man who seems interested in me at the hospital . . . I suppose I'll find out eventually."

The week passed quickly then and Kate found herself hurrying home each night to tend to Blake's needs. She found herself, too, looking forward to the exhilaration of her talks with Shen.

It would be two weeks before Blake could be moved. Janey was due back in about ten days. But Kate decided she would face that when it came. In the meantime, her apartment had become, at Shen's gentle request, the object of a duty roster for a handful of trusted comrades. Some comrades came during their lunch hours. Others—nightworkers—did shifts which left them only two or three hours to sleep. They entered discreetly by the back door, and brought their own food and tea, and expensive morsels, by Chinese standards, for their friend Blake to eat. There were little things sent by this wife or that: chicken broth or a wing of Peking Duck. Kate's apartment was kept spotless: even cleaner than she kept it. These highly disciplined, happy, eager young people saw to it that all was well with Blake and the good doctor who had befriended their cause.

But it was the nights which were special. Always at night Shen was there to help her with Blake. Kate had reduced her social schedule so that she could stay in. Once or twice Lu Chien and Wu Zhao visited. But they preferred not to. Only as many as were required to be there were allowed and Shen appeared to have made it his special responsibility.

For a time, for Kate and Shen and Blake, as he became well enough to sit up for the evening meal, it was like being part of a family again.

They all enjoyed being thrown together like this. And Kate and Shen enjoyed having a common purpose of tending to

Blake's needs. Shen often cooked—which surprised Kate. He took to bringing her little Chinese delicacies, too, as presents from Hwang's grateful network of contacts; and Kate took to bringing him little English and American delicacies to try.

On the night when it was to be Blake's first time actually sitting up at the table, Kate got away from work early and rushed home to cook a complete Thanksgiving dinner, with turkey and stuffing and cranberry sauce. There was hot cornbread and roast potatoes and all the wonderful fresh vegetables China was famous for. Afterwards there was pumpkin pie and angel food cake, and they drank wine throughout the meal and sang American and Chinese songs. Shen's favorite was "The Battle Hymn of the Republic." He took to it with great gusto and said all good Communists should learn the words—or at the very least the title.

# 23

*Blake's convalescence passed into its second week and always,* after work and during the night, Shen was there; quiet, observant, serious, warm, happy, and entertaining. Kate was grateful for the deep reserves of strength she found in him. She told him about her father and felt better for having someone to talk to about it.

Her mother had returned on the Monday of that week. Her father was now ten days overdue. There was still no news of him at all. Bette Richmond began to make inquiries through mission stations up and down the country to see if anything had been heard of Clem.

Kate tried desperately to keep her mind on her job and the task of Blake's recovery. For there was now a further complication looming. Janey was due back and Shen was anxious she should know nothing. This meant Blake would have to be moved early.

But Kate felt it was too soon and would risk reopening his wound. Reluctantly, however, she agreed.

So on the Wednesday night of the second week she and Shen helped Blake out of bed. They painstakingly dressed him with what help he could give them, and then they slowly and quietly walked him down the back stairs. They feared to use the elevator lest Ying Tai hear it and investigate. At the bottom of the stairs, just outside the rear door, Shen had arranged for a rickshaw to be waiting. As soon as they were all safely inside, the rickshaw took off.

The rickshaw runner, whom Shen assured Kate was friendly to their cause, seemed to be bumping them around mercilessly. The route they were taking—over cobbled backstreets—was hardly designed for a smooth ride. Kate feared what the jolting and shaking might do to Blake's wound. It looked healed enough on the outside but Kate knew this was no guide. The inner part was what mattered.

Eventually, coming out of the darknesses of the sideways and byways, they reached the back entrance of the Cathay Hotel. It was here that Blake kept a permanent suite.

As they began to help him out Kate realized that although he was not fat, his height meant he had a heavy bone structure. It was only with great difficulty and the aid of the rickshaw boy that they were able to prop Blake up between them and get him to the service elevator. The rickshaw boy pressed the elevator button and left. Kate and Shen waited and waited, but still it didn't come. Presently a waiter walked by and although Kate's inclination was to drop her head and hide her face, Shen quite boldly laughed as the waiter went by. "Our friend has had too much to drink and we thought it better not to risk him being seen in the lobby—you know how the foreign devils love to gossip about themselves," Shen said loudly, drawing the man into the confidence of the joke.

"You might have to leave him standing there to sober up," the waiter said, joining in the joke, "for the service elevator has been out of order all evening and the repair man cannot come until tomorrow."

"What a good idea," Shen shouted over his shoulder as the waiter disappeared from view. "We should leave him here to sober up all right."

But as soon as the waiter was out of hearing range Shen nodded to Kate with his head to drag Blake forward towards the front of the hotel.

"Should we really . . . ?" Kate asked with rising anxiety.

"There is no other way," Shen said. He took a deep breath and almost bodily lifted Blake.

Once again Kate was staggered at the strength in one so small. The memories of the youth in the alleyway came flooding back to her. What enormous power there was in those broad shoulders.

Kate never really knew how they got Blake up to his apartment. Ten times she thought they were about to be stopped and questioned. The lobby was full of Kuomintang officers, and every single one of them seemed to be staring right at them. What if one of them knew her! What if Yang Ho himself was there! But Shen laughed and joked with her the whole time, Blake all but propped on top of his right shoulder. She was sure it was Shen's superb coolness and confidence that got them through. "Keep talking to him as if he's your drunken lover or husband. If anyone comes up and tries to talk, just say, 'There, there, dear . . . but it was a good party, wasn't it?' and leave the rest to me."

But no one did come up. And foreign devils just a little the worse for strong drink were not exactly a rarity in Shanghai, or even in the lobbies of fashionable hotels for that matter. Certainly, the hotel staff, who knew Blake intimately, were not about to interrupt such a private occasion when he tipped them so handsomely.

So, miraculous as it seemed, they eventually got Blake safely to his apartment and Kate was soon tucking him up in bed with no visible signs of anything having erupted. But she would watch him closely for a few hours to make sure he was not regurgitating blood.

"Tea, Kate Doctor?" Shen said smiling. It was a joke between them now, him making tea and getting the word order wrong in English.

"Thank you," she whispered, as she stood taking Blake's pulse.

When she had finished and the tea was made, each sat down reluctantly. Both were a little sad to see this time in their lives ending. They would see each other again but it would be different: it would not be like a family—cooking and eating and laughing and singing together. Shen could not come and go at the hotel as he had at Kate's apartment. It would create too much suspicion.

"You know where to find me," Shen said quietly as he finally rose to go.

"At the signalman's hut," she said wistfully.

Shen turned to her and smiled once more. Kate thought it was the kindest smile she had ever seen in her life.

"My dear Kate Doctor," he said, "I cannot hope to tell you what you have done for all of us. If Blake had died, a secret so important it hardly bears thinking upon would have died with him. But even above this, we owe you another debt. We Communists are poor people who are used to being spat upon and beaten and treated as of no account. But you, at great risk to yourself, saw only our need. You helped in a situation few would have dared to. I suspect we will always feel a debt to you which we can never adequately repay. Whether because you were born here or for another reason, I know not—although plenty of others who were born here do not have your views—but you really do not see a difference between European and Chinese or even between one kind of Chinese and another. For you, truly, all men are one. This is a very special thing. You really do fulfill the old Chinese saying of 'a person to warm one's hands at.'"

"Oh Shen, what a lovely thing to say," Kate sighed. And then, as he smiled warmly back at her again, she stood up and walked over to him and hugged him. When they drew apart they looked at each other one more time and then Shen turned and walked quickly out the door.

Kate busied herself with Blake. She had drugged him with some laudanum for the journey to the hotel. But now it was beginning to wear off.

"Feel OK?" she said, kicking off her shoes and coming over to sit beside him on the satin quilt while she felt his forehead.

He nodded and forced a smile. Then, with what Kate thought was some difficulty, he said, "You're going to stay, aren't you?"

She smiled and nodded herself now. There it was again! That

touch of boyish vulnerability which made him so endearing. Underneath all the urbane bravado was the little boy who had never seen quite enough of his mother.

"Oh I don't think I can leave you just yet," she said warmly. She was taking his pulse with one hand and holding her watch with the other. "You're going to need someone with you for the next few days. I'd hate that wound to open up and no one to be here. All my good work would be for nothing."

He smiled again—but this time in the security of her remarks. In a few moments he was drifting off to sleep. She was sure he would not wake before morning.

Kate was very tired herself. The events of recent days had not occurred without strain. But she had had to hide her own feelings for the good of others. Now, suddenly, they threatened to overwhelm her. Now, suddenly, she felt vulnerable herself.

Quietly, in the half-light of the bedside lamp, she unbuttoned her blouse and skirt and let her underthings slip to the floor. She stood there naked for a moment, letting the dull yellow light play on her body as she looked down at it. Then, with a deep sigh of exhaustion, she pulled back the quilt and slid in beside him.

It had been impracticable to bring any clothes with her when she had had to help support Blake. She had only what she had worn, plus a stethoscope and extra sleeping draught in her jacket pocket. She would fetch her doctor's bag and some clothes from her apartment tomorrow. Lu Chien would watch over Blake during the day. Kate rarely wore night dresses except in the middle of winter, though she still sometimes felt a missionary daughter's guilt at such immodesty. In any case she was too tired to worry about it tonight. Too tired and too close to tears. She needed someone to be close to very badly. But even so, as she slid naked into the bed beside Blake, she was very aware that it was the first time in her life she had been in bed with a man.

Yet she felt comfortable. And as her bare thigh brushed against the silk of his pajamas, she felt a warm sensation deep within her. Instinctively she cuddled up closer to him.

Soon she was slipping into a deep, deep sleep, far out into a secure and gentle world, with her fears riding away on the nimbus clouds of the night, where the seven white dragons roam.

\*    \*    \*

In the days that followed Kate tried to keep herself as level as she could. She tried not to think about her father or about her deepening feelings for Blake.

But each day Blake got a little better—and now he was anxious to be up and about. Each time he asked her, Kate shook her head.

Then, on the Saturday morning, when she gave him a thorough examination and knew he was well, she began to feel very strange. She realized she was reluctant to pronounce him healthy because of what might follow. This fear threatened to overwhelm completely her desire to see him well because he was her patient. It was only with great difficulty that she finally said, "Fit," as she finished her examination. She had undone his shirt to listen to his chest, and as she began to do it up again she was aware that her fingers were trembling.

"Good," he said very quietly and levelly, pretending not to notice. "Good. You'll do me the honor of dining with me tonight then, here at the hotel?"

He had his old quiet assurance back and Kate became aware that what men saw as the natural order of things, which had been reserved for a time because of his dependence on her, had now returned. Yet there were things that would not be lost. The closeness and the bond that had been formed between them because of this thing would not be lost, surely? Would events or the passage of time diminish that?

For despite this longing for keeping things, she had never felt so strongly before the sense of grasping the present and holding it for all it was worth.

So in the end she found herself saying, "Yes, tonight then, here at the hotel." Then she finished buttoning his shirt and, picking up her bag, left the room without saying another word.

# 24

$O$n that same Saturday, in the forenoon, in his private chambers, General Yang Hung Ho called for his orderly. Presently the orderly came, carrying a silver tray with cigars and an upright brown stone bottle with a painted label. The orderly poured the clear liquid into the delicately stemmed liqueur glass and lit the general's cigar. Yang Ho tossed down the fiery mao tai and nodded for the orderly to pour another. Then he dismissed the man with a nod and settled back in his leather armchair.

It was ironic that with the death of the founder of the Chinese Republic, Dr. Sun Yat-sen, the year before, in 1925, the way had been paved for the rise of this brilliant young officer. He had risen to power quickly under the new commander-in-chief, Chiang Kai-shek. By the time he was twenty-seven, in 1926, Yang Ho was one of a handful of an elite corps of generals, many of whom were twice his age. Into their hands would be committed the sacred Nationalist duty of the extermination campaigns—the complete annihilation of every communist man, woman, and child.

Of all people who might have been chosen to head such a task, Yang Ho was uniquely qualified.

As the son of a warlord he had had an early apprenticeship in torture, beatings, and death. Such were the stock-in-trade of his father's rule. But even above this, his father was wealthy enough to send his son overseas to the Japanese Military Academy. Yang Ho was on his second tour there—for a refresher course—when Dr. Sun died. He was instantly recalled to China. He arrived back with his head shaved and shining, moustache clipped and magnificently attired in Nationalist uniform, bearing a first-class honors' degree in what the Japanese taught best—sadism.

Before his promotion to head the communist extermination, Yang Ho was placed in charge of the Secret Police, the Blue Shirts.

Though he appeared fully Chinese, Yang Ho was in fact Eurasian. And if the circumstances of his birth might have been considered strange by some, he knew this was only a further demonstration of how stupidly ignorant were even those Westerners who possessed a small knowledge of China. Actually, like Kate Richmond, he had a missionary background, although of a somewhat different sort. He was the son of a missionary's daughter as well as a warlord. His mother and father's union had been distinguished by the fact that it had been completely involuntary on the part of his mother. Her poor missionary father, with little or no education but a sense of deep calling from his Southern Baptist Bible Belt origins, had gone to China many years before with his wife and young child to preach the gospel to outlying areas.

His wife had survived but a few years before contracting typhus and dying. The missionary saw this as an act of the Lord which he did not understand. He continued his work.

But at one stage his itinerant preaching took him close to a warlord's camp. The warlord quickly beheaded the preacher with the ancient Chinese curved war sword, thicker at one end than the other, after the wretched man, still saying his prayers like countless martyred missionaries in China, had been blindfolded and made to bow before warlord Yang Hung in full view of his daughter.

The execution over, the warlord took the missionary's exquisitely beautiful young daughter, now fifteen, to his tent. There he raped her several times in succession, in between bouts of eating and drinking and one further execution, before sending her off with his keeper of concubines. He had his pleasure many times more until it was seen she would bear him a child. Then she was treated well until it could be seen whether the child would be a girl, who would be killed, or a boy, who would be kept. The baby was a boy and this pleased Yang Hung, who acknowledged him as his own, for this was only his second son, and sons were great manliness.

For a time Yang Hung placed high store by this white foreign devil concubine of his. But after a time, when it was seen she did not become full-bellied again and could have no more children, he tired of her. So she, too, fell under the sword, though not at the hand of Yang Hung, for he would not have it said of him that he had executed his own son's mother. Instead, he had a hireling kidnap her and do it away from the camp, telling the boy that bandits had taken her.

But this had been many, many years ago, at the turn of the century. The boy was now a man. And the man who sat in the chair this day, immaculately groomed in jodhpurs, khaki gabardine jacket, and polished Sam Browne belt, was China's youngest general. Despite the fact that he had the short stature of most of his race, he was still a striking figure. He had an air of great authority. But he also had the small, finely chiseled porcelain beauty of his mother, and it was only his shaved head and facial scar which prevented him from looking just the slightest touch effeminate. The decorations on his chest were numerous and hard-won in China's many wars, of which the Western world was so pathetically ignorant. The young general Yang Ho was a superb fighter and a master tactician. Into his hands, so many said, had been placed the future of China.

But today Yang Ho's thoughts were not on the future of China but on the beautiful young lady doctor, Kate Richmond. They had spent part of their school years together at the America-China school. She had always been kind and friendly towards him, which not all were, and he had fallen secretly in love with her. Sometimes he had longed to touch her young blonde body with a ferocity he had found hard to control. In his final year, when he was eighteen and she fifteen, he had asked her to the school dance. She had politely refused. He knew she had not gone with anyone else. He knew, moreover, that her parents were strict. Still, it had rankled. It had hurt his pride.

But even this might not have mattered if, the next year, she had agreed to attend the dance at the military academy with him. When she did not, he felt it to be a specific slight. She had not in fact refused herself. This time she had said she'd like to go but must still ask her parents. Her parents had requested to see the youth and explained they thought their daughter was still too young to go to such a dance. But she was by then sixteen and, according to Chinese standards, well into marriageable age. So the boy could not believe any parents would be so strict. Such prohibition because of age in Shanghai was nothing. Chinese noblemen openly took concubines much younger to dances. No, it was not because of her age but because he was Eurasian, he was sure.

He had seen little of her in the intervening years until that day on the ship. She had been a bright student and left to go to college in America—before starting her medical training—soon after the time of the dance. But he had never stopped loving her; wanting her. And now, after all these years, he was to have her. He knew that was going to happen as night followed day. Soon Katherine Richmond would have to come to him. Yes, soon she would have to ask his help.

He got up and poured himself another mao tai and stood by the window looking out. Then he walked back to his desk and opened a file which lay upon it. He read its contents for a moment, closed it, and stood up and walked to the long window once more. He was smiling as he stared down at the people on the busy boulevard below. He was dreaming of his future. Nothing could stop him now. He was going to deliver the Communists a body blow from which they would never recover and he was to have Katherine Richmond for his own as well.

At the same time as Yang Ho was pondering these things, Shen, whose position as the young communist leader was a closely-guarded secret, was in another part of town. He was walking towards the house of Ma Yen the Mandarin. It was Shen's birthday and he had come to have tea with his sister. He reached the house and stopped, announcing himself at the main gate. The gateman asked him to wait.

Although it was a long walk from Ling Ling's inner courts to the main gate, she always came herself.

Eventually, Ling Ling arrived and Shen entered. It was a lovely day and they walked through the gardens past the moon gate and circular windows set with beautiful blue wood fretwork.

They passed the lotus and lily ponds, and the artificial lake where the ducks swam. The ducks were white with orange bills. They had wooden wind whistles under their wings and made shrill music when they flapped across the water.

"And how does my sister—?" Shen Lung asked at last.

"She does well. And my brother?"

"Well also . . . and made better by my sister's joyful presence."

He still used the old forms of greeting, though he was not sure how much he—or she—believed in them any more. But they were a reminder of the past; of the good things of days gone by; of their childhood which had ended so abruptly for both of them.

When they reached Ling's courts a servant brought tea, and Shen and his sister talked polite chatter while it steeped. The moment the tea was exactly right, Ling handed it out herself, with some rice cakes.

Just then the old master shuffled in. It was his right in his own house to walk where he would. With a quick and mischievous smile he sat down and waited to be handed tea. His favorite wife had died the year before, and the best of his concubines had gone too, and the new concubines were so young and silly it didn't bear thinking upon. But he liked Ling Ling's warm heart and the way she always made him feel welcome over and above any politeness. So when word had come that his son Ma Yao, whose concubine Ling Ling was, had died mysteriously on some government business in the countryside, Ma Yen had immediately asked Ling Ling to stay on as his concubine. This meant that in time Ma Yen came also to know Shen. Although Shen was a common enough family name in China, Shen never risked using it except with a handful of comrades or someone like Kate whom he was sure he could trust. Under Hwang's and the professor's careful tutelage Shen had had, like his friend Wang Lee, many aliases.

The truth of the matter was, Ma Yen's son, Ma Yao, whom Wang Lee had murdered, had been one of the few who might ever have made the connection. Still, Shen had no illusions about what would happen to him if someone he trusted happened to divulge, either inadvertently or through torture, his identity. But Shen was fairly sure the old man did not know his real name or even remember the family name of his new concubine, Ling Ling.

And from the start, the old mandarin took to calling Shen "Young Ling," as if his sister's name were his also. Although Ma Yen must have suspected Shen had communist leanings, he seemed to like the lad for his strong spirit. So Ma Yen came often to take tea with Ling Ling which was not a thing he did

with his other concubines. He also instructed his gateman to tell
him whenever her brother arrived on a visit.

Ling always had a spare cup on hand. She poured tea and
handed it to the old one, with his long gray hair and gray-green
eyes and long gray thin beard, who sat in the most magnificent
embroidered robe and slippers.

"And how does my old master?" Shen asked. It was the
greeting of a servant to a master, but Shen did not mind. It did
not offend his conscience as it did some. He was practical
enough to know there were many they would not change, particularly the old Confucian ones to whom the Golden Age was
many centuries in the past. And besides, rich though old Ma Yen
was, he reminded Shen of his own father.

They talked politics and Ling pretended not to listen, for the
old man did her a great honor by allowing her to stay while they
conversed on politics.

Because the old one believed that the great Golden Age was in
the past, all modern governments of China came under his withering criticism as he drank down his second cup of tea with his
third rice cake, and, forgetting whose court he was in because he
was enjoying himself so much, clapped his hands loudly for
more tea. Soon the servant girl came.

Ma Yen turned now to Ling Ling.

"And tell me, little one, for I get out so rarely these days, are
you still the queen of the boulevards?"

"My lord is most kind. There are those who say I have some
face in the city because of my association with this great house."

The old lord chuckled. "You do this house great honor,
daughter. Great honor. The time will come when you will hold
great influence in this city, greater even than you do now, for I
hear all take note of you at the banquets and balls. I have seen
and heard the ladies in the great halls off the great square in
Peking and I tell you, and your brother here, you are a match for
any of them."

"My lord is most kind."

The old man crinkled his eyes in a smile. "And now it is time
for your brother's present," he said swiftly, with his eyes deftly
turning to the door at the side, as if to see that his orders had been
obeyed and the present brought. He clapped his hands loudly
again. Shen Lung and Ling Ling smiled at each other in surprise.

Presently, in marched a servant bearing a tall gilded cage, which sloped up at the top in curves to a gold ring and handle, with a beautiful bird inside.

"A nightingale for peace, a nightingale for peace," the old man chuckled in great glee.

"My old lord does me great honor," said Shen, standing.

"It has whistles under its wings, too, though I would not let it fly until you have trained it."

"I will do as my old lord advises."

The old man was finding it hard to contain himself.

"But you do not ask why a nightingale for peace—why a nightingale and not a dove? You do not ask—" he said gleefully.

"No, my lord."

"But you do not know—?"

"No my lord."

"It is well, it is well," said the old man, chuckling openly now. "It is well. I said you would not ask. I told my compradore who purchased it that it was a gift for you. And I told him what I would say. But when he did not know the answer and asked why, I said you would not ask. I said that although you honored me, you would be too proud to ask and would wish to find out for yourself. You people of the new breed are very proud, but it is a good pride for the new China, and if it cannot be better than the Golden Age, perhaps it can be as good. And it could not be worse than the governments I have seen in my time with so many starving and beaten and butchered."

"What does my old lord mean when he says 'you people'?" Shen asked.

"I mean you Communists."

"I am not a Communist." The secret had to be kept.

Ma Yen chuckled. "Of course not, of course not. I do not expect you to admit it. But you must allow an old man to suspect what he has come to suspect. Oh, do not fear—I shall say nothing of this to others."

Shen nodded, stony-faced.

"The day the Communists come to power in Shanghai," Ma Yen said, "I will give a big banquet for them. But tell no one I said it, tell no one I said it," he chuckled loudly again, and with that was gone as quickly as he had come.

Shen's sister stood up and hugged Shen as she said: "What a

good kind old man he is. Are all the traditional ways changing for him now in this city?''

"Perhaps, who knows?"

"Well, it is your birthday, and we may talk of such things another day. I have a present, too."

She went farther into the inner court to her bedchamber and presently returned with a large flat parcel, wrapped in expensive red paper.

"There was a time I would have thought the paper itself too generous a present," Shen said wistfully. "Perhaps I should, still."

"Nonsense. Are you not my brother who makes my life bearable in this city? Why should you not have expensive wrapping paper?"

"It is what the present may be if the paper is so grand . . ."

"Open it then, my brother, who is from such a poor family he is afraid of a rich woman's gift," she teased, "and see whether it is to your liking or not."

Shen Lung cleared his throat fully in the common country way.

Ling Ling laughed. Then, quietly, and with consideration, she took his hand and led him to the long, covered couch and sat him down. She brought a knife and sat by him as she loved to do. It was a memory of how they had sat together when young—before her sister had been born—when there was sometimes money for presents.

So they opened Shen Lung's present together, in a family celebration of two, and it was a rug of wool, of deep rich woven red wool so that he let out another exclamation. He had been forced to leave his beloved red rug behind when he had fled from his uncle.

"For a horse, for a bed, to make love on in winter, for a warrior," was all Ling said as she kissed him on the cheek and got up, shaking her full ripe body back into the cheongsam which had ridden up where she sat, and walking out towards the hall of her inner court to order more tea.

# 25

*Kate knocked on the door of Blake's suite that night with some* reluctance. She had never been more nervous. Everything she wore was the same as the night of the ball. She had had her hair done at Shanghai's most expensive and exclusive salon, where Janey was a valued client. It had been a present from Janey.

Yet despite the fact that Kate knew she really looked stunning, she was still nervous and very confused. That was putting it mildly, Kate thought, as she waited for the door to be opened. She knew Blake's invitation to dinner was certainly more than an invitation to dinner. And she wanted it to be more. But she knew, too, that whatever Blake might wish, and whatever she might hope for, he would also be the perfect gentleman. She had learned that much about him on the train. And now he respected her for what she had done for him. He would not force his attentions on her. There would come a point when Kate would have to indicate, however modestly, her willingness or he might turn back. Might treat her differently from his other conquests. Of course she wanted to be treated differently from all the others; but she wanted to experience the full gamut of feelings of having a man begin to want her.

She felt she should have shied away from the thought in horror. It was absurd, too, to think of giving herself to a man about whom she knew so little and whose reputation was, to say the least, regarded as unsavory. But however questionable and irrational it might seem, however calculating it appeared, she knew a very important part of her wanted it to happen.

The door opened and Kate's breath was taken away.

An imposing English butler in white tie and tails stood at the entrance. But beyond, over against the giant picture window which looked onto the vast expanses of the Shanghai waterfront and the sweeping avenues of the Bund, stood a full banquet table with more than a dozen hovering, white-jacketed Chinese waiters. Down from the raised platform, on which the table stood with settings for two, the Persian rug had been removed to reveal polished parquet flooring. Beside this, in a small alcove, sat a seven-piece orchestra in dinner suits.

"Doctor Richmond?" the butler asked. Kate nodded, still completely overcome and bemused by it all.

"I have the pleasure to announce the arrival of the guest of honor, Doctor Katherine Richmond," the butler continued.

Blake immediately appeared from behind the door where he had obviously been standing all this time. He was wearing white tie and tails.

"Welcome to my home—an official welcome that is—and to a special banquet in your honor, Kate. . . . Welcome . . ."

His voice was warm and deep and gentle.

He took her hands and led her in.

"I'm quite overcome," she said.

"It's my way of saying thanks," he said. "I wanted it to be special."

Kate knew banquets were an important part of Chinese etiquette, a method of fulfilling Oriental righteousness. Blake was paying her a great compliment by ordering one specially for her.

"You look good enough to eat," Blake said, as he took Kate's arm and led her towards the table.

"I'm not sure I could compete with the menu," she said mischievously, suddenly catching the mood of the occasion and elated by all the trouble he had gone to for her.

"Well I promise you one thing, Kate," he said, as he waited for the butler first to seat her and then him, "no one in China will eat better tonight."

"If the number of personnel are any indication, I can certainly believe that," she said. "And I presume there are more in the kitchen?"

He nodded. "And downstairs in the main kitchen."

"Of course. I have been told you never do things by halves."

"Who told you?" he said quickly.

Kate blushed slightly and realized she had given away the fact that she had been interested enough to ask questions about him.

"My roommate, Janey—Janey Edwards—she's had a crush on you since she was a schoolgirl," Kate said hurriedly.

He nodded, suddenly quiet for a moment. Kate had noticed this in him before—his occasional moodiness and silence at the mention of the Edwards name.

Blake had had the butler seat them close together, she at the head of the table, with an uninterrupted view of the harbor, and he at her left elbow. She looked down at the magnificent sweep of the Bund below, strung out like a ring of party lights. She felt very good about all that was happening to her and good about Blake.

"Why are you so silent?" she said, tenderly, leaning over towards him.

"It's an old wound," he said, "but nothing to do with Janey. I'll tell you about it one day. But this is your night and let me start by paying you a compliment. You remember that day on the train . . . ?"

"Of course. How could I not . . . ?"

"It was your voice," he said, "it was your voice that was special. There is something in your voice . . . I mean, of course I found you physically attractive. I'm not denying that . . . but it's your voice . . . there's something just completely honest and genuine and caring about it . . . it's a . . . well . . . it's a loving voice. . . . I think I fell in love with your voice that day on the train . . ."

Now it was Kate's turn to be silent. She had not expected this so soon.

"People sometimes fall in love with their nurses . . ." she said softly " . . . we went through quite a lot together in a short space of time . . ."

"I thought about that . . . I wondered about that, too. But I don't think so . . . I think our being thrown together like that just gave me the opportunity to get to know someone . . . get to know a person I might not otherwise have got to know . . . someone quite different from those I'm normally seen with . . ."

Kate looked at him. There were a thousand things she could have said but she just sat there and glowed.

As the meal began, the waiters hovered in hordes, intent that not even the slightest thing should go wrong for one paid such a high compliment by such an honored customer of the hotel as Captain Thomas Blake.

In all, they ate some fifteen courses, from sesame prawn to sea slugs, to shark fin soup, bird's nest soup, thousand-year-old eggs, Peking Duck, plum sauce, fresh lychees and pots of tea as well as mao tais and Chinese wine.

The orchestra played anything she wished.

When the meal was finished they drank liqueurs and coffee.

Blake smoked a cigar and smiled indulgently when Kate asked for a puff. He passed it over. Then he dismissed the waiters.

He took her gently by the hand and said softly, ''I believe this is my dance.''

She nodded and smiled, saying nothing, letting him lead her onto the dance floor from where she could still look out through the big picture window onto the world below.

He held her close and they began to waltz. The orchestra played tune after tune and each time he asked her if she had had enough, she shook her head.

They danced into the early morning and she nestled her head against his shoulder. Then, when Blake asked whether she would like to go for a drive, Kate nodded.

So he dismissed the orchestra and then got her wrap and they walked out to the elevator and down to the street where there was always a hansom cab waiting near the flower stall. The flowers were fresh from the market, still dripping with dew, and he bought her a bunch of tight red rosebuds as they climbed in and drove to the clip clop of horses' hooves on the early morning pavement.

They drove around the park, and then along the waterfront, holding onto each other, holding hands and kissing, kissing gently at first, and then deeper and deeper until it was time to return.

When they reached the hotel they rode silently up in the elevator. After he had closed the apartment door behind them, Blake moved slowly towards the bedroom to see if Kate would follow. She hesitated only a moment. Then, slipping her hand lovingly under his arm, she let him lead her in.

With her great capacity for loving, repressed so long in so many ways, repressed and sublimated in her early religion which was now receding, in her work and her love for her patients, in her love for those such as Janey and her parents, she now made the decision she had put off so long. With this great capacity for human love and understanding which was hers, which she was only beginning to find in herself, with this sense of the human spirit welling up within her now, choosing this moment to come out and change the course of her whole life, she knew what she would do. It was bubbling up like a well and bursting with such an intensity inside her that it was frightening. Yet it was also subdued and quietly her own like every really true and fresh discovery of human nature.

The room lamps were out but morning was beginning to come in through the venetian blinds. Kate could see that the bedcovers were turned back. Blake smiled at her in the half-light and came over and stood in front of her as he slowly began to roll down her long white gloves. Then he began to kiss her while his hands kept moving. Soon his kisses, which had started lightly, began to go deep inside her so that her tongue and mouth became strong in response. She barely noticed her zipper go. It was as if she heard a sound unrelated to her a long way off. Then she felt him ease her dress off over her arms and push it down over her hips to the floor. He was at her slip now, sliding it over her head and kissing her all the time. Then she felt the flats of his hands slide hard and firm over her buttocks and his fingers reach her suspender belt. When she felt him touch the bare parts of her legs she thought everything she had ever heard in her life about men and women failed to do it justice. In a moment she felt her suspender belt come away and her stockings fall around her ankles. Then his hand was on her bra and presently another was at her panties. She felt them go too as she stepped out and cuddled hard against him, feeling suddenly vulnerable.

He put his arms tightly around her and she felt her breasts rise high and erect against his starched shirtfront. It was like the finest of sandpaper and she knew this must be the last garment of his to go as her hand, her strong right hand with which she did so much work of another kind, found itself moving to the front of his body. She gently cupped her hand as she felt the delicate grapes slide against it. Then she was squeezing higher and harder. She heard him sigh and almost in the same instant she felt his hands go to the top of her buttocks. He kissed her all over now and the crescendo rose as both of them worked feverishly to rid him of the last of his clothes. Both were kissing now, kissing everywhere, a rising tide in each of them so that soon he took her by the hand once more and led her to bed, and there, on the wonderfully cool satin sheets, they made love as the sun came up.

Afterwards they slept. And then they made love some more. And then they ordered breakfast and ate it in bed. They sat alone together for hours after that, in the bath, replenishing the water, soaping and sighing and laughing and almost crying with the intensity of their feelings.

"I want to tell you something," Blake said tenderly as they sat in the bath.

"What?"

"All that softness and caring I spoke about in your voice . . ."

"Yes . . . ?"

"It comes through in your lovemaking, too . . ."

"But I'm so inexperienced," Kate blurted out, "I felt like such a fool . . ."

"You—? Never. I feel as if I've just made love for the first time."

"Oh Tom, what a lovely thing to say."

By the time Sunday night came, the time when the black dragons come out from the deep, when it was time for Kate to leave and go back to her apartment, she felt she had left a part of her behind.

On Monday—the day following her delicious weekend—Kate met Ling Ling by accident. Or so it seemed at the time.

She was hurrying home after work to shower and change when, right in the middle of the Bund, she saw Shen. He was standing, talking.

With him were two huge men standing beside a rickshaw in which sat the most beautiful Chinese woman Kate had ever seen. Kate did not have to be a Chinese fortune-teller to know who the woman was. It must be Shen's sister, Ling Ling, and the two men would be Hwang and Yu-Ma.

Although she was in a hurry—she was to see Blake again that

night—Kate could not resist stopping. She was anxious to meet Shen's sister and friends; and delighted to see Shen himself again so soon.

She stopped and Shen made the introductions. They all greeted her very warmly and with great Chinese courtesy—suggesting Shen had told them how helpful Kate had been. Ling Ling was particularly friendly. Kate liked her immediately.

Kate also at once knew that Ling Ling was indeed the one she had been thinking of as courtesan of the generals. But seeing her in the street it was hard to believe this—although she was very expensively dressed for her age. Kate wondered if there was a slight family resemblance to Shen. Perhaps. Kate was not sure. But in any case was it really wise for Shen to be seen in the open with Ling Ling like this? Some people in Shanghai must know Ling Ling's true family name and identity, surely?

Of course, although spoken of as a courtesan, Ling Ling was, in fact, a concubine. But her master, the old mandarin, Ma Yen, allowed her free rein. As long as she attended to his wishes, when he had need, she was free to come and go as she would, spending whatever she liked on clothes and using his sedan chair or rickshaw. Only rarely did the old mandarin venture out for a social occasion. But he liked his pretty concubine to be seen, for this gave him great face.

And so it was that Ling Ling, attended by one of the young eunuchs of her master's household, was always to be found at the most important functions—even more so than when her former master was alive—drawing to her like moths to a flame first the young Kuomintang Officers' Corps, then their superiors, and finally the generals themselves and the rich and influential of the city, all of whom delighted in her great good looks, vivacity, and warmth. Inevitably, many of these men also became her lovers, in addition to the aging Ma Yen. And of course the old mandarin knew and let it be known that he knew, and he got a cackling, gleeful pleasure from the fact that so many wise and powerful men wished the company of his humble concubine, Ling Ling. If he had not known, or had pretended not to know, he would have lost much face. But by permitting Ling Ling this open freedom, though some mocked him, most saw it as a demonstration of his power over her, his ability to give his property away and still retain it.

For Ling Ling it meant a growing fortune as she hid away the money she received—in the old wooden trunk hooped with metal which had been her dowry when she came from her father's house.

Kate looked at her now as she sat forward in the rickshaw a few yards across from the gardens at the busy waterfront.

She had a very round moon face and good healthy strong black hair cut square which hung full and neat to her shoulders like silk. And she was nineteen, full of the country ripeness of a girl that age. She wore a yellow cheongsam which filled out tightly at the curve of her hips. Her country thighs were strong where the dress split up the side and her full breasts overflowed at the point where the loops of the open-work bodice pulled the skin together at the top. Her feet were tiny and on them she wore very open high-heeled shoes with only a scalloped toepiece and no heel strap, as was the fashion in Shanghai at that time.

"What a beautiful cheongsam," Kate said. She meant it genuinely.

"It should be," Ling Ling laughed. "It cost me a fortune." She whispered a figure in Kate's ear and laughed again.

"But that's ten times what my dress cost!" Kate said, appalled into demonstrating bad manners.

"Of course, it is not my money. Perhaps you need to become a concubine too! Would you like that? I will speak to my lord Ma Yen, if you wish."

She went into peals of laughter, and Kate could not help laughing too. It was as though they were old friends. There was no boasting in Ling Ling's disclosure of the cost of her clothes, only delight, and her teasing was sisterly and good-natured. As they chatted, Kate was aware that, despite her peasant origins, Ling Ling had the same lively intelligence as her brother. She felt there was a promise of rich fulfillment in this girl, the feeling that she had much to give beyond the delights men might find in her body.

And it was not hard for Kate to imagine how Ling Ling, with her comings and goings up the boulevards, with her always new and exquisite clothes and her appearances at restaurants and banquets and grand balls, had become a known and popular figure.

Yet naked, without makeup, in the cold light of day after

lovemaking, Kate suspected that the wan little peasant girl would still be visible. She suspected this would even be part of her undoubted attraction for the generals and any who could afford her exorbitant fees: the stripping bare, as it were, the stripping off of expensive clothes and rubbing off of sweet fragrances of myrrh to reveal the peasant intensity of a maiden of the earth. This would be a pearl of great price indeed.

But if any of the generals ever managed to put a face to a face, and a name to the related face, and connect her with Shen, the pearl would be a far greater price than ever they imagined.

Ling Ling stepped down from the rickshaw with Hwang's help and they strolled on, all together now, on this sunny Shanghai day along the Bund. Kate wanted to excuse herself because she was now running dreadfully late.

Yet this chance meeting had the same feeling to it that all her encounters with Shen had—the feeling that it had been less of an accident than it appeared. Could Shen really have known the direction she would walk after work and at what time? Of course.

And in any event, it did not matter. For despite her urgency to be gone, she wanted to be with Shen, too. She was glad he had taken the trouble to seek her out, whatever the reason, and that he had kept his promise to introduce her to Ling Ling. And Hwang and Yu-Ma too. Now she knew them all—his family and friends—the ones who had been such an important part of his life. Kate's admiration for this man grew every time she met him. Some nights, during Blake's convalescence, she had waited anxiously, even expectantly, for Shen to appear. She knew what it was now. She felt easy with him. Easier than with Blake, in a sense. There were people you met with whom you were friends from the start and the rapport just kept growing. She had thought a lot about this at night, when she finally did get to bed, lying there thinking about the two men under her roof and how different they were. She had known she was falling in love with Blake from the first night he had been brought to her apartment, wounded and helpless.

But was she also falling in love with Shen? What was the thing inside her that kept turning and growing? Why was she prepared to interrupt the rush of feelings which propelled her towards Blake and stroll quietly along the Bund with this young

Chinese man three or four years her junior? Why did she feel a quiet, gentle, bubbling inside when she was with him? Or when she thought of him? Of course, for Blake, her feelings were like a bursting waterfall. Yet she knew some people spoke of a slow growth of love out of friendship, friendship based on respect and shared views and experiences. They even called this kind of love more "mature." They said mature love occurred when the physical and the emotional came together.

What nonsense! There she went again! Too much thinking and not enough action. Not enough letting go. Not enough letting it happen. Always having to rationalize it out in advance.

She told herself just to accept her love for Blake and enjoy it.

Then she was suddenly aware that Shen was suggesting they all stop for tea.

"You have been a long way off in another country, Kate Doctor," he said, getting the word order of her name wrong deliberately this time again to show he was teasing her. "Perhaps we all have need of some refreshment?"

Kate was just about to explain that she couldn't, and to excuse herself, when she felt Shen take her by the arm and, beckoning the others to enter the teashop, steer her aside, saying in a loud voice:

"The good doctor and I must talk and will walk in the sun for just a few more minutes."

As soon as the others had gone, Shen apologized. "I would not have taken this course," he said, "if an urgent matter had not come to my attention with which you may be able to help me. Shall we talk?"

Kate nodded and they began to stroll farther along the Bund. She felt butterflies in her stomach. She thought it was just that she was apprehensive about being seen with Shen. She had to stop herself mentally again and reassure herself that his identity really was the best-kept secret in China. But even so, what if Yang Ho were driving past and saw her out walking with one who looked so like the orderly who had brought him a message at the ball? Whatever the cause, Kate realized something was making her anxious. For once, she dispensed with the Chinese politeness ritual.

"What is it, Shen . . . ? What is it . . . ?" Her voice was excited and breathless.

Shen's reply was slow and measured:

"There is a possibility—nothing more—of a sighting of your father."

Kate's breath was taken away. She had no idea Shen had even been looking for him. "I can't thank you enough for taking the trouble . . ." she began.

"I emphasize it is a possibility only," he said. "There is no confirmed description. That is why I wish to talk to you. Your identification may be necessary . . ."

"Where? When? Tell me!"

"In the North—near where my parents live."

"I must go there immediately."

"Perhaps," said Shen. "But first hear me out. There is much more to going to the country—and you should weigh it carefully before answering."

Kate realized Shen's tone was very serious indeed now.

"Go on . . ." she said, quietening down.

"It touches our friend Blake," he said. "For reasons I cannot tell you but which you may indeed imagine, we must establish an alibi for Captain Blake for this coming Saturday and Sunday . . . an alibi which he himself will be unable to fulfill. He was unwilling to ask you what I now find it necessary to ask you . . ." He paused a moment and then continued. "The traditional Chinese values, which I still have not eradicated, feel shame that I should ask you such a thing, particularly when you have already been such a friend to our cause. But the new China in me wishes to ask you . . ." He paused again. Kate nodded slowly for him to go on. "The plan is that you should travel to the country with me this weekend," Shen said, "to search for your father. But it also means that if Blake must account for his actions, you could say he journeyed to the country with you. Train tickets in his name and all other things have been taken care of."

Shen paused and saw the concern in Kate's eyes.

"There really is news of my father?" she said anxiously.

Shen nodded.

"But Blake's wounds are barely healed and yet he is obviously planning something more," she said.

"Believe me, Kate Doctor," he said, "Blake will do what he

must do this weekend in order to honor a previous commitment, and nothing you can say or do will alter this.''

Kate looked at him. What on earth was she getting into! Did she care for Blake this much? Did she care for Shen enough to do this? Was she already beginning to believe in what the Communists were trying to achieve, although not in communism itself? But where would it all lead?

''You mentioned it was near where your parents live . . .'' she stammered out slowly.

''That was a personal weakness for which I apologize,'' he said. ''Seeing we must go to the country I thought, selfishly, we might also visit my parents . . .''

''Whom you have not seen since you left,'' Kate interrupted.

''This is true. But I also wish to remind myself how things are in the countryside—that I am not a stupid man who wishes to make rebellion for no reason . . .''

There was a silence. Kate had not heard anyone use the word *rebellion* before. Had she expected this was not Shen's aim? After all, he was their leader and this was their avowed aim—that was why members of the Kuomintang such as Yang Ho feared them so.

How was she to choose in the situation which now confronted her? What would she do if Blake and his alibi were not in the picture? She would certainly go for her father's sake alone.

''I know how it is in the countryside,'' she said slowly. ''No doctors for hundreds of miles except for the rich; and daughters like Ling Ling still being sold as prostitutes to feed starving families.''

A look of admiration passed from Shen to Kate.

''So you will come . . . ?'' he said softly. ''To help our cause?''

Kate looked at him. Had he known she might not come for the alibi alone? And yet she did not believe he would lie to her about her father.

''I will come in the hope that I might find my father,'' she said slowly. ''As for Blake and the alibi I cannot promise. But as you yourself say, he has not asked. It is true I would give almost anything for him, including, I suspect, my life. But I am neither Communist nor Kuomintang and I will not be involved in your causes. What Blake has it in mind to do I can only imagine. So we must see what transpires before I know how far I will go, and of course I shall try to talk him out of it.''

Shen nodded. He was smiling. "This is a very Chinese answer, as I should have expected," he said. Then, talking Chinese pleasantries as if nothing had happened, they quietly made their way back to the teashop.

The subject of what Blake indeed had planned for that weekend became the basis of his and Kate's first lovers' quarrel.

Although she was dreadfully late already, Kate sought him out immediately after she had finished talking to Shen. She and Blake had planned to attend a cocktail party.

Kate found him in his office. It was in his biggest warehouse, at the waterfront on the Bund. It was the first time she had visited him there. When Blake saw her through the glass partition he smiled and beckoned her in, dismissing his secretary as Kate entered.

Kate blurted out her story and Blake seemed vaguely amused.

"So Shen has told you," he said, smiling. "He's amazing, isn't he? Wish we had him on our side."

"On our side? What on earth do you mean? Aren't you and he on the same side?"

"Oh no. I'm a capitalist and he knows it. I'm only in it for the money, which really isn't very different from him. He's just looking after his investment in me."

"I don't believe it . . . I think he genuinely likes you."

"Perhaps. Dangerous, though—to form attachments in a business such as his."

Kate couldn't believe this was the same man who could be so tender to her at night. Still she had known from the start that he had two smiles. Had she expected him never to wear the other side of his face to her again? Or secretly pretended he would not need to wear it at all, now that he had her love?

"Anyway, he's told you," Blake went on. "He likes me so much he's told you to protect me and not himself—let's keep it that way for the time. He's told you—or asked you—and I wouldn't. He might like me but he's certainly prepared to put you in extra jeopardy. Damn smart, though. Gave you two good reasons—your father and me."

"I'm going to try to find my father!"

"Good. Fine. That's a good reason. Tell yourself that."

"You ungrateful . . ." Blake was within striking distance and Kate lashed out at him with her fists. He let her blows land on his chest but did not attempt to move.

As her hostility began to subside it came thinly through to Kate that Blake was trying to get her angry. He wanted to get her angry enough to refuse to go. She took a deep breath and stood back.

"Do you have to do this damned fool thing whatever it is?" she shouted, her fury turning to words now.

Blake looked at her. She knew nothing of the old enmity with Edwards. Nothing of the childhood scars and hurt. It was not his nature to tell people such things. And, in any case, she was Janey's friend and Edwards was Janey's father.

"It's time I delivered something," he said simply.

"It's the weapons—that same damned shipment of weapons you nearly got yourself killed for the other night . . ." She was shouting even louder now. "And if you don't deliver them you won't get paid—it's as simple as that, isn't it . . . ?"

"Believe what you will," he said, his voice at the same level at which it had started. "I promised delivery by a certain date and I'm overdue. In my business, delivery on time is everything."

They looked at each other then, silent and unable to talk. Eventually, Blake was the first to speak. He put his arm around Kate and walked her to the leather couch he kept in his office. He sat her down on the arm and held her hands while he said, "It's my business, darling . . . it's what I do for a living. We didn't ask to meet on the train—you and I—we just did. No one in his right mind would put us together—we're like oil and water. You're so good and kind and always helping people . . . and I . . . why don't we just enjoy what we've got while we've got it?"

Kate swallowed back hard and stood up. Blake put his arm around her. After a time he walked her to the street where he put her in a taxi and sent her home, saying he would call for her at seven.

When the taxi had disappeared from view he went back to his office. He poured a whiskey soda and sat at his desk without turning on the light. However much he cared for Kate there were bigger problems on his mind. She was right about the shipment of arms, of course. But the whole situation had changed since the night he was shot. It was no longer a matter of simple delivery. The question now was—delivery to whom? For if Yang Ho knew anything, anything at all, there might only be one way Blake *could* deal. And if this were so, and he did what he was afraid he might be forced to, would Kate ever understand or forgive him?

When they met later that evening it was as if nothing had happened; as if each had decided to pretend the argument had never taken place. Kate was light and frivolous—almost a touch too frivolous, Blake thought. But he said nothing and acted out his part well.

They swanned their way through the cocktail party, where several jeroboams of Bollinger champagne were in evidence, to dinner and dancing in the hotel dining room afterwards. Then later, somewhat the worse for wear, they made love again in Blake's suite with an intensity which amazed Kate. It was as if their argument had added spice to their lovemaking. Though she knew little enough of any techniques in this regard, she found her lips and body responding aggressively, demandingly, as if hostility which could not be voiced openly because of the mores of society were finding a very legitimate outlet in human sexual response. It was a new type of encounter for Kate, and the stirred intensity of her feelings were not lost on Blake.

At the end of the evening, as she dressed in the half-light while he still gazed at her from the bed, she said only, "I'll give you your alibi just this once, provided no one is injured or killed. If I find out anyone received so much as a bruise as the result of your plan, the deal is off. Agreed . . . ?"

"You don't have to do this," he said. "I was not the one who asked you. Don't commit yourself. You don't know what you are letting yourself in for. Reserve judgment until you know. You don't have to decide about the alibi yet. Besides, it may not be necessary. It's enough for the time being just to go with Shen and try to find your father."

She looked at him for a moment and then moved across the room to the bed. She was still in her underthings. Slowly, she took each garment off and discarded it and slid into bed once more.

"Thanks," she said softly, as she snuggled up and kissed him, somehow sensing that whatever the danger for him, he was not prepared to expose her to it, and that for this soldier-of-fortune who lay beside her, she was beginning to be an object of worth and care.

They made love again then and she fell asleep in his arms, no longer caring about the explanations she would have to make to Janey the next morning for spending the night away from home.

# 26

Kate and Shen left bright and early on Saturday for the country. It was a lovely sunny day and the countryside opened up before them. It had been agreed that they would take the train to the railhead nearest Shen's home, visit his parents first and ask in the town for news of Kate's father.

Kate soon realized the trip was a tonic for Shen. And she herself was excited. She sat opposite him and saw the change take place in his face as the mud flats and city gave way to the plains of the country with the hills of chalk-white and jute-brown in the distance. In the moist black earth beside the train, fresh green shoots were coming up.

At each new sight of the country, at a field richly planted and ready for picking, at fields of cabbages, layered green with such freshness, at an ox ploughing, at certain kinds of trees or birds, and later when the darker greens of cypresses and camphor trees came, Shen was alive with excitement, chattering to Kate with comments like a travel guide.

They saw some men fishing in a pond, using cormorants, and even though Shen must have known Kate would have heard the story of how these birds were used for fishing, he nevertheless explained, showing by reference to himself, how the porcelain ring is put around the bird's neck so it may catch fish in its beak for its masters but not swallow the catch.

Shen was in high good humor. The first sight of a field of poppies—red and orange and yellow with the black-eyed tendrils just visible—brought joy to his face. The flowers were always a sign of the season. But they were opium poppies as well. And although there were always some sown, Shen began to get annoyed as he saw how many there were this year—row upon row of them as far as the eye could see.

Kate said nothing and a short time later they got off the train. But while they were waiting for some horses they had ordered to be brought, Shen spoke to one of the coolies.

"It is a good year for the poppies then, Elder Born?" he said.

The man was very old and had few teeth and kept sucking his lips in continuously as if to hide his yellow gums. When Shen spoke he turned his head quickly as if to make sure no one was watching.

"Are you a stranger then, and an ignorant city fellow that you do not know this is the heart of the poppy district?"

"But it is a very dry year, Elder Born, like the great famine, and how can so much land be in poppies and it be good for the people?"

The old man wore a round squat black hat which was very dirty and dusty. His queue still hung down his back. He swiveled his head quickly again.

"Away with you, away with you. Am I a dirt farmer that I should know such things? Ask me about luggage and railway stations and I will tell you."

Shen now replied in the local dialect, in words that amounted to, "Thank you, Elder Born, we will ask of another."

At this the old man moved his head slowly from side to side, as if to say that would be unwise.

The horses came and they mounted up, riding along silently for a time.

The whole countryside was covered in poppies.

"What does it mean?" Kate asked.

"That they expect war. That the warlords and the landlords who control the countryside expect war and have planted extra opium to pay for it," Shen answered simply.

*  *  *

When they came within sight of his house, Shen's youngest
sister, who was now fifteen, was the first to see them. She came
running from where she had been working outdoors in the sun.
She had filled out. Kate thought how much like Ling Ling she
looked.

Next, at the sound of laughter and chatter, came his mother.
Her long hair was all gray now and as she walked in her blue top
and black pants she was portly and slow. Her right hand kept
straightening her hair as she walked.

"And how does my son?" she said as he dismounted and
swept his mother into his arms.

They stood thus for a long time and Kate wondered why his
father did not come. Then she realized how stupid she was
being. His father would be in the fields.

Eventually Shen broke off and, asking forgiveness for his
rudeness, introduced Kate.

Then she dismounted and they walked towards the house,
talking about Ling Ling while Shen asked of his father.

Kate thought Shen's mother seemed a little subdued and that
her smile avoided a direct answer. Once inside, Shen handed
over tea and rice cakes he had brought from Shanghai, although
his mother indicated there was plenty of tea now, thanks to her
son and daughter in the city.

Shen smiled but Kate could see there was a tenseness and
urgency about him. He turned to her. "Kate Doctor," he said,
"the field of Shen Fu my father cannot be seen from the path we
rode in on, but it is not far distant. Perhaps you would care to
accompany me?"

"I would be honored," Kate smiled, using the correct phrase
to fulfill Oriental righteousness.

"Good," said Shen, rising to go. "Let us leave immediately."

But as Shen Lung and Kate went to leave, Shen's mother rose
also. Kate saw that her face was now openly anxious.

Shen saw it too. "There is something . . . ? There is something . . . ?" he said urgently.

"He is much changed."

"But he is in health?"

"You will see what the change is when you come upon him.

But be kind. Much has happened here and we do not tell all in our letters.''

They mounted up and rode quickly then, urging the horses on where they could, although there was little more than an ox path in most places. And even then, this was hardened into rough high furrows so that they had to be careful how they took their animals lest they hurt them and made them lame.

It seemed a long time before they came upon his father's field. It was less than an acre in size but full of poppies in full bloom. There was no sign of a grain or vegetable crop anywhere.

They could not see his father and Shen became anxious.

He dismounted and Kate followed as they walked now, making their way quickly between the cultivated rows until Shen was certain his father was not there.

Then, just as they were about to leave, they saw in the distance the very top of a coolie's hat. It was at the far corner of the field, the cone of the straw hat just barely visible above the tall poppies.

They hurried through row after row of flowers until they came to the end of the field. A lone figure was sitting squat-legged under a hat. It could not be his father, surely? It was near noontime. It must be a laborer taking his *xiuxi*, the traditional Chinese two-hour rest break in the heat of the day.

Just then they heard a chuckle. And as they did so, they looked and saw. From where it had lain hidden, cupped in two hands below the elevated knees of the squat-legged position, a pipe emerged. The figure under the hat held it in two shaking yellow hands. Kate saw Shen recoil in horror. It was the first time she had seen him uncertain of what to do. He stood, unmoving, watching. And then Kate realized he was waiting. They both watched as the shaking yellowed hands took the pipe up again under the coolie's hat. This, for the opium smoker, is the moment of exquisite pleasure which none must interrupt. Kate saw the pipe draw, and heard the crackle of ignition, followed by a deep sigh as smoke went wafting in the air.

Shen walked over closer, squatting down himself so that he was almost under the broad brim of the hat. Kate heard him say very gently ''And how does my father?''

''He does well, he does well. Who is that?''

She saw Shen swallow hard and take one of the old man's

hands very gently leaving the other clutching the pipe in a grip like an eagle's claw.

Even at the touch of his hand there was no flicker of recognition in the old man's eyes. "Do you come from the landlord, then?" he said with a chuckle. "Only men of the landlord ride on horses."

"So you saw the horses, my father?" Kate heard Shen Lung say, hopefully.

"I have ears, I have ears," the old man said, and then added, "but why is it you call me father? This is not fitting." He chuckled again as if it were all some sinister joke to which only he were party.

"I am sorry, Elder Born," Shen said with great dignity, and close to tears again, "I forget myself." Then he added, with a faint hope still, "I have a father in these parts and for a moment I thought you were he."

At this the old man chuckled again. "Oh, there was such a one in these parts who was a fine farmer and I heard tell that he had a son who is in the city now. But no one has heard of the farmer for many moons and it is fitting that he is not here, for I hear tell he was a good man who would never grow the poppy flower—no, not even for food in bad years when there was a famine."

With what must have been a great effort of self-control, Shen spoke to the old man again and said, "Will you come and take a little food and tea, old one, for it is now past noon and there is a house nearby where we would be welcome?"

At that the hand which Shen held tensed and pulled him closer. For a moment Kate thought there was a flicker of recognition.

"The poppies," the voice said with a strange desperation, "I cannot leave the poppies. I must sit and watch the poppies. They are my life and death now. I dare not leave the poppies."

Shen Lung nodded slowly. Then, with great difficulty, he undid the vice grip which now held his hand, stroking the old man's hand kindly.

"Tell the landlord I sit and watch," the old man chuckled.

"I will, Elder Born, I will," Shen said as he stood to go.

But the old one was sucking again deeply, already far away in another world.

\* \* \*

They started to walk back towards the house. Kate could feel the tears in Shen's eyes. Quietly she took his hand and held it. She felt a need to do something more: to take him and hold him and comfort him. Perhaps it was the same feeling she had had all those years ago with the little boy in the alley. And yet there was something else also which she could not quite put her finger on.

When they reached the house Shen's mother was still standing outside.

"Who is it who has done this thing to my father?" Shen said. Kate saw the fear in his mother's face.

"The pains of old age came upon him after you left," she said, "and his back and legs which had carried such heavy coolie loads in his youth troubled him greatly—"

"There are medicines. Are we such a backward people that we think there is but one opiate? My father would not do this thing lightly," Shen answered.

"This is true, this is true," she said anxiously, fearing her son's anger might turn against her now for not preventing it. "He did not do it lightly. At first he took the cures the old one mixes."

"And then—"

"And then he took his first pipe and if it was for pain or for pleasure or to be seen as one who can afford a pipe on special occasions, who can tell?"

"With whom did he smoke his first pipe?"

The woman shook her head as if unwilling to answer.

"So many pipes cost a great deal. Who gave him the money?"

She feared to answer and stood cowed, bent like he remembered she used to bend to the cooking pots. But she was permanently bent now and bowed with worry and old age.

For all the love she bore the boy, it was a hard moment for the woman, now that it was here, this moment she had dreaded so long. But she had to tell him, she knew, and not hold back, though she feared for the consequences once the name was on her lips.

"It was your father's wife's brother," she said with painful resignation, using the formal form of address, her breath short and starved of air. "It was he who gave him his first pipe and then the other pipes until all the money was gone and our land too. And now it is he who is our landlord and we must plant what he says or there will be no more pipes and nothing to eat."

Kate looked at Shen forlornly. They all stood silent for a long time, staring off at the trees in the distance.

"Let us go in now, my mother," Shen said kindly at last.

They sat down to formal tea then, as befits an honored guest coming to one's house. And Shen Lung's mother and younger sister, Shen Tan, named for her mother, brought tea and rice cakes.

It was well after sunset when Shen Fu shuffled in and had only a bowl of tea before going quickly to bed with his pipe.

That night Shen took Kate to the inn in the village. He said he would now investigate the reports of her father. Kate wanted to go with him but Shen said that would be unwise. Because she was a *yang kwei,* people might not talk as freely with her there. Shen said he might be gone most of the night. Whatever happened, Kate must wait for him and not try to find him or start asking questions.

After Shen had seen Kate safely to the inn, he turned back and took another road out of the village. He found the spot he wanted and waited in the shadows. Just before dawn Guard Boy opened the door inside the granary and walked outside. He never knew what hit him. Shen came from behind, knocking him out instantly. Shen tied and gagged him and hid him in a corner. When, two hours later, Shen's uncle arrived to start his day's work, Shen was still waiting. As his uncle saw him, and a look of amazement and then alarm began to show on his face, Shen shot him through the temple.

It was now nearly fully light and Shen hurried. He doubted if any would recognize him but it was wise to be cautious. It was only with extreme difficulty that he stopped himself from running back to hug his aunt and cousins. The youngest, the little girl, would be fourteen now.

But he forced himself to go on. He had one more errand to do before he returned to Kate Doctor. He hoped his people were right. The old man had been unable to talk and had no identification papers. It seemed best to bring the daughter to him. It was fortunate the old man had been in the mountains only a few hundred miles from the village. If he'd been in the very far North it would have been impossible. Shen hoped his people had been right when they'd said the old man was well enough to be moved.

He reached the back of the teahouse where the night's carousing would have finished only a few hours ago. He knocked and stood back from the door in the shadows. Presently a man in a white apron came out. Shen waited for a moment until he was sure the man was alone. Then he stepped forward and touched him on the shoulder. The man turned and embraced him and they exchanged pleasantries. Shen asked about the man's wife and children.

"And the old one I inquired about—is he yet able to walk or do I bring the woman to him?" Shen said at last.

The man shifted uneasily on his feet. Shen could see the concern in his face. It was unusual to see him thus. He was one of Shen's best men, with responsibility for all those who had little red paper flags in that area. Besides, Shen liked him. And the man had always been fair to him. He had not resented Shen's being put over him at such a young age as some such as Li Po had.

"What is it, comrade?" Shen said gently.

"He is not here . . ." the man stammered out. "The Kuomintang took him on the way down from the mountains. I received the news only two days ago and there was no time to get a message to you safely. I hope I did right . . ."

Shen paused and inhaled deeply.

"Of course . . . It is a personal matter. Nothing must interfere with our overall plans. But it is strange the Kuomintang should show such interest unless they knew who he was and what he had been doing . . ."

The man in the apron nodded.

"They took him openly, on the way down . . . ?"

"Not fifty miles from here."

"To do something so open, when we Communists are not yet officially outlawed, is certainly unusual. They must want the old one very badly. Our men offered no resistance? No one saw our men were armed? No one was hurt or captured?"

"No, Comrade Colonel."

"Good. It is a pity about the old man but it is important nothing more was made of it. Timing is everything. They must not suspect . . . Do you have any idea where the old man is?"

The man in the apron shook his head slowly but then stopped and began uncertainly. "There was one thing," he said. "When they stopped our group, who looked just like peasants carrying a sick man to town, the Kuomintang leader said something unusual . . ."

"What was that?"

"First he told our people to hand the doctor over . . ."

"And . . . ?"

"You know young Chia . . . he is a bit of a hothead and perhaps I shouldn't have put him in charge but he really is very able . . ."

The man hesitated and Shen nodded.

"Well," the man went on, "Chia did disobey orders just slightly in one respect in that he said—in a very unpeasant-like manner to the officer—'On whose authority do you take this man?' And the officer answered him and said, 'On the personal authority of General Yang Ho.' "

"Interesting," said Shen. "Your people are quite sure he said 'Yang Ho'?"

The man nodded. "It means something?"

"Not yet. But I'm sure it will. No one has any idea the doctor is one of us—no one at all? Not even young Chia? You are sure?"

"I am sure. Even the ones he was training in the mountains knew nothing. Only that he was a *yang kwei*, willing to help."

"Let us hope that is how it continues."

"I am sorry, Comrade Colonel, truly sorry."

Shen smiled at him and put his arm around him. The man was twice his age. "Do not worry, my friend. We have not lost the good doctor yet. And it is a lot to ask of men to accomplish a mission without retaliating. But our time will come . . . And now I must hurry on my way or I will have problems of another sort."

"But you will take tea . . . ? You will sit briefly and take tea . . . ? My wife and little ones would never forgive me . . ."

"Of course. I would not come all this way and not see them."

And with that, each with his arm around the other, they walked into the house together.

\*     \*     \*

When Shen returned to Kate she was feverish with anxiety. It took all of Shen's self-control to say, in a matter-of-fact way, "I am sorry, Kate Doctor, to bring you all this way and have no good news. But as I said, it was the slenderest of threads. I am afraid my people were mistaken. It is not he."

"How can you be so sure? Let me see him."

"I am sure, Kate Doctor. I saw him and he looks nothing like your father. He is short and fat," Shen lied.

"Please let me see him."

"It is not possible. You must take my word."

"Of course. Forgive me. I'm just overwrought. I really do appreciate all you're doing."

"It is understandable. But all is not lost. We will keep looking. One door closes and another opens . . ."

Kate nodded and forced a smile. But she was very silent. They packed their bags and made their way to a mule cart which was waiting at the back of the inn. Shen was not even sure Kate noticed the cart took a long way around to another station along the route. Even in the train compartment she sat silent for most of the journey.

When the train finally began to steam into Shanghai station, Kate wanted to get off and run to Blake. She wanted only to hug him and sit in a bath while he poured her a drink and sat with her and listened to how disappointed she was. Then she wanted some scrambled eggs and toast and to be cuddled in bed until the pain started to go.

The full realization that her father was missing was beginning to weigh upon her. He couldn't be found and she might never see him again.

So as the train came to a final stop she turned to Shen and said, "I'm sorry to have been such terrible company. Thanks for being so understanding and leaving me to my thoughts." He smiled at her. "I will keep looking as if he were my own father, Kate Doctor," Shen said simply.

"I know," Kate said. "I know. And thank you. I'm so

terribly sorry about your father . . . But perhaps with time . . . I will ask if there are any modern medicines which might help.''

Shen smiled in thanks. "May I call you a taxi cab? I have some business at the station and must stay here.''

"No thanks. I'll find one myself.''

They shook hands formally and the next instant Kate was disappearing down the train corridor.

Five minutes later she was at the hotel. But when she knocked on Blake's door, no one answered. It suddenly occurred to her how stupid she had been. She had blocked out all thought of what he had to do over the weekend—all thought of how dangerous it might be. Why wasn't he there? Surely he must have known this was the first place she would look when she returned?

She rode down in the elevator to the lobby and asked for Blake's key. They had instructions to give it to her if she asked. When the clerk saw her he said, "Doctor Richmond, I didn't see you come in. Captain Blake phoned to say he had left a message for you in his suite. Shall I have a boy fetch it?''

"No thanks. I'll get it. Did the captain say when he'd be back by any chance?''

"No miss." He handed her the key. "Anything else?''

"No thank you.''

When Kate reached Blake's room there was a handwritten note on his personal stationery propped up beside the bedside lamp. It said:

Dear Kate,
    I have had to go away on business and shall be gone several days.

                                        Keep the bed warm.

                                        Love,
                                        Tom

This note, on top of everything else, was too much for her. She felt the tears coming and couldn't stop them and didn't try. The note didn't really tell her anything. Was he all right? Had he written it before his planned nefarious activity or after?

She kicked off her shoes and poured herself a strong whiskey as the tears kept tumbling down. Then she turned on the water for the tub and threw off her clothes and sat in it before it was full, hugging her knees up to herself. After a while the whiskey started to take effect and she felt a little better. She got out and found her cigarettes and got back into the tub with them and another drink.

Little by little she coaxed herself back into a better mood. She had been doing it since her teens. It was like a coach telling her she could do it. That there was no one to dry her tears for her—that she had to do it herself. She was not a little girl any more, however much she wanted someone to lean on. If anything was going to be done, she had to do it herself.

Then it suddenly hit her. Yang Ho! If Shen couldn't find her father, perhaps Yang Ho could. Of course. It was simple. Who was more powerful than Yang Ho? Shen had no army—only fellow believers who must hide and work in secret. But Yang Ho had hundreds of thousands of troops all over the countryside. They'd find her father. She was sure of it. What time was it? She reached a soapy hand for her watch. Nine o'clock. Nine o'clock on a Sunday night. Was it too late? Would he be home? Would he see her? Of course. She could at least try.

Then the thought struck her—how could she ask Shen's mortal enemy for help? It would be a kind of betrayal. But, she told herself, Yang Ho was her only hope, and she could not risk her father's life by not trying, however angry Shen might be, however much he might despise her. Surely he would understand. Surely.

And with that she jumped up, dripping from the bath, and began to dry herself quickly. She had only one work dress at Blake's suite. It was silly this thing of not leaving part of her wardrobe at Blake's. She could not go like that. It would be important to honor Yang Ho by dressing in style. That would give him face. She reached for the phone and rang Janey, whom she should have called sooner and felt guilty about.

"Janey? Hi. This is your long-lost roommate, back from the country."

"Katie? I'm glad you're back. Your mother's been calling to see if there's any news about your father. I suppose there is—you sound cheerful."

"No. Not really. But I just got an idea which might help—and I need a favor. Don't ask me to explain now, but can you lend me a dress and some underwear or bring some of mine over?"

"For a girl who started out late in life you're making me look like a slow learner. I'll bring you some of my underwear and some expensive perfume—is that the idea? I take it you are going fishing, in a manner of speaking?"

"In a manner of speaking, yes—although only that. But you know the old argument—you look and feel better if you know the layer underneath is right."

"Darling, you don't have to convince me—I invented the phrase."

They laughed. "Oh darling, I have missed you," Kate said now with feeling, "but I've been so busy and despite all the worry over Daddy it is wonderful to be in love, isn't it?"

"How would I know? It's been at least ten days since I was in love. Haven't met a decent man in nearly two weeks."

"Janey!"

"When and where do you want the goods?"

"At Blake's suite—now . . . is that possible . . . ?"

"Be over in five minutes."

"You're a darling. Thanks."

"Phone your mother, huh?"

"Sure. See you soon."

They hung up and Kate immediately telephoned her mother. Clem's disappearance had brought mother and daughter closer than they'd been in years.

"No news, darling?—"

"I'm afraid not, Mummy. I shouldn't have mentioned there might be . . . But I've got an idea . . . ."

"What's that, darling?"

"Oh nothing, really. Just someone I thought might be able to help. But don't get your hopes up."

"My faith is in the Lord, darling. I'm sure He will bring your father back. I'm sure there's some reason behind it all. Don't forget the power of prayer, darling. You are praying, aren't you . . . ?"

"Of course, Mummy," Kate lied. She had stopped praying a long time ago but did not tell her parents. "Must go, Mummy. I'll let you know the moment I have any news."

"Come round for a meal soon."

"Of course. Promise. Goodnight."

"Goodnight, darling."

She picked up the phone and dialed again, and when she got through asked to be connected with General Yang. She was trembling. There was a long delay, and she nearly put the phone down.

Then a voice said, "Yang."

"General Yang, this is Katherine Richmond. I wonder if I might come and have a word with you?"

There was the briefest of pauses. Then he said, "Katherine! What an unexpected pleasure. You do me much honor. Of course I should be delighted to see an old friend again. When do you wish to come?" Kate let out her breath. It was easier than she had expected. Too easy. A warning light flashed in her mind. "Tonight," she said. "Now. If that is possible?"

"Of course. Have you dined? Perhaps you will allow me to provide a modest supper?"

"You are kind, but there is no need. It is simply a matter of some urgency that I should like to discuss with you."

He did not ask what it was. "Then come as soon as you are ready. And when we have spoken of this urgent matter, perhaps you will stay a little and talk of other things too. It has been too long since we met."

"Thank you. In half an hour then?"

As she put the phone down, Kate's heart was pounding. There had been something in his voice, his tone, which alarmed her. As though he were a cat playing with a mouse. As though he had been expecting her call. But she would have to go through with it.

She sat down at the dressing table and put on her makeup. She had just finished when Janey arrived with the clothes. As well as black underwear she had brought Kate a black cocktail dress and some pearls. She offered to drive her wherever she was going.

But when they reached the street Kate thanked her and said she would take a cab.

The clock in the army barracks tower had just struck ten by the time Kate arrived at Yang Ho's apartment.

Yang Ho was politeness itself. Her old friend hurried to the door to greet her when he heard it was she.

"Katherine," he said. "How charming you look. But then you always did. I have not forgotten."

She could find nothing to say, and simply smiled. He looked

very suave, she thought, self-confident, very much in control of himself.

"Come, sit down," he said. "I have had a small supper prepared. It is less than I would have wished to offer to an honored guest, but . . ."

"I have come to beg your help," she began.

"Later, Katherine, later. First we will eat, and then we shall talk of what is worrying you."

She realized how used he was to command. If she were to refuse, it might anger him, though undoubtedly he would not show it. He had obviously decided that they should have supper, despite their earlier conversation.

"As we eat you must tell me all that has happened to you since our last meeting," he said. "We have both been away from China, have we not?"

He questioned her about her training in America, and she found herself answering freely. He was easy to talk to. As she spoke, his eyes were fastened on hers, and there was a strange intensity in his gaze. Once when she looked up she thought she had caught him staring at her breasts, but she could have been mistaken.

After the supper, he poured cognac, and as they lingered by the fire, Kate was at last able to explain her predicament, judiciously leaving out any reference to Blake or the weekend. It was the first time that Yang had really given her an opportunity to speak of her parents. When she had started to mention them earlier in the evening, he had always asked another question, changing the subject, as though he did not want her to ask him about her father. As though . . . as though he knew where her father was and that this was why she had come to him.

But that was nonsense. He would surely have told her. And if he knew her father's whereabouts, he would not now be saying, as she spoke of her concern for her father, that it did not sound like a very serious matter for him to find her father. Yang said he would send out an order to look for him first thing in the morning. "I am sure I will have an answer for you in a week or so, Katherine," he said. "When I do I will send my car for you and we will dine again and talk some more."

Kate smiled as he stood up and ordered his limousine to take her home.

She chided herself for her earlier suspicion. "Thank you for listening," she said. "And for being so willing to help."

"How could I refuse, Katherine? I am yours to command."

She was suddenly embarrassed. But as they made their farewells, Yang Ho still behaving with impeccable politeness, her heart was filled with gratitude, and she thanked him again.

Sitting back in the limousine, she was sure her troubles were over.

When Shen left the railway station that night he went straight to the house of his old teacher, Doctor Wu Zhao, who, with Kate's friend, his betrothed, Lu Chien, had first brought Blake to Kate. Doctor Wu and the elegant, intelligent Lu Chien were rich, cultured Shanghaiese of the ruling class. But, as teacher and student, they had become disillusioned with present and past governments. Wu was nearly forty; Lu Chien was in her early twenties. He was an academic. She was slender, slightly tall for a Chinese, and classically elegant in manner and pose. Yet she was a fervent member of the party. She believed, almost with evangelical ardor, that Communists must meet people on their own ground. So she attended the many large banquets and balls and generally made the social rounds of Shanghai, always displaying her great urbanity and kindly modesty, though there were those in the party who criticized her for these activities.

Wu was happy with his books and tutoring people such as Shen in all facets of communism, including Chinese gamesmanship at which he was such an expert.

He had attended military school in Japan, though not with the same love of it that others such as Yang Ho had shown. For a time, too, Wu had taught at Chiang Kai-shek's Whampoa Military Academy before they had a falling out. Wu, like Yang Ho, had fought, during World War I, incursions into Chinese territory. And, like Mao, Wu had fought briefly in the "First Revolution" of 1911 with Dr. Sun Yat-sen.

Although Wu was soft-spoken, with the leisurely polished urbanity of the classic mandarin, he was a visionary. To the communist movement he was invaluable. Many would say that he perhaps more than any other had given the young Communists who came under him the fire in their bellies. He supervised weekend shooting practice with the same quiet patience he exercised in classes during the week.

Shen had been his understudy in all things and he loved to visit the Wu house, for this learned and once-rich couple epitomized to him the heart of China. They loved their country above all else.

Over the years of their Communist party membership, Wu Zhao and Lu Chien had successively sold off their separate family fortunes—city houses of many courts and servants and summer palaces—until all that was left was a modest house and a small handful of their most-loved art treasures. They had let all their servants go. They had not yet married, because their Communist beliefs did not make it mandatory in such a situation.

On this particular night—the same night Kate had visited Yang Ho—Lu Chien, dressed in a slender, black cheongsam, with her black hair swept graciously high, bent to pour Shen Lung tea. Shen then quickly gave his account of his adventure to Wu.

Wu Zhao wore a simple cotton suit like Shen's, although with shirt and tie in the Western fashion. He had a full head of neatly parted black hair, with just a little gray at the temples. He had a military-trimmed moustache, and his body of medium-height, sitting easily in the chair behind the black lacquered table he used as a desk, looked fit and compact. The only things, indeed, which might have separated out this very precise-looking fighting man as also a man of insatiable appetites for the practice of ideas and learning—for ideas as bullets—were his spectacles. They were rimless, though with gold shafts to the ears. And somehow, in the way spectacles may change a person's entire appearance, they superimposed another person—a learned, quietly smiling one—on his soldier figure. One image did not conflict with the other. If ever the harmony of the elements came together, in the Chinese sense, it was in the quiet military erudition of Wu Zhao.

Shen told Wu everything and the other man sat nodding thoughtfully over his glasses. Lu Chien looked sadly in Shen's direction when he told of his father. They knew the history of his relationship with his uncle.

It was part of Wu Zhao's method that he was forever teaching, gently coaxing. As he listened to Shen he believed he knew just how close was the time when the Kuomintang would make their move to stamp out the Communists. There was so little time, and so much to be done. Still so many to be trained. Enough would be killed as it was—hundreds, perhaps thousands—before this fight with the Kuomintang, who called themselves "Nationalists" of all things, was over. They were so young, these soldiers of Wu's, these pupils of the streets who were the real nationalists. In his classes Wu had those of ages ten to twelve—around the age Shen had been when he'd come to them. Now Shen led them all—or most of them. Shen, like so many of the "Young Vanguard," was now a veteran.

It was the Chinese New Year of 1927. Wu, beginning to feel his age, feared what it might bring.

# 27

*The following week, with Blake away and with less anxiety* about her father gnawing at her, Kate threw herself into her work. She and Janey had their fun-filled long chats again. Kate spent an evening with her mother and was glad that their relationship was improving. And she had tea with Lu Chien, who seemed happier. It had been over a month since Blake had been shot. It appeared no one knew he was the man wounded at the arsenal raid and that she had helped him. Everyone seemed more relaxed. Everyone except Shen.

Shen had been a little touchy—which was unusual for him—on the one occasion Kate had seen him. It was on Monday, just one week after their return from the country. Kate had phoned up Ling Ling and said she'd like to talk to Shen. A meeting had been arranged at a teahouse during the Monday lunch hour, but Shen had seemed strangely preoccupied.

When she asked whether the delivery—which was so crucial

to Blake—had been made, Shen replied impatiently, "Not yet. Not yet." Kate wondered if he resented her asking. She explained she was really asking for Blake's sake, to know if his problems were over. Shen simply shrugged his shoulders. And when she asked if he knew Blake's whereabouts he insisted he knew nothing. She had the feeling he was forcing himself to be polite and that underneath he was angry—angry and annoyed—if not with her then with someone connected with her. She rose to return to work and smiled very warmly at him.

"I know a good lady doctor who is available for consultations if you need someone to talk to," she said impishly, "but of course she is a *yang kwei* and may sometimes unwittingly say things which may offend certain Orientals . . ."

Shen broke into a smile. "I am sorry, Kate Doctor. It is not you . . . It is I. I only wish there were someone I could talk to."

"Well, you know where to find me if you need me, as a friend of mine once said." They both laughed and Kate left.


Shen watched her go and sat down and beckoned for another cup of tea. It was the same teahouse in which he had sat, looking through the lattice, while Blake and the young man talked. He was known here and was reluctant to go to places where he was not known now. Everything was closing in on him. And Blake was such a worry. Only Blake knew where the weapons were—where Blake's people had put them on the night he was shot. Or where Blake had now transferred them to last weekend—if indeed he had moved them. Why had he not contacted Shen? Why had he not claimed his money? Surely he would wish to get it quickly?

The others might be unable to see that Rome was beginning to smoulder while they still fiddled at the bar of the Shanghai Club, but Blake was no fool. Shen's entire rationale in approaching him had been that he was a man dedicated to the pursuit of money and power. That he needed it to destroy his competitors who had generations of family money behind them. But if Shen had been wrong on this score, then the whole movement might be threatened.

The fat, balding teashop proprietor shuffled in with a fresh pot of tea. "You need some sleep, comrade," he whispered as he laid it out in front of him.

"Your excellent tea will have to do in its place," Shen said, smiling at the old man and grateful to have such a trusted companion.

"Well, we have been drinking tea together a long time, you and I, and I think it has been good medicine," the old one said as he turned and shuffled off again.

Shen nodded, back in the past for a moment. It was also to this teashop that Hwang and Yu-Ma had first brought him all those years ago. It seemed like a century ago. Was it true that this was how one felt on the eve of battle? Tired and weary and reliving the past?

When Kate got back to the hospital, there was a note from Yang Ho:

> Dear Katherine,
>     I have some news. If it is not too inconvenient at such short notice, would you care to dine with me tonight? I shall take the liberty of sending my car at 7 p.m. in the hope that you are free.
>
>                                   Kindest regards,
>                                   Ho

The limousine paused only momentarily before gaining admission to the great iron gates guarded by sentries. The sun was setting over the hills behind the compound, and as the big black limousine swept around a corner of the building, Kate found herself in a fairy tale garden. There were beautiful cypresses and rolling lawns and ponds and moongate bridges.

Inside, the building was full of ancient Chinese treasures of jade statuettes and wall tapestries and paintings and richly lacquered screens.

Kate was shown up the broad marble staircase to Yang Ho's apartments.

Whereas the other evening he had been in velvet smoking jacket, this night he stood in full uniform, an imposing figure with his back to the fire.

As Kate was shown in he said, "Ah, Katherine . . . Punctual as always, And because I am half European let us dispense with Chinese ritual talk for once. I have found your father and although he has been unwell it is nothing serious and he is now recovering."

Kate stood open-mouthed, her breath taken away. Yang Ho smiled. "I see I have made you speechless. Good. You see, you should have come to your old friend sooner. No matter. I think drinks are called for." He snapped his fingers and a tray appeared as if from nowhere. Kate took a sherry, Yang Ho a mao tai.

"Oh, Ho, I can't begin to tell you how grateful I am," Kate said as she sipped hers. "My father means more to me than anyone else in the world."

Yang Ho smiled again, drinking the clear liquid straight down and then snapping his fingers for another.

"Tell me where I can find him and when I can see him," Kate said excitedly.

"He is in the North," Yang Ho said slowly. "He caught a chill and a fever developed. For a time he was quite delirious. No one could understand what he was saying and for some strange reason he did not appear to be carrying any identification papers . . . As for seeing him . . . ? Come, let us eat and we shall discuss the logistics later. When and how you see him will depend on you . . ."

He indicated the dining room with his hand and Kate followed, smiling. The meal was one of the most delicious she had ever eaten. There were soups and crisp entrees and roast pigeon and some excellent European wines. Kate was feeling marvelous. Yang Ho really was very amusing. They were now talking about old times at school. He joked about how Kate had refused his invitations.

"I wished I might have gone," Kate said genuinely, remembering that they had been close once, as playmates at school often were, "but of course my parents were rather strict."

Yang Ho smiled. The meal was finishing and the waiters cleared off the last of the dishes.

"Coffee?" he said. "Of course," Kate replied, elongating the sentence slowly as a memory came filtering back, "of course.

Yes please, I mean. I'd love some. I was just remembering how you loved coffee."

"I tasted it first at your home, when we played together there in the garden in my early teens."

"So I am to blame for one of your vices," Kate said, laughing.

"Perhaps," he smiled, and then turned to snap a command to his orderly for coffee.

The coffee came and they were left alone.

"There is a favor I would like to ask of you," Yang Ho began, as he lit a cigar.

"I think you could ask me almost anything tonight," Kate said, smiling.

"In two weeks' time it is the military ball," Yang Ho continued, "I wish to ask you to accompany me."

Kate was caught off-guard. She had not expected this. But fortunately she had a very legitimate excuse. "Why Yang Ho, I'd love to," she said, "but unfortunately I have a prior engagement."

"On that particular night?"

"Yes. I've already promised to go with someone else."

"Well, perhaps another function on another night?"

It was getting difficult now. She did owe him a lot. But she also did not want to encourage him unfairly. "I'm afraid my nights are rather booked up," she said slowly and carefully. "If there is anything else at all I can do for you, I would be only too willing but I'm afraid at the moment there is someone I'm seeing . . ."

"To the exclusion of everyone else?"

"Yes."

"Thomas Blake?"

Kate went red. But it was pointless to lie. Half of Shanghai knew.

"Yes," she said, "Thomas Blake."

"A pity," Yang Ho said with deliberation. "I had hoped we might solve a little problem you appear to have in a more amicable way. Now it seems not. But I believe you *will* appear at the ball with me, Katherine. And I believe we *will* make love . . ."

Kate couldn't believe what she was hearing. "Ho, you can't mean that?" she said. "You wouldn't force me, surely?"

"No. I suspect you'll want to do it. I suspect you'll do it voluntarily. But you certainly are free to leave and never see me again if you wish. However may I suggest you hear me out first?"

Kate was beginning to feel weak in the knees. She could feel perspiration forming all over her under her clothing.

"Your doorman Ying Tai is mine," Yang continued, without waiting for her to reply. "We know you treated Blake for a gunshot wound in your apartment. It is now four weeks since you operated on him and you have still not reported it. We also know you took blood from your parents' clinic. We have seen the register there and it is not complete. We also have a sworn affidavit from Nurse Rhoda Dwyer that some blood was missing the next morning. Her affidavit says that you had signed the register, leaving the patient's name blank. Both things are illegal and very serious offenses. This places yourself and Blake in extreme jeopardy to say the least. But the matter of the blood being taken could also have very serious consequences for your parents . . ."

Kate's anger flared as she turned on him, barely stopping to think where her words might lead.

"It was my responsibility and no one else's. I signed out the blood."

Yang Ho was smiling. "The authorities might not see it that way. The clinic belongs to your parents. But I note that you admit it."

Had he deliberately set a trap which she had so easily fallen into?

"I admit nothing," Kate said, "only signing out some blood."

"It is of no matter, Katherine. You are now a grown and sensible woman. This is very different from when we were young. As you are no doubt aware, your friend Thomas Blake has left the city—or fled might be a better word. But soon we will find him and he will be arrested. I already have enough evidence to imprison him for life. But I wish for my own purposes to have a statement—signed by you, a European. You must say that Blake was brought to you by the Communists and you treated him for a gunshot wound. You must also identify the Communists. The moment I have such a statement, your father will be released and returned to Shanghai."

"How can you do this! Are you saying my father is a prisoner? That you are holding him hostage? That he is not free to come home?"

Yang Ho looked at her with a very superior smile. "My dear Katherine, are you really such an innocent as to have got yourself involved in such momentous matters without thought? Do you really not know we have suspected your father for some time of training communist medical personnel? Or that communist meetings have been held in your clinic?"

"That's preposterous—But even if it were true, it is not illegal to help Communists—they are not outlawed."

Yang Ho smiled again. "Oh yes they are. I signed the order myself tonight. It is now punishable by death. And helping one carries the same penalty. It might even be argued that Blake was one if he were engaged in nefarious communist activities . . . And of course this places you under threat of death for helping him . . ."

"But it wasn't illegal then . . ." Kate was stammering, "whatever I or my father did it wasn't illegal then . . ."

Yang Ho looked at her and sighed. "Oh I don't think anyone is going to quibble over a few days, Katherine, particularly when we're going to be rounding up all known sympathizers anyway. But enough of this argument . . . Are you prepared to sign a statement naming Blake as the European wounded and identifying the Communists who brought him to your apartment that night? Do this and your father will go free."

Kate was shaking her head, bewildered. "That would be as good as sentencing Blake and the others to death," she said. "How could I save my father at such a price? He would never condone a decision like that, even if it meant his own death."

Yang Ho seemed pleased. "I thought not," he said. "You people of full European blood are so predictable. Shall I show a little mercy at least for the time? Consider this as an alternative. Your father will be safe from prosecution under the new law provided you are prepared to give some token of your goodwill. He will remain in custody—but he will not be hurt if you cooperate . . ."

Kate could not believe it. How could all this occur in such a short space of time? How could one unintended meeting with a man like Blake on a train change one's whole life?

"I think I'd like a drink now," she said, desperately trying to steady herself.

"Of course. A brandy perhaps?"

"A mao tai."

"Of course."

He got up and poured her one. Kate drank it straight down and immediately asked for another. She felt glazed over, stunned, as if she were somewhere else.

"We were such good friends," she said, drinking down a third mao tai. "I liked you. I was kind to you."

"Yes, you were," he said. "Will you undress yourself, Katherine, or will I?"

# 28

When, *several hours later, Kate left Yang Ho's apartments,* she was still dazed. She found herself heading straight for the main railway station which was such an integral part of Shen's network. She had to tell someone. Talk to someone. And Blake was not there. Not that she would want him to know! He must never know!

She reached the station and after asking directions was shown towards the signalman's hut. But when she reached it Shen was not there. Bitterly disappointed, she was about to leave when Hwang and Yu-Ma walked in. She could have cried when the two huge men greeted her with such warm happy smiles. In an instant Hwang saw that something was wrong. He took her by the hand and said, "Sit here, good doctor. Sit here and rest and we will take tea."

She sat down gratefully. Then Hwang said, smiling, "I will go for our friend. But it will take half an hour—a quarter there and a quarter back if he is able to come immediately. You will wait?"

She nodded.

"Good. Others may come and go but you must not mind them. You will be safe here and the good Yu-Ma will watch over you. This is agreeable?"

She nodded again and without another word he took off.

It was nearly an hour before Hwang returned with Shen and Kate realized she must have been dozing. It was as if she had a concussion and her body was trying to hide itself in sleep and repair.

"I need to talk to you urgently," she said to Shen. He nodded and led her by the hand from the signalman's hut to the crowded public cafeteria where few foreign devils ever went and which was thronged with impoverished Chinese who had long hours to wait and sat there for comfort even though many could not afford a cup of tea.

Shen brought some tea and they sat and drank out of cracked China cups while Kate talked.

"I'm sorry," she said, nearly breaking down a dozen times as she told him her story, "I'm so sorry to burden you but I had to tell someone . . . I just don't know what to do. Blake is not here and I don't know where to find him and even if I did I couldn't tell him—not just for fear of what he might do but because of my shame. And I daren't talk to Janey because she knows none of this intrigue and I would not wish to involve her . . ."

Shen looked at her and Kate would never forget the look in his eyes. They were damp and sad and close to crying.

"There is nothing I can do, Kate Doctor," he said resignedly, his own voice half-breaking, "nothing that will ease the pain until we find your father again. I blame myself . . ."

"Don't," said Kate. "Yang Ho would have found a way to blackmail me, even if my father were safe and sound . . . I am sorry to have troubled you but I had to tell someone."

"Of course."

"Will the pain ever pass?" she said, not really sure why she expected him to know, but aware that she did; sensing that always in him there was a deep pool of human resource and suffering that would understand.

"It is the pain of humiliation," he said gently. "We Chinese know a lot of such pain. You have not betrayed anyone—and certainly not yourself. This thing was necessary for the moment. I am truly sorry that we have been the cause of such anguish for you.''

"Blake must never know," Kate said, anxious now, sure that he must never be told, the guilt rising like bile from her stomach and her temples throbbing as she felt as if every part of her had been stolen.

"Of course not."

"There is no sign of him?" Kate said, wanting his comfort desperately at the same time as hating him for not being there, feeling somehow that it wouldn't have happened if he had been. "We must warn him that Yang Ho knows," she said.

"To all intents and purposes he has vanished with his cargo," Shen said, more conciliatory now in his explanations of Blake's disappearance. "Believe me, Kate Doctor, when I say that we want to find him even more than you. Our situation has deteriorated very badly. Particularly with this most recent news you bring us.''

"We must warn him," Kate said, as if she had not heard Shen.

Shen smiled kindly. "The moment I see him I shall tell him you wish to see him, I assure you," he said. Then he added, "You realize, of course, that you hold all our destinies in your hand?''

Kate nodded. She was still stunned. She wanted the conversation to end. Yet it was time to ask the question she did not wish to ask.

"There is something else," she said, faltering.

Shen looked across the table at her. He knew what was coming. She had already helped them more than any had a right to ask. It was not her fight. Yet so much depended on her.

"You want to ask me if you will have to surrender to Yang Ho again," he said simply.

"Yes," she replied.

"Once one has tasted the bitter fruit it is never quite as sharp again," he said.

She forced a smile. "After all this, you, of all people, you, the leader of the young and the new, resort to the oldest Chinese proverb of them all."

"One should take wisdom where one finds it."

"This is true."

"You have no choice, Kate Doctor. Not just for us and Blake. But for your father . . ."

"I know it."

"But you hoped I might release you from your vow of silence to us. You hoped I might say something like, 'Tell Yang Ho who we are for we are no longer frightened of him and are ready to do battle'? You hoped you might be able thus to trade with him and win safety for yourself and family and perhaps even your beloved Blake?"

"Perhaps. I don't know what I had hoped. Perhaps I thought that. But this thing with Yang Ho will not be lightly over. He will want me again and again, I know."

"One may sacrifice part of the body and yet be free in the mind."

"Another proverb."

"In China we have need of many such."

"Isn't that the truth."

They finished their tea and got up and left.


Two hours later in another part of town a young man in a Kuomintang general's uniform knocked on the red lacquered door of the house of Ma Yen the Mandarin. It was well past midnight and he knocked lightly. Presently the huge gateman opened. He wiped sleep from his eyes and then looked again.

"So it really is you, comrade?" he said as Wang Lee's face broke into a smile. "I thought for a moment it was the Generalissimo Yang Ho himself."

"Do not let the real generalissimo, Chiang Kai-shek, hear you say that," Wang Lee laughed. "He still thinks he runs the army. He does not know how powerful Yang Ho has become. Or how dangerous. If Yang Ho is ever given his head . . ."

The big gateman nodded and ushered Wang Lee in.

"You wish my mistress . . . ?" the gateman said.

"I would not come at this hour if it were not important, comrade. But I do not wish to disturb her if she has callers . . ."

The big man looked down at Wang Lee and smiled kindly. He wished he might answer otherwise; or not at all. But the young man had the look about him of one who would like the truth.

"The last one left a short time ago, comrade," he said quietly. "My mistress will be bathing before retiring. I am sure she would wish to see you. Come, I shall take you to her head girl."

Wang Lee nodded and they walked together through the Garden of the Moon, past the Earth God Shrine and past the lily pond to Ling Ling's courts.

The big man ushered Wang Lee into the forecourt where the head girl sat. She rose swiftly at the sign of the Kuomintang general's uniform. Wang Lee wished she hadn't recognized it so quickly with such deference.

"Who shall I say is calling?" she asked. Wang Lee was uncertain whether the girl recognized him. In any case, Ling Ling had said all her girls were safe.

"General Wang, from Generalissimo Chiang Kai-shek's personal staff," he said, using a pre-arranged code so Ling Ling would know it was he. Like all intelligence experts the world over he tried to use names he could react to quickly and automatically. Wang was a very common Chinese name and there were two generals Wang on the Generalissimo's staff. It was a convenient cover.

The gateman smiled and left him. The girl disappeared for a moment and then returned, bowed, and said:

"My mistress is in her bath and says will you please accompany me to her?"

Wang nodded stiffly as a general would.

He was soon shown into the room where he and Ling Ling had first kissed. It seemed so long ago.

She sat in the bath at the far end of the room, propped against one corner. Only her head was visible above the wafting pillows of soap.

"You have eaten?" she said softly.

He shook his head—and then thought that this was a miscalculation. The head girl was still present and would certainly expect a Kuomintang general to have eaten well. He must be more careful.

"Some wine and cold duck," Ling Ling said to her head girl. "Are the lychees fresh?"

"By train from Canton this morning, mistress."

"Good. Some fresh lychees then for the general . . ."

The girl disappeared and Wang Lee thought once more how

caring this peasant girl of his, Ling Ling, was—how warm and caring and beautiful. He wished, despite all he knew about her work, that he might be with her always. Could that ever be? When he was with her he was tired of the war already, and it had not even started. He had been tired of the war since the day he met her.

"Will you bathe?" Ling said quietly.

"Yes. But I shall wait until the girl has come and gone with the food."

"As you wish it."

So they waited quietly then, smiling at each other, until the girl had returned, placed a tray on a table near the water's edge, and departed.

There was a large bottle of wine and some glasses with the food. "It is Western wine," Ling Ling commented, noticing Wang Lee looking at it, "champagne from France. I thought perhaps you may not have tasted it and would like to try it . . . it is very good but if you wish I can easily send it back . . . ?"

"It is not necessary . . . it is not necessary . . ." Wang said hurriedly.

"Good. Good. It is the wine of love and I have missed you so that I thought my heart would break."

"And I you, Ling Ling, and I you . . ." he found himself saying, wondering again why he felt so much at home with this one, as if each had known the other all their lives.

"It is better without clothes," she said, stretching so that her full ripe wet breasts arched out of the water towards him, "and besides, I want to watch you undress, to see every part of you that I will touch and love later."

He began to undress. But before he had gone far she had come out of the bath towards him and kissed him so that soon both were tugging at his clothes. They took each other then on the Persian rug beside the pool—both wet with the soapy water from Ling Ling's body—took each other with the speed and thrust of desperate lovers.

Her scream of pleasure was loud and breathless and his life force going into her was like a flood. And still they did not stop but only slowed and kissed lightly now, touching gently, letting that other deeper part of love they were both feeling wind them down in its own quiet way.

It was some time before they both sat silently together, naked, by the edge of the pool, eating and drinking, with the good drying feeling of each other's juices upon them. Wang Lee touched Ling Ling's cheek gently with the back of his hand and she took his hand and kissed it. They sat kissing, loving, knowing each other; and knowing, too, that ache of love inside so raw that tears would come if anything ever touched it.

They slept hardly at all, but lay awake, caressing, talking, prolonging the pleasure of just being close, lying side by side under the mosquito net and fan once more, knowing that the morning would take all this away. When they did sleep it was in little snatches, some part of each draped across the other, or nestled into a part of the other so that even in sleep they would know the other was there.

But morning did come eventually, through the round Moon Gate windows, the sun playing patterns on their bodies through the netting.

"It is serious?" Ling Ling asked, knowing the answer herself perhaps better than Wang Lee.

"It is serious."

"Blake is still missing?"

"Yes."

"So you have no weapons?"

"Practically none."

"And now that Yang Ho has signed the proclamation outlawing communism it is only a matter of time before he moves . . ."

"We believe so . . ."

"And my brother wishes me to see what I can find out . . . ?"

"With all my heart I wish this were a question of which I did not have to answer 'Yes.' "

She nodded and got out of bed and walked quietly to her chest in the corner. It was the old wooden chest with the common metal hooped around it.

As she bent her bare body to it Wang Lee stared at her tight olive flanks and buttocks and felt the ache in him starting all over again.

She walked back towards him, smiling. Her black hair framed her porcelain beauty at her head and between her legs. She carried an old brown paper parcel which looked as if it had been tied and retied many times with coarse jute thread. She curled the mosquito net up and threw it on the top of the canopy as she crawled back into bed and passed the package to Wang Lee.

"A gift for you and my brother . . ." she said simply.

Wang Lee looked at the package and began to open it.

He slipped the jute thread off sideways and suddenly half the packet split open. It was full of paper money.

"There must be thousands of yuan here," he said, the amazement showing in his voice.

"Yes," she said quietly, and when he looked at her again he saw her face was red. So he took her to him then and hugged her until she began to sob. They were deep sobs which kept rising up against him and buffeting him so that despite everything, despite all his Hong Kong-hardened youth and all the killing he had done already, the young chief of Communist intelligence began to cry also.

"There will be more," she sniffed, "more each month. You will come and get it . . . ? Come personally, for I will trust none other . . . It must be you or my brother and it will be safer for you, though I fear for both of you . . ."

"We cannot take it . . ."

"You must. For food; for guns; for medicines; for whatever you need to stay alive."

"It is the price of your freedom. You could leave here tomorrow with all this and live as a lady."

"And have it on my conscience that I might have helped buy life for my brother and the one I love if I had not been so selfish . . . ?"

Wang Lee was silent. After a time Ling Ling spoke again, gently. "Will you honor me and my family by taking this money for your cause?"

It was a formal request.

"Yes," he said bitterly, swallowing his pride. They needed the money desperately.

"And you will come each month for more . . . and whatever information I can find . . . ?"

"Yes."

"Good. Go now then before it is full light. I will get word to you or my brother the moment I know what Yang plans."

They dressed silently, side by side, Wang Lee in his uniform and Ling Ling in an exquisitely embroidered housecoat. They stood in the forecourt looking out on the Garden of the Moon while they waited for the gateman to come and escort him.

After Wang Lee had left Ling Ling rang for her head girl.

"I shall need the hot Szechuan dish of dumplings and a sedan chair for the forenoon."

"Yes mistress."

"Then return and make me ready."

The girl nodded, took the order to the kitchen, and within several minutes had returned with Ling Ling's full retinue of girls.

They spent three hours bathing, oiling, perfuming, and coiffuring their mistress. Then, when they had finished washing and combing her, they dressed her in her finest French underthings and her antique Chinese silk gown. At precisely 11:55 she departed in the sedan chair with a great China bowl of the hot Szechuan dish placed carefully at her feet in a wicker basket.

At Yang Ho's headquarters a servant appeared to carry the bowl upstairs. It was Yang Ho's personal body servant. Ling Ling knew he secretly admired her, as most men did. And one day, if it suited her purpose, she might let him have her once. But he would need to have a very great secret to tell, for if Yang Ho ever found out it would be the end for both of them. In the meantime Ling Ling kept him interested by being polite and civil to him, so that he gossiped to her, sometimes passing on useful pieces of information.

But her mind was on other things this day and hardly ready for the particular piece of gossip which he could not wait to blurt out while she waited in the antechamber to be admitted to Yang Ho's personal suite with her gift of the hot Szechuan dish he loved so. It would not do for a prostitute to appear forward and arrive unannounced. But to phone ahead and say she had prepared the dish her friend Yang favored so was acceptable and she had never known Yang Ho to say no. He invariably invited her to lunch when she telephoned, often canceling important engagements, and belched down great helpings of the hot dumpling and chili dish, which he believed to be an aphrodisiac, before taking her to the bedroom for the afternoon. He drank liberally, and these torrid afternoon sessions were often not without pain, but Ling Ling endured them because they were part of her plan.

She was barely listening to the body servant when suddenly she heard the mention of Kate's name.

"Doctor Richmond—are you sure?" Ling Ling said, unable to believe her ears.

"Of course I am sure. I know who goes in and comes out and how long they stay. And I know what I hear," the servant said.

Ling Ling knew this to be true. It was the body servant's job to guard the door to Yang Ho's bedroom with his life. No one entered or left without his master's permission. And there were no secrets from the servant. He knew Yang Ho often beat Ling Ling. He was a good boy, really, and once, after Yang Ho had left, she had been so sore and bruised she had asked him to rub ointment on her.

"You are positive about this?" Ling Ling now said to him, trying to sound as casual as possible.

"Of course. You are not jealous of some *yang kwei*, are you?"

Ling Ling shook her head. "And your master called for drinks?"

"Of course. Have you ever known him not to?"

"No," said Ling Ling, "no, I have not."

It was true. Ling Ling had never known whether Yang Ho called in his manservant because he really wanted a drink or because he wanted to show off his wares in front of another. Certainly she was sure he liked to humiliate the women he was with by exposing their nakedness to a servant.

Poor Kate! It was bad enough for Ling Ling. But at least she was a prostitute used to such things. And Kate would have had no warning. There was a small buzzer on the side of the bed which Yang Ho would have pushed. The first Kate would have known was when the servant burst in.

Ling Ling had no doubt the servant was telling her the truth. Each needed to trust the other in this sort of situation, or both their lives could be forfeit.

She had also no doubt Kate would not have submitted voluntarily. Given what she knew about Kate, and how she had helped her brother and Blake, Ling was in little doubt that Yang Ho must have found a way to emotionally blackmail her. If this were so, then it was likely Yang Ho knew about her brother and Blake—or at the very least suspected something.

So now Ling Ling had an added problem: whether to pass on this information or not. And if so, to whom? Yet she knew the answer to that already. Her brother must be told. But so must Blake. Ling Ling's growing sphere of influence revolved around certain key contacts. Most of these she slept with—except for one old powerful Buddhist priest—and most she traded information openly with. One of her most important contacts was Shan Li, head of the *Ching-pang*, Shanghai's infamous organization of "green gangs." It had taken the genius of Shan Li, an old street friend of Blake's, to link the *Ching-pang* with the often more rural-based and more respectable *pao chia*. Loosely translated, this meant "the organization of 100 families." Shan Li's goodwill was paramount to Ling Ling's career. Since the *Ching-pang* controlled all crime and prostitution in the city, Ling Ling could operate only with his permission. More than this, he allowed her to operate as a freelance, a privilege accorded very few. Not only did this mean she paid no commission, it meant she could pick and choose her clients—discreetly so there was no loss of face for her old lord, Ma Yen, who had been so kind to her.

But she also knew that Shan Li did not allow her this freedom just because he liked the delights of her body. He did it because she provided him, too, with valuable information.

It was a delicate and dangerous game she played, and in that game Captain Thomas Blake figured prominently. He and Shan Li were the closest of friends. Ling Ling had indeed met Blake many times at parties on Shan Li's famous floating casino. Ling Ling was under the strictest orders from Shan Li about Blake. Anything touching Shan Li touched Blake. No Chinese could pay a foreigner a higher compliment. Ling Ling knew the reason for this feeling and indeed it gave Blake great face in her eyes. Shan Li had told her that when he was a poor street urchin, hungry and with nowhere to sleep, Blake had befriended him one day after school. He had taken him home and given him food and hidden him in the boiler room of their apartment building. Shan Li had slept there for weeks without being discovered. And even then, when the boiler room coolie had finally caught him,

Blake had bribed the coolie with his pocket money to allow Shan Li to stay on.

Eventually, Shan Li was able to support himself. And Blake must have known he was doing it by stealing. But he said nothing—and he and Shan Li had been firm friends ever since.

So Ling Ling knew she must tell Blake. It was part of a debt she owed to Shan Li. But what Blake would do when he heard, she could only begin to imagine!

# BOOK IV
# The Red Sea

*1927–1933*

# 29

*Although he had planned that others should think to the contrary,* Blake had not, in fact, left Shanghai.

He knew he still held a trump card or two. Very much so. On the night of the raid, just before he was shot, Blake and his hired partners in crime had discovered an unexpected windfall—some extra "merchandise" they had not been expecting. Blake had promptly ordered its removal to a safe place. Only he and two others knew where it was stored.

All through his schooldays, during the years of afternoon neglect by his mother, Blake had been a Shanghai street urchin. This had given him, in later years, a network of powerful friends. Many of his former street colleagues had risen to important posts. Others were important by dint of their very insignificance. Some were hired coolies. Others were wharf supervisors; policemen; rickshaw operators; soldiers; members of the *pao chia* and *Ching-pang*. The latter secret society was headed by his friend Shan Li. Blake enjoyed Shan Li's patronage but remained clear of any criminal obligation. He saw his gunrunning activities as purely business, arguing that with so many warring factions in China, someone was bound to supply them and it might as well be he. Blake was nevertheless grateful he could never be asked to join the *Ching-pang* because he was not Chinese.

It was Shan Li who had provided—for a price—the personnel for Blake's raid. It was he who had later suggested that their intelligence had revealed that Yang Ho knew a great deal more than supposed and that Blake should go into hiding.

So on the night of the day Kate had left with Shen, Blake had made what he intended to be his last gunrunning foray for some time. When he was sure the precious contraband was safe, he had gone into hiding. He was, in fact, living in one of the *Ching-pang's* junks on the harbor. There were thousands of them, and they warned each other of approaching craft.

By the Tuesday of the following week—after he had been in hiding for ten days—Shan Li's people had secured more definite information. Yang Ho certainly knew Blake was the European who had been wounded. Yang Ho had obtained his information soon after Blake's raid. But he had wanted more detailed evidence and had been waiting for Blake to make a move in the hope of catching him red-handed or in the hope of Blake leading him to Shen. If this did not eventuate, he would arrest Blake anyway, and the lady doctor, too. Yang Ho now had men searching for Blake. The source of this information, Shan Li told Blake, was impeccable. It came from Yang Ho's most favored Chinese mistress, the girl they called Ling Ling.

Earlier, during his convalescence, Blake had thought a great deal about the likely outcome of the shooting. If he had been more conscious when they had first brought him to Kate, he might not have involved her. Perhaps he might still keep her out of it. But could he really betray Shen and the Communists to do so? And if he did, and Kate found out, would she ever forgive him?

He should really have known it was only a matter of time before one as expert as Yang Ho got to the bottom of things—particularly once a European had been shot running from the warehouse. But, of course, that was the very point—the reason Yang Ho wanted him so badly—because it had been a *second* warehouse Blake had been shot running from, not the first. Not even Shen knew about this and its importance.

But Yang Ho did. It was a second warehouse which had provided the unexpected bonus and made Blake rethink his entire operation.

The first warehouse had been relatively lightly guarded, as Shan Li's intelligence had said it would be. The Kuomintang were not expecting such a daring raid. Indeed no one was expecting a raid of any sort. They believed the Communists would not risk getting caught. And the idea of anyone else having the temerity to move against the Kuomintang was unthinkable.

Blake and his hired criminals carried out the raid on the first warehouse successfully. But during this raid an Edwards coolie-guard, whom they had bribed to help them, told of a second warehouse a short distance away. The coolie said this second warehouse was well guarded and watched over by Kuomintang soldiers. The temptation was too great. Blake and his band of thugs headed for the second warehouse.

As they approached the warehouse they could not believe their good fortune. Although there was a heavy guard of coolies, none appeared armed. There were only four soldiers—all armed—that they could see. The soldiers were all sitting together around an upended pork barrel playing cards. Blake's men were all heavily armed. It took little stealth for them to position themselves quietly near the coolies. At a set time Blake and three others stepped forward and overpowered the soldiers while the remainder of his men came suddenly into view with their weapons, threatening immediate reprisal should any coolie move. It looked like a fait accompli.

Blake could not believe it! The warehouse was full of dozens of the latest French armored vehicles with bolted metal plates and gun turrets and mounted machine guns. Blake had seen some in the closing stages of the war. But they had been relatively new inventions. And the ones he had seen had been like bicycles with mounted guns compared with these. These looked very bulky—big iron boxes with bolt-size rivets and upturned iron drums on the top. But he had no doubt about their efficiency. Nor any doubt what Yang Ho planned for these nightmare inventions of the mechanical age. These were not machines for the open country: these were street-fighting machines. It was obvious to Blake, with his military background, that Yang Ho was planning a battle in the streets of Shanghai. Any who took to the streets against this armor would be slaughtered. And he was sure the whole idea was to tempt the Communists into the streets, not knowing the army had these decisive, mass-killing, highly-mobile weapons in reserve.

Blake whistled. Whoever controlled these weapons controlled Shanghai—if not China. For it would start in Shanghai, nothing was more certain. It would start here in Shanghai, where the ferment of political unrest had always been cradled. Here, where, in such a cosmopolitan melting pot of insidious vice and non-existent virtue, schemes were plotted out in back rooms.

But if rebellion could be nipped in the bud and the leadership wiped out, the peasants in the countryside would have no one to organize them.

You had to give Yang Ho his due, Blake thought. He was a superb tactician. What a secret weapon to have in store! And what a gunrunner's dream! For if it were true that whoever controlled the armored cars controlled the future of China, then it was also true that that man could name his own price. But in so doing, he might well be deciding which philosophy, which belief system, would rule China—communism or capitalism.

Blake wasted no time getting as many men as he could spare into the armored cars and dispatching them. The venture was not without immense risk, of course. For whereas a long unused warehouse had been bought in advance to house the huge shipment of rifles, the armored vehicles had not been planned for. Blake's rule of not using his own warehouses for contraband immediately went by the board. When Shan Li's right-hand man, lent to him for the occasion to lead the others, asked where he should take the armored vehicles, Blake did not hesitate.

"To the last of my warehouses on the Bund," he said quickly. "Here. Take the key. You know the place?"

The man smiled knowingly and caught the key Blake threw him.

Blake and a few others remained behind. Two trips would be necessary to move all the vehicles. And although it was the middle of the night and his warehouse only a stone's throw away, Blake had never sweated so anxiously in his life. What if someone—anyone—let alone a soldier, saw one of these monsters trundling through the streets at night? They would be bound to report it. But not perhaps before all the vehicles were safely locked away and Blake and his men gone. And darkness and the lateness of the hour were also on his side.

The first of the drivers came running back. Blake immediately dispatched him into another vehicle. Then another arrived and then another. Blake remained behind, until the last vehicle was out. The driver waited with his vehicles while Blake bolted the warehouse, hoping to delay discovery until morning.

But just as he was locking the door a Kuomintang officer returned. The officer had obviously been out drinking or seeing a lady friend most of the night. When he arrived unexpectedly and saw Blake—and the armored car—he shouted and began shooting. Blake, running for the waiting vehicle, exchanged fire. But a bullet hit him just as he was jumping onto the running board and Blake barely managed to hold on until he was hauled to safety.

# 30

*I*t was now April 12, 1927, and according to Shan Li's sources, Yang Ho had positive evidence that Blake was the European who had been shot. He also knew Kate was the doctor who had attended him. However, Blake had subsequently moved the armored vehicles, on the previous Saturday night, to Shan Li's secret warehouses nearby. This meant Yang Ho had still not found either the stolen weapons or the armored cars. Blake suspected time was running out for him. If the Communists rose in the streets before Yang Ho got his secret weapons back, then Yang was in trouble. On the other hand, the Communists were unlikely to rise until they got their stolen weapons—the rifles from the huge train shipment Blake had promised them.

He thought about it all that first week in hiding, weighing the consequences.

They were weighty consequences indeed. Technically, of course, so far as Blake was concerned as a businessman, the small arms shipment of rifles and ammunition belonged to the Communists. They had contracted to buy them from him, paid him a fair price, and would have had them weeks ago if the government had not confiscated them.

He had organized the raid on the Edwards warehouse to

compensate for this loss and to honor his business commitment. He saw no reason to deviate from that now. Even in gunrunning one had to honor contracts. On the other hand, the armored vehicles technically belonged to the government. But Blake had possession of them and he had no doubt they would pay a handsome price to get them back. He was sure he could make a deal with Yang Ho to buy them—and buy Blake's silence for the sake of Yang Ho's superiors at the same time. Yang Ho would be sure to be keeping the disappearance of the armored cars a secret in the hope of recovering them before his superiors got to hear about it. Blake would get a signed document of receipt for the goods and explain he would make this public if it ever became necessary. This would ensure, too, that Yang Ho forgot what he knew about Blake being the European in the raid and Kate being the doctor who had attended him. The ledger would be ruled off. And it would certainly be a very neat and profitable way to do it.

But of course there were snags. If Kate ever found out—and he would have to try and ensure she didn't—there would be all hell to pay. He might argue that the armored cars were the government's anyway, but if they were used against Kate's precious Chinese poor people—even communist poor people—Kate would never condone it and he might lose her forever.

And Blake had to admit he did have a sneaking admiration for the Communists. Perhaps it had to do with having been poor and underprivileged himself when he was young. He was really only a street battler with some social veneer rubbed on the top. He had no illusions about himself and he knew most saw him as a soldier-of-fortune who would sell his own mother for the right business deal.

But that was not quite correct. And he wanted a life with Kate Richmond—probably more than he had ever wanted anything.

He began to wonder what the Communists might be able to raise for the armored cars. He supposed he could at least ask them. The Russians might lend them the money if it were important enough. And it was certainly that. But there was so little time. Would there even be time to get an answer back from Russia? And might not the Communists kill just as many as the Nationalists with the armored cars?

The wealth he had always wanted—wealth enough to eclipse

Edwards—was within his grasp. And yet he felt he was in a no-win situation. Whatever happened, the other side was going to blame him. Mind you, if the Communists got the edge because of the armored cars and tossed old Yang Ho out, it would be the start of the biggest revolution the world had ever seen—and Blake would be its official arms supplier. They would want all the weapons he could buy. It would take them at least twenty years to subdue all the Nationalists and warlords. It would be a lifetime job. Blake could retire to Hong Kong and keep them supplied from there while he became one of the richest men in the East. It bore thinking about.

Yet he knew that to deal with Yang Ho was probably the safest. The Communists were still an unknown factor. Yang Ho was not. Blake had not the slightest doubt how deadly effective would be any thrust Yang Ho made with those armored vehicles.

Was Blake about to decide in favor of Yang Ho? Perhaps. Perhaps he was about to take the safe and profitable route and try to keep the true facts from Kate. He loved her, but perhaps he was about to do that.

But just as he was about to make up his mind there was a knock at the door. He got up and opened. It was Shan Li.

"Do you have time for a visitor?" the big Chinese said. He was of huge proportions with a polished head and immaculately tailored Hong Kong clothes.

"Of course, if it is someone you trust and wish me to see and I know you would bring me none other."

Shan Li smiled and nodded appreciation at Blake's use of Chinese courtesy because he sensed the visitor was probably close by. Shan Li stood back and immediately Ling Ling moved forward.

"Why Ling Ling," Blake said courteously again, "how nice to see you. You honor my humble cabin with your presence."

Shan Li smiled and turned away. "I will send for tea," he said, as he closed the door.

Blake showed Ling Ling to a seat, noticing her serious look.

After she had sat down he drew his own chair up close to her and said, "I sense this matter is urgent with you . . ."

She nodded. "It touches Kate Richmond," she said, grateful that Blake had chosen to go straight to the heart of the matter, opening the way for her to do so, too. "She is being forced to sleep with Yang Ho. I believe she is doing this to protect you and my brother.''

Ling Ling would long remember the look on Blake's face. It was a look of cold-blooded murder. Shan Li had often said to her, ''Do not underestimate my friend Blake just because he is a round-eye. Not all are soft and stupid and he has a deadly hate all his own.''

In that moment Ling Ling knew what he meant. When Blake did eventually speak his voice was icy and deliberate.

''This cannot have been easy for you and I am very grateful,'' he said. ''It goes without saying that my house is your house and my wealth yours should you ever have need.''

''Thank you for that compliment but I am happy to help any friend of the honored Shan Li.''

Blake forced a smile. ''You know my friend Kate?''

''You have not seen her of late?''

''No.''

''So you have no way of knowing how she fares after this thing?''

''No.''

''Will you carry a message to your brother for me?''

''Tell him I have over one hundred of the latest French armored cars which Yang Ho had planned to use against him. They are his for the asking—for nothing—along with the other arms I had promised him.''

''I shall carry this message gratefully, Captain Blake,'' Ling Ling said with a bow.

''Thomas,'' he said quietly. ''My friends call me Thomas.''

She nodded again and smiled, rising to go. Blake opened the door.

''Goodbye,'' he said. ''May the day smile upon you.''

''And on you, Captain Thomas Blake.''


Blake locked the door from the inside and poured himself four fingers of rye straight up. He was furious. But he had been on the world too long to act before his anger cooled to reason.

He wondered when it had happened and why Kate had not told him. Perhaps it had only happened recently. Perhaps she could not find him. Only Shan Li knew where to find him.

Yet Blake also already knew Kate well enough to know that whenever it had happened she would not want to tell him. She would be too embarrassed. He knew she still saw him as very much a man of the world and herself as inexperienced.

Someone would pay! My God someone would pay! But he would need Shan Li's help. He unlocked his door and walked along the companionway to Shan Li's office. A big burly sampan sailor stood guard at the door but admitted Blake immediately.

Shan Li's floating office was full of exquisite teak furniture and priceless jade art objects. His gold-inlay antique desk had belonged to a Ming emperor. Shan Li liked to live well.

He gestured with his hand for Blake to sit in the chair facing his desk.

"Tea?"

Blake shook his head.

"Something stronger?"

Blake nodded.

"Of course. Whiskey?"

Blake nodded again and Shan Li held up four fingers to the giant sampan man. Shan Li made no attempt to speak until the man had poured two large measures without ice or water, handed them out, and left the room, closing the door behind him.

"You know the facts of this matter?" Blake asked.

"Of course. No one speaks to anyone under my protection without first telling me what they wish to say. You do not mind?"

"Of course not. I would expect it. Without your friendship I may not have received this information, for which I am very grateful. But because of the nature of this problem I must ask your help once more. Although it is a plan which may still yield us each a tidy profit as well as fulfilling my purpose of revenge."

"Speak on, my friend. We have both been in this profit business since we learned our terrible habits in the streets of this great city, have we not? What do you have in mind?"

"It concerns the armored vehicles which I found almost by accident the night of the raid and recently moved to safety in one of your warehouses."

"The lieutenant I lent you that night did mention something of it," Shan Li said with a wry grin.

"I believe Yang Ho would pay handsomely to have them back," Blake said casually.

"More than handsomely. What price did you have in mind?"

"One million pounds sterling."

"That is more than handsomely. That is a lot—even for Yang Ho."

"Your share would be 20 percent."

"I'm sure we can make Yang Ho see reason. My role would be to act as middleman, to keep you both honest, I take it?"

Blake nodded.

"Tell me how your plan would operate," Shan Li said as he took out a box of Cuban cigars.

"I will go to Yang Ho immediately and say you hold the key to a warehouse where the cars are hidden, on my behalf. If he accepts the deal, he must pass the money—all of it—to you at noon tomorrow in a pre-arranged spot. You will then send the money to me. We will allow one hour for me to count it or verify that it is not counterfeit, whether it is in cash or bank draft. Then, on my acceptance of the money, you will give Yang Ho the key and tell him where the vehicles are hidden . . . at least that is what you will appear to do . . ."

Shan Li looked up suddenly. "I like my word to be worth something, Thomas, and double-crossing Yang Ho is fraught with danger. I assume that is what you are planning—to raid my own warehouse and steal the armored cars back in the one-hour time gap allowed for verification of money . . . ?"

"Precisely. I am truly sorry about your word, old friend. It is indeed worth a great deal. What value would you put on it?"

"Oh I think something closer to 30 percent than 20 percent—what do you think? I don't want to be greedy."

"I think 30 percent is fine . . . Agreed?"

"Agreed." They both laughed and got up and walked towards each other to shake hands.

"It is a great swindle, Thomas, a great swindle. Yang Ho will be furious. Once word gets out he has paid one million pounds for armored cars he does not have—which were stolen from him to begin with and which he had already paid for—he will be finished. I doubt he would even get a commission in Manchuria. They will be duty-bound to court-martial him for misappropriation of army funds—which is exactly what you had in mind, I suppose?"

"Exactly. It also means, with Yang Ho removed, that it would be unlikely Kate or I would be prosecuted. Yang Ho has no real evidence he could pass on—only the flimsiest of reports from some apartment building spy, I suspect. Hardly enough for an international trial of two American nationals. No, he would have been hoping eventually to force Kate into a confession by his repeated humiliation of her.''

Shan Li nodded. "There will also be another end result, Thomas," Shan Li said, smiling even broader now.

"What's that, old friend?"

"The money, Thomas . . . the money you make from this deal will undoubtedly make you 'Numero Uno' in Shanghai—far richer than even your old arch enemy Edwards . . ."

"Yes, that is an interesting side-effect of the deal, isn't it?" Blake said, smiling garrulously to himself now, and then adding, "although, of course, it is always only 'Numero Uno' next to yourself, my friend . . ."

"True. But then you make the money legally . . . well . . . almost . . ."

They laughed again and had another drink to seal the bargain.

Then Blake went and showered and changed. Two hours later, in an enormous black limousine, he presented himself at the front gate of Army General Headquarters and asked to see General Yang Ho. It was time to trade.

Shan Li had not asked Blake what he intended to do with the armored cars after he stole them back, but that was a typical Shan Li response. Blake's business was Blake's business. Of course, the plan depended on both men trusting Shan Li. But Blake was sure Yang Ho would be arrogant enough to believe no one would ever dare cross him—not even the head of the *Ching-pang*. Both Blake and Shan Li, of course, were counting on Yang Ho not being around afterwards to get his revenge on them. But Blake really didn't expect to have much trouble persuading Yang Ho. The Communists could rise any day now that they had been outlawed. And Yang Ho could not risk being without his special armored car defenses.

If Blake's plan worked, he and Kate would be free. It would also be the beginning of the end of Yang Ho and his old enemy, Edwards.

The orderlies wasted no time in ushering Blake into the general's presence.

Yang Ho sat behind a large, ornate desk. He made no effort to rise. Instead he gave a cursory wave of his hand towards a chair. Rather pointedly he did not offer Blake tea.

"So, Captain Blake," he said, "let us forget, eh, Oriental niceties and get down to business. I have impeccable evidence that you were the European shot while escaping with a considerable shipment of government arms."

Blake went to talk but Yang Ho held up his hand and continued:

"It is senseless to protest. But there will be plenty of opportunity to do so under military law in due course if that is what you wish."

Blake smiled and saw that his smile unnerved Yang just a little.

"Let us not waste each other's time, General," he said. "I have not come here to protest, nor to give myself up. I am a businessman and I have come to trade. I have something I believe your government wants. It is available for a price, including a letter of indemnity, signed by you, that myself and Doctor Richmond dined with you on a certain night."

Yang Ho rose slowly from his desk and walked over to the big window which looked down on the boulevards below.

"Are you seriously suggesting I should provide you and your mistress with an alibi and that my government should pay for its own armored vehicles twice over? We *are* talking of armored vehicles, I take it . . . ?"

"Certainly," Blake said. "But are they your vehicles. Had you officially taken delivery of them? Or were they just stored in an Edwards warehouse awaiting delivery? If you hadn't taken delivery—and therefore presumably hadn't paid—does it really matter from whom you get them? Why pay your agent when they were so poorly guarded? Was not that his responsibility? Besides, the sooner you get this particular shipment, the surer you are that they will not fall into other hands."

Yang Ho turned sharply from the window and walked back to his desk.

A look had come into his eyes—a look approaching respect. He certainly had an admiration for a worthy opponent and Blake was proving to be that. He permitted himself a smile. "It may be possible to divert certain funds before they reach their destination," he said. "Such an action, of course, would doubtless have the effect of placing Sir Nigel Edwards close to bankruptcy, since he will still have to pay his suppliers. Such weapons cost far more than he will have at his command. And it will place you in a position of extreme wealth.''

"True.''

"What is the price?''

"One million pounds sterling plus commission for a middleman to act as an honest broker between us.''

Yang Ho looked at Blake again with even greater respect. It was an exorbitant price. Yet it was within what he might pay. It was true Edwards had not yet been paid. And Yang Ho did, as Blake knew only too well, need those armored vehicles. The communist threat was now grave. It was dangerous enough that even one outsider—Blake—knew of the existence of the armored vehicles. Blake was unlikely to tell the Communists what he was selling. But if one person could find out, so could others.

"One million pounds then, Captain Blake,'' Yang Ho said suddenly with a smile. "One million pounds.''

Blake then explained the conditions of delivery. Yang Ho refused.

But gradually Blake worked him around. Could he not trust Shan Li? After all, Shan Li had to live with the authorities in Shanghai. He was unlikely to do anything to incur the wrath of the man who some said was more powerful even than the Generalissimo Chiang Kai-shek himself. Yang Ho agreed with this proposition and said Shan Li was a worthy intermediary. He said he even understood Blake's position of having to be sure the money had been paid over before the goods were released and that the only fair way was to have an intermediary both sides trusted.

So in the end he agreed to the terms because, as Blake had known, he had no other choice. He needed those armored cars within twenty-four hours if he were to hold Shanghai. And if the Communists moved that night, Shanghai could well be lost.

So it was agreed that the transfer of money and arms would take place the next day at noon and one o'clock, respectively. At the same time Yang Ho would provide Shan Li with the alibi letter Blake had asked for, and a full receipt for the transaction, which Blake made clear he would not hesitate to publish if Yang Ho was ever tempted to ignore the alibi he had provided or say he had signed under duress.

* * *

Just before noon the next day Shan Li stepped ashore from a
motor boat which had brought him from his junk. He got into a
waiting limousine. The big black automobile moved a short
distance and then stopped opposite the Yokohama Specie Bank
of Shanghai on the Bund.

Yang Ho's limousine, with general's pennant flying, stood
parked outside the bank.

Presently a colonel emerged from the bank carrying a big
metal box and stepped into the rear of the automobile in which
Yang Ho still sat, and the vehicle did a U-turn to pull up beside
Shan Li on the river side of the Bund where there was a small
rest area. It was here the two men had chosen for their exchange
after Shan Li had phoned Yang Ho once the details of the deal
had been set.

Yang Ho emerged from his automobile with the colonel still
carrying the money and waited while Shan Li's driver opened the
back door of his master's car for them.

The curtained back half of Shan Li's vehicle was large and
sumptuous, and Yang Ho complimented him on it as he and the
colonel entered and sat down. They were offered drinks and
while they sipped them the metal box was passed over to the
front seat where a bespectacled gentleman immediately took it
and departed.

"A word on your own if you please . . . ?" Shan Li said
courteously to Yang Ho.

Yang nodded and the colonel stepped out.

"Now," Shan Li said, as soon as they were alone, "we must
move fast and it will be necessary for you to trust me even more
than you have done this day already . . ."

Yang Ho went to speak but Shan Li waved him silent.

"Nothing is more crucial to the future of Shanghai than what I
am about to tell you. In a few minutes' time Blake will raid my
warehouse where he has had stored the armored vehicles . . ."

A look of incredulity appeared on Yang Ho's face, but Shan
Li continued speaking without pause.

"But have no fear, he will not find the vehicles. I had them
moved last night and the moment Blake has the money as
agreed, you will get the vehicles as agreed. He will get the

money he wants, I will get my share, and you will get the armored cars. But Blake must have his indemnity. I must have your word on it and I must have the indemnity papers you promised him before I will release the vehicles to you.''

Yang Ho looked at him. His latest intelligence reports said the Communists would move that night.

"Blake had promised the armored cars to the Communists, then—?'' he asked of Shan Li.

"I do not know. All I know is that he intended for you not to have them, and the Communists are certainly a likely alternative. He wished you disgraced because you stupidly forced his woman into bed with you . . .''

Yang Ho's anger rose and his hand tightened on his riding crop. Then he thought better of it. Already he was beginning to have his own plans for Blake. In any case he could not afford a head-on confrontation with the leader of the *Ching-pang*. Besides, although few knew, Shan Li and Yang Ho were already partners in a number of brothels which Yang Ho encouraged his men to use. Yang Ho did not like not having the upper hand, but at least this way he would not be disgraced; he would get the armored cars and would only have had to pay for them once. As even Blake had pointed out, there was no question of paying Edwards. He would have to settle with the French suppliers himself. It would bankrupt him, of course—or bring him to the verge of it. But Yang Ho also knew he was as good at vengeance as Blake appeared to be. He would find a way to level the score.

"What of Blake's lady friend, Katherine Richmond?'' Yang Ho said.

"She is of no concern to me. She is a foreign devil . . .''

"So is Blake . . .''

"That is different. He was kind to me as a boy and took me home when I was a street urchin . . . Touch him and you touch me . . .''

Yang Ho knew what that meant. As leader of the *Ching-pang* Shan Li was like the head of a Mafia family—no, more—he was like the head of all the Mafia families . . . He had powerful friends.

"But I may do as I like with the girl . . . ? It is agreed?''

Shan Li looked at Yang Ho. One always had to give in on something in bargaining like this.

"It is agreed," he said. "Provided I have the indemnity documents, whatever you do to her is your business . . . only do not tell Blake I said so . . ."

Yang Ho nodded. His hand was already reaching into his tunic pocket.

"I believe you require these documents," he said, passing over the indemnity letter and the receipt which Blake had requested.

Shan Li perused them quickly and nodded. Then he leaned forward and tapped on the glass partition in front of him. The driver, who was his sampan guard, passed a small piece of paper through the glass partition and closed it once more.

"At this address . . . in one hour," Shan Li said as he passed over the piece of paper with some words typed on it.

Yang Ho stared at it. "It will take me at least an hour to get there," he said, astonished. "It is almost out of town."

"Exactly. That way we know we all trust each other because there is time for my men who stand guard there to be alerted and move the merchandise once more should you try to do something silly like trying to find Blake and take back the money."

Yang Ho grunted and pushed open the door nearest him, snapping his fingers. Immediately the colonel was at his side to hold the door wider and salute.

Shan Li reached out and placed his arm on Yang Ho's. The grip was vice-like.

"Never turn your back on me again, Yang. You are one of the few who have ever dared to do that. Today I have betrayed a friend and it does not sit well with me. But I will not have the Communists come to power in Shanghai. They would close the brothels and drug dens which support you and me so adequately. But be under no illusions that I like you or have done this to help you. I have done it for myself. You must move tonight and I have already held a meeting of my *Ching-pang* family heads. We have worked out a plan for you. We will supply personnel in plain clothes to help camouflage your initial thrust so that the Communists will be caught by surprise. Other criminal bodies— even some Western crime syndicates operating here—have agreed to help. The Communists must not come to power—here or anywhere else in China. You have a great opportunity to end the communist threat before it starts. Do not fumble it. We will arrange to have the back door of the International Settlement opened to you so you may strike first from that direction where you will be least expected. Quietly mobilize your forces now and be ready at the International Settlement by sunset . . .''

He let his arm drop from Yang Ho's.

Yang Ho was fuming. "You are trying to tell me how to mount a military operation . . ." he spluttered angrily.

"A military operation for which I am providing the armored vehicles and several hundred trained assassins. Do not think lightly of these Communists. Your men still fight in the ancient Chinese way of marching to beautiful music. These Communists fight like Genghis Khan's mongols . . .''

Shan Li slammed the door and motioned for his driver to move off.

When Blake found Shan Li's warehouse empty he was furious and drove straight to the dock area where he had agreed to meet Shan Li on his launch to collect the money. Shan Li's guard barred Blake's way as he saw him approaching. Blake's German Mauser pistol rested in his trouser band—a precaution he had taken on all his gun-running expeditions and which had probably helped save his life on the night he was shot.

Blake did not hesitate. He was angry; perhaps too angry. He was sure Shan Li had betrayed him. As he neared the burly guard he drew his pistol and butt-whipped the man across the head. The guard tumbled onto the deck with a thud as Blake jumped aboard and rushed below.

Shan Li stood in the cabin before him, making no effort to move.

Blake's gun was still drawn.

"How could you . . . !" Blake stormed at him, the gun raised, "how could you betray me after all we've been through together . . . ?"

Shan Li pushed a metal box across the table between them. "There is your one million pounds, Thomas, and Edwards is ruined. Was that not your plan?"

"You know damn well it went further than that . . . I wanted Yang Ho to pay . . . to pay for what he did to Kate. . . . Pay in such a way he could never threaten us again . . . her or me. . . . This deal was to buy our happiness . . . a life together without the threat of Yang Ho's retribution. . . . You . . . of all people . . . !''

Shan Li looked genuinely pained at the hurt and distrust he now saw in Blake's eyes.

"You are the last person in this city I would wish to betray, Thomas, you know that. You were the only one to befriend me as a poor orphan boy, and this is a debt not lightly turned aside. But I have people who depend on me for their livelihood . . . I have thousands of families of the *Ching-pang* and *pao chia* to support . . . I could not risk the Communists taking over in Shanghai, Thomas, you must see that. It would have been the end of business for me and my people . . . and for your people . . . the end of business for profit as we know it . . . the end of free enterprise . . .''

"The end of your damned drug trade and prostitution . . .'' Blake retorted, lowering his gun.

"True, Thomas, true. But I could not return to poverty again. Or even to money without power . . . in that we are both alike, you and I. . . . The streets taught us this indelible lesson very young. I am sorry you cannot have your revenge on Yang Ho . . . but then, revenge, too, can prove a costly merchandise. But you have your freedom, Thomas, you and your lady friend . . .''

Shan Li paused to throw a large thick envelope on the table.

"Here are the documents you were promised,'' he continued, "freeing you both from fear of prosecution. And if you will still take some advice from an old friend, you should seek her out immediately and both return to my junk as soon as possible, ready to sail. I will leave the launch standing by . . .''

"What on earth for . . . ?''

"The tide has now turned in Shanghai, Thomas. In a few hours this will be a very different city.''

Only a fool would have failed to understand what Shan Li was telling him; only someone as powerful as Shan Li could have known.

Blake was wracked with anxiety for Kate. Suddenly he knew nothing else mattered but to find her—and find her quickly. Shan Li had said he must find her immediately. And Shan Li was not a man to say such things lightly. The danger was imminent. It was now well past noon. Whatever raging, conflicting emotions threatened to toss even Blake's normally controlled nature, all else must take second place to the search for Kate. All his good fortune—the ruin of his old enemy, Edwards, and Blake's wind-fall profit—turned sour in the face of betrayal by his old friend and now the frightening danger to Kate. Somewhere out there were one hundred armored cars Yang Ho obviously planned to use—and Kate was on the other side, a known Communist sympathizer. Blake must find her, he must! But even as he picked up the metal box of money and turned to leave, throwing a preemptory farewell over his shoulder to Shan Li, another sickening thought was tugging at his insides. After all these years of philandering, after all he had done to claw his way to the top, he now had Kate to love, wonderful Kate, and the power and money he had always sought as well. At least he would have said so, until a few minutes ago. Now he saw his whole world tumbling down. His double dealings, despite his good intentions, could finally cost him the one thing he had ever cared about more than money—could cost him the beautiful, soft, blonde, winsome, yet strong person called Kate Richmond. He must find her. He must.

Kate was, in fact, barely a stone's throw away—at Lu Chien's house with Wu, Shen, Hwang, and Yu-Ma. She had received an urgent note at the hospital, delivered just before noon, and just after her last operation for the day. It requested her urgent presence, preferably with her medical bag, at Lu Chien's house. The note had asked her not to mention a word of this to anyone.

She had hurriedly filled her bag to capacity and taken, on an impulse, her larger, square bag of medicines also. She was convinced someone must have been wounded. It had even crossed her mind it might have been Blake again.

Fortunately she had nothing pressing for the rest of the afternoon and was able to arrange for another doctor to handle her private practice.

As she hurried out, clutching both bags, the sight of a waiting car did nothing to dispel her anxiety. Shen's people had so few cars.

When she arrived at Lu Chien's Kate was taken aback. She had thought at most there might have been a small demonstration, with troops firing into a crowd; or another abortive attempt to get the arms they so desperately wanted, with some of their people getting wounded. There were no wounded—but the house was like a battle command post. There were maps and weapons everywhere and dozens of people coming and going.

It was already, for Kate, one of those days when one is caught up in events which sweep you along; one of those days when you are part of a larger whole whether you like it or not; one of those times when a decision is made for you; one of those occasions when the timing of everything is heightened because of the nature of things happening, so that all decisions are telescoped into one, so that everything seems to happen in a split-second, to be viewed later.

How could she prevent herself from being drawn into this emotionally charged vortex in which she now found herself? Might she not, even now, return to the hospital? Even inside Lu Chien and Wu's house she could sense the whole tempo of the city quickening. And certainly inside the house no one left any doubt that the day of reckoning had finally arrived.

Shen was bending over maps spread out on a table, issuing commands.

"I am sorry to ask your help yet again, Kate Doctor," he said when he saw her, "but I fear for our people if they do not have medical help standing by. There are other doctors coming but there are so very few. You are the only non-Chinese. You do not mind?"

She looked at him. "Oh Shen, please don't," she said. She could see in her mind's eye the destruction of her beloved China in the events being planned that night. She was on the stage of the world and only dimly aware of all about her, but she knew it threatened the peace and tranquillity she prized so highly.

Shen looked at her and smiled a faraway, forlorn smile, a smile lost somewhere over the hills of China a thousand centuries ago. He sensed what she was thinking.

"Oh Katherine," he said at last, taking her aside from his maps for a moment, "oh Katherine, if only I could save your old China for you—yours and mine. But to preserve its things of beauty is also to preserve its age-old inequities. To preserve it is to preserve all the Yang Ho's, all the bad uncles, all the starving peasants and their children, all the years of failed crops and no medicines and no doctors. No, Katherine, the time is now. I have set my face towards the Forbidden City and will not rest until I reach it, though I fear it will be the longest march of all. But for the moment all we wish is to break out of Shanghai to join with other Communists in the North. But the authorities here will not let us leave, of this we are sure.''

Kate breathed a sigh of relief. "So you are not planning to try to overthrow the government of the city?'' she said.

Shen shook his head. "It is unlikely now. Perhaps that might have been a possibility once, but not now. Now we will be lucky to escape with our lives. We have received an intelligence report which we are having checked. I find it hard to believe but I have asked Ling Ling to check it and to do so she must put herself at great risk . . .'' He paused and then continued, as if making a deliberate decision to go further. "But there is news of Blake. He is all right . . . of this, too, I will know more later. I am sorry, but that is all I can tell you at present. We will know more towards nightfall.''

And at that he turned abruptly back to his map table.

Shen was greatly worried but trying not to show it. He had been overjoyed when Ling Ling had brought news that Blake would give them the armored cars. He had not even known of their existence. News of them had made armed insurrection a very likely possibility. But there was still no word from Blake. And worse—there was actually a disturbing report that Blake had sold out to Yang Ho. It came from a source within Yang Ho's own headquarters. The White Army—the name given to Yang Ho's Chinese Army to distinguish them from Shen's Reds—was also quietly mobilizing, the report said.

This was why Shen had put his evacuation plan into operation. If there was any chance—any chance at all—that Yang Ho was about to move and that something had gone wrong with the plan for the Communists to get the armored cars, then Shen's plan for armed insurrection was out of the question. They must flee—and the sooner the better.

He had sent Ling Ling to try to check these reports.

Blake had run out of places to look. He had been to Kate's apartment, but she wasn't there. He had been to the hospital—only to hear that Kate was off duty. He had been to the clinic—a place he had never visited before—but her mother had not seen her. And his visit there had unnerved him even more. The place was deserted. Kate had often told him how crowded it always was. And when Blake had remarked on this to Kate's mother, she had said, "True enough. This is the quietest day I've known in forty years. Must be a Chinese holiday or something—though I thought I knew them all."

Blake hurried even more now, in his chauffeur-driven limousine, to Janey's residence atop the hill overlooking the sea. He had heard she was sometimes there during the day.

"Where on earth have *you* been?" Janey said when she saw him. "Kate's been looking for you everywhere, night and day."

"There's no time to explain. Do you know where she is? I have to see her."

"Don't have the faintest idea," Janey said, shaking her head, "and it's just as well Daddy's not here, either, seeing it's you who's doing the asking."

Blake wondered for a moment if Edwards had already found out what he'd done. But he couldn't have. It was just Janey speaking of the age-old feud.

"I must find her, Jane, I must," Blake said urgently.

"There's always her Chinese friends," Janey said. "I know she's been seeing a lot of them recently, asking about you. I seem to have seen less and less of her since we moved into the apartment together. I rather surmised it was because of you."

But Blake did not respond. Her Chinese friends! Of course! How could he have been so stupid!

"Thank you, Jane, you've been most helpful," he said as he turned quickly and took off down the colonnaded stairs.

Shen! Of course, Shen! Who else? He had noticed their growing friendship. Blake wished he hadn't had to hide so completely. The fact that he and Kate had had an argument the last time they had met still worried him.

But a little relieved now, he jumped back into his limousine and ordered the driver to Shanghai railway station.

Yet ominously, when they reached the station and Blake ran inside, not one of the Chinese he knew could be seen.

He immediately thought of Lu Chien and Wu. But he no longer knew where to find them. He had heard they had sold all their goods and moved into the poorer part of town. The poor quarter at the back of the Bund. But would he ever find them? Or Shen? Shen had always contacted him. But if he could find Lu Chien, she might be persuaded to take him to Shen. Someone must know where she and Wu were living. Who did he know who knew them? He would have to try and backtrack through friends. Damn! It was five o'clock already. It suddenly seemed doubly urgent to find Kate before it got dark.

It was six o'clock before he got even the remotest lead on where Lu Chien lived—once again through the ubiquitous all-seeing eyes of the *Ching-pang* and Shan Li. But it was only the vaguest of directions. He knew the general area and hurried there. Then, with the dark now descending, and Blake sending his car away because a rich man's car would only be a hindrance in this poor neighborhood, he set out once more to find Kate. In any case, he would move quicker on foot. He knew the backstreets and gutter-language from his childhood. He pulled his coat collar up to hide his shirt and tie. His mood was as dark as it had ever been. Yet despite this, there was something else which worried him more and put an even greater urgency into his step.

First he saw it just at a house here, and a house there. And then, as he got farther into the poorest part of town where few ever ventured unless they had to, it was on every fourth house or so. And then every third. And then every second. And eventually every single one. Over each door post, or *lintel,* as it was once called, like a smear of blood, was nailed a large piece of cheap, red, Chinese New Year's paper.

As dusk set in, preparations in the Communist command post reached a fever pitch. But eventually, when it was fully dark outside, all except Shen, Wu, Lu Chien, Hwang, Yu-Ma, and Kate had been evacuated. Wang Lee was out scouting the city. Shen had decided that come what may, whether or not Ling Ling arrived with the information they needed, they must make their move that night. There were pre-arranged staging areas—such as houses and warehouses—all around the city. People were now being sent there for mass evacuation. The houses had to be marked with red paper because many of the people going could neither read nor write.

Just as Lu Chien was preparing a little food and tea, there was a loud knocking at the door.

Lu Chien, moving more urgently than normal, shuffled quickly towards it and opened.

It was Ling Ling. She stood there, obviously breathless. Shen, relieved to see she was all right, beckoned her inside.

"Forgive this discourtesy but there is no time for greetings," she said. "You must all leave the city immediately. The foreigners have let Yang Ho's men in through the back door of the International Settlement and any moment now they will attack the workers. You must leave or you will all be killed. Shan Li and the *Ching-pang* have also had paid informants among you. They are rounding up your leaders now. You have only minutes. I must go. Forgive me honorable friends. I must not be found here. I have brought a car for you. It is stolen. It is outside with the keys in it."

Because of those she slept with, because of the house she lived in, because of her range of high informants who sought her favors at banquets and balls, no one doubted the accuracy of Ling Ling's information. Wu was already moving hastily to pick up a bag kept near the door. Lu Chien picked up stitched padded jackets and pants which had been lying ready. For weeks, for months, perhaps years, they had known that sooner or later this night would come.

"And the armored vehicles with machine guns on top . . . ?" Shen cut in as Ling Ling paused.

Ling Ling turned towards Kate with a look of compassion Kate would long remember. Then Ling Ling turned back to Shen.

"It was Blake—as you supposed," she said. "The army ordered these vehicles to use against demonstrators. But Blake found them when he raided the warehouse. He has now sold them back to the army. Even now the vehicles are being ordered into the streets to block your escape."

"I don't believe it," Kate said incredulously. "He couldn't . . . he wouldn't." But her words sounded hollow. And she kept remembering his first smile, not his second; the hard cynical, world-weary smile.

"It is true, *Yang Kwei*," Ling Ling said gently, using the word for *foreign devil*, but with a tone of great compassion and kindness. "Yang Ho found out Blake was both the gunrunner shot escaping and the patient you would not name on the form for blood . . ."

"Capitalist running dog," Shen said vehemently, "I should never have trusted him. I should never have trusted a man whose main motivation was greed. All our worst fears of his betrayal have now been realized. I was right to suspect his motives and to mobilize for evacuation just in case. And yet I had hoped against hope that I was wrong . . . that we might still seize power and see victory here in Shanghai first. Now all that is lost and we must flee if we are to avoid being wiped out."

Kate was stunned; sick to the stomach. She felt like her knees were about to buckle. She felt like she was to blame. She could not believe the strength of Shen's reaction. He was usually so controlled. Then she saw Hwang, the usually kind and gentle Hwang, clear his throat and go to the brass spitoon in the corner and spit in disgust.

Wu, the ultimate master of controlled emotion, simply took his Mauser pistol from his traveling bag, cocked it, and said quietly, "We must leave now as Ling Ling says and be prepared to shoot our way out. But one day I shall return for Captain Thomas Blake and there will be a day of reckoning. His actions this day have put our cause back years."

There was almost more venom in his controlled, cold-blooded statement than in Shen's anger.

Lu Chien was crying.

Kate's initial disbelief was suddenly dissipating into deep, deep hurt at the betrayal of her friends; at her own betrayal. Blake must have known what this would mean to her. He had as good as put his lust for power and greed ahead of his love for her. She had thought he had changed. That she had had a softening effect on him. That her love had made him more humane. Now she could see that she had been wrong. Oh how wrong she had been! And now all her friends—her dear old trusted friends and her newfound friends—were in mortal peril because of him.

Just then there was the sound of rapid gunfire in the distance.

"I will drive you all to the edge of the city," Kate said, picking up her medical bags. "It will be safer for you. It will look better with a Westerner driving."

They all nodded gratefully. Kate was relieved to see their enmity for Blake did not extend to her.

Shen looked at his sister. "Will things go well with you?" he said urgently, as she turned to go.

She shrugged a little, to indicate who would know such things, and gave her courtesan's smile. It was slightly tense and forced.

"You are welcome to come," Shen said.

"This city and its ways are my home and family both. I will take my chances here."

"Even your old mandarin may not be safe," Wu cautioned as he narrowly opened the front door and cast his eyes into the street. "Come with us. This will be a very different government from the old one."

"Thank you, but I will stay," Ling Ling said. "If there is danger for my master, this is another reason not to flee. But you will be as dead men if you do not leave immediately."

Ling looked quickly around the room at them all one more time. Then she hugged her brother tightly and, before the tears could come, slipped out through the opening in the door.

As she disappeared down the street and around the corner on foot, the others hurried out to the car. Kate took the wheel and started the engine.

But as she pulled out from the curb, an armored car careened around the corner behind them, overtook them, and shot across their front, ramming them against the curb. The car stalled and Kate tried desperately to start it again but the front was stoved in. Just then the soldiers started shouting, "Champi, Champi!" —"Shoot, Shoot! Let them be shot!"—as they jumped out and ran towards them.

At these words, Shen, Wu, and the others drew their mausers and opened fire. Lu Chien screamed.

Taking an incredible risk—as two of the men in uniform went down and shots were still being exchanged—the superbly fit Yu-Ma jumped from the stolen car and with two strides covered the distance to the armored vehicle. Without looking or appearing to give it a second thought, he emptied three shots into the driver's seat from the crouched position in which he had landed.

With his fourth bullet he hit one of the uniformed men in the back. Shen, who had now joined him, shot the other.

"Pull out the driver's body!" Shen shouted. "We must take their car . . . Run . . . !" he shouted back to the others. Run . . . !"

They all immediately jumped out and made for the armored vehicle. It was not until she was halfway there that Kate realized the significance of what she was doing.

Her stomach left her. She stopped in mid-stride. People were filling the streets. Her friends were jumping into the armored car. She must go back. Another armored car might arrive any minute. She was not with these people! She was not fleeing. She turned and ran back towards the other car to get her bags, running in fear and feeling every muscle tense and every nerve twitch. She felt she would vomit as she ran.

She reached the car and wrenched it open. Where were her bags? She found and grabbed them and began to run once more. But where was she to go? She had been seen. Even if she tried to run away it would be no use. Even if she made it back to the hospital they would come for her. Once the shooting had started she was, in a sense, captive—a prisoner by force of circumstance. The others were shouting even louder at her now. She knew it was no use. She had no alternative. With tears in her eyes, and a medical bag in each hand, she turned and ran—ran for the armored car—ran stumbling and in tears.

Finally she reached the vehicle and fell into it. Wu was in the driver's seat. As he pulled out, Kate felt the sickly ache of loss beginning in her already. She knew that the shots fired had turned on her. The fortunes of war—the rise and fall of human nature—had added her to its list of victims.

She knew that until the time she had stopped and run back, she might have stayed in Shanghai. Until then she was just one running figure among other running figures—albeit the only white one. But once she had stopped, with people coming out of the houses, she was a recognizable figure. One they would have seen visit the house of the Communists in the street many times: the doctor lady whose photograph was often in the social pages of the newspapers. She had now been involved in the shooting of Nationalist troops and was identifiable as a Kuomintang enemy. By a sudden bullet of fate her whole karma had been changed.

By a sudden bullet of fate her lot had been cast with the fugitive Communists. By this same bullet she had been suddenly wrenched from the only man she had ever loved, who, she now realized through her tears, she might never see again.

And as if this were not enough, as they bundled themselves breathlessly into the Khaki Kuomintang armor-plated vehicle and took off at high speed along the bloodied street, she looked back and saw a sight that would haunt her the rest of her days. Staring back through the small oval visor at the rear of the car, she saw, in the distance, coming around the corner quickly to the sound of shooting, the one person no one in that car wanted to see except she. Blake! Had the others seen him? No. They were all too intent on looking to the front. Did *she* even want to see him? She felt her stomach heaving again.

It would have been enough anxiety for a lifetime to have been shot at, at almost point-blank range, as she had a few minutes earlier, without all these other things tearing at her as well. To be cut off from one's deepest love, cut off suddenly and without warning, and to have to handle this at the same time, was almost more than she could bear. But on top of that it had to happen by betrayal, and a particularly selfish, violent betrayal by one . . . By one with whom she had been so intimate!

It all seemed, in that moment, to threaten her very being. And, as if this were not enough, there was still the chaotic tumult of the escape. Here she was, by no fault of her own, suddenly part of the Communist revolution. She had had no say in it. Suddenly she had been catapulted right into the middle of it. But she tried desperately to push the tumult of present external events to the back of her mind as she attempted to deal with the emotional chaos heaving inside her.

How could Blake have done this to her? For, whatever he had done, she felt it a personal slight. He had done it to *her*. She loved him so—or had loved him—or might still, she was so confused. Yet he had done this to her! Had their nights of passion, their lingering moments of tenderness, meant nothing to him?

She continued to look back.

He was still running after the car, shouting something, something she could not hear. She tried desperately to make out the words. And then, as she could lip-read what he was saying, her confusion worsened and turned to tears. He knew she was there! He must have seen her jump into the armored car and he was shouting out to her—shouting out aloud for all the world to hear the words he had so often whispered to her in the middle of the night but which were the last words she wanted to hear this day because she felt so betrayed. He was shouting, she was sure, "Kate, Kate, I love you," and she couldn't handle those words today. She didn't think she ever could again after what he had done.

She looked back until he was lost in the distance.

Wu and Shen sat in the front seat, Shen giving directions as they tried to run the blockade in their stolen French armored car.

Yang Ho's Kuomintang had indeed launched a surprise attack through the International Settlement, as Ling Ling had said. It was obvious to Shen, given the strength of Yang Ho's attack, that he must have had help from Western allies anxious to stop the rising tide of unionism and communism in Shanghai. It was not until later that he learned that some of the men riding around in the armored cars, dressed in Kuomintang uniforms, were the armed guards of Shanghai mobsters, sent by their masters to capture and kill those who would oppose their Shanghai operations of drugs, prostitution, gambling, and professional kidnapping. Yang's troops had moved in from one side, and the gangsters from the other—from the European settlement which the Communists had considered safe.

Kate and her friends in the car were desperately turning corner after corner in an attempt to head off another confrontation and escape into the night. But as they swung into a main street leading to the Bund—which they could not avoid if they were to get away—they came face to face with the horror of that infamous night.

Even those in the back could smell and hear, and of this night that was enough.

In the side streets the noise of gunfire and the cries of people had been muffled.

But once into a main thoroughfare, in the uneasy light on the Shanghai night, there was suddenly the exploding noise of rapid fire, the pungent smell of cordite in the air, a drifting pall of smoke, cries of death and anguish, people running and shouting, and a sewer smell of gutted, dripping bodies, as armored cars charged people.

Everywhere was that rampaging shout of "Champi!" "Champi!"—"Shoot them! Shoot them!—Let them be shot!"

Kate was now sick all over herself. They swerved and swerved—around people and vehicles—as they drove on in this nightmare of a night.

What they were witnessing, Kate now began thinly to realize, was a massacre. The troops—Yang's troops, Chinese troops of the Kuomintang, the army which had been part of the First Revolution of 1911—was now systematically annihilating its own people because the revolution had gone too far.

Kate feared, from her knowledge of China, that events had now been set in motion for which neither side would ever forgive the other: events which, in terms of murder, lust, and intrigue on the grand scale, would make the drama of ancient Rome look like a poor performance by an unknown theatrical group.

Somehow, miraculously, Kate and her group eventually got to the edge of town. From the start they had been heading in the direction of the mouth of the Yangtze. Shen's military genius was already becoming apparent. The entire thrust of Kuomintang had been to contain the Communists within the city, surrounded by Kuomintang troops on three sides and by forces of the secret societies on the fourth side.

But Shen believed the Kuomintang would not have been able to bring boats up to block the river without alerting communist leaders in the city. And the entire aim of the operation had been to surprise and contain the Communists within the city itself—probably the greatest concentration of Communists in China at that time.

Shen's view of the Kuomintang's river strategy turned out to be true. He and his party abandoned their armored car in the lee of a bank and walked cautiously to where Shen knew of a group of sampan families who were Communists. They had a good smart young leader who, at the sound of the shooting in the city, had readied their two boats for sea. The leader had been a little reluctant to leave immediately, for fear he was abandoning his city comrades. His willingness to wait had probably saved their lives.

As soon as Shen and his party were aboard, the young man ordered those of the great, long pole tillers to push out. Soon, as the great Yangtze wind caught the sails, the giant tidal river was picking them up and carrying them to safety.

Shen and Wu looked at each other and then across to where Yu-Ma and Hwang stood beside Kate and Lu Chien. Each knew what the other was thinking. For all their learning, and for all their classes in political theory, the one with no knowledge of communism, because he could not speak or hear, had acted the most bravely and wisely.

On this and subsequent nights the death toll rose to thousands as the purge continued to flush out and destroy every last Communist. They were shot dead in the streets where they stood, and in their homes, and while fleeing. No one escaped: not men, nor women, nor children, not relatives nor friends.

The terrible events that began on the night of April 12, 1927, became known as the Shanghai Massacre. When it was finally finished, and the streets were stained red as a monument to communism, everyone said that at last the evil had been wiped out. But of course they were wrong. It was a beginning, an important turning point.

# 31

*In the days that followed that fateful night of April 12, 1927,* Kate and the others, hidden in sampans and barges, slowly made their way up country. They were homeless now, on the run, without money or influence and completely dependent on the peasants of the countryside to hide them and then pass them along from village to village.

It was the time of the Blue Shirts, the secret police. They controlled local police forces everywhere and encouraged people to inform on their friends. Many Europeans, it was said, were volunteering their services to spy on their Chinese friends.

There were soon refugee columns by the thousands on the roads as Yang Ho continued his purge. Always there was the sound of gunfire in the distance. None of their party was in any doubt about what would happen should the Kuomintang catch them, or a peasant betray them. They slept close together by night to keep warm. Wu Zhao and Lu Chien side by side, then Yu-Ma and Hwang and Kate, with Shen on the outside. The men took turns on guard.

Usually they were so tired they fell asleep instantly. But one night Kate could not sleep. She lay awake, fighting back the tears as the magnitude of what had happened—and how it had dramatically changed her life—engulfed her.

Then she felt Shen tugging at her sleeve. "Kate Doctor, Kate Doctor," he was whispering, "Kate Doctor . . ."

"Yes?" she answered.

His voice, now that he had her attention, dropped suddenly to a soft and more sympathetic tone. "Kate Doctor," he said, "we have great need of good doctors—great need. There are many who will stay alive because of you—many more than if you had stayed in Shanghai. You will save the lives of thousands. And you will see your family and friends and beloved Shanghai again, this I promise you. We will take the city you love so much—take it effortlessly as if it were an obstacle of small consequence. We will walk in it again, you and I. When we have built and trained our army. Before we are finished the whole of China will be free. So do not be downcast. There have been nights of terror and there will be more. But there will be nights, too, to tell your grandchildren about. This is a great enterprise we are involved in."

Actually, she didn't believe a word of it except the part about there being plenty of wounded for her to tend to. But he had made her feel better—like a parent makes a child feel better with tales of princesses and knights in shining armor. So she took his hand, the one which a few moments ago had been tugging so fiercely at her coat sleeve, and put it to her mouth and kissed it.


Lu Chien was sobbing quietly. Wu Zhao tenderly stroked the soles of her feet. Each day they got more sore. They had not been made for walking. Because Lu Chien was of high birth, her feet had been bound from the moment she had come out of the womb. They were now barely more than three inches long.

"I cannot go on," she was saying to Wu. "I will be a burden to you all."

"Hush, my little one. They will harden. It is just that you are not used to so much walking. Try to walk just one more day for me . . ."

She nodded against his chest and after a while her sobbing eased. When her voice was a little clearer, she whispered to him again:

"But I will not be a burden. When the time comes that I cannot go on, I will know what to do as befits an honorable daughter of a mandarin."

"Hush. Do not talk nonsense. We are Communists now. Go to sleep and get some rest."

"Yes," she said quietly, "rest."

# 32

*In Shanghai, the international city which flourished with every* form of capitalist vice and virtue—and which therefore had the most to fear from communism—there were two new heroes.

The first was General Yang Han Ho, the supreme commander. His policy of merciless opposition to the Communists had been vindicated. Thousands had been killed. The new armored vehicles had been an unqualified success. A few renegades had gotten away. But they were in columns, straggling north. And bit by bit Yang Ho's troops were mopping them up. No one was in any doubt that in a few weeks—a few months at the most—the communist threat would be over.

In all the adulation of success it did not seem to have occurred to Yang to ask whether Shen had been forewarned. Ling Ling went about her courtesan duties and was seen more and more in Yang Ho's company. Knowing his moods well, she sensed he had another secret, like the armored cars, which he was keeping to himself. But her intuition told her not to seek it out yet.

The other hero of Shanghai was Captain Thomas Blake. No one was more surprised to find himself cast in this role than Blake himself. Indeed, he was furious about it. As the death toll mounted, he told himself that he should have foreseen the massacre even more than he had when he had first thought of giving the Communists the armored cars; that he should have been more alert to Shan Li's capacity for treachery. It was, after all, his stock-in-trade. But it had not even entered Blake's head that he might turn the tables on him after their childhood friendship. Of course, Shan Li didn't see it as betrayal. He saw it as protecting Blake from himself: as protecting capitalism and ensuring that Blake still got his money and his immunity from prosecution; and Shan Li had even warned Blake to get Kate out of town.

Blake had no doubt that Kate was now in one of the refugee columns staggering north. He would never forget that sinking, stabbing feeling he had felt when, rounding the corner, he had seen Kate falter, go back, and then finally run forward towards the armored car. He had called and called but she had not heard him.

Yet he knew she had been right to flee. She had certainly been recognized. Yang Ho's Blue Shirts had wasted no time in getting the story out. Her picture, together with Blake's, had been on the front page of the English-language daily the next morning. It had called Kate one of Shen's "red bandits," the daughter of a known communist sympathizer. It said she had been part of a group of escaping Communists who had shot Kuomintang soldiers dead.

The story in the newspaper about Blake was somewhat different. It quoted General Yang Ho. He said Blake was a hero. It made no mention of any previous government order of armored vehicles from Edwards & Co. It said only that Yang Ho had placed an order for armored cars at short notice with Captain Thomas Blake, to help to try to avert the suddenly worsened communist threat. It said Captain Blake had responded magnificently:

"There is no doubt that his ability to lay his hands on such strategic merchandise at such short notice saved Shanghai, the heart of free enterprise, from communism."

The story was cleverly worded but read like the betrayal of Judas Iscariot. A betrayal which, in this instance, the business community, with all their vested interests, saw as an act of great heroism. Yang Ho had even had the sale price for the arms included in the small print. The high price was justified, he said, because of the shortness of time.

The article also praised Yang's military genius for thinking of the idea.

Blake knew that Yang had released the story out of spite, though he could hardly have told the real story. But it was praise Blake could well have done without. He feared for when Kate read the newspaper or heard reports of what it said—if she had not already. He must somehow get word to her—or try to find her. But because Blake had promised the armored cars to Shen and they had finished up with Yang Ho, he doubted anyone would believe him. He was also one million pounds richer—a fact easily verifiable by the communist intelligence network which under Wang Lee was formidable. If he took the money—which he had no intention of not taking—how could anyone believe he had not deliberately set out to betray the Communists? He would find that story hard to swallow himself. And this was why Yang Ho had released the story. If Yang could not have Kate, he was determined Blake would not either. He was determined to blacken him in her eyes for all time. By his clever little public relations exercise of planting a false story about Blake in the newspapers, Yang Ho had implicated Blake in the bloody Shanghai massacre—Yang Ho's massacre—of thousands of innocent men, women, and children. Yang Ho knew that to someone like Kate, this would be the ultimate crime. He was determined she would hate Blake as much as he was sure she hated him.

The very thing that Blake had been trying so desperately to avoid, his greatest fear—that if he helped the Nationalists against the Communists Kate would never forgive him—had now been realized by no fault of his own.

As he went around Shanghai, praise being heaped on him from every quarter, he did so with a heavy heart.

\* \* \*

Blake tried to see Ling Ling several times. Each time her gateman refused him entry. In the end he had to prevail on Shan Li to arrange the meeting. Finally, late one afternoon, some days after Kate and the others had fled, he was shown into Ling Ling's inner court.

"It is very gracious of you to see me, Ling Ling."

"My honored friend Shan Li requested it. But if it had been anyone else . . ."

"I understand. I ask only that you deliver a letter for me to our mutual friend Kate . . ." He took a letter from his inside coat pocket and went to hand it to her. It was in an envelope marked "Doctor K. Richmond." It was a full explanation of what had happened. He was sure if Kate read it she would believe him. How they would ever then link up was another thing. But if the letter could be delivered, Kate could get a message back to him. Then he would find her and smuggle her out to Hong Kong where she would be safe.

But as he held the letter out, Ling Ling took a step back. "This is something I cannot do," she said emphatically.

"Please, Ling Ling, please. It explains everything. Please take the letter . . ."

She shook her head. "There is nothing to explain. And even if I knew where she was, I could not take it . . ."

"But Wang Lee will know . . . Surely you know where to find him . . . ?"

Ling Ling looked suddenly frightened. Why did Blake mention Wang Lee in connection with her? She knew Blake knew Wang Lee from the affair over the guns in the first place. Her brother had told her that. But she had not known Blake also knew of the connection between herself and Wang Lee. That could be very dangerous. How could she ever trust Blake again? . . . What if he and Yang Ho were co-conspirators . . . ?

"I know no one called Wang Lee," she said simply, "though it is a common enough Chinese name."

"Have it your own way, then, Ling," Blake said. "But please take the letter . . . Or at very least send a message to your brother that I wish to see Kate . . ."

Ling Ling looked at him. She knew how it was to be separated from one's love. She ached for Wang Lee.

"I will take the letter," she said, weakening for a moment,

"but I cannot promise it will ever be delivered. Even if I knew how to arrange this, there might be others who would refuse to take it . . ."

"I understand," Blake said. "I'm very grateful." He passed the letter over and went to shake her hand appreciatively. It was a *yang kwei* gesture and one from which she immediately recoiled.

"I must be about my business, now, Captain Blake, if you will excuse me," she said rather pointedly.

"Of course. I have taken up too much of your time as it is. Thank you . . ."

She nodded and indicated her outer courts where her head girl was waiting to take Blake back to the gate.

He forced a smile and turned and walked out.

After he had left Ling Ling walked with the envelope to her old wooden trunk in the corner. She took off the cover, opened the lid, and threw the letter inside. Then she closed the lid and replaced the old Chinese shawl she kept over it.

When Wang Lee arrived later that day, he bluntly refused to deliver the letter. He said he would not even carry a message to Kate that Blake had tried to contact her. As far as anyone in the communist camp was concerned, Wang Lee said, Blake no longer existed. At least not until they returned triumphantly to Shanghai and put him on trial for murder.

Wang Lee could stay only a short while so they made love hurriedly and he departed—with what little extra money Ling Ling had been able to earn for supplies.

After Wang had left, Ling meant to have the letter returned to Blake, but something diverted her and she forgot.


The business community, with its usual display of loyalty, immediately shifted sides from Edwards to Blake. They all knew there was no middle ground in this fight—you were either on one side or the other. Besides, it was well known that Edwards had been left holding the financial bag, as it were. He had broken the capitalist law of "Thou shalt not take a loss." He had had to pay the French suppliers from whom he had bought the armored cars.

But Yang Ho had said the government had no intention of paying him for vehicles which had been stolen while in his care. There was nothing Edwards could do. He could hardly sue them.

Because of the Kuomintang's desire to keep its weapons' capacity from the foreign powers, it had been an arms-length transaction—the sort, admittedly, which was carried on all the time by governments. But in gunrunning there was no honor among thieves and the golden rule was never to get caught. There had been no question of Edwards being able to insure such questionable black market merchandise, whichever country it had come from. For all anyone knew, the armored cars might have belonged to the French Army originally.

Two weeks after Blake's coup, the annual elections of the Shanghai Club took place. Nigel Edwards had been elected president unopposed for thirty years. As he shuffled into the club for this year's elections he was carrying a heavy hangover. He had been nursing it for days—since he had first known of his pending financial ruin. It was only with great difficulty that he rose to address the meeting. The members sat before him among the mahogany paneling and brass spitoons and padded leather armchairs, shiny from years of use.

"Gentlemen," Nigel Edwards said, the sun coming in from behind him and highlighting the tufts of white hair over his ears, "Gentlemen, I vacate the chair for the annual elections and hand over to the deputy president to conduct the ballot. In so doing I again place myself in nomination for another year."

"I nominate Captain Thomas Blake," a youngish voice said from the back of the hall. The president and his deputy had barely had time to change seats.

Edwards stared forward through the cigar-smoke towards the back. It was the voice of Fox, one of his former managers. The one from the North of England who had accompanied Janey to the club ball. Edwards had never liked his North Country ways. Never should have allowed him into the club. He'd heard from his general manager that Fox had recently gone over to Blake. Well, Edwards would have to get back into the business himself now—give Blake a run for his money.

But even as he told himself this, he knew the delicate balance which sometimes separated number one from number two in the business world had been disturbed. Even if he did get back full-time into the business himself, and even if he'd lost none of his old acumen, he'd be lucky to be number two. He wondered if a merger might be the answer. If Blake would agree to that. He doubted it. He wouldn't have at Blake's age. The young bull and the old bull. It was the oldest business story of them all. And now it was happening to him.

The voting was going on but he barely heard it. A few of the old guard stood by him. A few, not many. It was always money which counted in business. Nothing else, really. They said they liked you. They pretended they liked you. But when it came down to it, there was only money. That was what business loyalty was all about—money. That was the business motive; the profit motive.

Did this fellow Shen have something different? Perhaps. The voting was ending now. He coughed again and had trouble stopping. Damned cigar smoke. He'd been coughing a lot lately. Well, it was time to be gracious. The deputy president was announcing the result:

"I am happy to inform honorable members that the new president of the Shanghai Club is Captain Thomas Blake. As such he is the first American in the history of our club to hold this office."

Loud ovation. Of course. All the world loves a hero. Well, here was the hard part.

Sir Nigel Edwards, looking his full sixty-five years and then some, stood up and walked down the aisle between the chairs towards the back where Blake was standing. The way cleared.

As he neared Blake he held out his hand. "My dear Captain Blake . . . my heartiest congratulations. It is, I believe, by club tradition and certainly by desire, my privilege to buy you a drink. What is your pleasure, sir?"

"A bourbon, thank you."

"A bourbon it is indeed! Two, thank you, barman," Edwards shouted as they walked towards the bar. "Two bourbons and the rest are on me. Whatever is your pleasure, gentlemen."

They all moved to the bar then, as if nothing had happened. And after Edwards had bought his round, it was Blake's turn as the incoming president.

Edwards stayed for a few minutes more and then prepared to go. It was Blake's day and he would leave him to enjoy it. But before he left he turned to Blake.

"You'll come to dinner at the house, of course—tonight if you're free? My daughter has been asking after you and I know she'd love to see you."

All the bar had heard the invitation. Blake looked at the old man, the old man he had hated and fought so long, and had now beaten, but who was showing such grace in defeat.

"I'd be delighted to come, Sir Nigel, thank you."

"Eight o'clock then?"

"Eight o'clock."

# 33

At a village near the junction of the Yangtze, Shen and his band came upon a young woman and a man who said they were going south to find a communist band. They said that near Canton, Communists were being allowed to live in safety.

The girl said she had been an actress in Shanghai. Her name was Song Wei. The man, whose name was Po Bai, was huge. He was of Manchurian blood and looked a match even for Hwang. The girl was short with the characteristic high cheekbones of the North and the prettiest eyes Kate had ever seen.

When Shen asked them how they came to be in the village, they said that they, too, had fled on the night of the massacre.

Shen immediately liked the idea of going south. Wu urged caution.

"How do we know there is really a group of comrades in Canton?" he said to Shen. "They say they are living openly without persecution. I do not believe it. I do not believe it is possible."

"It could happen. Canton is close to the border. Yang Ho is not stupid. He would not risk a bloodbath on the foreign powers' doorstep."

"I still think we should continue north. At least we know there is a large group there with Mao."

"We think there is. But it could take months or even years to reach them and many would die. We have little food, no arms, no warm clothing, and must travel in winter over the Great Snow Mountain. It seems impossible. Whereas Canton is close and in a warmer climate. If we could live openly there as Communists it would give us a chance to consolidate and build an army."

"Even if Communists appear to be living there safely, it could be a trap—that is the sort of thing Yang Ho would do to tempt you out into the open."

Shen looked at his old teacher with his clipped military moustache and graying hair and smiled. "I will defer to your judgment if you insist on it," he said gently. "We have not come this far to be ruled by the impulsiveness of youth."

Wu looked at him and smiled back. "Nor by the reticence of aging ex-colonels," he said. "You are in charge and must make the decision."

Another look passed between them. "We go south then," Shen said.

"So be it. But be careful. We do not really know these people."

Shen nodded.


From the village near the junction of the rivers they headed first for Nanchang. But by the time they reached there, in August, bitter fighting had commenced. Yang Ho's armies were now in the countryside, trying desperately to stamp out the remnants of communism.

Yet despite her personal knowledge of Yang Ho and his tactics, Kate was totally unprepared for what happened on that chill autumn day and which struck terror into her heart.

They had been unable to avoid some of the fighting at Nanchang, although they had circled around as best they could. Shen was determined not to get caught up in minor skirmishes until he could build a viable military unit to fight back.

But as they approached a ridge just out of Nanchang, Shen, who was leading, motioned for them to be silent. They knew the procedure. Either he or Hwang would climb up carefully to make sure they were not walking over a hill right into enemy fire.

Shen crept up quietly. He appeared to look carefully, and then after a moment returned, beckoning them all to lie down. Kate could see he was frowning. He looked at her. Then he appeared to decide something. He slid closer to her.

"Do you want to see what the enemy is really like?" he said, his teeth clenched in a way which indicated he was obviously holding in an enormous amount of anger.

Kate nodded slowly. "Yes," she said. "Why?"

"You will not talk or utter a sound, whatever happens—you promise?"

"I promise."

"Then follow me."

She nodded and he took her hand. What was it he had seen that had changed him so? A moment ago, despite the steep slope, they had all been laughing.

Nodding now to Hwang and Wu to keep the others in place, Shen led her carefully along the slope of the hill and then climbed up to where a bush stood on the perimeter. From the cover of this they could look down, unobserved, into the next valley.

At first Kate could see nothing except the usual Chinese scene of peasants in the field.

She looked at Shen.

He pointed to another hill on the far side of the valley. Kate strained and thought she saw some movement.

She looked at the field again and realized that the peasants bending at the rice shoots in the mud were all women. Some were just girls—from seven or eight up to their teens.

She looked at Shen once more. Then suddenly what was about to happen dawned on her. Her mouth fell open and she was sure she was going to scream. Shen's hand moved like lightning to stop her. He held it tightly over her mouth.

"We can do nothing—absolutely nothing," he whispered, "or we will all be killed. Keep perfectly still and do nothing."

Kate nodded and he eased his hand away.

She saw that the movements on the other side of the hill had now become shapes. They were moving quickly. Suddenly, all the hill was alive with a marching Kuomintang army. Now the women in the field had seen them and started to run.

But, as if from nowhere, from each corner of the field, army scouts emerged, obviously placed there well in advance. They ran with rifles held aloft, firing warnings.

Soon they were herding the women into lines like cattle. Suddenly, too, the main body of troops was forming. They marched in line as they reached the bottom of the hill.

Kate saw the first soldier step forward. The girl in front of him was barely thirteen. Two of the military scouts held her by the arms as the first soldier came forward at double march. His movement barely slowed as he placed his rifle on the ground. His hands went out and ripped at the girl's blouse, tearing it open so that both her breasts popped out. His hands kept on mercilessly. He ripped at her flesh in a downward, nail-clawing motion. Kate saw the blood gush and heard the girl's anguished cry.

But by this time the soldier's hands were at the girl's black peasant pants, pulling them down, clawing. The pants came away and Kate saw the girl's whole pubic region exposed. The flimsy black cotton material was around her ankles now but the soldier made no effort to remove it. The other two men still held her as the soldier fell upon her, pushing her back heavily into the mud. He gnawed at her like an animal at meat while his hand pulled feverishly at his own trousers and groin. Then he had his penis in his hand and was thrusting it into her with such a fierce stabbing motion that the girl let out another horrendous cry.

Shen took Kate's arm and with some difficulty pulled her back down the side of the incline. She was heaving with deep sobs.

As soon as they were back with the rest of the group she turned on him:

"How dare you! Why did you show me that? What was the point of it . . . ?"

"So you will hate the enemy as much as we do," he said. "So you will know what will happen to you if you are caught . . . and to give you fortitude for what lies ahead. When there is not enough food, or the winter wind is piercing, hate is a great nourishment."

Kate looked at him. "How did you know this was going to happen?" she said.

"It is how some commanders keep their troops sated. The men are allowed three minutes each—no more. They must do it on the run. That is why they do not pause long enough to take off all the girl's clothes. It is not unusual to find a field full of girls naked except for one ankle still caught in a trouser leg."

"A field full—?"

Shen looked at her gently. "Yes, Kate Doctor . . . a field full . . . They shoot them when they have finished with them and perhaps that is just as well, even though they do not do it for humane reasons but to stop anyone from talking."

As they moved off, Kate was silent. She could feel anger rising in her stomach. What right had Shen to decide what kind of person she should be? What was happening to her carefully planned future? Suddenly, everyone had been taken from her— her father, her mother, Blake, and Janey. Her surgical career had been abandoned for the delta mud of China. But if Shen's aim was to make her impervious to pain and suffering by giving her such an impossibly large dose all at once, he was succeeding. She was beginning to feel numb all over, as if with a local anesthetic. She trudged on, barely aware where she was, but knowing she would never be the same again.

# 34

*In Shanghai, at the Edwards mansion, Blake, Janey, and Sir Nigel sat at the long oak table in the dining room. The meal was finished and coffee was being served. It had been a sumptuous meal, with excellent French wines. Edwards had been his affable best.*

He looked down the table to where his daughter sat at the

other end, and then across to his left where Blake sat. The butler brought the port decanter and retired. Janey looked radiant. She had moved back into the house the previous week. Edwards had known she'd be all right once he got her back under his parental wing. And Blake did cut a dashing figure, he had to admit that. Edwards had certainly underestimated him. He still hated him, of course.

Yet there was a little admiration, too. Blake would be an excellent match for Janey. And there was no one else. No one with the right business acumen. Janey still spoke of taking over the business herself but there was precious little left. No, a marriage and a merger would be the thing—a merger which retained the Edwards family name on the firm. He thought Blake would go for that. It would give him the respectability he had always wanted. "Edwards, Blake and Company," or "Blake and Edwards." It didn't matter. And he was too tired to think about it any more tonight. He'd got them both together. The rest was up to Janey now. He had no doubt she would be equal to it. And even as Edwards thought this, Janey said:

"You look awfully tired, Daddy. I'm sure Captain Blake would excuse you if you wanted to retire early."

"Would you, Tom? You're sure you wouldn't mind?" He had taken to calling him Tom and the sound seemed to fall all right on his ears. Better than he had expected. And he was tired. So terribly tired.

He was tired a lot lately. Tom was a good name. He wondered if the boy knew he had named him—that his mother had asked what to call him that would sound respectable in Shanghai. That was a lifetime ago. He hadn't thought of Tom's mother in years. Or of the boy in connection with her. It was a pity the hate between them had gotten so out of hand. The boy could have been his son, really. He'd never allowed himself to think that before. In those times barely a day had passed when he hadn't made love to his mother—mostly on the soft leather couch in his office which he'd always retained. Even when her sailor husband was home they still made love.

Yes, he liked to think the boy could have been his, but he knew he wasn't. Yet he could have let himself feel the boy was his son. He could have helped more. For his mother's sake.

He stood up from the table and felt a little whoozy. He

steadied himself with a hand on the edge of the oak table. Went back to Tudor times, that table. They didn't make tables like that anymore. He doubted even the Communists could make one like that. Edwards walked slowly down the table and kissed Janey.

"Goodnight, darling."

"Goodnight, Daddy."

"Goodnight, Tom."

"Goodnight, sir."

Blake had taken to calling him "sir." That was nice. That was respectful, like a son should be.

Edwards smiled one more time with a wave of his hand, opened the big wooden door, and walked towards the stairs.

"I must admit you're handling it well," Janey said as soon as her father had gone.

"What?"

"Betrayal."

Janey picked up the port decanter and walked along to where Blake sat. She positioned herself with the decanter opposite, took out a cigarette, and waited rather pointedly for him to light it.

"I'll probably never see her again," Janey said. "Kate will probably finish up in one of Yang Ho's prisons or be peeled alive naked in public . . . And you also betrayed my father . . ."

"Don't forget the Communists," Blake said cynically, "everyone says I betrayed the Communists . . ."

Janey exhaled deeply. "Well no one is weeping any tears for them, least of all me . . ."

"No, like most people in this city, you never did like them, did you?"

She shook her head.

"I love this city," she said, wistful for a moment. "I love this city and it is my home. I've never known anywhere else and I certainly don't want to see the Communists sweep in and destroy it and turn it into some drab, gray mausoleum . . ."

Blake nodded. "About your father . . ." he said. "There can be no betrayal when people are not friends. I think he knows I beat him in a business deal and that he'd have done the same thing to me if he could have. I think he even half respects me for it. I certainly respect him for the way he's taking it. He knew that in the particular sort of business your father and I engage in, while the profits are very high, the risks are correspondingly enormous and the result can be disastrous if something goes wrong."

"You men and your goddamned business profits . . . !" Janey said. "Always wanting to be bigger and better and richer than each other . . . That's what it's all about, isn't it . . . ?"

"That's part of it . . . and your father understands that . . ."

Blake could think of other things, too. He had not forgotten his hatred for Edwards for being his mother's lover, and what Edwards had done to her. But he was not going to say anything about that to Janey.

"And if it comes to it," Blake went on, "you've got the profit-motive in your blood as much as anyone."

"Nothing justifies betraying Kate," Janey said angrily, although she knew Blake was right about the profit motive.

"No one betrayed Kate, least of all I," Blake said. "If Kate hadn't happened to be at Lu Chien's place with that damned Shen, who was always trying to manipulate her to his own ends, she would be here now, safe and sound and free."

"He wasn't manipulating her . . . she genuinely likes him and wanted to help . . ."

"Good . . . She is going to have plenty of opportunity."

"And how can you say you didn't betray her . . . ? All of Shanghai knows you did . . . by getting those armored cars . . . You got one million British pounds for them . . ."

Blake shrugged. He knew it was useless to argue. "Believe what you will, Jane," he said.

"Are you denying you got the money?"

Blake shook his head.

Janey wondered if Blake really did believe what he was saying—that he hadn't betrayed Kate. Money and power—those were what he really loved. Most people would condemn him for that, but actually she understood. It was true of her father, too. It was also in her own blood, as Blake said.

In fact, she realized she didn't hate Blake half as much as she had always told herself she did. She realized it had just been part of the family feud. She had been expected to dislike him. In fact there was something quite likable about him. He never pretended to be other than he was.

Blake poured another port and pushed it across to Janey.

He knew he could argue until he was blue in the face and no one was going to believe him. Why was it that something published in a newspaper had such a ring of inevitability and truth to it? Even after libel actions were proved, people still tended to think there was something in the original story.

"Heard from Kate lately?" Blake said cynically.

Janey shook her head.

Blake knew his cynical moods had been returning of late, his world-weary moods. For a time he'd lost them almost completely. He realized how much Kate had changed him in a short space of time. But now . . . Now she was gone and he would never see her again. He had known his letter would not reach her and what had arrived in the mail today had confirmed that. His letter had never been delivered. Yang Ho had done his job well. Every last Communist in the country believed so fervently that Blake was guilty, no one was prepared to deliver even the shortest verbal message from him. But someone—probably Wang Lee who would be crossing the lines at will if Blake was any judge—had been prepared to deliver a message to Blake. Probably only too happy to! Probably knew what was in it!

The letter—from Kate—which he'd found in his hotel pigeon-hole that evening, was burning a hole in his pocket.

He'd read it several times on the way over in the limousine. His "Dear Tom" letter.

Fragments kept coming back.

Well, Blake thought, now was as good a time as ever to tell Janey. He poured himself another port and slowly took the letter out of his pocket.

"I know someone who's heard from Kate lately," he said, as he pushed the letter across the table towards her.

Janey was stupefied. She took the letter and began to read while Blake sipped his port.

Dear Tom:
    You will appreciate that it would be pointless for me to identify day or time or place. It has crossed my mind several times that you may have tried to get in touch with me. Please don't. It is hard enough without that. I feel so very sorry for you. Sorry for both of us. But

more so for you. You would probably feel better if I said I hated you. But I don't. I loved you and probably a part of me always will. But please don't try to see me again. Please. For my sake if not for yours. They would kill you on sight, you know. And I don't think I could stand that. Although I know I'll never see you again, I know I'll think of you often and ask what went wrong and how it might have been avoided. And so, my *darling*, I will call you that for the last time. I don't know what you might say to me if we could talk again, but let me say this . . . There is a sense in which I will always love you . . . but as far as you are concerned, I am dead.

Say hullo to Janey for me and give her my love. But tell her to treat me as dead also . . .''

Janey looked up at Tom. There were tears in her eyes.

"There's a finality about that letter that is chilling," she said.

"Isn't that the truth?"

"Well, there's nothing we can do now," Janey was saying. "Call it destiny or force of circumstance or just plain bad luck . . . call it what you will there's nothing we can do now. Her lot is cast with the Communists forever . . ."

Blake nodded.

Janey was desperately unhappy and distraught for Kate. But she was also trying to come to terms with the fact that her best and closest friend was now a wanted criminal. Not only had Yang Ho called her a "red bandit," he had offered a reward for her and for any others identified as being part of the group responsible for the shooting of Kuomintang soldiers outside Wu and Lu Chien's house. If Kate ever returned to Shanghai—or was captured anywhere else in China for that matter—she would be brought to trial and shot.

Janey looked at Blake and Blake looked at her. There are times when an unspoken word is better than a spoken one. Both had had an enormous amount to drink. The night had not been without its tensions. There had been cocktails before the meal, wine during it, and several glasses of port afterwards.

"I must go," Blake said.

"Oh must you?" Janey said, suddenly hearing her own words and realizing there was a genuine meaning in them.

Blake looked at her very directly now. "No," he said, "I don't have to go. There's nothing I have to do for a long time . . . perhaps never . . . But seeing we have taken very liberally of one of the two oldest drowners of sorrows in the world and it has not worked, I thought perhaps it was time to suggest I go . . ."

He was close to being drunk. They both were.

Janey poured them each another port and passed his across. "Skoal," she said, tossing hers straight down.

Blake followed suit. "Skoal," he said, pouring two more the moment their glasses were empty.

He was now quite drunk and so was she.

"I don't suppose you would care to join me in partaking of the other oldest drowner of sorrows in the world . . . ?" he said with slurred speech.

Janey gave him her half-cynical smile. "I'd hate myself in the morning," she said with feeling. "You might even too . . ."

"Isn't that the truth? . . . Your place or mine?" he said very deliberately.

"Yours," she said, rising unsteadily. "I'll get my wrap."

# 35

*After the mass rape Kate became obsessed with the idea of* escape. Hong Kong was only two hours by train from Canton. If Shen and his group reached Canton, she knew of missionary friends of her parents there who might help her escape. They could smuggle her out to Hong Kong on the train, or even by car.

Anything would be better than this. She was not cut out for this type of life at all, she had decided. The thought of Canton followed by Hong Kong kept her going. She had been a fool ever to come home to China from America. Well, she would rectify that error very presently. She would take that teaching post under Jonas Elms. Or go into private practice. In New York. In New York! No one there cared much what happened in China. They certainly didn't know the most momentous revolution in mankind's history was about to take place. A revolution in which millions would die!

Some revolution! If Shen thought he was Moses leading his people out of bondage into freedom—and the Chinese countryside was the land flowing with milk and honey—then he should head for America via Hong Kong immediately, preferably with some help from the Almighty. It was no good staying in this God-forsaken land with this motley crew a moment longer. A revolution to start from this? It was preposterous. A pipe dream of a few old men like Wu who were past their prime. They had gotten hold of a few young men like Shen and trained them. It was ridiculous to think these boys were any match for the Kuomintang. She hadn't thought this earlier, though. No. But that had been before the mass rape in the valley. Only one thing mattered now—to get away—to get away from all of it. They could patch up their own damn dead.

But the farther south they went, the fiercer the fighting became. Government soldiers dogged their march at every step, sometimes with the support of gunboats from the river.

The new man, Po, was proving himself a fearless fighter and they could not have done without him. His young female companion, Song Wei, fought too.

Song Wei was of peasant stock, from a village in the North called Dawn Blossom. At first Kate thought she was too fragile and feminine. She had dark, stormy hair and high cheekbones and sharp features, and her temperament was mercurial—laughing one minute and furious or sulky the next. Perhaps that was why she had come to Shanghai to be an actress, because she could assume any mood she wanted. But she was not acting when she went to fight, nor was she fragile and feminine. As a soldier, she was the equal of any man.

Although she was never overtly offensive, it was clear that she disliked Kate, who puzzled over her animosity, and then came to wonder whether it was jealousy. Although she was Po's woman, Song Wei looked sometimes at Shen with more than interest in her eyes. Perhaps she resented Kate's friendship with Shen. Kate had tried to make friends with her on more than one occasion but was always repulsed, even when she complimented Song Wei on her prowess as a fighter.

Kate herself sometimes wished she had been trained to shoot like the communist women. Still, she was not truly sure she had the stomach for it, and in any case there were not enough weapons to go around. Po and Song Wei would have been welcome if for no other reason than that they had brought their own weapons. The others were still armed with their German mauser pistols.

There was more heavy fighting at Swatow. But again they swung wide around it, desperate now to reach Canton and join up with the Communists there before the Kuomintang swept down towards the border. It even crossed Kate's mind that Shen might be trying to reach Hong Kong himself. She desperately hoped so. From Hong Kong he could journey to Russia where he could borrow money to form an army before crossing back into China from the north.

Wu, of course, had fought and commanded before, and he was invaluable. He taught as he went, whispering warnings, cautions; telling when to advance and when to retreat; when to fire and when not to fire. The classroom lessons were now becoming the battlefield lessons and soon they all felt like seasoned soldiers.

Sometimes, it seemed to Kate afterwards, when she thought about it, that she had lived a whole lifetime in that first year. It was now, unbelievably, nearly a year since they had escaped. After one of the bloodiest massacres in history they had fled by river. Then they had marched across country to the "Three Cities" of central China. Next they had gone south at the time of the Nanchang uprising, in the August of 1927. Surviving this, they had traveled farther south again—into the tropical belt of fresh lychees—only to run into the gunboats.

Then, still later in 1927, after Swatow, they had turned to go even deeper south to the Canton, or "Kuangchow," commune.

But as they now neared it, word came that it was being beseiged. They raced on, covering *li* after *li* in record time. But they were not quick enough, and by December the so-called "Canton Commune" was back in Kuomintang hands.

It was a bitter disappointment. Their band, which had swelled to more than twenty now, with horses and mules taken from dead Kuomintang troops, stopped by the roadside to spell the animals and think.

They had been traveling hard all day. It was noon. The tropical sun was high and harsh.

But the fields were green because they were far south. Wu commented that a few hills more and they would have been able to see Hong Kong. Kate could have cried. Now that the commune had fallen, she saw before them only long years on the run. Even if they were to head north, where it was rumored there were small *soviets*—small areas of communist government—it was a pilgrimage none wished to undertake this day. Kate kept thinking of Hong Kong, two hours away, where she might take a bath. That wonderful, jostling, cosmopolitan city; a city where foreign devils and Chinese all gathered together; where cabbages sat as high as green mountains in the open market place; where fish and poultry and rich tender pork and beef and all the subtle sauces of the whole of China sat on the air; where under trees and in shaded teahouses one might sit and contemplate what was his or her pleasure. The idea of this, as Wu mentioned Hong Kong, was too much for them all to bear.

It was the heat, of course—the harsh high heat of the sun and the humid heat of the tropical lychee jungle which had made them feel this way. At least that was how they explained it later. They said the heat had reminded them of the beloved Shanghai, and the good meals and fun and fellowship they had enjoyed there, before they had been wrenched so wickedly from it.

After they had rested, Shen took a vote and it was unanimous.

Whether there were soviets to the north, whether there was a place one could live openly as a Communist or not, of one thing they were certain. Somewhere in the central mountains there was said to be the start of a communist army. It was said to be led by a young man called Mao, who had a price on his head of a quarter of a million Chinese dollars.

Perhaps, if enough Communists did what their band had decided to do this day, and there was the start of an army, then there would be a bigger army, and then a bigger one yet until, as group joined group, and with training and arms and good fortune, they would start a march different from the dejected, disappointed, and defeated one they felt themselves to be on this day.

So they headed towards the central mountains and Kate found herself walking with them. Might she have made it alone to Hong Kong? Would the Kuomintang troops who controlled the South have let her through? She would have been arrested as a matter of course without proper papers. She wondered where Blake was. It was over ten months since she had written her letter to him. Might he be in Hong Kong where she had first met him? Or selling arms to the Communists in the North—under some assumed identity? What of Janey? And her mother? And her poor father for whom she had all but given up hope?

Yet she knew that this endeavor, which she had been forced to become a part of due to force of circumstance, was bigger than her or Blake or even the whole of China. Things were happening here, right where she was, which would one day shake the world, she was sure. A war was about to be fought, a war about the right of individuals to choose their way of life, a war about freedom, she supposed.

So Kate, too, walked on, noticing that Lu Chien's feet, bound half her early life to the ideal golden lotus shape of three-and-a-half inches, had started to bleed again.

# 36

*I*t was strange that although thousands of Chinese had been slaughtered, life in Shanghai continued as normal. It was 1928. The foreign powers were carrying on as if nothing had happened.

Janey got out of her bath and stood in front of the mirror. She was examining herself prior to dressing for an outing with Blake. She wondered what she really wanted of him. And what he wanted of her. In the months since that first night when each had sought solace in the other, they had seen a lot of each other, but had not slept with each other again. It was beginning to worry Janey just a touch.

What would she wear—white underwear or black? Crimson? Beige? Chartreuse? Well, why not? It was delicately laced and satined—just the thing for the wind to blow at on an idyllic summer afternoon on the river. They were to picnic on the Yangtze. Janey smiled as she put the tip of a finger to a cut-glass perfume bottle and then ran the finger down from her navel to her deep dark maidenhair. Then she began to step into her underwear. She dressed quickly now, almost with a cavalier air about her, her joie de vivre high as she went from drawer to drawer and closet to closet until finally she stepped into her shoes; stood once more in front of the full mirror; looked approvingly; and then picked up her broad-brimmed hat, gloves, and purse, and swung out of the room.

They drove first in his open emerald green Rolls Royce to a place where they could take a punt—one of those flat, rectangular barges which the English dons at Oxford had invented to make love in. Janey noted with wry satisfaction that the bottom of the punt was padded.

The uniformed chauffeur took the wicker basket and champagne bucket from the car and placed them carefully in the punt. Then he helped both of them in and pushed the punt gently out into the water. He would wait there until they returned.

The river was beautiful at this time of year. At every bend delicate Chinese willows dipped into the water like soft lace curtains.

After a while Blake nudged the punt in towards the bank. It slid gently under the overhang of the trees.

The sun was sifting through the soft green in broken patterns, gently warming them and providing a dappled light which played on their faces as they looked at each other.

Janey was the first to talk. She wanted to make it easy for him, although she felt his look said everything. She was not sure why they had not made love since that first night. Perhaps because each had felt slightly disloyal despite Kate's letter. Each had been able to excuse that first night because of the amount of liquor consumed. Their relationship since then had been much more formal—yet increasingly friendly in recent weeks. And both knew that the passage of time was healing and changing things.

When he had phoned to ask her on the picnic, she thought he had decided the time was right, but she still wasn't sure. But she was sure that she wanted him to.

"Oh Tom, what a lovely day—what a lovely place," she now said lightly, with the warmest of smiles, and then leaning over, touched the back of his hand with hers. "Thank you for bringing me here."

"My pleasure," he said, smiling beneath his dark moustache. "A little champagne, perhaps?"

"Of course."

He uncorked a bottle and filled their glasses, and they clinked them and looked at each other and smiled again.

"Hi, friend," he said in his soft, methodical American drawl.

"Hello."

After the first sip he leaned across and kissed Janey on the lips. She made no effort to draw back. His lips were still moist from the wine and his breath smelled of tobacco.

As they came apart, Janey, sitting with her back against the padded rear of the punt, with her feet towards him, asked would he mind taking off her shoes. Slowly, carefully, he slid them off and lightly stroked her stockinged feet. He was sitting very close to her feet now, facing her. He slid a few inches closer, lifting and placing her feet in his lap. Slowly, Janey began to move her stockinged feet back and forth.

It was that gentle rising, unhurried ecstasy that all lovers hope for. They lingered on it a long time—sipping, refilling, looking at each other, smiling and talking Shanghai small talk.

When the first bottle was empty, Blake said simply, "Another?" Janey shook her head and said softly, "Not yet."

She might have said a hundred different things and the meaning would have been just the same. Her tone said everything. Silently, Blake slid himself up beside her and drew them both down together. Slowly, very slowly, he began to undress her, kissing her all the time.

Janey went to work with him, shedding her dress, underwear, and stockings in orchestrated movements, pulling up first one knee and then the other, her hands touching his and moving with them until she was naked on the bottom of the boat with him kneeling over her, kissing her up and down and the sun playing patterns on them both.

Then he paused for a moment, kneeling astride her, as he undressed himself. She made no effort to move but stared, enjoying the full uninterrupted sunlit view. Then suddenly he was on top of her, entering her quickly and with passion, as she knew he would. But soon he slowed to a gentler, more deeply penetrating rhythm, riding her high on the clouds of ecstasy for a long time until finally she could hold herself no longer, nor he either, and they both went riding in together as her back arched and the tide came in.

# 37

*A*fter Canton a change came over Shen. Kate noticed it immediately. He seemed more determined. More eager to fight. And he no longer seemed young to her.

It was at this time, with their small numbers, that Shen first developed the classic communist guerilla tactic. The Chinese White Army led by Yang Ho was still very traditionalist in outlook. Although Yang was trying to modernize it, many generals still held the idea of warring armies facing each other on opposite sides of the field of battle. Formation was everything.

Shen immediately saw what an advantage this gave him. He chose his ground carefully so they would always fall unexpectedly on Kuomintang soldiers in tight formation.

The Communists hit hard with whatever they had and then withdrew quickly before the larger enemy force could regroup. Shen's band always attacked only a selected part of the enemy— the front, middle, or rear, depending on the terrain—and fell back immediately when they had their objective for the day.

At first the Communists' objectives were very simple—ten rifles; some pistols; extra rounds of ammunition; some bandoliers. Sometimes they attacked the Kuomintang at rest, sometimes their tightly formed marching ranks. Shen, Po, Wu, Hwang, Yu-Ma, and Song Wei were always in the forefront. They would sweep down on the selected enemy position, firing as they went. Kate followed with the women and children. While the main communist force covered them, Kate's group grabbed the discarded weapons. Then they retreated to higher ground, some old ex-soldiers assigned to her group giving Shen and the others covering fire while they retreated last of all.

At Shen's insistence, Kate learned to shoot. But she refused to shoot in battle, although she found herself starting to enjoy the raids on the enemy, realizing what an opiate the excitement of battle was.

She noted, too, how well the intellectuals of the party had done their job. This was just how they had set out for it to be. They had taken youths such as Shen, who had been beaten and maltreated, and made them swear to find a better way. They had taken them and trained them with their best professors and gunsmiths and masters of military tactics. It was as if these young men had been in full-time military service since their teens.

Yet Shen had a breadth some of the others did not and Kate hoped he would not change too much. She hoped she would not. How much harder could one become? Did fighting make you want to kill? Did scenes such as the one she had witnessed the other day fashion you for all time? Would she ever come to kill? What if, in the heat of battle, she were suddenly faced with that decision? And what of the Kuomintang wounded she had to leave behind in order to tend her own wounded? Was that not leaving them to die?

# 38

*In Shanghai, Nigel Edwards was working late in his godown on* the Bund. The big Edwards & Co. sign still hung outside, as it had for more than fifty years. But everyone in Shanghai knew the giant warehouse no longer held anything more valuable than a few crates of Edwards' personal stock of whiskey. He had let all his staff go except his trusted old head coolie, F'eng. F'eng had been his compradore. A few months ago F'eng had been one of the most influential Chinese in the city. Now with his master's back broken, F'eng had lost much face.

Edwards closed the ledger he had been working on and rose to switch off the light. It was finished. That was the last of the books. Now they were ready for the takeover. Well, it was being called a merger—Blake had been gracious enough about that. But all the city knew it was a takeover. Edwards pulled the cord of the threaded brass balls which hung from the green baize light on his desk. He turned to go. But just as he did so, he heard a noise outside the glass door of his office. He could see a dull glow through the glass.

"F'eng, is that you—?" Edwards got up and moved over closer to the door.

As he did he saw a shadow move outside the glass. Slowly Edwards put his hand on the handle and turned the knob. Then he carefully opened the door and walked out to where a single dull light had been switched on near the door. It cast a triangular yellow glow over the part of the warehouse near his office. The rest was in darkness.

"F'eng—?"

There was still no answer.

Damn him, where was the man? Edwards thought. He needed him to switch off the lights and lock up.

Just then Edwards heard a shuffle, followed by the sound of breaking glass.

"F'eng—? For God's sake, man, come out here where I can see you."

Several moments passed and then Edwards heard another shuffle and saw the old man emerge from the darkness. His thin beard was scraggly and his long black gown dirty.

"What was that sound, F'eng?" Edwards demanded firmly.

"Nothing, Tai-pan. Nothing."

Edwards looked at F'eng's long black gown. It was wet around the bottom.

"Did you have to steal from me, F'eng, after all these years? Did you have to take my last thing of value? Did I not look after you and your family? Were you not like family to me? I would have given you a bottle of whiskey if you had asked me. Here . . . take the whole case . . . the whole lot. But don't steal from me."

Edwards shook his head, bewildered, and was about to move away. But as he went to turn, he heard a quick emission of air like a hiss and then suddenly his face felt wet on the side. He put his hand up quickly. It was wet . . . It couldn't be! But it was. His own head coolie had spat at him. As the terrible realization began to come over Edwards he heard the words that followed the ultimate insult:

"Capitalist . . . capitalist . . . dirty imperialist capitalist running-dog foreign devil."

Edwards reeled back towards him as a further realization suddenly came over him. He had always known that Blake's information must have come from someone inside his organization. "You . . . !" he shouted, his anger rising into fury now. "You—you were the one who let Blake in and told him about the armored cars . . ."

But his words trailed off as he felt a sharp pain in his chest and fell to the ground clutching it.

As far as Yang Ho was concerned, the continued freedom of Shen Sun Lung was a thorn in his side: the one thing which stood between him and ultimate authority.

But Yang was determined to find him. For Yang's aspirations went far beyond those of a hero-general. And he knew the price one must pay in eternal vigilance to have absolute power. As far as the public was concerned, the Communists were in full flight and would soon be no more. But Yang now knew, from reports flowing in, that Shen had changed his tactics. Shen had stopped running. He and his group of followers, of whom some were now having the temerity to call an army, this was the group it was said the Richmond woman was with, had started attacking local Kuomintang patrols. A few of his own soldiers were even said to have gone over to Shen. Yang did not believe this. But it would not do for it to get out.

Shen must be stopped. He must not be allowed to become any more popular. That was the stuff of which legends were made. There was a sense in which one such as Shen Lung should never have been allowed to leave the city. A country boy is better kept in the dark alleyways of the city where he is not at home. He should never be allowed to return to the fresh air and his beloved peasant ways, lest the combination of those ways, and what he has learned in the city, cause him to draw a peasant army unto himself.

Yang Ho poured another *mao tai,* lit a fresh cigar, and walked once more to his favorite window. No, Shen must not be allowed to grow another month older. If the armored cars could not do it, perhaps another invention of modern warfare would. When the airplanes arrived, Shen's column would be cut to ribbons.

# 39

*It was past midnight when Blake rang Janey's doorbell.* He had no stomach for the task which lay before him this night. He kept thinking of Kate and how much better she would do it.

Janey answered the door in her black dress and stockinged feet. She had a lighted cigarette in one hand. Surprise showed on her face.

"Tom . . . I was expecting Daddy . . . I thought he'd forgotten his key again . . ."

"It's about your father that I'm here . . . may I come in . . . ?"

"Of course." Her face was clouding over. "What's wrong? There's nothing wrong, is there—?"

"Yes, darling, there is," Blake said quietly, entering and closing the door. "Your father's had a stroke. He was found dead on his warehouse floor."

Blake put his arm around her and walked her gently over the black and white marble foyer to the study. She was sobbing deeply. Blake poured her a whiskey, and then one for himself.

"Oh Tom . . ." she said as she gulped it, in between sighs, "Oh Tom . . ."

"There, there," he said, holding her against his chest. "There, there. It'll be all right."

"Give me another," she said, and quickly drank down the second whiskey when he handed it to her, and then held out her glass for more.

"Don't you think that's enough?" he asked gently.

She shook her head, and after a moment or two he gave in and poured her another finger.

"I should see him," she said. "I'd like to see him. Is he all right? Can I see him?"

"Of course. In a little while. They're laying him out now. In a little while."

She nodded. Then, her voice still heaving with heavy sobs, she said:

"Take me upstairs, darling, there's a dear . . ."

"Of course."

Janey grasped at the crystal whiskey decanter with her free hand. She still held her drinking glass in the other as she walked towards the door, Blake following.

When they reached her oak-paneled Tudor apartments in the west wing, Janey walked straight on through the sitting room to her bedroom. She put the decanter and her glass down on the bedside table and threw back the covers. Then she sat on the end of the bed and put her hands up under her skirt to unhook her stockings from her suspender belt. She carefully rolled each stocking down over her legs in turn. As she did so her skirt rode up but she made no effort to push it down.

"Light me a cigarette, Tom, there's a dear." Her voice was not at all slurred but there was a strangely dispassionate tone to it.

"Of course." He lit one from his gold case and handed it to her. Janey drew deeply and handed it back to him while she stood up, reached a hand around to the back of her dress, and fiddled with her zipper.

"Damn. Fix that, too, will you darling?"

"Of course." He handed the cigarette back to her while he cleared the zipper all the way down.

Janey shrugged her shoulders and stood out of the dress.

She inhaled deeply again and then walked to the bedside table where she put out the cigarette in a huge blue crystal ashtray.

She poured herself another whiskey.

"He was a damn good father, whatever you thought of him," she said. "He was never other than good to me."

"Of course. I came to like him." It was true, though at the same time he hated him. But he could not tell Janey that. Perhaps her father and he had been too much the same sort of men, and the things he had liked in Nigel Edwards were the things he admired or at least accepted in his own character, and the things he hated . . . No, that part would not be true. He looked at Janey. She was her father's daughter all right. "You were alike, you and he," he said.

"Isn't that the truth?" She pulled her black satin slip up over her head.

"It all had to do with my mother, Janey. That's why I didn't like him at first. Kids are funny that way."

"We're all funny that way all our lives." She had both her hands around her back now and in a moment the clip gave way and she stood there topless. "I'm going to miss him," she said, as she bent to her black suspender belt, deliberately twanging the elastic as she sent that, too, flying. Now only the black lace panties remained and as she stood there in them Blake thought he had never seen her looking so beautiful or so vulnerable.

"Of course you'll miss him. We both will."

She smiled laconically and pushed both her hands down in a sliding movement.

"What you see is what you get," she said, as she kicked her panties sideways.

He hesitated. "You don't mean that. Not tonight. Shall I find your nightdress?"

She shook her head. "No. Hold me, Tom. Hold me."

Blake came over and held her naked against his chest. He could feel her sobbing through his suit.

"We have to talk about the business," she said, between heaving sighs, as if she believed talking about something close to her father which had a life of its own—however tenuous—would take the hurt away.

"In a few days—after the funeral," he said.

"After the funeral. Yes. After the funeral. We're a long time dead, aren't we? You know that?"

"Yes, I know that."

"So where's it all get you? You and Daddy and the whole damn lot? You make all that money but where's it all get you in the end? God I envy Kate. At least she's got a purpose."

Blake nodded, saying nothing but wondering—wondering just how much for him Janey was Kate, and Kate, Janey; and whether, in some strange way, he hoped to exorcise one with the other.

Janey walked over to the window and stood looking out. It

was a full moon and the silver-yellow light streamed into the room mingling with her auburn-brown maidenhair as she turned back towards him. "Please, sir, will you come inside me and make me forget that the world exists?"

# 40

*More peasants and scattered groups were joining Shen's* army every day now. They seemed instinctively to trust him. And the bigger and stronger the Red Army became, the more it had to fight to secure food and weapons.

There was still no news of Kate's father. Shen knew the best way to gain intelligence on where Yang Ho was keeping him— assuming he was still alive—was to send Wang Lee back to Shanghai. Wang Lee was champing at the bit to go. And they were desperately short of funds and medical supplies once more. No one questioned that Wang Lee had a genius for such matters. But Shen hesitated because he knew the source of much of Wang Lee's genius. Each time he sent Wang Lee on a mission, Shen knew he exposed his own sister.

For a time Shen could justify keeping Wang Lee with them for security reasons. It was too soon after the massacre. It was still not known how much the Shanghai authorities knew about Wang Lee or his physical appearance. The communist organization within the city had been decimated. But a few comrades remained underground, including, surprisingly, the old professor, the lady who had helped to train them all and said she was too old to flee. Shen was anxious to protect what he had left of his network until more was known of how dangerous it was to be seen with Wang Lee.

But this threw everything even more squarely back onto Ling Ling's shoulders. Shen knew she and Wang Lee were lovers.

And the old-fashioned side of him found this hard to accept. He knew Wang Lee had not fled the night of the massacre like the others. Nor the night after. Or several nights after that. He had, instead, slept in Oriental splendor in Shen's sister's bed, while thousands died outside. Then, with his usual cavalier bravado, he had slipped quietly out of Shanghai, dressed as, of all things, a young mandarin. Apparently he and old Ma Yen had become such friends that the old man had lent him some of his dead son's clothes to escape.

This had not made Shen happy. And yet he knew that some of Wang Lee's personality traits which infuriated him were the very reasons Mao had chosen him. Not one in a thousand could have escaped from Shanghai at that time. But Wang Lee had. And he was prepared to go back. To keep going back, knowing that every fresh visit greatly increased his chance of being caught. They desperately needed him to go. But to expose his own sister thus . . . ?

Shen reluctantly agreed.


When Wang reached Shanghai, traveling this time as a Kuomintang colonel, he made his way to Ma Yen's street and waited for the cover of darkness.

Then he walked to the end of the street and knocked on the red lacquered gate.

He heard the stout oak door behind it begin to creak and was relieved to hear the voice of Hsing-tao the gateman singing. But any sense of relief he felt disappeared the moment the door opened and he saw Hsing-tao's usual happy expression change to one of dark concern. Hsing-tao's eyes moved quickly from side to side while his head remained stationary. Wang Lee's reflexes were as sharp as ever. Instinctively understanding Hsing-tao was trying to tell him to go away, Wang Lee stepped swiftly to the side. Just as he did so, he heard the voice of another, a voice which sounded strangely familiar, say:

"Who is there, gateman?"

"No one, master. I suppose it is children playing. When I opened there was no one."

Wang Lee now moved like lightning, melting into the shadows until he reached the corner. Then he looked back cautiously.

Kuomintang colonel's uniform or not, he would not risk ignoring Hsing-tao's warning. But what had happened? Where was the old mandarin? Why did Hsing-tao call another "master"? And where was Ling Ling? Was she inside? Or had something happened to her? One thing was certain. He would have to find out.

As he walked, more quietly and with some dignity now, a plan began to form.

He did not wish to use any known contacts except one. It would be impossible to tell who was watched and who was not. Yet he must find out what had happened. And, reluctantly, he knew there was only one way to do this. He must also seek the help of a European. An influential European. One who would have a reason not to betray him.

It was not foolproof. But, then, what was these days?

He was at the main thoroughfare now and hailed a rickshaw, giving the address of the Cathay Hotel.

When he reached there he went in and booked a room. No one took any notice of an officer without luggage. It was automatically assumed that after a phone call his mistress would arrive discreetly and go straight to his room. A quiet meal and then a night of love. If not a mistress, then one of the girls from the high-priced escort services. It was expected. Those who carried the weight of office needed such respite. Besides, as Wang Lee had anticipated, he was treated like a hero. All Kuomintang— particularly senior officers—were heroes after the routing of the Communists. Wang Lee had no doubt that whatever service he might wish rendered that night, there would be no bill when he left in the morning.

He took his room key but tarried in the foyer until he saw a phone booth free. Then he idled over and casually closed the camphor-wood and glass door. He asked the operator for a number and, when she had found it in the directory, asked her to connect him.

The phone rang and rang. Eventually a woman's voice—a European voice—answered.

"Miss Jane Edwards—?"

"Yes."

"This is a friend of Doctor Richmond's. Please do not make any comment. I have news of her and wish to speak to you. Please tell no one of this and meet me in one hour at the

Teahouse of the Jade Dragon. It is in the old quarter. Sit at the fourth table on the left as you enter . . .''

He clicked the receiver down and waited. After a few more minutes he picked it up again and gave the number of the teahouse. When the proprietor answered Wang Lee said simply:

"Is service as normal or have these traitor Communists who have disturbed the city also affected your business?"

"Service is as normal," the proprietor said quietly, recognizing the voice.

"Good," said Wang Lee. It was a pre-arranged signal. "Please listen carefully. In one hour an English round-eye will come and sit at the regular seat. Give her tea and tell her to wait. If, after half an hour, you are sure no one has followed her, come and find me in the usual place."

Again he clicked the receiver down, turned to look swiftly around the crowded foyer, and then slipped quietly out of the booth and into the elevator.

He rode to the floor above his and then came back down the fire stairs. He walked past his room twice, the full length of the corridor, to make sure it was not watched before opening the door and entering.

There was a little time yet. He stripped hurriedly and ran a bath, thinking of Ling Ling. As he sat in it and let his tensed muscles relax, he knew that one way or another he must find her that night. If they had caught her, there might still be time. But if anyone had hurt her . . . He was under orders not to kill except in self-defense, so as not to risk undue attention. But if anyone had harmed one follicle of the hair on her tiny precious body, they would have to deal with him that night, and they would die slowly, in screams of agony, whatever the cost.

Janey arrived at the Jade Dragon just before 9 P.M. She had had to leave a house full of dinner guests, including Blake, on the flimsy excuse that an old school-friend was ill.

She walked in and sat at the appointed table. Presently a fat old waiter in a dirty white apron shuffled up to her:

"Your friend has sent a message that he will be a little late. He asks that you wait . . . Is this agreeable . . . ?"

Jane nodded.

"You will take tea?"

She nodded again. "No one followed me, saw me come in, or for that matter knows where I am, if that's what you're worried about," she said.

The old waiter said nothing but smiled and Jane saw it was a smile of relief. Nevertheless, she sat over her tea for half an hour before she saw the old man slip out the back door of the teahouse.

In the alley at the rear the old waiter stood under a single light as he had so many times before. He stood thus for five minutes, smoking a cigarette. If he finished it and did not immediately light another, the coast was clear. If he lit another, or even another after that, in the chain-smoking manner of so many Chinese, then it was still not clear. While he smoked anyone waiting was not to come in.

But there was no sign of anyone this evening so when he finished his first cigarette he did not light another. Soon he heard Wang Lee's voice coming from close by:

"She is there?"

"Yes."

"And it is clear inside?"

"It was when I left. Give me three minutes more and if I do not return, come in."

"It is good to see you well, comrade," Wang Lee said kindly. "They never suspected you? You were always one of our best."

"It is good to hear your cheeky voice again, too, comrade," the old man said. "The others are well?"

"Skinny but well. We build an army."

"It is the only way now. We will build our network again so that one day you may return and liberate us."

Wang Lee had to choke back emotion at the old man's dedication.

The proprietor shuffled back into the shop then. After a few minutes, when he did not return, Wang Lee slipped in quietly past the kitchen to a corridor which would lead him unseen to the seat behind the chipped, red-lacquered fretwork screen.

He sat down and leaned forward.

"Miss Edwards . . . ?" he whispered.

"Yes," she said, startled to hear an unseen voice behind the screen.

"I am sorry for this secrecy but it is for your safety as well as mine."

"I understand. But what is it you want? You said you had news of Doctor Richmond. How is she . . . ?"

"She is well and of great service to us."

"Where is she?"

"She travels with the First Red Army."

"Of course. I did not mean to pry . . . How are you called . . . ?"

"Wang."

"Wang who?"

"Just Wang."

"That is like a European saying Smith or Jones."

"Precisely," he laughed.

"Well I'm grateful for the news of Kate," Janey said. "Please tell her her mother is in good health and give her my love. You said you wanted a favor of me . . ."

Wang Lee found himself warming to this woman's directness and cynical humor.

"Katherine is anxious to get a message to the girl they call Ling Ling," he said cautiously, inventing a lie which he hoped would ensure Jane's silence. She would surely not wish to betray her friend. "Apparently the girl has moved from her last address," Wang Lee went on.

"Well I can't see that I can do any harm to tell you that," Janey said. "Yes, she has moved. When Yang Ho routed the Communists and declared martial law, he commissioned the house of Ma Yen the Mandarin for his own residence. No one knows what has become of the old mandarin, but Yang Ho took all his concubines, including Ling Ling, and set them up in an expensive officers' brothel in Lafayette Avenue. Ling Ling is now in charge. Only the very senior officers are allowed to use it. And Ling Ling is to remain at Yang Ho's personal beck and call. It is said he keeps her for himself and very important visiting dignitaries . . . Is this information helpful to you . . . ?"

"You are very well informed, Miss Edwards," Wang Lee said, trying to keep his voice as unemotional as possible. "But tell me, where exactly on Lafayette Avenue is the house of Ling Ling?"

"It is the old stone house with the rolling English gardens."

"But that was owned by a British trading company . . . ?"

"Yes."

"You mean Yang Ho requisitioned that, too?"

"Strangely, no. They just moved out after the purge."

"Interesting."

"Yes. I knew you'd say that. Not all *tai-pans* are completely skeptical about the Communists ever coming to power . . . Just most . . . like me . . ."

Wang Lee laughed. "You have been very helpful, Miss Edwards, and I can assure you that *when* we come to power I will do my best to try to protect you. Perhaps if I come to town again, we may meet and talk some more and I may give you further news of Doctor Richmond . . . ?"

"That would be most welcome."

When he returned to the Cathay Hotel, Wang Lee marched boldly up to the front desk.

"Get me the number of the special house for officers in Lafayette Avenue and put it through to the booth," Wang said in a commanding tone. "But make sure you connect me with the madam in charge, for I will speak to none other. My friend General Yang has said I am to speak to her and her alone . . ."

"Of course, sir, of course." The reception manager behind the desk obviously knew the rule that the madam in charge was reserved for special officers. He probably assumed Wang Lee was an intelligence officer—a member of the infamous Blue Shirts.

Wang nodded and walked slowly over to the booth, taking out a cigarette and inserting it in his holder as he did so.

By the time he reached the booth and picked up the receiver, Ling Ling was on the line.

"Yes, this is Madam Ling . . . who is this, please . . . ?"

"Do you recognize the voice . . . ?"

"Why, General Wang, from the Imperial General Staff . . . how nice to hear from you again . . ."

"Are you able to visit me tonight at the Cathay . . . ?"

He heard her hesitate at the other end of the line. Then she answered slowly. Her voice sounded strained. "Perhaps I could come for a short visit. But I would not be able to stay. Is this agreeable . . . ?"

"Of course. Room 101. The door will be unlocked and the room dark. Open slowly."

"I understand."

It was after 2 A.M. before Wang heard the click of the doorhandle to his room. He had sat for hours in the darkness, waiting, his German mauser pistol in his hand. The window behind him was open and the light cast its glow over his right shoulder. When the door opened, the light from the corridor would silhouette anyone coming in. He would have the light from the window to shoot by and the window was open as an extra precaution in case he needed to escape by the fire stairs at the back.

The door opened slowly. A woman's gloved hand came around the door frame. Wang Lee sat motionless and silent. Gradually, little by little, more of the woman came into view. It was Ling Ling. But still he did not speak. It was not over yet. He waited for her to enter fully and close the door. It would be impossible for her to see him sitting in the darkness.

"Move over against the wall and wait," he whispered.

She glided to one side.

If any were coming, they would come now. If anyone had followed her—for whatever reason—he or she would come now, in that crucial moment when they were sure you felt you were safe the threat was over.

Wang Lee sat perfectly still with his gun poised. He waited five minutes. He could hear Ling Ling's breathing. It was all he could do to contain himself and keep his eyes on the door.

When the five minutes were up he eased himself out of the chair and moved silently around the wall in the darkness towards her. He could see her in the shadows and smelled her perfume as he slid silently past her and slid the bolt home on the inside of the door.

He walked to the window and drew the blind, leaving the window open behind it. Then he switched on the light and looked at her. She ran to him and hugged him.

"I cannot stay, truly . . . I cannot stay . . . ," she said, as he began to tug at her clothes. But the next instant she was at his.

Then both were together on the floor—hurrying, breathlessly hurrying, as if in a field with the sound of a marching army close by.


She stayed, in all, only twenty minutes. But by the time she left, Wang Lee held another bundle of money—a staggering amount of money for food and supplies. She had also given him two messages—both of which were for Kate—and some valuable information about what Yang Ho planned.

But he feared for her. As he checked out of the hotel soon after she had left, and the reception manager winked and said, "Business concluded satisfactorily, sir?" he feared for her. Yang Ho was not stupid. How long could Ling Ling continue to fool him? And in addition to gleaning information from Yang, and keeping from him the full extent of the money she was making, one of the messages Wang Lee had to deliver to Kate made it quite clear someone else had involved Ling Ling even more directly in espionage work. However protective of Ling Ling both Wang Lee and Shen might have been, the aging lady professor had now asked a favor of Ling Ling.

The truth was, the singularly most important Communist in China at the moment, whether he and Shen liked it or not, was not even a Communist at all. The most important—and therefore the one in the most danger—was not Mao or Shen or even Wang Lee. It was the chirpy, warm-blooded but deep-of-soul peasant girl named Ling Ling, whom he loved, and who seemed so blithely unaware of the danger she was in. For after they had made love—so ferociously that his elbows and knees were skinned—she had delivered what she called her "important" messages, including some information about Kate's father. Then she had chatted on animatedly as if nothing were wrong, telling him how glad she was that Yang Ho was paying for her to take singing lessons.

But perhaps she was whistling in the dark to keep her courage up.

As Wang Lee boarded a Kuomintang troop train at the station bound for the country and slipped quietly out of Shanghai he did so with a heavy heart.

\*       \*       \*

In the communist camp all was not sweetness and light. As their numbers grew it was inevitable they would lose some of the sense of a tightly knit family they had had at the start. It also became necessary, because of their increased numbers, to appoint a deputy. There was no question of it being Wu. He was needed in the planning tent, poring over his maps, filling in the details for Shen's inspired battle plans. Even Wu agreed that Shen had little choice but to appoint Po. The man had proved himself in battle and, whereas not as daring in planning as Shen, he was a fine tactician.

Did Wang Lee sense some dissension in the camp the moment he arrived? Perhaps. But he was certainly not ready for the broadside he received when, overjoyed at the information Ling Ling had secured on their behalf, he shouted out to Kate, "There is news, Kate Doctor, news of your father . . . !"

Kate ran over. "Tell me, tell me!" she said breathlessly.

"Not yet, comrade," Wang Lee said shaking his head. Despite his garrulous, cavalier nature, he was careful how much he said and in whose hearing. There were too many people around. He smiled and put his arm around Kate. She was dressed like so many of them now, in baggy thin khaki battle tunic with large patch pockets.

Whether Song Wei meant for Kate to overhear what followed they never found out. But as Kate and Wang Lee moved off towards Shen's tent, both heard the unmistakable sound of Song Wei's voice:

"So is this all our fine Chief of Intelligence returns with after his special mission to Shanghai . . . a personal message for our own white foreign devil whom he dares call *comrade* when she is not even one of us?"

From the day Shen had made Po his deputy a strange metamorphosis had come over Song Wei. Her place in the hierarchy established by Po's position, the former actress had shown just how sharp her fingernails could be.

At Song Wei's remark to Wang Lee, Kate went to turn on her when she felt Wang squeeze her arm. Then, in his best Hong Kong gutter Chinese he swung towards Song Wei and shouted:

"Are you some stupid peasant woman that you think I run off at the mouth in public with all I know? What I discovered on my mission is for my commander and him alone. As for my friend,

Kate Doctor, here, if you as the Communist you say you are had done as much for our cause as she who is not has done, then you would earn the right to speak but not before.''

And with that he turned sharply back towards Kate and put his arm around her once more.

"Her influence grows," Wang said quietly as they walked.

"I know."

"Well let us not spoil good news. It is good news, by the way."

Kate squeezed him around the waist as they walked. "Oh Wang Lee, how can I ever thank you enough?"

"By your eternal smiling presence—by your presence and concern for our lives. Without you we would be only half an army. Besides, I told you on the ship you had created a debt of honor I would one day repay."

Kate smiled. But it was true. And whether she was half an army or not, she was certainly needed. She had learned more surgery in one year—was it already that long since Shanghai— than most do in a lifetime. Yet she knew the worst was yet to come. They all knew that. No one had any illusions anymore.

When Shen heard the news about Kate's father he was over-joyed. Ling Ling had actually found out where Yang Ho was keeping him prisoner.

"Kate Doctor, Kate Doctor," Shen said excitedly, "it is on our way—right on our way—a detour of only a few miles, no more. A day or two's extra march at the most. It will take a few months before we reach it, but in the meantime we will form such a plan to rescue him that not even Yang Ho and all his Blue Shirts will be able to stop us."

Kate looked at her dear friends then—Shen, Wang Lee, Hwang, Yu-Ma, Lu Chien, and Wu—and for some reason she just burst out crying. She cried for a long time and could not stop. She just stood there sobbing and being comforted and hugged by each of them in turn, even the giant Yu-Ma, who, when he walked up to Kate and tenderly put his arms about her, had the most caring and protective look Kate had ever seen in her life.

## 41

*They kept pressing on to where it was rumored Mao had set up* a mountain garrison.

It was still a great way off and winter was coming on.

Mao, who had not been one of the Shanghai leaders, had led his own peasant uprising in Hunan. He had been defeated but it was said he had escaped to the Chingkangshan Mountains. There was supposed to be a soviet there. This was a term the Chinese had borrowed from the Russian Revolution. It meant simply a council elected by the workers and soldiers of a district.

What concerned Shen was that if he knew about Mao and his possible whereabouts, Yang Ho might too. The sooner Shen and his people reached Mao to reinforce him, the better.

So soon, whenever they could, they traveled by night as well as day. Yet in those months when they were on their way to the mountains—walking or by mule—not one peasant betrayed them. No one asked for money. But in line with communist policy, Wu gave written IOUs.

Kate often wondered at the spirit of these peasants. So few were Communists. But they were prepared to give away their last food.

The Kuomintang continued mounting their frightening purges.

Late in December 1928, Shen's army came within sight of Chingkangshan. They were several hundred now, with more joining every day.

They marched into Chingkangshan singing, swinging in great columns towards the narrow entrance to the pass. Suddenly heads appeared from above rocks everywhere. And then a cap or two waved—green cotton caps with red stars on them. Then presently the hills all around them were alive with men, women, and children cheering.

This was the first major linkup of communist forces, and those cheering on the hills could not believe their good fortune. They had heard of another band—a small band straggling back to the mountains from the south. But here was no motley group. Here was an army, a real army. Combined with Mao's army, these several hundred extra would be a formidable force.

As Shen and his band finally stopped, and he dismissed them, pots were quickly put on the fire to boil. Soon all were sitting around with steaming tea and hot noodles served by their new-found comrades-in-arms. There was great reverence shown. For all knew that those who formed the nucleus of this army were the survivors of the Shanghai massacre.

After Shen and the others had rested, and were passing around a single cigarette between them, a strange-looking man, who appeared as if his arms did not belong to his body, strolled up to them. Although circulated pictures were still uncommon, Shen recognized him immediately from descriptions. He was unusually tall for a Chinese, and he stood erect and thin, though with a slight slouch from the shoulders. He had an unresponsive-looking face, which would have been thin if it had not been for the fully covered cheekbones which, with the shock of thick black hair parted in the middle and flopping down on either side, made the face look fuller than it was. There was strain in his eyebrows. He wore a creased cotton battle jacket with large flap pockets. Although his cotton pants were khaki, his jacket, which buttoned to the collar, was navy. His arms flopped down straight at both sides so that it made the sloping away of his shoulders seem even more exaggerated. His hands had the fine long fingers of a calligrapher and his skin was smooth like a woman's. A half-smoked cigarette hung limply in his right hand. It looked curiously casual, like his clothes. But the rest of him was serious and his brow creased vertically in towards the center and his mouth was tight, giving an almost patrician, superior look.

"Well, comrade," the tall man said as he came up, "I suppose you must be Shen. We had expected you—but not with such an army! You are already making quite a name for yourself."

Shen looked up. "I wouldn't want Yang Ho not to know where to find me, Comrade Mao," he said with a smile. They both laughed out loud then, and the others joined in. Wu and Mao were old friends, and greeted each other warmly, having fought in the First Revolution together under Sun Yat-sen. After Wu and Mao had reminisced for a time, Shen introduced Kate and the others to Mao. They all talked on into the night. But there was a faraway look in Mao's eyes which Wu later told Shen and Kate he did not remember from before.

Mao was now in his mid-thirties. He had always been a poet visionary, of course, as well as a fighter, so some of the preoccupied look was to be expected. But there seemed a special tiredness and world-weariness in him this day, despite his efforts to greet the new arrivals.

They soon learned that Mao was already facing the first of many revolts within the party. Li Li-san was challenging Mao's policies. Li was an advocate of city revolution and wanted to move against the cities first, setting up communist governments in the big centers of population before tackling the countryside. This was against Mao's avowed policy that a peasant uprising should take place first.

"And what do you think of urban revolution, little commander?" Mao said later to Shen as they all talked quietly.

Shen smiled and said:

"I think that you are a peasant, and Hwang is a peasant and Yu-Ma is a peasant and I am a peasant and Wu Zhao and Lu Chien are converted peasants, and the ones who helped us along the way were peasants, and that this army and this cause will stand or fall not in the cities but in the countryside and fields. It must be a peasant army. We must fight here first where our strength is and then take the cities."

Mao nodded thoughtfully. He had heard of Shen's outspokenness. But they were very much of a mind on this. Although others in the group around the campfire in the hills that night had different ideas. And they argued for a long time before Kate excused herself and retired.

For the first time since their march had begun, they had a temporary home. Perhaps this lulled them into a false sense of security.

They had come from a string of successful battles in which they had been the aggressors. Kuomintang propaganda put all communist raids down to "bandit attacks."

Shen's "Young Celestials"—the name given to his crack regiment of young men who had been the backbone of his army and formed the vanguard of every major battle so far, and with whom Kate invariably traveled—were tired. Winter was coming on.

They were having such a happy time for once. All the peasant villages welcomed them, but the one surrounding the Ching-kangshan camp had been particularly warm. The peasants joked with the soldiers, calling them "notorious red bandits" and laughing.

There was much singing around the campfire at night. There was hot food. Their beds were dry. There was a sense of great purpose.

And there was fun and laughter. There could, of course, be no false modesty in a camp of this nature. They were all living in the open together. But poor Lu Chien, the mandarin's daughter, now married to her beloved Wu in a simple communist wedding ceremony, still found it difficult. She found herself unable to bathe communally in the mountain streams—or use the communal toilets.

Quite early on in the march, Shen had returned to his peasant habit of having a pee in the nearest bush whenever it suited him, much to Lu Chien's embarrassment and Kate's amusement.

For the women, panties, underclothes, or padding for their menstrual periods were things of the past. Any cloth was used for bandages. Yet Lu Chien, however hard the battle, however cramped the circumstances, would still not go against her conservative upbringing. Somehow, on all their journeyings, she managed to refuse the call of nature until a quiet, unobtrusive way could be found.

Her friends joked with her and she took it all in good humor, but she refused to bend on the bathing and toilet arrangements.

And for some reason, best known to herself, Song Wei joined Lu Chien in her stand. Some said it was because she was an actress and gave herself airs.

One Sunday, when they were all relaxing and the sun was out, the camp was not quite as alert as it might have been.

They had decided to bathe with some soap which Wang Lee had brought from his last trip to Shanghai.

They all stripped off their clothes on the grassy bank and ran

into the stream—laughing and running and jumping to keep
warm, and throwing the two cakes of soap between them. There
were Shen, Kate, Hwang, Yu-Ma, Wang Lee, and some of the
women. Wu, out of deference to his wife, watched from the
bank. Lu Chien, as usual when such things were going on, was
nowhere to be seen.

Kate loved it. It was a great leveler, a good source of camara-
derie, and a good outlet for letting off steam. Once they all got
rid of their reserve it was great fun.

Wang Lee was delivering Ling Ling's second message to Kate
as they stood side by side, quite unselfconsciously, taking turns
to soap each other's back and Kate congratulating Wang again
on remembering the soap despite such a difficult mission.

The first message, of course, had been of her father. But Ling
Ling had also given Wang Lee a second message—the one
which Wang had been annoyed about because the old lady
professor had contacted Ling Ling directly.

Wang Lee was explaining to Kate that he did not hold it
against her personally, but he thought it very dangerous for the
old lady to expose Ling Ling by a direct contact. No one knew
how safe the old lady was anymore. Besides, he doubted the
message was worth it.

"Does the name John Carpenter mean anything to you, Kate
Doctor?" he said.

"Yes it does, Lee," Kate said slowly, "I knew him very well
once." Wang Lee thought he detected a tone of nostalgia, almost
of warmth. "I was at medical school with him in America,"
Kate continued. "But he dropped out after the second year . . ."

"To become a journalist . . . ?"

"Well, to study at the School of Oriental Studies in London,
which so many journalists do . . ."

"He is one of the new American wire service representatives
in Shanghai. He wants to interview you and Comrade Shen . . ."

"He what?"

"Wants to interview you and our leader. The old lady says he
is sympathetic to our cause. Or that he is not completely unsym-
pathetic. I think the old one is getting senile. She says, according
to Ling Ling, that she trusts him completely and it is time we
started to try to counter the Kuomintang propaganda with some
stories of our own.

"She even took him to interview Shen's mother. Took him to Shen's home because he promised not to reveal the identity of Shen's mother or the name of the village or use any photographs. She says he kept his word and the story was quite favorable . . . ."

"John is certainly trustworthy," Kate said quietly.

"But what if Yang Ho ever got hold of him . . . ?" Wang Lee countered. "I think we've got enough trouble staying alive as it is without revealing where we are to someone . . ."

"Perhaps. Maybe I'm just being selfish. I'd like to see him. But I'll do whatever you and Shen decide."

Wang Lee nodded. He and Shen had already decided to go ahead if Kate agreed and appeared to trust Carpenter. As their army grew they would need more and more arms from other countries—and they had to do something to combat the Kuomintang's lies. Neither liked the old professor involving Ling Ling, but both had agreed that she was, as usual, right.

"I'll talk to Shen about it and let you know," Wang Lee said.

Kate nodded. Shen and the others had been busy talking a short distance from them.

As they all got out and dried themselves, Shen explained to Kate and Wang Lee what he and the others had been talking about. But Kate was barely listening. Did she know John Carpenter? Know him! He had been her beau at medical school, had even asked her to marry him. But she had not been ready for that, nor had she cared for him sufficiently then. And now, after all these years, he was in China . . .

She turned her attention back to Shen. He was saying they had decided it was time for a very belated wedding present for Lu Chien—Madame Wu. He, Hwang, and Yu-Ma had already done some preliminary scouting. A short distance from the camp they had found a stand of stout mountain bamboo—ideal for the present Shen had in mind.

So when everyone was dry, they went and cut the bamboo. Then they took jute cord to bind a seat, walls, and door. And finally—when they were all finished—they presented Lu Chien with what they called "Madame Wu's Pee House," amid great laughter.

They insisted she try it. Reluctantly, she agreed and bent her knees to sit down. This caused even greater merriment. The pee

house was too small! They were just preparing to enlarge it when
the first sounds of artillery fire were heard.

The laughter died instantly as they ran back to their defenses.
Barrage after barrage landed. Within a few hours it was obvious
this was no random attack. The casualties were too heavy. This
was no local White Army detachment making a sporadic sortie.
Kate was soon up to her elbows in blood and Shen was engaged
in their bitterest and bloodiest fighting so far.

The other side—the Kuomintang—were easily visible from the
elevated position of their mountain stronghold. In the forefront,
quite clear to view, was Yang Ho himself.

No one asked if Kate was a Communist. In fact they made a
point of not asking her so as not to embarrass her. Her medical
bag had been life itself so many times to so many comrades—
those from other units as well as Shen's. She was as much a part
of the army as anyone.

Kate's medical capacity doubled—particularly her capacity to
improvise. She lived off the land with herbs for healing in the
same way they lived off the land to eat.

She took from the dead to help the living—even if sometimes
it was only clothing—for in the mountains there was a chill in
winter such as Kate had never known.

As she moved among the bodies, no one looking on would
notice she was not Chinese, except for her blonde hair.

If she had been trained for no other thing, if some canon of
providence had decided before she was born that she should be
trained for this very moment of history in which she now found
herself, she would have counted herself lucky. She had an
opportunity few would ever have. An opportunity to serve, to
work at her healing in circumstances in which few would ever
find themselves. She had an opportunity, moreover, to be part
of—to see at firsthand even if she did not believe in what it stood
for—one of the most momentous revolutions of the twentieth
century.

For, as day followed day, as muleteers with stolen gun carriages rode by, as supplies were freely given by starving peasants, Kate knew that the wind the Kuomintang had always feared
was blowing, blowing in the wild grass. She was thrilled to be a

part of it. Thrilled to march with Shen's Young Celestials. They treated their lives so cheaply, these young warriors. They loved their country and their peasant families so. Kate knew she would see many more die. But perhaps she could keep as many alive as possible.

She wondered about Blake and what he would think of her now. A pacifist doctor engaged in war! A pacifist doctor with a price on her head. She could never forgive him but she still missed him, and was her crime really so very different? She was no longer against gunrunning—at least not for her side. She might not be a Communist, but she wanted her side to win. The war had certainly done that to her. Grass and mud floors and wooden operating tables in the open, running with blood, did that to you very quickly.

She wondered about Blake a lot. But the months rolled on and the casualties got higher. She asked about him. She still asked. She asked the commanders where they got their weapons. Were there not some gunrunners bringing them in? Could he disguise himself so as to fool the Communists—and would he dare? No, there were no gunrunners, they said. Would to the gods of the earth there were. The Communists were always so desperately short of arms they would buy from anyone. Yes, anyone.

Yang Ho continued to siege Chingkangshan. He ordered up reinforcements, and White troops massed in even greater numbers against the mountain stronghold of the First Red Army. But the garrison position had been well chosen in the mountains. There were natural rock and shale walls for defense—and springs of water near crop-growing areas to help withstand siege.

But despite the siege, recruits managed to slip in and the army continued to grow. Some were White Army defectors. Shen took them all. There was little doubt in anyone's mind that a massive battle was looming. Shen was now effectively commander-in-chief, with Mao spending more and more time on organization as political commissar.

Another influx of defecting White troops boosted their ranks. But even so, the Whites surrounding them still outnumbered them twenty to one.

Because of the long siege, food now became perilously short.

In January 1929, Shen decided to try to break out. In the mountain passes he had been regrouping; training; consolidating his army.

When they did break out it was with an army such as the world had never seen. The days of lax Chinese armies were gone. The Red Army which broke out of the mountains that day moved as one man—with unbelievable morale and determination. But it was not only this which caused the world to sit up and take notice. The poorly armed Communists had employed for the first time what was to become the classic Chinese communist guerilla tactic to overcome the disadvantage of inferior numbers and poor equipment. The Red Army was completely outnumbered. But they had trained so hard that they were able to hit with their entire force and regroup quickly. They were able to move in quietly, hit quickly at one spot while the enemy still had its several armies spread out, and then regroup and move on quickly to a second army. After immobilizing it, they moved farther on still to savage a third army before the news of the first attack had barely reached the second.

This was the classic Chinese communist battle tactic: hit hard and run. It became commonplace later, but then it was revolutionary. Yet it was no skirmish. It was a concentrated, obliterating attack, making up in intensity what it lost in duration. The Reds were too few and too poorly armed to sustain long battles. So they had to accommodate their fighting to their resources. The hit-hard-and-run attack was the main vehicle of these tactics. And the main resource was the spirit of the men themselves who believed in what they were doing, with a daring and determination that broke column after column of White troops until they were forced to flee.

Their new tactics might be successful, but there were still large numbers of wounded—so many that Kate had to ask Shen to assign some of the women to her as assistants. Song Wei complained bitterly when she was among those selected, saying she was of far more value as a fighter, the equal of any man. She stormed into Shen's tent, and the others outside could hear her shouting angrily at him. He replied in quiet, measured tones, persuading her that she was desperately needed to help Kate with the wounded. They talked for a long time, and when she came out, Song Wei was smiling.

She went to Kate and said, "That Shen, he's wonderful, isn't he? I'd do anything for him. Well, here I am. What do you want me to do?"

In the weeks that followed, during which it seemed to Kate that she had not moved from standing knee-deep in blood beside her makeshift wooden operating table, one person became her strong right arm—Song Wei. Everything Kate had ever thought about her was forgotten. She could say anything she liked, so far as Kate was concerned. Perhaps Shen's placating words had had their effect. No only would they have been lost without her bandage supply, but Song Wei also was invariably there to sluice the blood off the table when it needed sluicing; to wipe Kate's forehead when, despite the intense cold, it dripped with perspiration; and to hold the hurricane lantern close over the wounded long into the night.

Yet despite Song Wei's help, and that of a few others, Kate realized she was still hopelessly understaffed to handle battles of this magnitude. She needed a whole group of women with properly assigned tasks. They must be better prepared—well in advance. With this in view she went to see Shen.

It was the day after the battle in which the Whites had been put to rout. But Kate was up early making the rounds of her "hospital beds." Most of these were beds of pine needles under the deep fir overhang of the branches, which gave some protection under the trees from falling snow. Her orderlies were getting the tea out. Kate inspected the worst cases first and then collected two cups of tea—one for herself and one for Shen—and walked towards his tent.

It was 6 A.M. It never occurred to Kate that he might not be up. He was always up early. It was stupid of her, of course, for whereas she still had patients hanging by a thread, whom she could not leave for more than two or three hours, his main work had been done for the time. And he certainly needed a rest.

But as Kate pulled back the flap of his tent and bent her head inside, two cups of tea held carefully in one hand, her eyes met the full frontal naked form of Song Wei.

There was no mistaking where Song Wei had been. The red

blanket on the ground, where Shen still lay asleep, was turned
back at the edge nearest Song Wei. Kate had entered at the
precise moment the former Shanghai actress had chosen to jump
out of bed. She stood naked for a moment as she looked for her
clothes.

When she saw Kate she made no effort to cover herself,
although it was freezing cold and her nipples stood out like
cow's teats. Well, Kate thought, it was certainly true what Lu
Chien and Wu had said of her. They claimed to have seen her
naked in a Shanghai club for the rich before she became an
actress and before they had become Communists. They had said
her body was alabaster and black mink. It was the most beautifully
formed figure Kate had ever seen. Everything was in proportion,
from the tightly rounded full breasts to the neatly-swelling hips.
Kate was transfixed for a moment with the unexpected spectacle.

But Song Wei was equal to the occasion, as always. She
simply smiled casually but conspiratorially to Kate and put an
index finger to her lips to indicate not to wake Shen.

She found herself feeling jealous. Was it simply jealousy at
Song Wei's dark perfection? Or was it jealousy because Song
Wei had had a man's comfort on a cold night and Kate had not?
Did it go even beyond that? Was she jealous of her sleeping with
Shen? Kate forced herself to smile. "I think that's the most
beautiful body I've ever seen, Song Wei," she whispered warmly,
handing over one of her cups of tea. "It seems a pity to cover it
but you'd better put something on or you'll catch your death of
cold."

Song Wei nodded and put the tea down for a moment while
she bent over and rummaged for her pants and battle jacket. The
jacket was stained with blood as Kate's was—there had been no
chance to wash clothes yet—and it reminded Kate why she was
there and how much she owed Song Wei. She felt guilty about
feeling jealous. On an impulse, as Song Wei stepped into her
pants and put her arms into her battle jacket, Kate put her tea
down, moved over to Song Wei and quietly did up the buttons.
"Sorry there isn't warmer clothing for you, little one," she said,
kissing her lightly on the cheek. "You of all people deserve it. I
couldn't have managed without you." And with that she picked
up her tea and disappeared from the tent, leaving Song Wei
looking quite overcome.

No one thought another thing about Song Wei after that. She and Po had become such indispensable parts of the group. But when Kate suggested to Shen that he appoint Song Wei head of a women's committee to help with medical duties, including the scrounging of supplies, Shen seemed reluctant. He pointed out to Kate that it would involve Song Wei's moving outside their main force a great deal—and even behind enemy lines.

"I realize this," Kate said, "and it worries me, too. I'd go myself for the supplies, I need them so badly. But unfortunately this is not possible and someone has to do it. Who better than an actress who is a trained fighter?"

"You are right, of course, Kate Doctor," Shen said disconsolately. "I'm just being selfish."

"Perhaps for the first time in your life and with just cause. She is very beautiful. Are you very much in love?"

"Love? Who knows? Who asks such questions in these times? I know only that for a few minutes each day I gaze on beauty, and feel warm flesh, and know that all is not war always."

"So it is good for you and good for her and good for us. That cannot be all bad."

"No," he laughed, "that cannot be all bad. And tomorrow we might all be dead. So it is decided, then . . . Song Wei is your head nurse and gatherer of bandages."

# 42

*Captain Thomas Blake and Jane Carruthers Edwards were married in the Episcopal Cathedral of Shanghai on April 9, 1931. It was the biggest Easter wedding the city had ever seen and there was a lavish party at the club afterwards. Everyone said it was the wedding of the year.*

But the business merger, once thought inevitable, had not

gone through. The Edwards business, although on the verge of bankruptcy, would continue as an independent firm. A few days before the wedding, Jane Edwards had been officially installed as its managing director and president.

She had announced she would seek new avenues of business in an effort to save the company. Everyone said it was impossible.

The truth was, Blake had been more than willing to agree to a merger. It had been Janey who had vetoed it. When Blake had pressed her, she had simply smiled and said, "Dear Tom, if you want to marry me it must be because of what you found on the bottom of the boat that sunny afternoon. For the rest, I intend to live my own life and run my own business my way. I will have your children and run our family, but I want to see to it that my father's business survives as well."

Blake had nodded. He was, in a sense, past caring. It was just a marriage of convenience. Both knew that. Kate was now a dull ache. But she was still there—and probably always would be. They spoke of her only rarely these days. And he and Janey had a lot in common. She was the perfect hostess and oiled the social wheels of his business with great charm and finesse. It was still not really sanctioned that women ran their own businesses, but Blake had never been a follower of convention and made no objection. Janey loved him for this openmindedness. There was a deep bond of friendship between them and certainly a lot of physical attraction. Perhaps other things would grow.

And so they were married. But not without feeling a chill breath blowing in the wind that afternoon as the bridal party stood on the steps of the cathedral for the wedding photographs.

The breath belonged to Shen Sun Lung. It blew down from the mountain reaches of Chingkangshan with the news that not only had the siege of the Communists been broken, but the Red Army had put the Whites to flight. Yang Ho had failed to rout the Reds and now he was returning in defeat! It seemed impossible. After all, the Whites had outnumbered the Reds twenty to one!

No one at the time believed Chingkangshan was the beginning of anything—everyone thought it was just an isolated victory. But it gave them all cause to ponder. Today Chingkangshan, tomorrow the world? What was it the poet had said? Something like that. Shen would know better. They said Shen was a poet. A soldier, politician, intellectual, and poet. Could he really be a better leader than Yang Ho?

When Ling Ling heard of the wedding, she decided, in her wisdom, that Kate Doctor would probably prefer to know about it.

Even so, it would take months to get word to her. Although Wang Lee had built up his network once more, many of the links were still uncertain, particularly in the villages away from the railhead. It was a tenuous system at best, comprising rail, car, muleteers, and peasants on foot.

Ling Ling wrote out a message, enclosed a cutting from the daily paper, and placed it in an envelope ready to send. Perhaps Wang Lee would come himself again soon.

As Yang Ho's power and influence had increased, so had Ling Ling's. In the sumptuous group of apartments set aside for her on the top floor of the house on Lafayette Avenue, she was waited on by servants and free to come and go except when her master needed her. Her aged mandarin benefactor, Ma Yen, now lived in a small house with one servant—Hsing-tao, his former doorman—all paid for by Ling Ling. The old man, in his night-time meanderings and mutterings around the house, seemed strangely disenamored of the new regime and had even been overheard to chuckle on more than one occasion, "Yang Ho's a butcher, Yang Ho's a butcher . . . he'll get a different price than he bargained for from the slaughter of Shanghai."

Now everyone knew that the elder born was past the age of reason and no one would take any notice of him, but neverthe-less Ling Ling feared for him lest his words reach the ears of someone in authority and be misunderstood. So she determined to protect him. She was the only one he listened to. And she loved him dearly for being so good to her and was determined to make his days as happy as possible. She could not believe that if Yang Ho found out he would do anything, although she determined to keep the secret from him.

As she readied herself for her master Yang Ho's return, she knew their meeting would not be a happy one. He would want to see her as soon as he got back, she knew. He would want to exorcise the anger of his defeat and she had to be prepared for what might come. Fortunately, when he beat her, it was always where others could not see—for he would not have it said of him that he beat his concubine. Usually he used his hands and only occasionally his officer's plaited leather riding crop. If she had to enjoy a beating or two to remain in his confidence and so save others' lives, what matter? The important thing was that Yang Ho must never suspect she sought information. If he ever had the slightest inkling, then he might not get as drunk during their sexual encounters as he usually did. And if he were not as drunk as she thought, and woke to see her at his document case and knew she had found the secret of its lock, she had no doubt as to what would befall her.

# 43

*Shen's army now reached the point at which it had to detour to find Kate's father.*

Kate was excited and insisted that she go. Despite the danger, Shen saw the wisdom of this. His whole plan depended on split-second timing and there could be no slip-ups. The main force would be waiting nearby and could not, at any cost, be threatened. With Kate part of the raiding party, there would be no question of her father not being prepared to leave. The moment he saw Kate he would know it was safe.

Shen had ascertained in advance from Kate that her father could ride. He had learned on his father's farm in Georgia as a boy and although that was a long time ago, it would be adequate for their purposes. Kate herself had learned to ride during their forced marches. They had precious few horses but Shen insisted she ride whenever possible. This not only enabled her to rest, it also gave her practice in riding. As their medical officer she was high on the list of those to be saved at all costs in an emergency and had to learn to ride for this reason alone.

The group responsible for the raid was small: Hwang, Yu-Ma, a couple of Shen's trusted Young Celestials, Song Wei and Kate. Song Wei was necessary because as scavenger of medical supplies and therefore the one most frequently outside the camp. She was their local geography expert.

On the day planned for the raid they were up early. Song Wei was sent ahead to scout.

There was thought to be nothing particularly significant about the actual geographical location in which Clem Richmond was being held. When Yang Ho's intelligence had picked up that there was a white doctor helping train young communist recruits in emergency medicine for battle conditions, he had simply ordered his nearest army unit to capture him. It was only later he had discovered what a prize he had.

While he used Kate's father against her, Yang Ho saw no reason to have him moved. Indeed, just the opposite. Moving always involved risks. So Clem Richmond had remained where he had been taken when captured. This was a walled compound within the ancient city of Nanking. It was also the main White Army base for that area. Because it was walled and well guarded, Clem Richmond enjoyed virtual "house arrest." After a time he had even been allowed to help in the compound's infirmary.

In this infirmary was a young orderly called Lin Teh. He was the son of a small market vendor in the town who was always denouncing the Communists. In fact, both father and son had been Communists for years. Months before, when Shen had sent a general message to all his people to be on the lookout for a *yang kwei* doctor called Richmond, it was Lin Teh who had finally replied—via a message hidden in a basket of his father's best fruit sent by rail to a certain destination in Shanghai and relayed by Ling Ling.

Lin Teh was an important part of the plan. Shen, as was his invariable policy with his undercover people, had told no one of Lin Teh's existence—not even Kate. Wang Lee knew, of course, as Chief of Intelligence. He could recognize Lin Teh on sight. But no one else could.

The plan was this. On the day set for the raid, Lin Teh was to take Clem Richmond to the back gate of the compound. This was really the tradesman's entrance and Lin Teh had made sure that he had developed a pattern of Clem Richmond being seen there and having a reason for going. Lin Teh was an energetic, likable young man who had seen to it that Clem Richmond liked him. It had then been an easy task to persuade the doctor to come with him to the gate to meet his honorable father who brought the fruit to the hospital. After that they both went regularly to the gate to have a piece of fruit and supervise the delivery for the hospital.

So the routine had been established. The back gate was still heavily guarded. But nowhere like the front gate. On the day of the raid Lin Teh was to tell Clem Richmond who he was and what was about to happen—but not before.

The raiding party was to be dressed in the same clothes as the peasants of that area. Song Wei was to go ahead to the gate and nod when the others arrived if all looked normal. Fortunately, there was a system of a kind of Kuomintang militia—a hangover from warlord days. So the plan was that Hwang and the others would pose as a family of well-to-do farmers, wishing to join the White Army to fight the Communists whom it was said would take away all the landowners' land. This also gave Hwang and the others an excuse to come armed and on horseback. The army would expect them to demonstrate their ability with weapons and provide their own horses. As for Kate, she was to be disguised as the youngest son—minding the horses at the rear—with her hair up under an appropriate cone-shaped hat covering most of her head. Song Wei was not to appear connected with them in any way. Then, if something went wrong, she would not be caught and her crucial scavenging for medical supplies stopped. She was to be a lookout only—and any messages which passed between her and the group must be by eye contact alone. For the rest of the time she would mingle with the peasants at the gate and pretend to be one of them.

It seemed like a good plan.

An hour after Song Wei had left to reconnoiter, Kate and the others set out on their horses for Nanking. The distance was not great and they reached the outskirts easily, swinging wide around the main part of the town towards the camp which stood on a separate perimeter.

When they came within sight of the compound wall—made of irregular gray stones like on a cobbled road—they dismounted and walked, not wishing to attract the attention of the guards positioned on the top of the wall. These guards, and how they reacted, would be crucial. Hwang and the others could easily deal with any opposition from the guards at the gate itself. But if the alarm were given and their party had to retreat under fire, they could expect the hail of bullets from the men on the wall to be merciless.

They were quite close now. They kept moving up steadily until they could see Song Wei. She nodded her head almost imperceptibly. That was the signal. It meant Kate's father was visible inside the gate. Song Wei had been told nothing of Lin Teh, but Kate's father had been described to her in great detail. Lin Teh had alerted Clem Richmond to look for his daughter under the cone-shaped straw hat. When he saw her he was to walk quietly out and get on the white horse.

On Song Wei's nod the group ambled up to the gate. Kate stayed back—on foot—holding the horses by their bridles. She tilted her head up just the slightest bit under her hat so she could see. The gate was open! She could see her father! Her heart was pumping furiously. She could feel her armpits and hands running sweat. Any moment now Hwang would make his move. He and Yu-Ma would overpower the guards and her father would walk quietly out and mount Shen's own horse, which he had lent for the occasion. At the same instant she would lift her head right up so her face would be clearly visible to her father.

Hwang and Yu-Ma looked at each other and smiled. The two Young Celestials were close by. Kate saw Hwang move one foot forward. He was like a crouching animal ready to jump.

Just then Song Wei's pistol went off. Her horse reared and bolted.

The next moment all hell broke loose as the Chinese words Kate had come to hate were being shouted from the battlements:

"Champi, champi!"—"Let them be shot, let them be shot! . . ."

Her head jerked up in a reflex action as she saw the gate—the precious gate inside which, a few feet away, stood her beloved father—slam shut. Had he seen her? It didn't matter now. She had seen enough of war to know that. Wang and Yu-Ma were instantly beside her and she felt herself being yanked bodily into the air. Yu-Ma swung her high and wide into the saddle while Hwang grasped the reins. Then they both jumped onto their own mounts as Hwang whacked the flank of Kate's horse and shouted "Ride, Ride!—Ride for dear life, Kate Doctor! . . ."

The shots were raining down on them already. As they took off Kate couldn't believe how unreal it seemed. Bullets were splattering down into the earth all around her. She could see the dry earth sputtering up in tufts of dust as she rode—racing her horse away. Then she felt her neck jerk back and thought she had been shot until she realized the wind had caught her hat and whipped it off against her neck. Her long blonde hair fell out as she rode. The wind was in her face. Then an instinct—who knows from where?—told her to tuck her head down beside the horse's. Just as she did so, a bullet whistled overhead.

At the sound of its sharp crack the sense of unreality left her. It now gave way to fear. Her body spasmed and she wet herself against the saddle. Her urine was hot as it ran down her legs. Yet in a moment she began to feel strangely safe. It had to do with the animal against whose head her own was nestled. She could hear his nostrils snorting and smell the adrenalin in his breath, as he knew a race was on and was determined to test his own deep-flanked strength against that of the earth below and the bullets above. It gave Kate heart. Somehow she made it to the edge of the trees around the compound. But there was no stopping. Hwang was shouting for her to keep going as they galloped around to avoid the town once more and move up country before circling back.

She rode and rode, her heart nearly breaking. She had been through so much and had tried so hard not to cry. Now the tears came tumbling down. She had been separated from all who were close her—Blake, the closest of all; Janey, her dear friend; her loving mother; and her kind father. Only the thought of seeing him again had kept her going. She needed his love and affection and tender, caring strength so much. To be promised it once more, only to have it wrenched away when he was actually in sight . . . visible through the open gate of the compound— seemed monstrously unfair. Was there no justice in this world? None at all? Shen had known what it had meant to her. That's why he had gone to such lengths to find her father. And now . . . ! Now she was convinced she would never see him again. Yang Ho would not take a near-rescue lightly. His way, to ensure it did not happen again, would be to kill the prisoner.

Kate was devastated. She rode on, the tears streaming down her cheeks now as the wind whipped at her face.

When they returned, Shen was furious. He hated any battle plan of his to go awry. He made his annoyance quite clear. He immediately ordered the army to break camp.

In the meanwhile, Shen ordered Song Wei sent to him. He walked with her a short distance from the main force but they could all hear them shouting. "It was an accident," Song Wei shouted, "I had my pistol hidden in my saddlebag, cocked, ready to use in case something went wrong, like I was instructed. My horse stumbled on a pebble and the pistol went off."

It was true these had been Song Wei's instructions. It didn't matter; in the eyes of the camp she was guilty already. Was she not the only one allowed outside the camp? Because of her beauty, temper, and ambition she had never been a popular figure. Even her help with the wounded many saw as an attempt to ingratiate herself with Kate and the hierarchy. And the trips outside the camp—were they not so she could steal tasty little morsels for herself and Po when all others went hungry?

And, as if to confirm their opinions, the argument continued.

"It was an accident, I tell you . . . an accident!" Song Wei kept shouting. "Anyway, why do you care so much for the White Foreign Devil . . .? You have jeopardized the lives of all these good people you are supposed to lead on the march by sending an expedition to look for her round-eye father . . ."

Shen looked at Song Wei, his eyes blazing. She stopped suddenly. She knew she had gone too far. She had challenged his authority, openly, in the hearing of others.

"They are not even Communists . . ." she stammered, trying to justify herself now. "Why protect them so . . . ?"

Shen looked at her again, perhaps seeing Song Wei for the first time. He was going to miss her from his bed, there was no denying that. But she had to be made an example of.

"The *yang kwei* doctors," he began, in a voice loud enough for those listening to hear, "both father and daughter, have served this cause of ours a lot longer and harder than many others such as yourself, Song Wei, who are newcomers. When we started to build the beginnings of a revolution all those years ago, a revolution such as the world has never seen, and knew we would need trained medical personnel, only one doctor would help us. He even allowed us to meet in his home and clinic. That doctor was Clem Richmond. Later his daughter also helped us. Both these people have saved the lives of countless comrades and suffered deep, deep personal grief on our behalf. It is true neither is Communist in the sense you might use the word, but they have been Communist in spirit to us and that is all we ask. And if you think we Communists are not loyal to our friends, you know nothing of communism . . . nothing . . . We have survived on loyalty to our friends and their loyalty to us, for we certainly have no money to pay them. You have now challenged that loyalty of our friends by asking why we protect them. We protect them because they protect us. Moreover we do so because it is common humanity and no less applicable to communism than any other belief on earth. I would go to the ends of the earth, and so would every soldier in any army I command, to rescue one such as Clem Richmond or his daughter. As for you, you put your fellow soldiers at risk by needless carelessness. The cadres did not train you to handle firearms carelessly. This you learned yourself and you must be disciplined. You must be re-educated in the Communist way. As punishment you may no longer go outside the camp alone. You are not to approach my tent or speak to me unless first specifically spoken to. And you will be on permanent latrine duty—to teach you humility—until further notice.''

The crowd began to disperse. Kate had been standing with Hwang. They had heard everything. Even Hwang believed Song Wei's action had been deliberate. ''Cunning and deliberate,'' he told Kate, ''so we could not be sure it was intentional.''

''But why would she do such a thing?'' Kate asked.

''To hurt you perhaps. You know how she hates anyone who is not Chinese.''

''But we have become friends.''

''Surface friends,'' Hwang said.

''Well, we've had our differences . . . but I don't believe she'd do anything intentional to hurt me . . . I believe it was an accident . . . a terrible accident . . .''

She broke down and started sobbing again.

Hwang put his arm around her. "That's why we all love you so dearly, Kate Doctor—because you always believe the best of people . . ."

As the army moved off, Wang Lee rode up to Shen. "You didn't actually believe her?"

"Yes. I think it was an accident."

"You're letting your heart rule your head. She's a spy . . . if ever I saw one . . . she and Po . . ."

"I agree Po is a possibility . . ."

"A possibility! He fought with Yang Ho . . . on the same side . . . !"

"So did Wu. So did half the men in this army . . . many Communists were Nationalists once . . . many fought in the First Revolution. Should I regard them all as spies . . . ?"

"Of course not. Only the ones who act suspiciously. You can't tell me that was an accident . . ."

"I'd told her to keep her pistol ready . . . ready to protect Kate at all costs . . . we all know that . . ."

"Yes. And we all know Song Wei is one of the best shots in this camp . . . that she is very expert with firearms."

"It could happen to anyone. What would you have me do, put her before a firing squad and shoot her . . . ?"

"Yes."

"She may be innocent. Time will tell. But if she is a spy . . . if she and Po have something planned, we are more likely to find out what it is, if we at least know who to suspect. If we banish them, others will simply be sent in their place whom we will not suspect. . . . Sometimes we get dozens of white defectors a day joining us . . ."

Wang Lee knew Shen was right. But he didn't like it.

"Sometimes, Leader Shen, you are impossible," he said brusquely, reining his horse off to the side leaving Shen to ride on alone.

In the days and weeks that followed, Kate believed Song Wei's power over Shen was broken. Although she did not rule out the possibility that such a talented ex-actress might rise again. For if Kate's time with Shen on the march had shown her his many strengths, it had also revealed one weakness. And as the weeks passed into months, with Song Wei removed from his immediate presence, Kate saw loneliness gathering over Shen like a cloud.

## 44

*No one celebrated Christmas because it was not part of the* Chinese calendar.

The New Year's Festival approached—but Shen remained disconsolate. Kate was lonely, too. It should have been a time for happiness: to welcome in the New Year of 1932. It was the "Year of the Monkey" on the Chinese calendar. This was supposedly an important year for Shen, whom the old opium-faced soothsayer had christened "the Monkey Warrior" all those years ago.

But nothing would budge Shen from his depression and Kate was nursing a bitter disappointment herself. Since the failure of the mission to rescue her father she had become extremely worried about him and what the Whites might do to him. Then, on top of this, news had arrived from Shanghai.

Ling Ling had judged correctly that Kate would like to know of Janey and Blake's marriage. She tried not to be jealous but she was. It was a terrible silent cross for her to bear. The army was desperately short of medical supplies again and Kate found herself urging Shen to let her go to Shanghai on one of Wang Lee's missions.

"It won't help to see them, Kate Doctor," Shen said kindly. "What is done is done and will not go away."

It was the worst period of vulnerability she had ever known. She found herself thinking of Blake again, and how good and warm the nights with him had been. Thinking of her need, if she were honest, to have someone the way Shen had had Song Wei. Someone to hold her; someone to gaze on; someone to feel close to; someone to make love to; someone, something—warm and moving and human against all this death. She kept looking at Shen and the loneliness she saw in him. She wished she might say something. But she feared to go to his tent as she used to. She was frightened of what she might let herself do—might want herself to do—if he showed the slightest sign of wanting to comfort her or be comforted himself.

It was made doubly difficult due to the barrier between them because of Song Wei. And Kate sensed that for the sake of Shen's pride, he would have to be the one to break it down. She was certain that he wanted to, but could somehow not quite bring himself to do so. Yet in another sense they were closer than they had ever been. Each was aware of the silent sharing of the other's pain. They spoke little to each other in words. And when they did, it was of the most mundane things. But their eyes would meet and all the unspoken thoughts would pass between them. In some strange extrasensory way, Kate knew that he believed her future lay with his, and knew too that the same certainty was in her own mind, and that it was what both of them wanted.

Before Song Wei came, they often used to walk in the countryside, just a short distance from the camp, when it was safe and the army resting. But for a long time there was very little rest for the army. Then when there was, neither Kate nor Shen seemed able to suggest a walk.

But finally, one afternoon, quite without warning, when there was a chill wind blowing and snow against the mountains, Shen came up to her. He was wearing a blanket over his shoulders. "Walk with me a distance, Kate Doctor," he said quietly.

She nodded.

They began to walk slowly. Then, when they were a little way from town, Shen slipped one of his hands into Kate's battle jacket pocket to keep warm.

He had often done this in the past, but somehow this time both knew it was different. And when Kate's hand found his, it locked and unlocked almost in desperation. They walked on a little farther until they came to a cornfield.

For a handful of minutes—no more—they left the march. He was not a soldier and she was not a doctor.

Shen was silent as he took the blanket from his shoulders and laid it on the ground. Kate sat down quietly. Shen followed. Slowly, very slowly and deliberately, they began to kiss.

On that chill of the cornfield near the town, on the hoary grass and hard flaxed-out stubs of corn now gathering ice, they looked at each other. Alone together for the first time since the march had begun, they marched to no sounds other than their own, though tuned with a fine and desperate intensity as if they might not come this way, or do this thing, again.

Still wrapped close together in the blanket on the hoar-frost ground, their sighs eased as their movement slowed. He was still inside her, with one of his legs resting gently over hers, as they lay side by side and smoked a cigarette.

"So," said Kate with a smile, turning to him and brushing his hair from his forehead, "is it different with a round-eye?"

He smiled. "Of course."

They both laughed quietly.

"Good," said Kate. "Do you still miss Song Wei?"

He looked at her quietly. Each knew the look. Honesty was at the root of their friendship. Deep, caring honesty.

"Yes, I still miss Song Wei, Kate Doctor. Do you miss Blake?"

It was her turn to look at him. "Yes, I do," she said, "I still miss Blake."

"Of course."

Kate thought how kind his tone was, despite all Blake had done to him. It was a tone of concern.

"Although he betrayed us," Shen continued, "it does not necessarily follow that he betrayed you, Kate Doctor . . ."

"How could that be . . . ?"

"There is a suggestion . . . just a suggestion . . . that in your case he may have acted from a slightly higher motive . . . It would make a difference . . . ?"

"I doubt it. I said I miss him. Like you miss Song Wei. There is a love in everyone's life, I think, if you are lucky . . . where there is a desperate intensity of feeling that swamps all else. I had this with Blake. I think you had it with Song Wei. But Blake for me in the long run . . . ? After what he has done . . . ? I doubt it. One should never say never, of course. But could I live with a man who, for whatever reason, had helped to precipitate the Shanghai massacre? Even if there were a loftier reason involving me, he must have known what the consequences would be. Without those armored cars many fewer would have been killed. Hundreds more could have escaped. And at one point in time Blake was the only person who knew where those vehicles were . . ."

"He and Shan Li, of the *Ching-pang*," Shen said.

"But Blake is not of the *Ching-pang*?" Kate asked.

"No. He knew Shan Li from schooldays, from playing in the streets and alleys with him. But he has been a valuable source of information—for him and us."

"For us . . . ! You don't mean we use the Chinese Mafia to gain information . . . ?"

Shen smiled. There were still traces of Western thinking in her.

"Not directly," he said. "But an informant of ours has contact with them. It was from Shan Li that we first heard of the impending Kuomintang attack on Shanghai . . ."

"But Ling Ling brought that news . . ."

He smiled again. "Of course."

"Don't rule out Song Wei," Kate said softly, changing the subject, as they smoked another cigarette together before returning to camp. "She is very young. And you still like her. She will grow. She will mature. She just overplayed her hand. She is very young for all this war and the machinations of communist politics as well."

"To marry her would be to have a tiger by the tail."

"To be a communist is to have a tiger by the tail."

He smiled.

"She is very ambitious," Kate went on. "Perhaps that would be good for you. And never forget the attraction of the flesh, as they say . . ."

They looked at each other then, feeling their nakedness and flesh together under the blanket, and laughed.

"No," said Shen, "the attraction of the flesh is a very powerful thing, as well as an affinity of the mind."

"Isn't that the truth?" said Kate, suddenly feeling him alive again between her legs as once more he began to drive deep, deep inside her and they were lost in their own march of time again.

# 45

$Y$ang Ho's enjoyment of his adulation had turned sour. After news of his defeat by Shen at Chingkangshan, he was no longer the toast of Shanghai.

He paced his room once more.

So Kate Richmond was still alive, was she? There seemed little doubt that the intelligence reports which placed her as present at the attempt to rescue her father were accurate. He had now ordered her father sent even farther into the North. He could have him killed, of course. He would like to have him killed. But that would be foolish. He was obviously much better kept alive as bait for his attractive daughter.

Yet in the meantime there was something else Yang could do.

He walked to the big picture window and looked down on the boulevards below. Did he still dream of ruling in Peking? Did he still dream of taking Kate Richmond with him? He had been too kind to the girl! Too considerate! His warlord father would never have tolerated such things. One ruled by force or one did not rule at all. And, in addition, someone on his staff, someone close to him, had betrayed him. Someone had passed on information to the rebels and perhaps was still doing so. Well it was time to strike back! This should get their attention and flush them out. He pushed the buzzer on his desk. His deputy instantly appeared. He was an older man, with a face pitted with pockmarks like a rock.

"You have the document ready?" Yang Ho snapped.

"It has been prepared as you ordered, sir."

"Good. Bring it immediately."

The deputy, who was a little stiff in his movements from old war wounds, disappeared for a moment and then reappeared carrying a large document. It was the official proclamation of martial law. Yang Ho raised his pen to sign. The Richmond woman was a known communist sympathizer, if not a communist herself. She had been part of a group which had shot Kuomintang soldiers. She was part of the army which had caused Yang's humiliation. Yang Ho lowered his pen and signed. When he had finished he stretched and turned to his deputy:

"The older woman doctor . . . the Richmond *yang kwei* who runs the clinic—the mother of the wanted woman . . . Arrest her."

The deputy nodded. "On what charge?"

"Collusion—collusion with the enemy. Running a clinic known to have provided aid to the Communists."

When the document had been cleared away, Yang Ho rang for his orderly.

"Mao tai and cigars and the prostitute Ling Ling!" he barked.

"Yes sir."

"I want her here in five minutes. Understand?"

"Yes sir."

The orderly disappeared and made a phone call. Then he reappeared with the liquor and cigars, hurrying out the moment he had poured a glass of the clear liquor.

Yang Ho drank the schnapps-like liquid straight down and poured himself another. Then, with a glass in one hand and riding crop in the other, he paced up and down while he waited.

When Ling Ling arrived, she entered timidly. She had little doubt what was going to happen. He had beaten her many times before and she knew what that riding crop meant. Whenever things went badly for him, he beat her. Sometimes he just made her lie naked across his knee so he could spank her.

But these times were never the worst. The worst were when he was so angry a simple spanking would not suffice.

The moment she entered this day she knew it was such a time. But even on the occasions when he made her bend over the end of the bed, and beat her mercilessly with the cane riding crop with square plaited leather tip and plaited leather handle, he never broke the skin. Never left any bruises where they might show and cause him to lose face by others knowing he had beaten his concubine. She often wondered where he had learned to punish so professionally. Her breasts and buttocks and the flesh between her legs could be sore for days, and her buttocks might be so sore with great red welts that she could not lie down at night—but at least she was not humiliated in public. She was beaten, roughly raped, and left. But at least no one but her head girl, Mei Lai, and Yang Ho's orderly ever knew. After Yang had vented his anger and stormed out, his butler would quietly ring Mei Lai to come and get her. That was how it worked.

She knew he was angry at his defeat by the Communists in the mountains, but just how angry she could only guess.

"Take off your clothes and bend over the bed!" he shouted as she entered the anteroom, before even the butler had had time to leave. "In there and be quick about it or I will come and rip them off myself."

She hurried into the bedroom. But she was nervous and her fingers were taking too long at the loops on her cheongsam bodice. Even as she fumbled again, she heard him enter from behind and the next instant she felt a horrendous whack across her cheek as she went reeling. He had hit her with the leather handle of the riding crop. Hit her straight on the face. She stumbled and tried to get up. But even as she did so, he hit her again, raining blows on her back and buttocks through her clothes as she put her arms up and tried to shield herself. But it was useless! He just kept hitting her on the arms and hands until she pulled them away in pain, exposing her head and body again.

"I said to be quick about it!" he shouted, pausing momentarily, stepping up to her and pushing her back down with his boot, so he stood over her with her body facing up.

She was terrified. And aching all over. But she began to fumble with her buttons again.

He walked back and lowered himself into a chair, smiling the most evil smile she had ever seen in her life, while she feverishly tried to get her clothes off. The loops finally gave way and she stepped out of her cheongsam. She unclipped her stockings from her suspender belt as she sat on the edge of the bed and winced in pain. Her slip and panties came off almost in the same movement as her belt. But she was so nervous she could not undo her bra clip. She tried again and again and then mercifully it gave way.

She sat on the edge of the bed, naked, vulnerable—more vulnerable than she had ever felt in her life.

He rose from the chair and tested his crop in the air.

"Bend over!" he snapped. Quickly she slid down onto her hands and knees, turning around and arching herself over the bed so her buttocks were the uppermost towards him.

"How many others have you had while I was away fighting . . . ?" he shouted as he began to walk towards her. "One hundred . . . ? Two hundred . . . ? You have made me the laughing stock of the city . . . The general's rich whore is everyone's rich whore. Well, you will be a poor whore by the time I have finished with you . . . We will have to punish the body which has betrayed me and see if that will teach it obedience . . . Let us see if your capacity for pain is as great as your capacity to be Shanghai's biggest whore . . . !"

She still had her back to him and heard him coming, the crop swishing. She thought to run, yet even as she thought this, she knew the beating would be worse if she did. Well, at least the money was safe. She was sure he would never find that. Fifty thousand British pounds for her brother and Wang Lee. However hard Yang beat her she would not give that up. So he had found out she had been seeing others to make extra money! So what? At least he had not found out that she was spying. Or that Shen was her brother. As long as he and Wang Lee were safe nothing else mattered. She heard Yang Ho stop behind her.

# 46

*The man on the country railroad station* pulled his hat down over his forehead and peered deeper into the now thickening dusk. He hoped they would come soon. He did not care to be alone out here, even in the daylight. The civil war was spreading now, as the Communists marched north. It was not easy to travel anywhere anymore. It was not safe anywhere. If you had travel documents from one side, and the other side found you, your chances of eating breakfast the next morning were not great.

He had White Army traveling papers, otherwise he would never have gotten this far. But now he was being passed from village to village by people who did not say they were Communists yet did not say they were not. It was a hazardous journey, and often he was left waiting for days on end.

There was no guarantee that anyone would arrive this night—no guarantee at all. He might wait here for days and still they might not come. Some bandits of one sort or another would come soon, though, he was sure of that. There must be some in the area, perhaps watching him through their binoculars even now, stuck out on this open, dusty, far-country railway station with his cargo for all the world to see.

He shivered again and wished he'd had the good sense to put on his warm clothes and overcoat. At least he'd had the good sense to bring them. But he did not wish to undo his suitcase at this time, although it would be more sensible. He looked at the leather suitcase, mid-brown in color and only a couple of small patches the size of coins left of its original surface. The rest was scuffed, dry, and worn down, like a second layer of exposed skin. There was a strap with a big buckle around the outside. His gun was inside the case.

He should have carried the gun. Should he get it out now and change into his winter clothing at the same time? That way, if bandits came and let him go but took his case, that way he would still have his winter clothes and gun. But a gun was not a good idea. They knew if you were carrying one on you. They were suspicious enough without that. It was not a good idea. But the warm clothes might be. And he could still fill his pockets of the army greatcoat with the things from his case which he must keep with him at any cost. Perhaps if he put on all his clothes, the winter ones over the summer ones, and put his pistol in the waistband underneath, they would not notice. Then he could put the other things in his pockets, or under his greatcoat also, and put his gloves on, and carry the whiskey, and then he wouldn't need the suitcase. It was stupid, really, to carry it. But on such trips he always brought as many essentials as he could as far as he could. Damn. There was the first-aid kit, too. Where would he put that? Would he sacrifice the whiskey for it? No. He must find a way to take it, too. Perhaps the whiskey would fit in the small cardboard case, like a doll's case, with a red cross on it and a tin handle.

It was more than a first-aid kit, really. It held the best of drugs. He was used to this sort of operation. Tired of it but used to it. He scratched his stubble. He had not shaved for two days. He scratched his eyebrows, too, checking for lice unconsciously as he did so. Then he scratched at his fair hair, ruffling the parting, though it was careless about staying in place and the wind kept wisping at it.

He stared into the dusk again. The cold night air and the hurrying dark now made his blue eyes look steely and gray.

God, where were they? He knew they would not come on time, if they came at all. But where were they?

He would change. It always helped to do something when you were frightened. He wasn't so frightened of the Communists, really. He didn't think there'd be too much in those Red bandit stories the Whites put around. That would be propaganda. He was more frightened of the Whites. He'd seen enough of them marching in the countryside.

He was down to his last two bottles of whiskey. He uncorked one and drank down two gulps. That was better. Now he'd transfer everything from the case as he said he would. He bent to it and slowly, methodically, like a haberdasher checking his stock, went through everything, trying it, folding it, seeing if it would fit best here, or best there.

When he had finished he wished for another drink of whiskey. But he dare not. It must last. Damn them, where were they? It was almost completely dark and he had no light other than his half dozen boxes of matches. He lit a cigarette to warm himself, holding onto the smoke as long as possible.

God he was tired. Now he wished he hadn't unpacked his suitcase. He felt so stupid with all those layers of clothing on. But still, he was warm, and the pistol did feel good next to him. If it came to it he'd shoot a couple of the bastards before they got to him. The two whiskeys had given him a little bravado and now he had a third whiskey and said to hell with it, he'd damn well have another mouthful or two if he felt like it, because if he wasn't alive for breakfast it would be a pity to waste it.

He wondered yet again whether it was all worth it, all this, just for a journalist's interview with the Communists—but an interview that no one else in the world, probably, could get.

Just then he thought he heard a car.

He peered around the edge of the narrow sentry box-type building, kicking his empty case out of sight as he did so. His boxes of cargo were off to one side in the dust. The headlights of the car threw up enough light for him to see a Kuomintang pennant atop the radiator. A car usually meant an officer, and a fairly senior one. But then some of these were members of the secret Shanghai opium rings and worse than ordinary soldiers. He decided to stay hidden. He withdrew completely, behind the outhouse, pressing his body flat back against the chalk-painted timber.

He heard the car stop. He heard the sound of one person get out. Good. He carefully put one hand on the butt of the pistol and drew it clear and held it close to the outside of his overcoat. He had decided to fight if it was necessary. There might be a carload of them, of course, but he rather thought not. They were always so anxious, these Kuomintang, anxious to the point of officiousness. They'd all be out buzzing around like bees if there were more than one. But an officer traveling alone? That didn't make sense either. Where was the driver? Of course. There were two. It was the driver who was out looking around. There would be an officer still in the car. Could he hope to shoot the driver and the officer before the officer could get his pistol out of its leather clip holster? What if he was an unusually good officer and kept his pistol out at all times on a night such as this near Red territory? Jesus, it was going to be hard to get out of this one.

Just then he heard his name called. In English! "Mr. Carpenter, are you there? Are you there, Mr. Carpenter? We must keep moving. Please show yourself if you are there."

He was still cautious, but common sense demanded that no one would know his name other than those who were supposed to meet him there, the information passed along from the last village from where he had been sent with a muleteer to this station to wait.

Slowly he walked out—his pistol still in his hand but hanging down—into the misty, dust-filled headlight beam to be greeted by a smiling young Chinese. He was strong and fit-looking, with a bandolier across his shoulder, a captured Kuomintang Russian automatic weapon in his hand, and a peaked green cotton drill cap with a red star on his head.

He spoke in impeccable English:

"I apologize for being so late. It is of course a great pleasure to meet you but if you do not mind, we must hurry. We have taken the liberty of stealing a White Army car for two such honored guests, but the enemy appeared to be fairly close behind at the last village we passed through."

Carpenter wondered about the second guest but there was no time to argue.

They hurriedly loaded Carpenter's things and then Carpenter got into the back seat while the young man roared off into the night.

It was dark in the car, which was curtained. But Carpenter could dimly see a young woman slumped across the seat with her head resting in the far corner.

"Is she all right?" he asked.

"Oh yes, she is just sleeping," the voice replied from the front seat. "She has just come from long weeks of war before our army broke out of the mountains."

"And she has slept through all this?" Carpenter said.

"Oh yes, from the moment she got in the car and despite the

Kuomintang chase some miles back. She understands this may be the only comfortable rest she will get for some time."

Carpenter nodded. "Cigarette?" he said, offering one across the back of the front seat.

"That would be a great luxury. Thank you, sir."

"The 'sir' is not necessary."

"I understand. It is a formality."

"You were in Hong Kong?"

"Until the purges. Then I came home."

"To fight for the new China?"

"There was no pleasure in the old. Is it long since you were home in America yourself?"

"Four years."

"Your Chinese is good, then?"

"That is for you to judge."

"That is a very Chinese answer. But then you were at the School of Oriental Studies in London, were you not?"

"For a time. But yours, too, is a very Chinese answer. The subtle lesson is that you Communists are so smart you know all about me."

They both laughed then and talked Chinese after that, and smoked another cigarette. When Carpenter had put his out he lay back in his seat and thought about sleeping. But as he did so, he looked across at the woman in the corner and only then did he realize she was not Chinese, as he had supposed. She was white—beautifully and gloriously blonde where a tip of her hair which had not been showing earlier was now visible under her headscarf.

He sat back smiling. So he had found her! It was almost exactly eight years to the day since he had last seen her.

"She did not know it was to be you," the driver whispered from the front seat. "She was told only that there was an important visitor we would try to link up with. We thought it would be a nice surprise for her to see an old friend."

He paused and saw Carpenter in the rearview mirror nod in agreement. "And the interview with Comrade Shen?" he said.

"This too may be possible."

"Thank you. How are you called?"

"Wang. Just Wang."

"Colonel Wang Lee—head of Communist intelligence?"

"It is dangerous even for a journalist to know too much."

They both laughed then and smoked another Chunghwa together.

As he drove, Wang Lee wondered if Carpenter would be quite as friendly when he heard the conditions they intended to impose on his interviewing.

Shen and Wang Lee had decided to allow Carpenter to interview Kate. They knew this was a good story for the American newspapers—an American lady doctor who traveled with the Communists; who had been with them from the start. This would help counter the Kuomintang propaganda.

But they would hold back on the interview with Shen for the time being. Once Carpenter had interviewed Kate, they would send his copy—his newspaper story—back through their own channels to his office in Shanghai. Wang Lee would take it personally. Their network had improved sufficiently so that he could now make it in about two weeks. This would be as fast as Carpenter himself could lodge the story, failing stopping at Kuomintang cities where he might telegraph it. But he would not wish to do this any more than they, because he, too, would know the Kuomintang would censor it. The story would never be sent.

The Communists had also decided to allow pictures for the first time. Pictures of Kate and Shen!

When the Red Army received reports back on how the American papers had treated Carpenter's story on Kate, a decision would be made on the Shen interview. In the meantime Carpenter would be invited to remain behind—to stay with the army and see how they lived and worked and fought. It would be made clear, in effect, that he was to stay until they saw the results of his work.

Kate was still asleep when the car finally reached the communist camp. They decided not to wake her. Carpenter was shown to his own tent. Although they were pathetically short of everything, they had made a typically Chinese effort not to show it. There was steaming hot water for a bath. And there were scented towels, tiny hot scented towels in the oldest of Chinese tradition. They had been scented with the last of Lu Chien's French perfume, the last dreg of a tiny bottle she had carried with her since Shanghai.

Carpenter washed thoroughly, sitting in the small wooden tub they had brought him and sipping the clear fiery mao tai from a brown stone bottle they had placed beside him after apologizing most profusely for their lack of whiskey.

There was a brazier in his tent and some hot soft towels beside it. How did they do it? He knew it was all done specially for him. He knew how poorly off they were. But he also knew what an insult it would be to refuse. Even the mao tai would be scarce. He would drink it sparingly and hold back on the whiskey so he could leave them a bottle when he left.

He had been drinking too much recently. He had covered the Shanghai massacre and some of the battles from the Kuomintang side and he wasn't good at seeing all that killing. He wondered how Kate had coped with it. He'd known after his second year he could never be a doctor. At least a journalist could look at the bodies quickly and then cut and run. You didn't have to stay behind and try to stitch them up with intestines oozing out from gunshot wounds.

But what would happen when the airplanes came? Should he tell them? Could he tell them? Would it break a journalistic confidence if he did? Would it end any possibility of ever getting a story from the Kuomintang again?

He stepped out and took a towel and dried himself and was just finishing dressing when he heard Kate's voice outside the tent flap.

"John? Are you decent? May I come in . . . ?"

"Sure."

The flap was turned back and Kate stepped into the tent and let it fall back again.

She had not changed clothes and still looked very sleepy.

"Sorry I didn't greet you earlier. I wish they'd told me. But I did need the sleep . . ."

He nodded. "It's good to see you, Katie."

"And you, Johnno. How are you . . . ?"

He went to put his arm around her and gave her an affectionate hug but she drew back.

"What's wrong . . . ?"

She smiled awkwardly.

"Katie . . . ? What is it . . . ? We're friends, surely? Tell me what it is."

"I'm embarrassed . . . I'm not used to Americans . . ." She hesitated a moment and then went on. "Look, would you mind awfully if I used your bathwater before it gets cold? The Chinese, of course, would never ask. But it seems such a pity to waste it and I am filthy. Although you've got to promise you won't write about us using second-hand bathwater . . ."

Carpenter found himself swallowing back hard.

"Please promise . . ." she said again, more earnestly this time.

"I promise," he said. "I'll go outside for a smoke and leave you to it."

"Not on my account. And it's bitterly cold out there. Turn your back if you have to, but I tell you that after all this time on the march that's the last of my worries. All things are relative. Being seen naked is very low on the totem pole compared with bathwater which has been used only once by a relatively clean stranger . . ." She smiled and with that began to strip. Carpenter turned away and fumbled in his case.

"Tell me when you're in," he said after a few moments. Then he heard the sound of splashing water.

"In," she said enthusiastically, "deliciously in."

He handed her a cake of Cussons Imperial Leather soap.

"Oh John," she said, "oh John, you don't know how much this means."

"No," he said. "You're quite right. I don't. But I can imagine. I would have refused the bath if I hadn't thought it would have offended their sense of Chinese Communist pride."

"I know," she said, a sound of trailing nostalgia in her voice. "I know. Tough on the outside and soft as a marshmallow inside. You haven't changed much. Still concerned with other people's feelings. Still wanting to right the wrongs of the world, I suspect. A traveling agnostic newspaper missionary."

"I see you have lost none of your mental edge . . ."

"That's about the only thing I haven't lost . . . Oh Johnno, I love these people dearly . . . but have you any idea what it is like to see a friendly face . . . ? Someone of your own kind . . . ? Someone from home . . . ? It's so very, very good to see you, old friend . . . So very good."

"And you, Katie."

"And you're to stay a little time . . . ?"

"I would expect so—if your Shen lives up to his reputation for cunning . . ."

Kate laughed. "I've never thought of him that way . . . A military genius, certainly. But cunning . . . ? I don't know . . ."

"Well, that's how the world is beginning to see him . . . as a brave little fighter who keeps upsetting the odds with his cunning . . ."

"I suppose you're right. Anyway, I'm glad you're staying. It will give us time to have lots of long talks."

"I hope so. Would you like a whiskey?"

"An honest-to-God, Scotch whiskey . . . ? I would kill for it."

"That will not be necessary. Will a Glenfiddich be OK?"

"Like heaven."

He poured her one and himself another mao tai, and they sat talking about old times until her skin wrinkled up and the water turned cold.

# 47

*In* Shanghai, with the aid of her Hong Kong lawyers and accountants, Janey had set up a new branch of the business, albeit in the same warehouse on the Bund from which her family had operated for generations.

The new business had already caused a stir. Its prime aim—indeed its sole aim—was to advise trading houses and individuals how to get their money out of China before the Communists came. For this service Janey charged a flat fee of 10 percent. Her firm also offered to act as broker for any business wanting to sell off its entire stock. If she acted in this way, Janey made a flat offer for the stock. In other words, she expected the seller to give her a substantial discount for cash because she was the entrepreneur, the risktaker. She might have to hold the stock for months before she could sell it. Or she might be caught with it, she argued, if the Communists arrived in the meantime.

At first Janey's only clients had been a few women wanting advice on family money which they held independently of their husbands. In each case Janey had persuaded them simply to transfer it to an American bank in Hong Kong. There it would earn interest and they could still draw on it in China. It was simple and effective and the money was safe from communist takeover.

After a time, a small businessman came to Janey. He offered her his entire stock and arranged for her to sell off the freehold of his property in Shanghai. Then, on Janey's advice, he leased back space in what had been his own warehouse to continue trading with all his assets safely in Hong Kong. Her next customer was a German firm. Then small French and British interests. The business began to grow.

The Shanghai business community had remonstrated with Janey several times about this rather unusual practice. They said it was uncouth and unnecessary. That it was causing terrible problems and the authorities now saw it as a direct challenge to morale.

Janey simply smiled sweetly and said, "I appreciate that no one believes the Communists will ever reach Shanghai—that Yang Ho will stop them or the foreign powers will intervene. If this is so, then why worry?"

But she also smiled quietly. "On the other hand," she chuckled to herself, "if Wang Lee is right and I can stick it out until a day or two before the flood, then I'll make a bloody fortune."

Blake, looking on, smiled too. He had a fair idea what his wife was thinking and he wasn't altogether convinced she was wrong.

He had been amazed at how her father's death had changed her. She had always been independent but now this side of her nature had blossomed. It was also becoming very apparent that she had her father's head for business—although she was more adaptive and modern in approach than he was.

Yet Janey was not the only one who had changed. The whole world was changing. Her father's passing had signaled the end of an era. It was December 1933 and Shanghai would never be the same again. The giant tai-pans such as Nigel Edwards were a dying breed. The world would not see their likes again—these legendary traders who had stamped their feet on necks for profit all over the Far East. Blake, of course, had taken Edwards' place as number one—that was what the election at the Shanghai Club had been all about. And Blake's business was now bigger in terms of net value than Edwards' had ever been. But it was not the same. Blake knew that. The others knew it, too, although they would never admit it. The old world was passing. Even if Shen and his band of cutthroats didn't make it, the days of the Raj were numbered in China. The businessmen still acted as if Shanghai and its trading concessions—loaded so hopelessly in favor of anyone who was *not* Chinese—would go on forever like some illegal gambling house on the edge of town which everyone pretended did not exist.

It was amazing, really, that the Chinese had let it go on so long. The sign over the Shanghai park still hung there and said it all:

"No Chinese or Dogs Allowed."

Blake's thoughts turned back to Janey. Their personal relationship had changed too. She cared nothing for him, and he thought she had probably married him only for the status it would give her.

If only he'd had the sense to marry Kate. No doubt she hated him now, for what she must see as betrayal. If only it were possible to get a message to her.

It was then that he thought of Ling Ling.


Ling Ling lay in a darkened room in her upstairs apartment overlooking the river. She knew Wang Lee was in town but she had refused to see him. The communist network was strong again and they trusted her as one of their own. She had a staggering ten thousand pounds in her drawer for them to pass on to Wang Lee. But under no circumstances would she see him, she said. The comrades understood. They promised. But even so, she was expecting Wang Lee to come bursting through the door at any moment. Almost hoping he would. He was like that. Daring, courageous, almost foolhardy in his pursuit of his goal.

There was a knock at the door and it made her start.

"Madame Ling?"

"Yes." It was her head girl.

"There is a gentleman here to see you."

"You know I am seeing no one."

"It is a European gentleman."

"You must send him away."

"I told him Madam, but he insists . . . insists he must see you urgently . . ."

"There are no exceptions . . ."

"No madam. But he asked that if you refused I should tell you his name . . ."

"What is it?" Ling Ling said wearily.

"Blake, madam. Captain Thomas Blake."

Ling Ling sighed. "Bring him up, then, Mei Lai. But tell him the curtains must remain drawn and I can see him only for a few minutes."

"Yes madam."

A few moments later Blake was shown into the darkened room.

He could barely make out Ling Ling reclining on a couch in the corner.

He saw her motion him to a seat and wait for the girl to leave.

"I heard you were ill and came to see if there was anything I could do," Blake began.

"Who told you this?" Ling Ling said, irritation showing in her voice.

"Shanghai is a small town. I have informants."

"Of that I am certain, Captain Blake."

"Damn it, Ling Ling, I want to help."

"Why should you want to help me?"

"Because you were a friend of Kate's. Because Kate liked you . . ."

"And you think that by helping a friend of hers you will assuage your guilt for betraying her?"

"I came here because I heard you were ill and I wanted to help, but I also happen to know that if anyone can get a message to her, you can."

"Now we come to the truth."

"I didn't betray her, Shen Ling, that I can promise you . . ."

He heard Ling Ling catch her breath in the corner. She was stunned. Overwhelmed. That was the first time anyone had used her family name in years. How had he found out? Should she try to pretend otherwise? No, one such as Blake would not say such a thing lightly. Besides, what did it matter now? It was almost a relief. She would be dead soon anyway.

"So you know who I am, Captain Blake. So the cards are now on the table as you *yang kweis* say. Will you also now betray me . . . ?"

"I didn't betray anyone, and one day when you people do your homework you may find out . . . in the meantime I must find a way to see Kate . . ."

"It is impossible . . ."

"Wang Lee could arrange it . . ."

"If he were here . . . perhaps . . . But I do not even see him anymore."

"Please," Blake said. His voice sounded pleading.

Ling Ling felt a moment of sympathy for him.

"I can promise nothing . . ." she said.

"But if you will think upon it . . . you will see if there is a way to arrange a meeting . . . ?"

"I will think on it—that is all . . ."

Blake nodded gratefully.

"Will you take some money for their cause?" he said.

Ling Ling was astounded. "From you—? Of course not."

"You are incapacitated and cannot work. You cannot let those who pay you fifty pounds a visit see you as you are. You will need extra money to keep up the quota you have set yourself."

"You know too much, Thomas. . . ." She paused. "You understand that if I accepted it I could tell no one where it came from? They would never accept it from you."

"I understand."

"Then I will accept it for medical supplies for Kate Doctor. This way I do not dishonor my brother for I believe even Kate Doctor would accept it from you to save her beloved wounded. But I cannot promise she will ever know. Is this agreeable?"

"It is agreeable. Is there nothing I can do for you?"

"You can keep my secret."

"Of course. Nothing else?"

She shook her head, touched by the tone in this strange man's voice. Could it be he was telling the truth? She remembered his letter. What was it she had done with it? She was too tired to think now. "Nothing, thank you, Thomas."

"You know where to reach me if you change your mind?"

"Yes."

"At least come and dine with us when you are well. Janey would love to see you."

"When I am well . . . ? Perhaps."

"I have the money with me. It is all in cash. I will leave it here on the seat."

"Thank you."

"Goodbye, Ling Ling."

"Goodbye, Thomas."

He stood up, placed a large manila envelope on the seat, and quietly left the room. The envelope held 100,000 English pounds in thousand-pound notes.

Wang Lee saw Blake go and wondered. He had been watching the house in one disguise or another for days. Now he wore the uniform of General Wang of the Kuomintang again. But General Wang had been rather overused. He would need a change of disguise soon.

What about Blake? Was it possible Ling Ling was playing both sides of the street? Yet even as he thought this, he knew it was unthinkable. She would never betray her brother. Was Blake a client then? The thought of it made his flesh crawl. Yet he knew it was possible. But Blake had not really stayed long enough for that. Wang Lee had seen him come and go.

Did Wang's normal caution get the better of him in that moment of seeing Blake exit? Was it jealousy? Was it impatience? Was it simply the blindness of love? Was he, the consummate spy, as vulnerable as anyone else when it came to this? Was there just that fraction of a second of blurred judgment as he began to cross the road from the cover of the trees to the house of ill repute? Just that momentary pushing back of caution as he crossed and knocked boldly on the front door? The door was opened to him, and when he was told Madame Ling was not receiving visitors, he pushed the girl roughly aside and went bounding up the stairs even as he saw her move to an alarm bell and push it.

He tried three doors in quick succession, each occupied with soldiers and prostitutes who huddled to each other in surprise as they saw a general full of anger throw open their love nest doors.

The fourth door was locked and he paused momentarily. He aimed with the heel of his boot for the lock's most vulnerable spot and then kicked.

The door flew open and the room was in darkness but he knew he had found her. The perfume was unmistakable. Her unique body smell. And then her voice: "Oh darling, darling, why did you come? I told them not to let you in and now they have sounded the alarm and a whole troop of Kuomintang will arrive if we cannot stop them in time. Mei Lai . . . Mei Lai . . . !"

She was shouting now and presently the girl came running.

"It is a friend. A friend. Ring the barracks and say it is a mistake. Quickly. Quickly. Then run and tell me when they have left . . ."

The girl nodded and ran back down the stairs.

"You must go," Ling Ling said breathlessly. "There are back stairs leading from the door behind me. Only Yang Ho uses them. I have a car now. It is at the bottom of the stairs. Take it and go. I will say you have stolen it. Take the envelope on the seat. And this other besides . . ."

She reached towards a drawer in a round table beside her.

"I will not go. I will tell the troop of soldiers I am General Wang and it is a mistake."

"That will fool no one. Much has changed in this city since you were last here. They know you now. They have a full description. Such an excuse would fool no one. Particularly not the Blue Shirts' captain who commands the troops. Here, take the money and go. And here are the keys to the car. Please go . . . they could arrive at any minute . . ."

He took one envelope and reached out for the other she held and the keys. Just as he did so a shaft of light from a gap in the curtains flicked momentarily across her face. It was so quick; so brief. And yet it lit her indelibly in his mind for all time like a flash of thunder.

"Who has done this?" he exclaimed, his full anger rising now.

"Go," she pleaded. "Go. Can't you see that was what I was afraid of . . . ? Why I didn't want you to see me?"

Wang Lee stormed to the curtains and threw them back.

He had seen, in the chink of light, one hideously swollen eye and bruised cheekbone. Now he saw there was not an inch, not one single solitary inch of her face which had not been systematically worked over.

"Take off your robe," he shouted. "Take off your robe."

"Please," she implored. "Not that. Anything but that. Please go. I fear for your life."

He had to know.

He walked quietly over to the couch, took her gently by the hand, and stood her up. She offered no resistance. He noticed her movements were very stiff. Gently he kissed her and pulled the single band of material at her waist. Then he slipped the robe off her shoulders, looked at her front and back, and gently replaced the robe. She had been beaten from head to toe. Her back and buttocks and breasts showed whip marks. Her nipples and other parts of her breasts had stitches in them, as if they had been cut with a knife.

"Please go," she pleaded. "Please."

Then she realized Wang Lee was sobbing. "The sun will not set tonight with the one who has done this still alive, that I promise you," he said through his tears.

"Promise me you won't . . . promise me exactly the opposite," she said. "If you go looking for him you play into his hands. Don't you see that is exactly what he wants? You must take the money. That is what is important now. There is over 110,000—10,000 of which I earned in my spare time and for which I was beaten. You must take it to my brother . . ."

"And the other money . . . ?"

"It does not matter. It is American money for medical supplies. Please go . . ."

"I will find a way to see you before I leave," he said. "I will send a message with the *yang kwei* Jane. Do what she says."

And with that he was out the door and down the stairs. He reached the car and started it just as a Kuomintang truck swung into Ling Ling's drive. Wang Lee did not hesitate. There was just room to get by. He accelerated and roared past it, the truck's driver having to swerve to avoid a collision. As he careened out the sanded drive onto the main thoroughfare, he could see the truck turning in his rearview mirror. They gave chase but their truck was big and cumbersome and by the time it had turned around he knew he could lose them before they could catch him.

# BOOK V
# The Long March

*1934-1935*

# 48

$S$hen *now faced the biggest decision of his career.* Word reached him that Yang Ho was massing an army of 1 million troops. In addition, the latest fighter planes had arrived.

The Communist First Front Army now numbered over 50,000. There were also several thousand women and children. They often had to move in single file along narrow mountain paths.

On the roads they were even easier targets for pursuing airplanes.

Shen had to decide whether to stand and fight or run. If he fought he risked the whole force. But if he ran there was no guarantee of success either. The planes could strafe just as many running away as those standing and fighting. Fewer might be lost in battle. But Shen was not ready for his all-out fight with Yang Ho yet. He knew he needed an even bigger army.

Even if he ran they would have to fight every inch of the way. Yang Ho would deploy his 1 million troops across Shen's path. But he would avoid an all-out battle. If they could reach the North—the very Far North up past Tibet and close to the border—they might be safe. They might wear the Whites down. He might buy them enough time to build the army he really wanted.

And every mile farther into the North the Whites went the harder they would find it to supply their men. Shen and his people had become experts at living off the land. Or starving, and still being able to fight! The Whites had not. They were used to being supplied.

Shen was convinced it was the only way. It would mean a march—a march longer than any in history. And many would die—even women and children. But if they made it, the communist nation would be saved.

Yet there were bitter struggles in the Communist Council

when Shen made his plan known. Po openly opposed him. Because of the way their organization was now structured, Shen could not depose Po without the permission of the council. And whereas some—including Wu—favored Shen's plan, others did not. It was too daring, they said. Too dangerous. Better to be killed on the central plains than in the snow of the North. Some even said they should try to make a deal with the Whites. Either way, no one could ever survive such a march—not even superbly healthy soldiers who were well supplied.

In the condition they were in—without any proper food, ammunition, or medicine—it was suicide. Perhaps they might defeat the Whites if they stayed. Po certainly seemed to think so. Perhaps he should command.

In the end Shen had to deliver an ultimatum. Him or Po. Stay or go. He finally won but it was a bitter, narrow vote and a terrible way to start the worst and most arduous journey of his life. Not only must he carry the full burden for all his troops, plus women and children, but he must fight knowing that at any minute half his army might defect or choose not to go on.

And they would still have to fight their way to escape the already encircling White Army. He was not in any doubt about that. Then they would have to outrun the Whites. The Red Army would stand or fall on one consideration—its stamina to survive.

They would have to cross the three largest rivers in China. And then the infamous Tatu Gorge. And the Great Snow Mountain. And then the Great Grasslands, filled with quicksand.

But if they managed to survive, the Red Army would have made the longest march in history. They could rebuild for the day they swept down from the North to Shanghai.

Quietly, that night of October 16, 1934, the Ch'and Cheng— "the Long March"—began from Yutu.

From the hills and valleys where they had hidden their pitiful bundles of rags, the procession started. They pulled bicycle carts, and handcarts, and oxen wagons, and converted rickshaw cycles. Some had coolie poles. There was such a paucity of any "transport" that it made the use of the term highly debatable. But from these hills and valleys a paper dragon procession of sorts had begun. Of all the great refugee movements in history, this one seemed the most unlikely. Women and children and elder borns thrown together with an army?

It was ridiculous, they said in Shanghai and Nanking. Reconnoiter again. Even the Reds wouldn't do that.

But for days and nights, with the main movements taking place in the very darkest parts of night, Shen and his Young Celestials kept the line moving. Soon it was fifty miles long; and all carried something—guns, food, ammunition, and machinery.

So it was true! So they had broken out? So what? they said, in the Kuomintang officers' mess in Nanking, where Chiang Kai-shek now had his capital. So the Vanguard of the army, that special force that always led, commanded by the young General Shen Lung with his fanatical Young Celestials . . . so they had broken out and were setting a cracking pace. Striking north, were they? Out and cutting and running, clearing the way for the main force? Where did they think they were going? Did they really think they were going north? North, to link up with any other moth-eaten bands of Reds they might find on the way? It was farther than to the Arctic Circle and back. And the terrain just as difficult. And they had women and children!

As well as all those used car parts! Yes, that's what they were, used car parts. For machines and weapons. How could they ever put them together again, these stupid Reds?

The generals ordered another round of mao tais. The small cylindrical glasses with turned-out lips carrying the fiery clear liqueur came immediately on a silver tray carried by a waiter in a spotlessly laundered white jacket.

"Well, they'll never reach the Hsiang, of course, let alone the Wu or the Yangtze," said one. "That's where they'll be heading sooner or later—can't go north without crossing the three great rivers. But they'll never make it."

"Even if they did," said another, "they'd sink with those damned spare parts they're carrying. Rusted already a lot of them, you know. But they're such a mean, poor lot they'd rather drown than lose one rusty nail. So they'll drown with all that machinery in their pockets."

They all laughed at that. Of course the Communists were no threat. No one could swim the Yangtze at this time of the year. Fifty miles of people in single file, loaded with weapons, machine parts, and women and children? How many of these peasants would be able to swim anyway? None! They were country yokels, all of them. All the White Army had to do was wait for them to drown.

These were the young generals speaking. The ones who had trained in Japan like Yang Ho and had the Japanese hatred of the ordinary Chinese soldier. There was an old general present who was out of favor with Yang Ho. He had been pushed aside, but not demoted. He had less and less stomach for killing Reds these days.

It seemed that that was all he'd been doing for the past several years. But the Reds kept on going and doing the impossible. Now they were doing another thing everyone said they'd never do. Once or twice he had even secretly wished he'd been fighting on their side. In terms of military brains, they'd run rings around his own people. That was where he'd fallen out with Yang Ho. He'd wanted to start using Red guerilla tactics against the Reds themselves. But Yang Ho wouldn't hear of it. The out-of-favor general believed it would have meant a loss of too much face for Yang—that that was why he'd said no.

Well, there'd been a bit more face lost since then. The entire White Army had had the Reds surrounded and down on their knees not once but twice. Now they had broken out again. It seemed unbelievable that they should ever make the North. They would have to cross some of the most inhospitable wastes of China. No, that was impossible, even for the Reds. And whereas he gave them grudging admiration, he had no particular love for them. He knew how he and his family would fare if the Reds ever came to power. He was the head of a very old landholding family. At best they would lose everything they owned. Oh well, he'd better help these insolent young puppet generals of Yang's, if only to protect his family holdings.

"Well, of course, the Reds will never make the Yangtze," he said. "But perhaps we should order out the planes now, rather than keep them in reserve—just to be sure."

Order out the planes? Excellent, old chap. There was a topping idea. Order out the airplanes now. Why wait until they were all out in the open?

Shoot all the blighters from the air as they crept along those mountain passes. Shoot them before they got a chance to drown. Now there would be a proper extermination campaign. Now they'd get them all—women and children, too. Strung out in single file over the hills. Soon they'd have to march in the day as well as the night. How could they miss? Must check on where the planes were, and how many squadrons they had.

But although the breakout had taken the enemy by surprise—and although the high command had not at first treated the reports of the night marches seriously—now there was heavy fighting. Not all the Kuomintang line generals were fools, and the ones at the front now engaged the Red Army in a bloody battle as the main column of refugees tried to move on.

And, as if they did not have enough to worry about, Kate suddenly saw Hwang returning in the distance from the front of the column. He was marching back towards her. And he was walking beside a stretcher! Kate's heart sank. Where was Shen? Because of the women and children it was the first time she had not been at the very front of the line with him.

She ran towards Hwang, pushing past as much as she was able for there was only a narrow one-way strip. As her thin figure pushed forward, she felt her stomach knock something hard so that she winced. She had stupidly knocked into the back of the wooden frame of a bicycle cart. But the pain she had felt left her in little doubt about an anxiety of another sort which she had been carrying since fourteen days after she and Shen had last made love. She had been ovulating and her period had been due in seven days. They were to all intents and purposes sleeping in the one tent now. Po was furious and so were many of the elder born. Despite their liberating communism they still saw the liaison of Chinese and white as degrading to the Chinese.

For the time being Kate and Shen were too much in love to worry. And the sharp stab of pain she had just received—worrying her that she might miscarry and lose Shen's baby—terrified her almost as much as the thought of him being wounded.

When she got within range of Hwang and the two stretcher-bearers, she began to shout. But she could not make herself heard above the noise of the crowd. So, angry now—angry with even the people who held her back, and ashamed of herself for feeling so—she began to shove harder. She was pushing now, pushing with her shoulders and elbows and shouting at the people in the great proletarian line of followers, following stupidly they did not know where, running away, so it seemed to her at that moment.

And just as she thought this, she was within sight of the stretcher and she saw Shen's face. It was bandaged and her heart missed a beat.

"Oh, Shen!" she shouted. "Oh Shen." She ran up to the stretcher when he did not respond. She burst into tears. Hwang took hold of her then and held her close to his side so the people would not press too much against her. They walked side by side together for a moment, she sobbing and the kindly Hwang trying to comfort her.

"I must examine him," she said, though she knew it was Shen's invariable rule that the line must not stop for anything, not even for the wounded.

"When we stop," Hwang said quietly, "when we stop. He is without consciousness but he is alive. He took a piece of shrapnel just above the eye. But he is still with us. This is good fortune, for we have lost many of our comrades today."

Po was now in charge and Kate was worried that if he did not call a halt soon she would lose Shen. As much as she could see the stretcher being bumped around while they continued to march, the cut was deep but not wide. She would have preferred it the other way. The shrapnel had gone dangerously close to the brain. She was also very worried about whether he would lose the sight of his right eye. She wanted to run to the head of the column and remonstrate with Po. Perhaps Wu would be able to prevail on him to stop. But even as she thought this, Kate knew she could not do it. Shen would not want it. Nor would Wu help her. The safety of the whole group had to be put before the life of even the commander.

So she made a split-second decision. She had about a fifty-fifty chance. If she made it, Shen would be all right and she might save his eye. There must be enormous pressure there already. But if she slipped, there was a good chance she would cost him both his sight and his life, or at least irreparable brain damage. She could see just the tip of the shrapnel sticking out. It would have to be drawn out immediately. And there was no possibility of her cutting around it. Somehow she had to get hold of it—get a very firm grip on it—and pull it out. The trouble was, how was she to grip it firmly enough? And even if she achieved this, would she have the strength? It was a difficult enough operation standing still—on the march it seemed impossible.

She hurried to the bicycle cart which carried her two black bags and rummaged in the larger one until she found a pair of stainless steel baby forceps. She examined the jaws. Were they too big? Probably. But her other forceps were like tweezers. She needed something in between. It was not the first time, nor would it be the last, she would have to improvise on the march.

"Hwang!" she shouted to the big man above the noise of the march. "I need a pair of pliers . . . ordinary mechanic's pliers. Can you manage that?"

Fortunately, Hwang was already used to Kate's medical requests and did not query her. He simply nodded and handed the corner of the litter he was carrying to Yu-Ma. Yu-Ma now had two corners. At the front were two of Shen's most trusted Young Celestials. They had come back from the front line with the stretcher. They would stay, fully armed. There was no reason to suspect anything, but it was best to be careful. These were difficult times—both inside and outside the party.

Hwang arrived with a pair of pliers. Kate uncorked the last of her tincture of iodine, poured some into a small metal kidney dish from her bag, and dropped the pliers in.

Lu Chien had now come up and Kate handed her the metal dish while she scrubbed from it herself. Then, signaling for them to lower the litter as much as possible, she bent carefully over Shen, unwound the bandage, and reached for the wound.

Just as she was about to grasp the piece with the pliers, the ground became uneven and the stretcher rose towards her. God, this was murder! It was impossible! She steadied herself again and realized she would have to wait for a straight stretch of ground. The blood had dried around the wound so she left the bandage off. Strange how a foreign body which can do so much damage can also stem the flow of blood.

Hwang realized what the trouble was and now shouted to her, "In a few more yards Kate Doctor . . . there is even ground for a time. I will tell you when. . . ."

Kate smiled and nodded. She told Lu Chien to have another bandage ready. She tried to concentrate. Mentally to rehearse how and when she would pull.

She realized that keeping in step with the litter was essential.

Just then she heard Hwang shout, ''Now, Kate Doctor!''

She bent with the pliers, determined to come at the piece carefully. Holding them firmly, she slowly brought them to within an inch of Shen's head. There was just half an inch of metal sticking out, no more. She grasped and felt the jaws of the pliers close on the hard surface. She concentrated with all her might on keeping in time with the marchers. Then she ever so gently began to tug. Shen was still unconscious—which was just as well. All pain-killing drugs had gone a long time ago. The marchers were now dependent on occasional gifts from peasant villages of the strongest local spirit.

As the litter rose and fell, Kate tugged harder. But she was making no impression. She would have to pull really hard—it was the only way. So, summoning all her strength, she yanked with all her might. The pliers came away and her arm flew back. She nearly went tumbling head over heels.

She knew now there was only one thing to do. She had hoped it would not come to this. But she had thought it might. It was terribly unfair.

''I'll need Yu-Ma!'' she shouted to Hwang. Hwang nodded and called an elder born up from the column to handle Yu-Ma's corner of the litter.

Kate and Yu-Ma had always had a great unspoken communication. It was not hard to indicate with the pliers and sign-language what she intended. Yu-Ma had seen the shrapnel sticking out. And what he might lack in speech he made up for in mental agility. Kate pointed to the pliers; then to Shen and herself. She shook her head to indicate she could not do it and handed the pliers to Yu-Ma. He seemed to understand immediately.

She washed his hands in iodine and waited. Her heart was in her mouth but her eyes and face beamed smiles of confidence. The strongest and most agile of them now bent over the young man who was like a son to him; the one whom Yu-Ma always guarded with the fiercest determination.

Yu-Ma was bending by Shen's side like a great sinewed panther. Kate saw the measured, nimble steps as the big man paced each stride to get the rhythm of the march. The pliers looked tiny in his giant hand.

Then suddenly he crouched lower. Kate could see the perspiration on his brow. Like her, he brought the jaws of the metal instrument closer inch by inch. Then she saw him lock on.

Would he try to pull it slowly first? To pull hard all at once was best. It was the only way. And the sooner the better, so you didn't risk the implement slipping down onto Shen's forehead. She wished she might talk to Yu-Ma; say something to him; reassure him.

Then the next instant she saw Yu-Ma's hand fly clear of hers. But there was a difference this time. The shrapnel was held aloft and blood was spurting from Shen's forehead. Quickly Kate swabbed the wound with the remaining iodine, sutured it, and applied gauze and bandage. Just as she did so she heard Shen groan. The next moment he opened his eyes. "Can you see me?" she asked anxiously. "Wink your eyelashes if you can see me!"

He smiled and she saw them move. Thank God! But she was still not satisfied. "Can you see out of each eye—? Wink in turn if you can. First . . . right . . . then left."

She watched as one by one he blinked both eyes.

"Thank God," she said, "thank God."

Then she ordered the last of the plum brandy for him and tried to make him as comfortable as possible.

The next day the strafing began.

# 49

*T*he airplanes were from Germany, flown by Chinese and German pilots. They swooped down, breaking the line of marchers again and again and making the refugees flee for cover. Hwang and Yu-Ma seemed constantly to be dropping the stretcher, with Yu-Ma always throwing himself on top of Shen as a shield.

There was no question of marching only at night and resting

during the day. It was still many, many *li* to the first river they must cross—the Hsiang—and they had to get there before the enemy had time to regroup.

Shen was in constant pain. To make matters worse there was bickering among the other commanders. As time went on they learned more and more about Po. Like Wu, he was a former Kuomintang officer. Before coming to Shanghai he had commanded a local White Army garrison in the province in which his father was still military governor and through which they must pass on the march. Certainly, in one sense, because of age and experience, he should have outranked Shen. With Shen wounded, and Po in command, the march took on a very different character. Po was a traditionalist and led the marchers in precise mathematical formations.

They were sitting ducks for the airplanes. Shen had no alternative. On the second day after his wounding he took charge once more—from his stretcher. He sent for Po and a heated argument took place with Shen shouting and Kate trying to quiet him.

"We must make this a proper military operation so that there is no pattern at all!" Shen shouted. "We must rest different groups. We must march some slow and others fast. Then give cover for those lagging. One day we must rest a great deal, where we have caves or find some shelter such as in a forest. Another day we must double or triple march and not stop while in the open. And we must zig-zag! It is the first, elementary, and natural thing to do when fired upon from the air. Then we must soon organize ploys to deceive the enemy. We must organize false marches by our best people—feigned marches to give the weak ones time to move on while the planes and enemy chase our crack troops on false trails. Then, even if we sustain losses, or these men never make it back, it will have been to some purpose. And some volunteers should surely be left behind—to fight on and impede the enemy's advance and to remain even after that to liberate villages, train cadres, and consolidate the territories we have passed through."

Kate smiled quietly to herself. Shen was getting better. But he had also made a bad enemy within his own camp.

Three weeks later they finally reached the Hsiang—but it was to a barrage of artillery fire that they arrived. The White Army had beaten them there.

For a whole week the Whites' artillery kept them pinned down, giving Po ample opportunity to sow more discord among Shen's officers.

Shen was looking for a weakness in the Whites' strategy. He kept sending scouts out, and sometimes, at night, a small patrol. Although Shen would not have admitted it, the wound had been a blessing in disguise. It had been his first proper respite from fighting, his first forced rest—albeit in a stretcher—in nearly two years. Now, despite the hunger which always gnawed, and having to watch out for Po, he was sharp and ready.

On Monday afternoon—at the start of the second week of the Battle of the Hsiang—Shen decided it was time to silence the White artillery.

They waited until it was dark. Then he and his Young Celestials moved quietly forward. At least they did not question his tactics! They knew them too well. They would go anywhere with him these men! They knew he had been waiting until he was sure he knew the full disposition of all the enemy artillery; until he was sure that however heavy the fire was, there were not more guns waiting in the hills to be moved forward when the refugee columns started to cross.

The Young Celestials moved silently forward until they came within sight of the enemy's thinnest position—the farthest along the bank where the artillery emplacements finished. Shen—with all but twenty of his men—took up position on a level bank. The other twenty stripped to the waist. They then took jute bags—which held the army's few precious automatic weapons and grenades. They would hold them over their heads while they swam. These men had been chosen for their endurance against the fierce currents. It was essential to Shen's plan that they got far enough across to convince the enemy his force had broken through to the other side.

The men entered the water and Shen concentrated on looking at the enemy through his field glasses. It was a good moon. He noticed how well dressed those of the enemy were compared with his own men. It was hard not to be a little jealous. They were sitting by campfires and all looked fully fed and warm. Their officers wore jodhpurs and Sam Browne belts. They had smart peak caps, with polished leather frontal straps. The foot soldiers had webbing packs—with ration and ammunition pockets—

and even a place for a small shovel down the back. Many wore German helmets which covered the back of the neck and were cut out square in the front.

Shen looked towards the river. His men must be a fair way across by now. Soon they would make the opposite bank.

A runner arrived to tell him that Wu was in position. Kate and Wu were in charge of the women, children, and old ones.

They were in a tall clump of reeds immediately to Shen's rear.

Shen wondered if he had been right not to rope the women, children, and old ones together. The river current was wild and dangerous. But if he roped them together, those who were shot would act as deadweights and pull the others down.

Surely it must be time now! His men must be across! But even as he thought this he heard someone open fire from the other bank. Good! That was the signal.

The next few minutes would be crucial. Shen signaled the men close to him. He had two companies in position. The startled White troops were now dousing their campfires and running forward. As they did so, Shen's men opened fire. The Whites went down in droves. They were caught in the cross fire from both sides of the river.

A second wave of White troops replaced the first—and Shen's men dealt just as severely with them. Then a third wave went in. This time Shen signaled for grenades. They had precious few left but not one was wasted.

The enemy now began to panic. It was what Shen had hoped for. He moved quickly forward with his main force, swinging in a wide arc around the battle area to the river. He splashed into the water, taking a flare pistol from his belt. It was an old brass pistol with a polished wood butt, which had been a present from Wu. Shen clipped in the cartridge-like flare, snapped the pistol shut, and fired into the air.

The sight they now saw, standing waist-deep in the freezing water, brought tears to Shen's eyes. Wu, his old military teacher, watching the fighting closely, had quietly repositioned his people as the fighting moved. They now emerged behind Shen in a direct line. Shen waved the first of the refugee line through. Then, leaving another of his officers in charge, he returned to the fighting.

It was imperative they now move quickly into stage two of his plan. Having established a beachhead, it was essential he clear out the enemy on this part of the bank and mine the approaches to the crossing.

By dawn, as the first light came up, the river was a sea of bobbing heads. But the mines had stopped the main White Army from getting within firing distance.

An hour later they were all across. Some soldiers were dead. A few old ones had succumbed to exhaustion or stray rifle fire. But, as Shen remarked, that was a better result than the original Red Sea crossing, and he and his people had not had the benefit of a miracle.

# 50

*A few weeks later they had crossed the Wu river and were* racing for the Yangtze. It was already December and the weather was turning.

For a time, winter became the main enemy. But the bad weather also gave them a temporary respite. As they neared the Yangtze a thick fog settled in, so that for the first time since they had started the march they were free from attack.

In January 1935, a Politburo meeting was held in Tsunyi Kweichow. Mao was officially elected leader of the party.

After a few days rest, and with the fog still holding, they were off again—this time at such a crack pace that Kate wondered how any of them would ever survive.

There was a new heart in the army and in the people—but a new speed was being demanded, too.

Everything now seemed to depend on the greatest of all rivers—the Yangtze. They could see the trucks and men of the Kuomintang going up daily, etched out in lines along the tops of the hills in the distance, going up to reinforce the few places one might attempt to cross.

Shen started counter-marches once more to confuse the enemy. Kate was convinced they were marching around in circles. So was Po. On the night of the fourth day Po stormed up to Shen at the small campfire they had made during a brief break for an evening meal.

Po was a big man, in some ways more Manchurian than Chinese. He had Chinese features, but they were big and hard. He still wore part of his old Kuomintang uniform.

"I demand to know where we are going!" he shouted, without even pausing for Chinese politeness first.

However hard the march got, however tired and short of temper they might all become, this was not something Shen would easily forgive. Chinese politeness went deep into him, back to his father. And Shen would give his right arm rather than sacrifice this part of his heritage.

"And how goes my General Po, this evening?" Shen said, as if there were all the time in the world and he had not even heard the other's first sentence.

"We are marching around in circles!" Po shouted, even angrier now.

Shen looked at him. "Yes," he said, "we are. Your family does well?"

"So you admit we are lost?"

Suddenly Shen's voice went ice-cold. His whole expression changed. It occurred to Kate that this was how he would be in battle. She had never seen him close up in actual hand-to-hand combat. It was chilling. It almost frightened her. She felt uneasy. The whole group did. It was as if an executioner had suddenly silenced the crowd with a look.

"I will explain my decisions when you command this army and not before," Shen said in a tone that cut the air like a knife, "though if you had asked with civility and the interests of the army at heart, I would certainly have told you. But enough of this. You are no longer a general—you are demoted to colonel until you can learn to follow the chain of command."

"The council will never allow this," Po shouted. "They will overrule you!"

"The council will allow what I tell them to until further notice or they may appoint another such as you to command," said

Shen. "I am sick of fighting a war by committee and will do so no longer. I either command or I do not command . . ."

There was nothing to do but to have a hastily convened council meeting there and then. Shen won—but by one vote. And as Wu and the others who had supported him pointed out, there were those who would never forgive him. The doctrinaire Communists—and Po—would now actively work against him.

Shen agreed, but said with his usual pragmatism, "I had made a mistake so it had to be corrected. Generals can kill too many people in a war. So can colonels, but the number is likely to be fewer."

Still, he was annoyed with himself for having to do it. He had wished he might have been able to keep some of Po's goodwill until they had crossed through Po's father's territory. But first he had to turn his attention to the Yangtze.

Later that night, as he had always intended, he and Kate and Lu Chien gathered to say goodbye to Wu.

Kate thought how beautiful Lu Chien looked despite everything. As she bent to talk gently to an old one here, who had not much longer to live, or a wounded one there, she was still incredibly beautiful and refined and emanating peace despite the terrible pain her bound feet still gave her.

Wu, his once black hair now much grayer and his mustache gray and no longer clipped in the military manner, was being stoic too, as befitted his once-noble status.

But he had taken a piece of shrapnel in his right thigh in the last of the thickest fighting and would not make the distance. So, with all the old ones past their prime, and with those too wounded to travel farther, Wu was being given his last command.

"If there was any other way . . ." Shen was saying, close to tears. He, Kate, and Yu-Ma were saying their farewells.

"I know," said Wu. "But there is not . . . at least not for the pupil who is worthy of his teacher." He and Shen hugged each other then and after a time Shen and the others moved off to give him and Lu Chien a few minutes alone.

In the middle of the night, when Wu's group was long gone, Shen quietly moved his main column out in the other direction towards a valley he had chosen.

\*     \*     \*

It was now some months since Carpenter had been with the rebel forces. His article and accompanying pictures of Kate had been an unqualified success. Flashed around the world by wire services, the idea of a young American female doctor traveling with a band of rebels had caught the imagination of the public.

Carpenter had been scrupulously accurate as always, taking no sides. But he had told the Reds' story honestly and Shen had agreed to an interview also, determined that the communist view be put forth as well as that of the Kuomintang.

But that had been some months ago. Carpenter had been back to Shanghai, then to the battle of the Hsiang, and now, with the battle of the Yangtze looming, he was traveling up-country once more—this time to be with Chiang Kai-shek. There was no love lost between the two—particularly after Carpenter's reportage of the Reds. But Carpenter was determined to be fair to both sides and it was Chiang's turn.

The Battle of the Yangtze was now seen as so serious that Chiang Kai-shek himself had come up to take command. The Reds must not be allowed to cross the greatest of all rivers. This would be too much of a blow to the pride of Imperial China, represented by the Generalissimo himself.

Chiang stood as a modern-day emperor in the Imperial tradition, determined to bar the rebel Reds at all costs. He would take charge himself and wipe them out. Then Carpenter would have something to write about! Something for America and the foreign powers to listen to!

Chiang set up his headquarters in Yunnan-fu, the capital of Yunnan. With him were Madame Chiang Kai-shek, Carpenter, and a subdued Yang Ho who had lost much face by the Generalissimo himself arriving on the scene.

The war was beginning to turn very sour for Chiang Kai-shek. His famous "extermination" campaigns, masterminded by Yang Ho, had failed to exterminate the Reds. Each time, the military genius of the Red leaders had been superior.

Moreover, Chiang already faced dissension from within his own family. Madame Chiang was none other than Soong Mei-ling, sister to Soong Ching-ling, widow of the most famous and beloved revolutionary and founder of modern China, Dr. Sun Yat-sen.

Madame Sun Yat-sen, who was in fact part of the Kuomintang

Nationalist movement now headed by her husband's successor and sister's husband, Chiang Kai-shek, led a group of dissidents. They said Chiang no longer stood for what Sun Yat-sen had wanted for China when he led the First Revolution of 1911—the revolution in which Mao and Wu had fought alongside Sun Yat-sen. The dissidents resented Chiang's increasing military dictatorship and said openly he was not acting in China's best interests.

It was against this background that Chiang arrived in Yunnan-fu, determined to silence his critics and end the communist threat for all time, furious that he had already been forced to flee from one set of field headquarters at Kweichow.

As Chiang Kai-shek massed his forces for the last great battle to exterminate the Red Bandits, blocking route after route to the river, the Reds continued to march. Everyone said they were marching around in circles. Where were they going? Had they gone mad for lack of food? Was that it? What was the point? Were they really heading for Tibet, as the rumors said? That would get rid of them for sure—all those priests and cold mountains. The Kuomintang officers' mess at the Yangtze headquarters was alive with rumors.

Shen pored over his maps and marched some more. Then, without warning—for in all this marching who knew where the communists were from one day to the next?—word came to the Yangtze officers' mess about another sighting. A message said that the communists were inside the Yunnan border.


In the comfort of Yunnan-fu, the capital of Yunnan, Chiang Kai-shek was settling back once more in his chambers with his wife and Carpenter, who had been invited in for a drink before dinner. Chiang Kai-shek was conducting himself with mandarin courtesy to impress the foreign visitor when Yang Ho was hastily ushered in.

"Excuse this discourtesy, Excellency," Yang Ho began and then, seeing Carpenter, added:

"If I could perhaps have a moment of your Excellency's time, in private . . . ?"

Chiang obviously had no idea what was coming. Or did he? Carpenter was never sure. Had Chiang given the original order? Or Yang?

"Speak!" the Generalissimo snapped. Even Yang Ho knew it was useless to argue when he was in that mood.

"The Red Bandits are reported within sight of the city, Excellency . . ."

"The what . . . ? Where is our Yunnan army . . . ?"

"At Kweichow, Excellency . . . where you were previously . . . sent there to protect you as ordered . . ."

"I gave no such order . . ."

A look passed between Chiang and Yang.

"No, Excellency."

"Well get them back, then . . ."

"There may not be time, Excellency . . ."

"Are you actually proposing I flee a second time . . . ? How will that look on the A.P. and Reuter's wires?"

"Excellency, believe me . . . it is essential. I cannot guarantee your safety if you stay."

Reinforcements were urgently ordered up from the Yangtze. Even Carpenter knew enough of Red battle tactics to see what was happening. By a series of brilliant unexpected moves, Shen was forcing the Whites to weaken their strategic Yangtze defenses to reinforce Yunnan-fu.

The Red Army near Yunnan-fu now engaged the Whites. There was bloody fighting and even some artillery fire. Chiang eventually capitulated and fled with Madame Chiang Kai-shek. Carpenter opted to stay. He was sure if the Reds overran the city they would respect his neutrality. Besides, he had a hunch they were going to make it across the Yangtze. And if they did, he was going over to write it. If the Reds crossed the Yangtze, it could be a turning point in the war. The river itself was symbolic. And the military genius required to do it was staggering. If they crossed, the world would know—know finally that the Red Army was a force to be reckoned with.

There'd be a lot more selling out hurriedly to Janey then, a lot more, Carpenter thought cynically. He had dined with her and Blake several times on his last tour to Shanghai, after Kate had asked him to visit them and find out certain things for her.

He had a lot of news to tell Kate, including some she would not want to hear.

Carpenter and Yang were barely on speaking terms. Kate had told Carpenter what Yang had done to her, and Carpenter was sure Yang suspected this. Besides, Yang had not come out of Carpenter's interviews with Shen and Kate as exactly a knight in shining armor.

The moment Chiang left, Yang ordered Carpenter sent to him:

"You are to leave immediately," Yang said without any formalities. "I am barring all civilians from the war zone."

"But the Generalissimo said I might stay."

"You may stay in the region, yes. You may do what you like. But you may not stay in a battle area if I, as commanding general, do not decree it."

"Fine. I was intending to go over and cover it from the Reds' side again. I'll just leave a little earlier, that's all . . ."

"I hope you do not get caught in the cross fire, Mr. Carpenter. It would be a pity for papers such as the *London Times* and the *New York Times* to lose such fine, balanced dispatches . . ."

"Oh I'll be all right, Yang Ho, don't worry about that. I want to stay alive long enough to write a human interest story—a sidebar to the war—a story of how one of China's most senior generals is such a sadist he beat a poor, simple, loving prostitute half to death . . ."

Carpenter saw Yang Ho freeze. He obviously had no idea he knew about Ling Ling too. Carpenter should not have told him, of course. He should have written the story first and sent it. Yang Ho could have ordered him shot and made it look like a battle accident, blaming it on the Reds. But White troops were defecting every day now. Yang could never be quite sure that the man he ordered to do the killing might not defect and tell his story to other correspondents. Then again, Yang could have the assassin shot, too.

"Have a good war, General," Carpenter said as he turned on his heels and left without waiting for Yang Ho to reply.

The planes overhead bombed mercilessly. In the rain they bombed all the approach routes to the city. In the clouds of dust they bombed. The reports said this was the main column all right. They'd got them. They'd bottled them up at last. They were wiping them out.

But then, unbelievably, a big refugee column was reported near Lengkai in the city of the Yangtze. The Whites could not understand. How could the Red Army be in two places at once?

Carpenter was still getting his things together, ready to leave, and bribing an orderly to steal some whiskey from the officers' mess for Kate when the news arrived—news which caused him to start chuckling out loud.

So there were reports that the Red Army had been seen in the vicinity of the Yangtze, were there?

"Impossible!" said Yang Ho's staff generals. "Impossible! The Red Army was even now at the city's gates."

But as Wu's force of old men and wounded soldiers continued to engage the enemy in battle, and some of Wu's men started to fall, the awful truth began to filter through to Yang Ho's operations' room. This was no real Red Army! This was a decoy army! An army of the badly wounded—of the old and lame and sick and infirm. An army of all those too ill to travel.

While Wu's army had been engaging the Whites so heroically, the main Red force, marching largely by cover of night, had struck west. The Vanguard, led by General Shen Sun Lung himself, had swooped down and taken the crucial Loushan Gorge in one day of prolonged and intense fighting.

Now the whole Red Army, yes, the whole army, except for this handful of old people, had broken through and was hell bent on the Yangtze. Coming like a flood to the Yangtze.

The White general who had so much admired the Reds' battle tactics smiled to himself again. He recognized Wu as he was brought in. So that was who Shen had helping him! Here was the master to the pupil. Arguably the best military brain China had ever produced! And he was a Communist! What hope did the Whites have? What spirit! To force-march that distance in a week! He would have thought it impossible even for a fit army!

As Wu and his remnants marched by him, the old general saluted. He was past caring what Yang thought any more. These were the most magnificent Chinese fighting men he had ever seen.

Having escaped the Yunnan invasion by the old people's army, Chiang Kai-shek, from the safety of his base close to the Indo-China border, cabled to his forces on the Yangtze:

"The Red peril must be stopped."

All the crossings were strengthened. Chiang sent another order:

"Burn the boats. Take them to the far side and burn them."

All available Kuomintang troops within hundreds of miles were now ordered up to the Yangtze—or to Chiang Kai-shek's personal command where, with every available local warlord, he began pushing from behind the Red Army trying to catch them in a pincher movement between himself and his men who were stoutly defending the Yangtze.

Thus would the Long March become the short and finished-for-all-time march, he boasted.

The Reds were now in close formation, varying their ploys between three and four columns, pressing right on towards the Lengkai crossing on the Yangtze. The Vanguard was already there. Reports said they were building a bamboo bridge. Well, of course! With all the boats burned they'd have to. How else would they hope to get their thousands across? But they'd all be dead—all of them—before that bridge was built. And if any of them did get on to it, well watch out. The White airplanes would bomb the bridge to hell.

But the next morning the Vanguard was gone and the bamboo bridge abandoned.

Shen had kept a division well back and hidden.

At night he pulled out. The plan was quite simple. They had to march nearly one hundred miles in that one night and the next day.

Just before dusk on the following afternoon—in captured Kuomintang uniforms—Shen and his men slipped quietly into the heavily fortified town of Chou P'ing. They surprised the officers' mess, captured the officers in charge, and made them order their men to lay down their arms. Shen and his men then proceeded to secure the one remaining crossing over the Yangtze.

But they still needed boats. The town itself was not enough. This was a big operation for engineers as well as infantry. Shen sought the help of his ever-dwindling group of volunteer swimmers. They swam across swiftly and returned to say there were indeed boats on the north bank. They had not been burned. The Reds had heard of the Kuomintang order through Wang Lee. But government troops were notoriously lazy. "If it had been a Red order we would have carried it out and ended the war," the swimmers boasted to Shen.

But there was still the problem of getting the boats to the south side to start the ferrying operation. Shen called for Wang Lee.

"Can you impersonate a boatman?" he asked Wang.

"I can impersonate anyone or anything," he said cockily. "The local dialect is a little tricky, but I know some of it."

"Walk down the bank and call for a boat. Say a big artillery piece has arrived and must be taken across urgently."

"You think they will believe it?"

"They were stupid enough not to burn the boats."

"This is so."

"Tell them the Generalissimo has ordered the gun to be in place by morning."

Wang Lee nodded and went off smiling. Half an hour later word came back to Shen that a boat was on the way. When it arrived, Shen's Vanguard—all of whom were still in their stolen Kuomintang uniforms—took the boat and crossed the Yangtze. They overpowered the troops on the far side as easily as they had the troops in the town. The Yangtze crossing was now secured.

But the resting force had not been idle while Shen's division had been opening up the crossing. At daylight the first of the Long March line began to arrive. Yet working all the boats, it still took nearly two weeks to get all the marchers across. How they managed this, without any fatalities before Kuomintang intelligence was finally able to locate the main Red Army again and organize reinforcements, was a miracle. But by marching at three times the pace of normal soldiers in a day—and superb strategy—the Red Army had managed once more to give itself the precious time needed to keep its nation ahead of the Kuomintang.

The great battle of the Yangtze was over—it had not taken place!

The battle that was to have been the greatest of the civil war, an epic struggle to remember for all time, the story of how the Red peril was finally stopped, had been won without a single loss of life!

When the first Kuomintang troops finally arrived, all the Reds were safely across the river. With great ceremony the women and children burned the boats in sight of the Kuomintang.

# 51

*The winter frosts, which had provided such a pattern of lace*-work on every living thing, thawed into an early spring. And there were no guns fired! Not one single, solitary shot. For two days—it was the start of a peace but they did not know it then—it was quiet. On the third day the sun came up.

Kate and Shen went for a walk in the pine forest nearby. There were some camphor trees, too, and the scent hung on their nostrils, mixed with the pine. The sunlight threw yellow shafts between the trees from high up. The dark trees and the pine-needle floor, still touched with snow, were wonderfully alive in the first morning light.

Kate had one hand in Shen's greatcoat pocket.

"I've started having morning sickness," she said very quietly.

"Yes," he said, "I saw you the other day. I was going to say something but I thought it might just be the bad food—or the lack of it. Then I thought if it was something else you would want to tell me in your own time and way."

Kate smiled and grasped his hand tightly.

"What is it?" he asked.

"I was thinking how like my father you are," she said softly. "Stoic, caring. Noticing everything. Mentioning nothing until I do. The doctrine of individual responsibility. You don't mind about the baby, do you—I mean, babies shouldn't stop because of war, should they? Even if I could have prevented it, which I couldn't, you don't mind, do you? You don't want me to get rid of it—You don't mind . . . ?"

He looked at her then, and stopped her where she walked, and took her by the hands and turned her to him. Gently he kissed her. Then he smiled at her and said, very quietly, "My dear

Kate Doctor, I have not minded anything you said or did since I
first met you in that alley half a lifetime ago.''

She kissed him then on his face, softly, as she leaned across
and said, "Oh Lung, what a lovely thing to say."

They stood together holding each other for a long time. Then
they walked on in silence until they came to where a large patch
of sun reached the pine-needle floor.

There they lay down and made love with Shen's greatcoat
over them.

Later they walked back together, warm inside, and talked no
more about the baby—whether it was right or wrong or good or
bad to bring it into such a world—until the day Kate gave birth
and it was a girl. They called her Angelique.

# 52

Nearly a year had passed since the battle of the Yangtze, and
the lull in the fighting continued. But all knew the peace could
not last. Both Kate and Shen knew Yang Ho was not the sort of
person to take defeat lightly. They could not believe he did not
have some sudden, swift, and bloody retribution ready—and did
not stop to think that perhaps, just because of the distance, it was
simply that they hadn't heard.

Then Carpenter arrived, many months later than he had intended. He had indeed followed them across the Yangtze. But by
then they were miles ahead of him as usual, setting a crackling
pace. So he filed his story of the victorious Yangtze crossing and
was about to give chase when he heard of the temporary peace.

He took the opportunity to return to Shanghai in case the
Whites really were going to sue for a proper truce, although he

doubted it. As soon as he was sure it was just another Yang Ho ploy, he headed north again to find the Communists.

When he reached their headquarters he soon realized there was news from Shanghai affecting Kate which she had not heard. Even Wang Lee did not know it. Wang Lee told Carpenter he had not been able to return to Ling Ling after escaping down the back stairs. Nor had he had time to contact Janey. The Nationalists had been searching for him everywhere and he had soon realized that, with so much money for the cause at stake, it would be irresponsible to do other than return as quickly as possible with it. This meant he, too, had left without hearing the vital news. Then they had been so tied up in fleeing from the Whites once more and crossing the Yangtze that he had not had a chance to try to reach Shanghai. But he would have to, soon. The money was all used up. They had to pay exorbitant sums on the black market, of course, for any arms and medical supplies which they could not capture. They were always short of both. And food. Some 80,000 of them still remained, although at one stage there had been nearly 120,000 on the march.

So Carpenter had to break the news to Kate. Her mother had been executed. Kate would not at first believe it. She was stunned. Shen came over and tried to comfort her but she kept shaking her head and crying. She kept insisting the news must be wrong. "Things get mixed up in war," she shouted. "Yang Ho wouldn't kill her—he wouldn't. He would not dare. There would be too much of an outcry."

"Times have changed, Katie," Carpenter said softly. "Shanghai isn't the Shanghai you remember anymore. The locals are scared. The foreign powers won't intervene against Yang or Chiang Kai-shek because they're even more frightened of communism. Imagine what the foreign powers stand to lose if the Communists ever gain control. Millions. Billions. Land and buildings and multimillion-dollar trading interests all confiscated overnight. Your mother is just another old lady caught in the cross fire in a street battle with communist rebels. That was the official version. That's the way we had to write it. We can hint that she was executed behind prison walls but we can't prove it. And what we can't prove the papers won't run. The Western world is scared. It doesn't want to upset Chiang or Yang. People remember the Russian Revolution and see the whole thing happening again in China.''

"It's because of me, isn't it—?" Kate shouted, her grief now flaring into anger as she turned on him. "It's because of me! The damned American government thinks I'm a Communist and doesn't care about my mother being killed . . . about my parents who have done more for the United States in this part of the world than all their damned ambassadors put together . . . ! What about my father . . . ? What effort has the government made to find him? He's still an American national! It's because of me, isn't it? They think I'm a bloody commie, don't they? They think my father's a commie. They probably even think my mother was one!''

He looked at her, pained.

"Yes, Katie, they do,'' he said simply.

"But I'm not a Communist! And as for my mother . . . !''

"I know that. I even said so in my article.''

"But they won't believe it?''

"The Kuomintang propaganda against you has been very effective. Yang Ho has seen to that.''

"Don't they understand that I was caught up in this from the start? From the first coolie on the ship? From the night I tended Blake to the day the massacre started . . . all I was doing was tending the sick or helping with medical advice . . . That's my job . . . Doctors don't have to take sides any more than journalists . . .''

She was in full flight now. She was beginning to accept the news of her mother's death as it spilled out in her anger. But Carpenter had more to tell her and would rather she hear it all straight away.

"Katie,'' he said, gently, "They also know about you and Shen. Don't ask me how but they know. They know you and Shen are lovers and that you are the mother of his child . . .''

"How could they possibly . . . ?''

"Who knows . . . ? Word gets out. Even from a communist camp . . . You don't really expect you are without a Kuomintang spy or two in your midst, do you? I'm sure your people have them in Yang Ho's camp . . . You couldn't have succeeded the way you have without them. I know your people would be harder to infiltrate, and that your people are more loyal, but it's kindergarten stuff to think they might not have one or two . . . ''

"So in the eyes of the world I'm the communist general's whore, am I, and the mother of his illegitimate daughter . . . ?"

"Something like that . . .''

"Is that all? Or do you have some other piece of good news you have failed to bring me today from the wire services of the world . . . ?"

"That's all—except they do also say there's even dissension in your own camp about your relationship with Shen."

She looked at him, was about to say something more, and then burst into tears and threw herself against him, hugging him fiercely and sobbing and saying, "Oh Johnno, it's true. And it's all so damned unfair. But I'm not a Communist. I swear. I just love these people and want to help them . . .''

"I know, Katie, I know," he said, gently stroking the long run of her blonde hair with his huge hand, "I know. Come on . . . show me the baby . . . that's what it's all about—new life."

They walked off hand in hand.

Shen, who had witnessed the entire exchange from a distance, felt suddenly alone. When he turned to go there was a tear in his eye. Hearing her say the words "But I'm not a Communist, I swear . . .'' had hurt him more than anything else.

In the weeks that followed, a strange metamorphosis came over Kate. She had always wondered how the exposure to so much war—so much violence and hatred—might affect her.

Was this why she had denied the death of her mother so vehemently? Using denial as a shield against the hate and violence she feared might be in herself?

For in her heart of hearts she had known—really known—that such a terrible act of retribution was precisely how Yang Ho would behave after a catastrophe like the Yangtze.

Kate longed for her father. But he was not there.

Perhaps it was true that Kate's other trials and tribulations had been wearing her down; perhaps if they had not occurred she might have been able to resist the change she now felt sweeping over her; perhaps if she had not seen so much killing she might have been better able to contain the anger and the hatred, the hatred and revenge, which she now felt rising in the gorge of her throat. Kate could not get over the feeling that her mother had died as a result of her actions and however much she told herself she was not to blame, she knew she would have to live with this knowledge until the day she died.

But if this were true, it was also true that Kate herself had been at the mercy of other people's actions which, once put in motion, she had been powerless to control. When she had ordered blood to save Blake's life, she had not, in her wildest dreams, ever believed it could lead to the death of her mother. But what if she had known? Would she have denied Blake life? It seemed so unfair that in pursuing her oath of healing she had been cast irrevocably into a chain of events which had dramatically altered the pattern of all their lives.

Well, there were no more "what if's." What had happened had happened and she didn't think she'd ever get over it. We all had these "abominable snowmen" somewhere in our lives—the "Yeti" who came out of the mist when we least expected them—and it was really how we faced the Yeti that counted. She knew no other way than stoic endurance. And yet, at the end of the road, at the end of the road they were now starting out on, the end of the road back, there had to be some revenge. Forgiveness? That was going out of fashion in a world gone mad. So Kate changed. And the change that was taking place in her was this: This time she was looking forward to the war.

The mutterings against her continued. Against both her and Shen. Were they wrong to sleep together? To have had a child? Many other communist couples had. Ah, but there was the problem. She was not a communist. Nor was she Chinese.

Kate had no illusions about the origin of these critical remarks. A few might come from old women for whom tradition was the most important thing in the world, but most of them were inspired, she was sure, by Song Wei. She hated Kate for being a *yang-kwei*, and even more for having usurped her own place in Shen's bed and in his affections.

Carpenter did his stories, stayed a few weeks more, and then left. Shen was kept increasingly busy with battle plans. Wang Lee was on his way back to Shanghai to try to raise money. Wu was gone. Lu Chien was more and more withdrawn. Hwang and Yu-Ma were constantly away by Shen's side. And Kate could not move around as freely as she once had because she was breast-feeding—although she was producing little enough milk. She had never felt so alone.

She wished she had sent the baby away with Carpenter. She had actually discussed it with him. Had actually tried to find a wet nurse who would travel with him to Hong Kong. That's where she wished her precious Angelique might be—safely in Hong Kong with Mumma San. She was sure Mumma San would look after her. And Carpenter had agreed to make the detour if that was what she really wanted. But both knew it was impracticable. Besides, did she have the right to take the child away from its father? Yet Kate was so confused—grieving over her mother, angry for revenge, and isolated by some communists because of her relationship with Shen—she felt that she should use the excuse of safety to send her baby away. She thought that if Angelique were not there as a constant reminder of the mixing of Asian and white, the problem might go away. She and Shen could stop living together and things could be as they once were. But she knew she could never part with her baby.

Besides, she realized, though dimly, that people had not really minded them being together at first. Some of the old women had even chuckled in an affectionate way, saying how important it was for the good doctor to have a man to lie with, particularly on the cold nights, and what a comfort it must be for their leader, too.

These same women, when they needed treatment for an ailment or had to come to Kate if one of their men was wounded in battle, now drew back from the intimate affectionate talks they had once had with her and which she now tried so desperately to initiate again.

Then one day she overheard something. In the latrines, of all places! Or rather next to the latrines, in the bushes, as she was hurriedly pulling up her pants after wiping herself on some broad but none-too-soft leaves. Paper was at such a premium. It was kept for packing wounds, or, occasionally, if there were a little over, to give to the women who bled heavily during their menstrual cycle. Many did. Kate knew that perhaps half of this extra bleeding was probably due to early miscarriages because of the heavy work the women were called on to do. She never mentioned it.

The latrines consisted of two pieces of timber, two by four and several feet long—suspended parallel above a trench. The dirt from the trench was packed hard at each end to support the two pieces of timber which ran along the length of the trench. Sometimes there was just sapling timber or stout bamboo, instead of the two by four. Sometimes nothing at all, and then one just stood. Timber was a luxury afforded only by an extended stay. If there was timber you sat on it across the space.

Kate had been on the latrines alone. Then she had slipped into the bushes to look for leaves. The latrines were usually dug near bushes where at all possible for this very purpose.

Just as she was pulling her pants up, Kate heard Song Wei's voice. Song Wei, still on latrine duty, was talking to one of the women whose voice Kate also thought she recognized.

Kate was not greatly surprised by what she now began to hear—it tied in with what Carpenter had told her, and the venom in the speaker's voice was nothing new.

"The Western newspapers are calling her the Red Bandit's whore . . ." Song Wei was saying. "Is this what we want for our leader . . . this sort of disgrace . . . ?"

"Perhaps the Kuomintang have said it," the old woman replied. "They make up such lies. The good doctor is hardly a whore. Many of our people sleep together on the march . . ."

"After a simple communist wedding ceremony . . ."

"It is true most marry first. But the good doctor is not a Communist, so how can she have a simple communist wedding ceremony . . . ?"

"But that is just the point," said Song Wei, seeing her chance and pushing it home to advantage. "She is not one of us. She is a *yang kwei*—a foreign devil."

"A most unusual foreign devil," said the woman, whom Kate was warned to see did not give in to gossip easily, "a most unusual foreign devil to come all this way with us and treat our wounded although she is not one of us . . . The leaders offered

to help her escape to the North through Russia many times . . .
she could be back in her own country now if she wished . . ."

"And isn't it strange she is not . . . ?" Song Wei whispered in
a deep conspiratorial tone.

"She cannot go now anyway," said the woman, "not now
that she has a baby to look after. And who wants her to go . . . ?
Who would tend to us if she went . . . ?"

Song Wei ignored the question.

"What if the baby is not the only reason she stays . . . ?"

"What do you mean . . . ?"

"She is white . . . and the Kuomintang who fight us are
called White because they are like Europeans . . . Who is to say
she is not one of them . . . perhaps she sends messages of our
whereabouts through her friend the American correspondent
. . . Once a foreign devil always a foreign devil . . . there are no
good foreign devils . . ."

Suddenly the anger of the woman sitting on the latrine trench
flared:

"Away with you and leave me in peace. Can I not even rid
my body of its waste without hearing your biting tongue? Away
with you. There are good and bad foreign devils like there are
good and bad Chinese and good and bad Communists. But as for
me, you will never hear a bad word against the good doctor from
me."

Just then Kate recognized the voice and could have cried. It
was the woman whose son's hearing she had restored. But not all
in the camp would be as loyal as she. No wonder there was so
much feeling against her! Re-education through latrine duty! In
the hands of a performer like Song Wei, it was like putting a spy
in the powder room, or the men's toilet. For the men also used
the latrines Song Wei had to clean, and Song Wei was not
exactly the ugliest person in camp. Imagine how she must have
played her injured-party little game with some of the men,
vulnerable and tired after battle.

Kate was trying to think how best to combat Song Wei's
campaign when all hell broke loose again.

# 53

*They crossed into Szechuan Province under a hail of heavy* artillery fire. Szechuan—where they should have been safe! Szechuan, where Po's father was military governor.

Although the fire did begin just before they crossed the border, it was hard to tell where it was coming from and who was responsible. But when they finally got out of range Shen's worst fears were realized. Po and the malcontents he had gathered around him had disappeared. Strangely, Song Wei had not. Po's defection was a bitter pill for Shen to swallow. It was he who had supported Po traveling with them in the first place when Wu had cautioned against it. That decision had cost him dearly several times. But none as dearly as this time.

It was not just the numbers Po had taken with him, although Shen was short enough of soldiers at the best of times. It was what Po might do from a base in Szechuan. In all the other provinces, while there were some local White Army troops, most had to be moved in from outside. So White troops had to fight on terrain which was foreign to them, without a great deal of help from the locals. The Communists, on the other hand, often had the advantage of expert local peasants to guide them. In some cases they had their own partisans who had been fighting there as Communists before the main force came through. Now, if Po and his father decided to ambush Shen—and Po's father certainly still had a sizable army loyal to him—local knowledge and tactical advantage would be lost.

But it was not even this which Shen feared most. If he were

Po, and really bent on destroying them, he would not even risk an ambush at this stage.

He would use his base in Szechuan to get word to Yang Ho, while his men, who knew the area, scouted the Red Army's every move. Then, when Yang's main army arrived, it would be a perfect time to ambush the Communists in force.

And in addition to all this, it had been impossible for Shen to keep his main strategy from Po, who had been one of his commanders. Po would be able, if he chose, to give Yang exact details of where and how Shen planned to cross the Great Grasslands. Of all their obstacles, this was the one place where their communist guerilla tactics would fail them. There would be no chance to cut and run there. It was a sea of quicksand among the grasses. Crossing would be painfully slow, particularly with the women and children. If a wise commander wished to deal a death blow to the young communist nation on foot, this would be the place to do it.

They had not eaten for four days and Kate decided to use this as an excuse to suggest some hot rice. An ulcer had broken out on Shen's leg because of malnutrition. Lu Chien looked desperately weak and pale. She herself was mere skin and bone and somehow she had to keep Angelique alive too. But even rice would only fill their stomachs. Well, hardly that. She must find some greens for them to eat.

Everyone was sick with dysentery of one kind or another most of the time. And scabies. They all had scabies. Kate wondered if it was time to make them eat grass. Shen had told her he had eaten it as a boy. For many on this march it would not be the first time. But they all put it off as long as possible. It was the final thing one did. Perhaps it was the idea that it made one like an animal. Well, they were that on this march. And there would be no shame in it. But perhaps it was not time yet. Perhaps tomorrow. Tonight they should enjoy the last of their cooking oil and rice, the last hot rice. There was no salt. And no tea. But if the flame of the cooking oil lasted long enough, perhaps they might cook some hot water to drink.

Then it would be a race for the Tatu. The commanders on both sides knew what that meant. Neither would have wished the fighting to extend to the high-precipice Tatu river, with its fatal waters below. But now it had.

As they stopped to eat, Lu Chien shook her head fervently, a terror in her eyes at using the last of the food. The fear of this seemed greater than the fear of the enemy. Kate could see it even affected Shen.

It was an old Chinese thing, this not using the last of the food. It was as if while food remained, one was not destitute, not starving—the family was not dependent on others and their handouts. While one had rice, one was not poor. Kate understood well enough. Too well. The use of the last of the food seemed to destroy, too, the illusion that some good fortune would turn up. There was always the faint, final hope that something would happen. "Oh well, and perhaps some good fortune will befall before we have to eat the last of the rice."

They ate the last of the rice silently.


On the night before the battle of Tatu, Hwang came and took Kate aside. Hwang's ability to get information passed along from railway station to railway station had always been an important adjunct to the work of Wang Lee and his men.

"There is a report in from the Village of Wild Grass," Hwang said.

Kate looked at him with the slow terror of expected pain.

"They have murdered Shen's family," Hwang said simply. "Every member of it." There were tears in his eyes as he saw back over the years to the young boy who had joined the train.

They told Shen together.

"This is why we are Communists . . . this is why we fight," he said quietly, and he went off to be alone.

Kate wished she might comfort him. She thought about all he had been through. Had it been worth it? He would have a few ghosts. She had a few herself. And getting more every day.

Had it really been worth it for any of them? They had lost so many loved ones. There were so many good and bad memories. But the memories were important. They were the heritage of the next generation—and that was all there was. In the joy and pain, that was all. This was the rise and fall of human nature. The fortunes of war. One worked to make the memories of experience better for the next generation—for as many of the next generation as possible.

Her thoughts turned to Angelique. Most of the time Hwang and Yu-Ma took turns carrying her, and when Kate was working sometimes she would be lucky and the child would be asleep, needing no looking after. But when she demanded attention it was usually Lu Chien who nursed and cuddled and rocked her.

So far Kate had not reached a stage of desperate worry about her child. She must be tough—she had survived these dreadful conditions, and colic and diarrhea and coughs and colds. Not surprisingly, she cried a lot. Kate liked that, irritating though it was. What she feared was a listless silence which might indicate that the baby was beginning to loosen her tenuous hold on life.

She must find a way to keep the baby alive. She must. And Shen too—as he faced the Tatu.


The Tatu had a pivotal place in the history of China. It was the scene of both triumphs and disasters. But in the previous century the Manchu Imperial Army had put the rebel force of Prince Shih Ta-k'ai—the T'ai-p'ing Rebels as they were called—to rout. The message, as Chiang Kai-shek saw it and wired ahead to his massive army, was clear. The Tatu was the place where rebels were defeated.

But the Tatu was a double-edged sword. Its very gorge-like nature could make it difficult for big armies to maneuver.

Shen put himself in charge of the assault. He had never wanted a command more.

There were still one hundred miles to go—over the icy, muddy, rainwashed rock ledges and paths that led to the infamous Tatu bridge—the Luting.

Shen's repressed anger of the previous night now erupted. He and his men, like most of the marchers, had been without any footwear for weeks. Barefooted, with some of his men's feet still bleeding from the forced march through the forest, he now set out to conquer the mountain passes in record time and secure the bridge for the mass crossing.

Pain had long since ceased to matter.

There was hardly a man whose family had not been touched in some way by the Whites—a member killed, a friend or relative shot or raped.

They did not look like soldiers anymore. Not one of them

looked like a decent bandit. Their clothes were in tatters, and they were all taut skin over bone. They were barefoot, and they moved over the mountains like a gang of Shanghai street beggars. The Whites could never quite believe that what they were fighting was an army.

But if the journey over sharp rock and ice were enough to test the courage of the stoutest, the sight of the bridge was doubly so. It became suddenly obvious that not all Whites were stupid. Local Whites.

The bridge across the Tatu was nine giant chains, perhaps a foot apart, stretched parallel to each other across the raging waters below. Even when they were not in flood, as they were now, they boiled with a Niagara intensity. The chains were locked into giant iron eyelets at each end, and these forged eyelets in turn were anchored deeply in huge blocks of wood, set into the rock cliff-face of the Tatu gorge itself. The weather was dark and overcast. The water, because of the light refraction from the black rock cliffs around it, had the most hideous black look. This should have been less stark because of the white froth from the cascading churling water, but in fact it looked more evil because of it, whipping around like some great black frothing atavistic monster of the past standing guard over the most impossible of crossings in China.

Yet if there was unrelieved gloom in these black hills, and in the sheer drop from the bridge to the deadly water, this was still not the worst of it.

Straight across the bridge, right at the far end of it across the river from where they now looked, was a tiny upward-curving pavilion, arched like a roofed gateway over a long straight drive. And underneath this pavilion was a row of machine guns. They had an uninterrupted line of fire straight into the bodies of any who would cross the bridge. But more than this, there were gun emplacements high up and to the side, giving great angulated lines of fire. If the Red Army were to cross here, they might lose everyone.

Yet even the thoroughness with which this particular White commander had anticipated and prepared for the Reds in the placing of his guns was outdone by his strategy on the bridge. This man would have burnt the boats if ordered. He would have thought of doing it himself. For, as the Reds looked again at the bridge, their hearts continued to sink. The principle of the chain bridge was, of course, that between two chains were laid wooden planks, with thin vertical iron stanchions every twenty yards or so to keep some tension in the chains and to act as supporting handrails for those crossing.

But arriving before the Reds, the Whites must have crossed the bridge first and then retraced their steps, taking up half the planks as they went. So now, in addition to the strongest concentration of fire on a single spot which Shen had ever seen in his life, the planks had been removed to halfway across. And the bridge was half a mile wide! It seemed impossible. He must think out a plan. But there was no time to think. The whole of the Red nation was on his heels, urged on by their leaders at his command. And every moment's delay meant the possibility of the White Army arriving in greater numbers.

Shen had sent a Red Army detachment—under Wang Lee—around to the other side by a longer route, but there was no chance of them arriving in time.

Well, he would go himself. That was a start. His chances of surviving were nil. But it had to be tried. It was the only thing to do. Perhaps some volunteers. He and seventeen others. Two on each chain. With grenades. They were all as good as dead the moment they put their hands on that chain and hung down from it vertically.

He called for volunteers and all stood forward. There were only twenty-five in his original Vanguard left. It seemed unfair not to take them all. Their eyes wanted to go so much. They had fought so long and hard together and all were tired, so desperately tired.

He chose the youngest and the fittest. It seemed a terrible waste to kill the best. But only by being willing to lose his best could he give his army, and the whole Red Army which would follow, a remote chance of victory. He himself was as fit as any, he knew that. "The strength of a peasant is the strength of a peasant," he quietly recited to himself.

He nodded an order and they all stripped down to their pants. Those who were not to go shared out the best belts with grenade clips on them.

Then, giving over his command to his second-in-charge, Shen took hold of one of the outside strands, which he believed would be the most dangerous of all because the outside chains would receive angle fire as well as straight-ahead fire. He hung waiting by the big timber block at the start of the bridge. The others joined him in position. Then, on a nod from him, the first wave of nine started across. The second wave was to wait only long enough to give themselves adequate swinging distance before starting.

It should have been done in the night. Of all operations it should have been done in the blackest of night. They did not need to be able to see to swing from one hand to another. Indeed it might have been an advantage not to be able to see down. It would certainly have been an advantage not to be able to see across. Though there was precious little time to look either way as the bullets started to come—sounding like thunder cracks when mixed with the tumultuous roar of the river below.

Shen's instructions to his men had been simple. Their only hope was to swing as widely and erratically as possible. They had to be moving targets—never stationary ones. They must keep dodging and weaving, never, even in swing, staying in one position long enough to give the enemy time to aim and fire.

It was not long before they all heard the shout of the first man to go. Then Shen heard a thud beside him. There was no cry but he knew that the man had gone too. He must not think about it. His obligation was to get across. They must get as many across as possible. Was it possible to get "any" across?

"Swing," he told himself, "swing." His short sinewy frame, no longer stocky, with not an ounce of fat on it, bounced around the chain. His knuckles were bare already.

He tried to make his swings as violent and as quick as possible. He kept going—hearing the bullets close all the time. He heard and felt others going off. Once, he even saw one young one—who had done so well he had gotten ahead of Shen— receive a direct hit in the face and go down in a blood-splattered cry. The young soldier's speed had given him a consistency of pattern to let someone aim carefully at him, Shen thought.

Consistency of speed! He varied his own immediately, consciously slowing down for a moment, then speeding up twice as fast as he finished his slow swing. Speed as well as side movement, that was it. Concentrate on nothing but developing a pattern of which there was no discernible pattern. Wide, not so wide, very wide, very narrow, very wide, not so wide, hang almost vertical, fast forward, fast side, slow, slow, slow-fast, wide. And so it went on.

He had no idea of how many men were left. But he believed he was nearly halfway across the open space. If he could get to the planks, if he could just get to the planks, there would be a blind spot under them where he might rest just for a moment. If two or three comrades, perhaps even half a dozen, could reach there, they might stand a chance of hauling themselves up onto the bridge and running far enough to release their grenades.

Just then he thought he heard the sound of a second lot of firing. Had the main Red Army arrived? He kept swinging. A few yards more. Wide, very wide, very very wide, slow, narrow, fast. Yes, they had opened up behind the Whites. It must be Wang Lee's detachment. That had been his assignment.

It made only a negligible difference. But it was something. One machine gun diverted or slowed down was something. And some of the angle-fire gun emplacements were having to turn. Yes. They were turning. The angle fire was becoming less intense. Now he and his men had a chance! A slim chance, but a chance nevertheless. He swung all the more violently, intent on not getting shot now that he was so close. So close. And one of his men had made it! Well, almost. He was on his last swing. Then Shen saw a wave of machine gun fire hit the youth and down he went.

Shen could feel his hands wet now. He knew it was blood. Well, so what? His feet had been bleeding on and off for days. He just hoped the blood flow would not get so strong that it would make his hands slippery. That's what mattered. Damn the blood! Damn the pain! But damn the fact that blood was wet and if you bled enough it made your hands slippery. What a terrible way to be defeated. To go down by your own blood. He could not! He must not! He must hold on. "Swing, swing, swing Shen, swing," he told himself. "You can make it. You must give your comrades a chance. If you can get one decent grenade down the alley of that bridge, your comrades have got a chance. If you can get that Pagoda gun emplacement, the others might cross the bridge. One grenade . . ."

He was nearly there, but the fire was more concentrated now. Their aim was better. He was closer. It was heavy now. They had him in their sights now. The bullets were coming like tracer fire. Only a few more yards and he would be there. But the fire was too heavy. He must do something or they would have him.

Could he swing-jump underneath the bridge? He was not really close enough. Yet with the intuition of a thousand frosty nights and mornings of battle, he knew—absolutely knew—that the next round of fire would find him. Whatever else happened he must not be there. With all his force he swung back as far as he could. Then he pushed with all his might and let go—swing-jumping not to the front but to the first chain across from him. He had no sooner grabbed this one than he swung again—jumping for the third chain as he saw a narrow gap underneath the planks where there was room for his hands. He grabbed, almost missed, then grabbed harder as he felt himself slipping, and then, with his arms feeling as if they were coming out of their sockets, he was hanging vertically under the timber of the bridge.

He looked around him. Suddenly someone swung in beside him.

"Which wave are you?"

"The second, sir."

Another man, a veteran of the Vanguard and of many years of fighting with Shen, swung in two more across.

"Which wave?" gasped Shen.

"The second sir. You are the only one of the first wave left."

Shen nodded grimly and carefully turned himself half around, hand over hand, for a moment.

Only three of them had survived.

The chains were all empty. But he must not dwell on it. He turned back and nodded to the others. "Ready?"

"Ready, sir."

What men these were, he thought. What men. There would be others to follow. His deputy had orders to keep sending them across as long as they lasted—but not to send foolishly, and to wait until he saw what they managed to do with their grenades. There would be others. But what men these were. And the old one. He must be over forty. He was older than Wu. What strength and agility.

Shen gave the signal and they began to haul themselves up onto the planks. The fire would still be heavy, but they would have more room to maneuver.

The next minute they were all up and running—grenades out and ready. He must get one in really close. He was dodging and weaving as he let the first one go. He unclipped and let off another—and another.

His eye was still troubling him and it was like seeing through a dark curtain. Never mind. He went a lot on sound in battle. Sound and smells. You could tell a lot about the numbers dying if you listened and smelled. No time to stop and listen though—one more and then out to the right.

Running, breathless, with bleeding feet again but with the blood dry on his hands, he unclipped his last grenade and threw caution to the wind. He held it perilously long until he got in close enough to let it go underarm—let it go for the village of Wild Grass. Let it go to take half the damn White Army with it, let it go for the women and children. Let it go for the slow and wounded, let it go for Kate and Lu Chien and Wu Zhao, the patriot and warrior, let it go for all the unborn babies in the belly of China.

He let it go and fell, struck by a bullet ricocheting off a rock.

For his part in capturing the bridge, Shen Lung, along with the other heroes of Tatu, was awarded the Red nation's highest honor, the Gold Star.

It was at this time that his men, who had seen his epic swing on the chain across the river, started calling him "the Monkey General."

Fortunately the bullet which hit Shen had only inflicted a small flesh wound, little more than a scratch, on his shoulder. But weariness and the sudden sharp pain had caused him to faint. He did not regain consciousness until after others had come across with more grenades and until Wang Lee's detachment behind the Whites had broken through and secured the bridge. Wang Lee, with his typical inventiveness, had brought doors from a nearby village to put over the chains to bring the others across.

Yet if the bullet did not seriously wound Shen he was nevertheless close to the breaking point in those triumphant days after the crossing of the Tatu. As the line of refugees moved on, singing their songs again now, and even Lu Chien appeared a little better, Shen told Kate he had a tiredness near death. Every limb of his body was like lead. He had a perpetual headache. Kate had nothing to give him but love and understanding. He needed food and rest. They all did.

Kate was amazed that somehow, as he had done a thousand times before, Shen walked on. Kate wondered how many times you could force the human body to do this. Was there a limit? Was there a point at which it just rebelled and stopped? Of course there was. They lost as many that way on the march some days as in battle. There were those dying all the time, just out of sheer exhaustion—because the complicated and intricate mechanism of the human body had just stopped like a clock, its owner unable to rewind it. This was how Shen felt, Kate knew, day after day after day. And yet, day after day after day, she saw him put one foot in front of another, take another exhausted debilitated step, take another deep breath, shrug himself deeper into his thin cotton battle jacket, the only covering on his top, and move along the trail of the Great Snow Mountain.

Kate was very tired herself. She daydreamed all the time now. She daydreamed of Yu-Ma's pony back in Shanghai and what she would give to have it now. She daydreamed of Janey and her father and Ling Ling and the old mandarin. She daydreamed of Hong Kong and Mumma San. She daydreamed of Blake and what life with him would have been like.

It was, perhaps, their worst day, although they often said that. They could see Tibet. Kate knew that had to have something to do with it. It was where the Yeti lived. The Yeti and Shangri-la—in the one place. Hell and heaven together, in one country. It seemed ridiculous. Was she doing more than daydreaming now? Had the hunger and exhaustion really gotten to her? Was it because her bare feet were bleeding now? Could she feel that? Good. Her senses were not completely gone, then. Even in the snow and ice and numbness she could feel that. Perhaps her senses were just misplaced for the moment. Or perhaps they weren't misplaced at all. Perhaps, really, there was a Shangri-la up there, up ahead on the top of the world lost in the mist.

There was certainly a Yeti, so why shouldn't there be a Shangri-la? A place to rest. To stop and rest. A place of peace. Of tranquillity. A place of food and rest and happiness. Perhaps she'd just rest now for a moment, here by the side of the trail.

Others were resting. Others were sitting down. Good God no! Get up. Get up all of you. Not you Lu Chien! God no, not you! Yes, my feet are bad too, though not as bad as yours. Here, let me help you. Just a little farther.

So on they marched, these heroes of Tatu. On they marched like tiring Arctic explorers, slipping, sliding, falling down, getting up, and pushing on, this mule train without mules except for the precious few to carry the machine guns and who must not be eaten, this army without shoes, this nation without food or clothing or shelter or territory of its own other than the *via dolorossa*—the true path of suffering—beneath it which it had chosen for itself.

They could see the mountains of Tibet closer now. Over rock and ice they went and the numbers dying of exposure got greater all the time as if to ridicule the triumph of Tatu.

When there was not rock and ice and sleet and snow, there was mud on the high passes in between. Mud so slippery and treacherous because of the sheer height at which they walked that it had to be covered with cut bamboo.

Then Shen started to worsen.

By the time they had stopped to rest for the night, he had to be carried. Kate made him as comfortable as possible in the cleft of a rock high up in the Great Snow Mountain of China with Tibet in the distance. They laid down some of the bamboo poles, dirty with dried earth, which had been used for fording the mud earlier in the day, and on top of these Kate placed the worn but ever highly prized red blanket. Hwang sat on the rocks waiting. Yu-Ma had disappeared.

Angelique began to whimper, and Kate asked Lu Chien to take her outside so that she should not disturb Shen.

Song Wei looked terribly concerned. Shen was as pale as death. Kate could not see how he could survive another hour. He was absolutely exhausted. The wounding of his eye plus the ricocheting bullet had been too much on top of the malnutrition from which they all suffered. Kate took from her doctor's bag a small stone flask of mao tai. She had purchased it from the village at the Tatu river with the last of her personal money for just such an occasion.

She held Shen up, cradling his head in the bend of her left

elbow as she put the flask to his lips and encouraged him to
drink. Shen suddenly smiled.

"So it was not the last of the rice," he whispered.

"No," Kate said, swallowing hard, "it was not the last of the
rice."

"It is well, it is well," he said, taking a little more of the
liquid.

Just then Yu-Ma arrived back.

They saw he was smiling. And then—unbelievably—they saw
Shen was smiling too. They looked along the line of his eyes to
Yu-Ma's hands. In them the giant man, who was quite out of
breath, held two enormous red peppers. Where had he gotten
them? And oil—he had a little heating oil and was motioning to
the others. They quickly moved to get the cooking pot out and
scoop up some snow.

They put the cooking oil in a cut-opened tin and put the snow
in a small wok. They heated the snow over the fire and then cut
the peppers into the water and boiled them up.

When it was hot they gave Shen a little of the pepper stew to
drink and then some of the peppers to chew. Little by little they
fed him more and more, and Kate made him take another sip of
mao-tai. Then, thankfully, he slept. But even so, his strength
had been wasted and he was still so exhausted and pale that Kate
kept checking every few minutes to listen for his breath to make
sure he was still alive.

Although they were all desperately hungry, none of them
would have any of the pepper soup.


The story of the red peppers was hard to ascertain from
Yu-Ma by sign language. But as far as Kate could deduce, it
appeared Yu-Ma had arm wrestled a man for the peppers and oil.
Yu-Ma's hand drawings in the air seemed to indicate one of the
Szechuan tribal guides. In each area they passed through, the
leaders always tried to persuade locals to help guide them through
a particular stretch of territory. This of course often helped give
them their advantage of speed over the Whites. Sometimes the
guides were paid in money, if the army had enough, or in
captured guns and ammunition. Sometimes one or two young
communist leaders stayed behind to start a communist group

with the guides and harass the enemy passing through. It was forbidden to take anything from the locals without paying, but none of them had any money anymore. Whether betting may or may not have been frowned on was an arguable point which no one was prepared to debate that night. The strength of the good solid hot vegetable may well have saved Shen's life.

Hwang was all in favor of calling him "Red Pepper" rather than "the Monkey General." Instead, they composed "the Red Pepper Song," which later became a Red Army favorite.

Shen, when he got a little better, said a boy who was doubtless destined to be a warrior could do a lot worse than being called Red Pepper. It was a good strong warrior's name.

In the days that followed, he regained a little of his strength.

Then, after a few weeks, he was able to walk around again.

In July they reached West Szechuan. They knew there was supposed to be a Red base there, and when they found it they were overjoyed. There was goat's milk for Shen and Angelique. There were beds of straw; fresh vegetables; some noodles. The comrades in that area were desperately short of food themselves. But at least they had some fresh things and Kate took sparingly what she felt was needed for the desperately ill to help them regain a little strength before they moved on.

Yang's armies were still pursuing, according to intelligence reports, and they would not be safe until they finally crossed the Great Grasslands which lay ahead.

Still, it was a blessed resting place for a few days, although their joy at this and Shen's renewed strength was marred by one thing. Their party was one member short and would remain so now. Ten days ago, on the lower reaches of the Great Snow Mountain, as they made their way down from those terrible passes to the relative safety below, they had received word that the beloved Wu Zhao had died. He had been buried with full military honors. This staggered them. It had never happened to a fallen Red soldier before. But apparently some aging White general had insisted on it.

They had seen so much death and buried so many comrades, but this was the first personal tragedy that had encountered their little group since that night a lifetime ago when they had fled from Shanghai.

Kate thought again about Shanghai and Ling Ling, and the

terrible suffering she had undergone on their behalf at the hands of Yang Ho. When Wang Lee had told Kate about it she had gone off to be alone and cried. She, perhaps more than anyone else, understood; she who had also been humiliated at his hands. Kate found it hard to hate. But if she hated anyone, if she wished anyone dead, dead of a slow and agonizing death, it was Yang Ho. She thought about Ling Ling and how alone she must feel. She thought of what the knowledge of her niece, Angelique, would mean to her. She had not yet been told.

They all deeply felt the loss of Wu Zhao. He had been like a father to them, and although he had left their little group, his presence had remained with them and they had hoped to be reunited one day.

Now the local Reds who had been so kind to them when they first arrived began openly to argue with Shen. They could not believe that he still intended to go on. The army led by Shen had traveled nearly 5,000 miles on foot. There was still another 2,000 to go. How could any of them hope to make it alive?

Shen should remain, for the sake of the communist nation. They seemed to find the idea of a tattered, worn-out, emaciated army, less than two-thirds its original size, an indication that the march had failed. The local leaders said the only answer was to consolidate them—and march back and fight the White Army still massed south of the Yangtze. It was madness, and Shen told them so.

Besides, there was now another enemy. It was 1935. The Japanese were striking out towards the north of China. And no one, no one except the Communists, and the tattered worn-out Communists at that, seemed to care.

The talking went on, and Kate watched as Shen, in his anger although still weak, said his piece. It was unthinkable to turn back now. What had they fought for? What had all the comrades died for? For an idea. For the idea of them all finding a place to live in freedom and launching the fuller war from there.

Shen was a full general, with a full army at his command. He wore the Gold Star of Red China. He was one of the heroes of Tatu. He was listened to with respect.

At the next meeting of the Politburo, to his complete surprise, he was elected to take the place vacated by the death of Wu Zhao. He had just turned twenty-nine. Kate, looking on, felt old and unfulfilled.

# 54

*It was time to move again. They had rested for more than* two weeks—the best rest, perhaps, of the entire march. But it had not been enough, particularly for Shen. Sometimes all such a rest did for those who have been running so long on adrenalin and stamina was to slow them down. But perhaps, when they got moving properly again, the rest would have done them good. Shen did seem very much improved. The baby was growing too. Unbelievably, after two weeks on goats' milk, she was actually putting on weight.

Yet if Kate had known what lay in store, would she have risked going on and these loved ones going with her? Would she have spoken out for them to remain? It was no shame to stay. Many had decided to. Even some of the leaders. After a disagreement of tactics, one could have made a choice to stay without dishonor. Would this have been better for Shen and Lu Chien and Kate and the baby? Better for them all? No one could have known, after all their trials and terrible losses, that the worst was yet to come; that before long they would be in the Great Grasslands—infamous and dreaded always—crossing there as across a desert without water; crossing there across an innocent-looking plain of grass, but as through a minefield, for there were quicksands at every step, and it was a ten-day journey to get through even in record time.

But even before they had entered the Great Grasslands, their troubles started again. Not that they were ever in any doubt about crossing the Grasslands. They knew they must to reach their destination. But with so dangerous and tortuous an obstacle, the question always was which route was the best to take. Would fewer be lost if they tried only to touch the edges of the

Grasslands, swinging as wide as possible around them in the hope that most of the hidden quicksands—which made them so infamous—could be avoided?

The problem was that this time the Whites appeared as out of nowhere. A few days out from their rest at West Szechuan, Wang Lee brought news of a terrible and massing White Army, hot in pursuit, bigger than all the armies so far, and running, yes running, faster than the Reds could run. Kate was filled with terror.

Their health was too broken. It was too much.

Chiang Kai-shek was preparing for one last, final battle to end the civil war.

But despite their rest, Kate and her friends were on their last legs. She was not in any doubt about that.

Shen was certainly not fully mended from his last ordeal. Yet he and the other communist leaders now made a classic communist decision; a decision of daring. They must go straight across the most difficult part of this vast moor of China, rather than around it. They would strike for the heart of it. They would dare the enemy to follow. Yet the loss of life would be acute. And the task of keeping the Long Marchers together would be nigh impossible.

Shen and his "Young Celestials"—the crack vanguard of troops he invariably traveled with at the head of the column—prepared to move off. Kate often traveled with them. It was where the fighting was usually the most intense. But this time she hesitated.

"So many of our friends and the young ones are so weak and tired . . . I should stay with them . . ."

"It will be safer in the middle of the column—safer for you and the baby."

She nodded. "I hate not being with you and the others . . . And yet I feel I am needed more here . . ."

"So do I."

They embraced and she watched while Shen and the Vanguard rode off into the distance.

Kate stood on the edge of the Great Grasslands and looked as far as she could see.

Enormous bogs, soggy, grass-filled fields, stood before them now, in the encroaching twilight. As she looked upon the land there was a desolation about it that made her heart sink. What a terrible misnomer the term "Great Grasslands" was. What lay before them, in mile after mile of interminable flatness—for so many miles that it was said it took ten days to cross at the barest minimum—was a swamp. A putrid, decaying, smelling swamp. Grass there might be, but it was rotting, dank grass, more black than green, set in black stale mud, giving off the most pungent of gases from mold and vegetable decay. The gas rose like fog over a deserted moor. The smell was stifling. There was not one inch Kate could see where the mud looked solid enough to walk on. Here was hidden death at every step.

Everything else that had happened on the Long March would now be as nothing compared with this.

Kate looked at the others. They had been march-running all day to keep ahead of the Whites. Shen had now moved to the head of the column, commanding the army, although he was really too weak and ill to do so. She looked at the baby. So far she sat quite happily wrapped in the red blanket, sitting in a pack made from a shirt, on Hwang's back. Either Hwang or Yu-Ma carried her and she was brought down when it was time for Kate to feed her from her breast as she walked. Apart from this the two men carried her in turns, to save Kate's strength for helping the wounded.

Kate looked at the others and felt them to be her responsibility. They had always been that, she knew, from that first night in Shanghai. They had been her patients, her friends, her family, her responsibility. Now she felt it ten times over. Kate looked for some rope but there was none. They were as short of this as everything else. She quickly told the others to take off what they could spare, to use anything at all to knot into a rope. Soon they were all bare to the waist—the women too. Even the quiet and shy and sensitively elegant Lu Chien finally acquiesced. Kate smiled kindly at her as she put her into line. Kate knotted their blouses and tunic tops into a rope—so that anyone falling into the mud might be rescued.

Kate organized the line so that Hwang would lead. She would have preferred Yu-Ma because he was stronger, but she could not risk having a deaf man leading. He might never hear a call for help from behind. So she put Hwang first, and then Lu Chien, with Yu-Ma behind her and herself last. This way she could be mouth and ears for Yu-Ma and still be near Lu Chien. She had given considerable thought to who should carry the baby. Hwang was the leader and the one with the cloth rope. He must be free to move quickly if any got into trouble. Besides, he could not be hampered by a baby on his back while testing which path in the mud they must take. Nor would she want the baby to be thus at risk if Hwang made a mistake and they had to rush to pull him out themselves. It was unfair to ask Lu Chien, who was little better than a cripple herself.

Song Wei was almost strong enough to carry her. But the best choice, and the one she believed most able to shoulder the responsibility, was Yu-Ma. She would entrust the baby to Yu-Ma, with Lu Chien walking in front of him and Kate behind. It seemed the only way.

There was a moon, thankfully, although another feature of the badlands, of the grasslands, soon became apparent. It rained almost incessantly. From night to morning, morning, noon, and night, it rained, throwing a dark curtain over any natural light which daytime or the moon might have given them. It was bitterly cold.

Perhaps that first night was the worst night of their lives. They seemed hardly ever off their hands and knees, any of them. All around them they heard cries of people falling, shouting for help, and then the chilling asphyxiating gagging of a breath expelled and urgently sucked in, in a last swallow of life, as someone drowned in the mud.

They went on. They were too terrified not to. But they were terrified, too, to move from one piece of mud to another. For this was all they had at the best of times: a foothold on a few square inches of mud. There was no path. None crossed frequently enough on this desert plain to wear a path, even if there had not been continual rain to wash it away. One worked on the assumption that grass which was pushed back or pushed aside might indicate a way someone had traveled before, but whether they had traveled for safe or ill, the grass had not left a sign to say. So on they went, death all around them, and farther back still was the sound of rifle fire and the rearguard of the army engaging the Whites. They pushed on.

First light and a slight cessation of the rain brought a frightening realization of how heavy the losses had been in the night. The worst thing was people wandering off and getting lost, as group wailed to group. Kate could not see how they could last. It was a miracle their group had stayed together so long. But what if Lu Chien or one of them wandered off? One could lose one's direction in one footstep in this country.

One thing became obvious. They could not travel at night. However sorely pressed from behind by the Whites, however anxious to push ahead to avoid any possibility of the Whites moving troops in to block their advance as they came out of the marshes, they could not travel at night. If they did, they would lose everyone—every last man, woman, and child. Although, by now, there were fewer than fifty women left in their immediate vicinity. Kate went to send a runner on to suggest they must rest at night, but just as she was about to, one arrived from headquarters at the front of the line. They had already taken this decision.

After a brief rest for breakfast, they were off again. They had brought a little food with them from their last stop, where the leaders had organized a supply of the only food available.

There was some green rice and they ate it now.

At night it rained and rained and rained. They had no tent. There were no trees on this distant prairie. They tried to shelter under some bushes, in the end uprooting them and pushing them together to try to make an umbrella of sorts. But nothing stopped the rain. Day after day and night after night it came without pause. They were all wet throughout the entire time and Kate feared for the baby. They could not cook. Anything they might have used to start a fire—to cook on or to warm themselves by—was wet throughout.

On the fourth night, at Kate's insistence, they took off all their remaining clothes and got under the red blanket together. It was, of course, also wet. But they huddled together, all of them, and each gave the other the only sort of warmth possible in this dank, dark, putrid place, a transmitted skin warmth for themselves and the children.

Their clothes were still wet by day, and even at night parts of their bodies got wet, but at least for some time they felt parts of them dry and a little warm.

\*    \*    \*

The Whites followed them farther and farther into the marshes, showing some of the fighting agility and determination of their opponents.

They fell upon the Reds while they rested, cutting into the groups of frightened peasants huddled together, cutting and running as the Reds would have, and not fearing where they put their feet or how many of their soldiers lived or died, but content to have struck the enemy a withering blow in return for all their escapes and tenacity and sheer courage and fighting ability.

And so it continued, day after dreadful day, night after dreadful night, in the terrible cold and rain until the spirit of all but the stoutest was broken. Lu Chien thought again about what she had promised to do before the march if she ever felt herself becoming too much of a burden.

Yet they went on. They went on because others were still going on and there was no going back.

On the fifth day, as they neared the halfway mark in the thickest part of the marshes, the Whites hit them again.

It was the bitterest fighting so far. And the bitterest part of it all was that with each fresh assault there was always the same figure on horseback at the front of the attack: Po. He was fighting with the tenacity and determination of a Communist!

However much they feared the marshes, they must go on. Yet the faster they went, the more the ambushes continued. Shen was in little doubt now about what had happened: Po had joined with his former friend Yang. Yang had no doubt offered him a general's post in the White Army. Perhaps even the military governorship in place of his father.

After one week, after the White ambushes—the blood and the dying all around them again now from battle and Kate up to her elbows in doctoring again to keep as many alive as possible—they were all at the breaking point once more. Some began to believe that a false step in the mud might be a blessed relief.

Whether it is possible to tempt the fates by such a mood is a matter of conjecture. It was certainly true that on this day, at that hour, on the eighth day, when they awoke, if that is the right word when one has hardly had any sleep, when the light came up and it was time to rise again, and it began to rain the hardest of any day since they had started this march of death in their stupid idealistic ideology so many centuries ago, it was true that on this day, at this time, they all felt that things couldn't get any worse and death would be a blessed relief. They kept it to themselves. But they could see it in each other's eyes.

Yet they pulled on what clothes they had left, their still-wet clothes from the previous day, which they had slept on as usual, pulled them on wet, under the blanket, not from any sense of modesty but because it was warmer and drier there, if any spot was drier this day, and because they were reluctant to leave the warmth of each other's bodies.

As they got up, Yu-Ma started to vomit again. He had tried to keep it quiet but Kate had noticed. It had been going on for days. It was the green rice. They had all had touches of it. But Yu-Ma was the worst. He had had dysentery for a long time now; they all had—and the green rice had made it worse. The continual strain was taking its toll. Yu-Ma was pale and debilitated. Yet he still managed a smile. Kate wished she could do something for him. Were any of them going to make it out of this bottomless pit? If the strongest was now becoming weak, what would happen to them? Kate knew that someone her size could live on less than Yu-Ma and that something like the Long March could be a worse disaster for a large-framed man.

So when they arose this day, Kate could see that Yu-Ma was in no condition to carry the baby. But who was to carry her?

Hwang must remain unimpeded at the front. Just then Lu Chien said quietly, "I will carry your daughter, Kate Doctor." Kate put her arm around her and marveled again at the quiet, inner strength of her old and dear friend. But even so, she wondered if she should let her do it. And why not Kate herself? Surely that would be better?

Yet what of the wounded? For several days now she had had to keep breaking away from her place in the line to attend to the wounded. She had practically no medicine; only some saltwater in canteens, now, to wash the wounds and try to make them sterile, and cardboard bandages—yes, strips of cheap thick country paper like cardboard from the last village to pack the wounds. She tied the cardboard on with strips of jute or whatever she could find. Could she deny these wounded persons her medical help to carry her baby? She was tempted. She was sorely tempted. And she believed she was about to say she would carry it, about to make the decision and blot out her other responsibilities, when Lu Chien said again quietly:

"I will be all right, Kate Doctor. You must tend the wounded."

Kate smiled. "Are you strong enough to do this yet?"

"I am as strong as any who are left . . ."

"That is true."

Kate nodded then, and put her arm around Lu Chien again and was proud of her that in this time of defeat and desperation for all of them, she found a little extra strength, elegant strength to keep going out of nothingness.

Kate had no way of knowing, nor did Lu Chien, that she was in that euphoria of adrenalin stage that comes with tiredness, when one believes oneself capable of taking up an extra load.

And so, on this dampest of damp days, with the chill wind blowing the rain and sleet at them, with the rain coming like ice at them, they started out again. As they did so there was a momentary cloud break and the rain eased just for a second. It might have been better had it not. Kate looked out on unrelieved gloom as Lu Chien shouldered her precious pack and began to walk.

They were on one of the dark and deserted plains of the world. Yet even a plain may have an ending. How could this be a plain? Miles wide and hundreds of miles across. Was it a plain without an ending and had they all been following each other around in circles for days? Perhaps they were no farther advanced now than when they had started. Perhaps they would never get out now. It was a deadly game the Whites had invented. They waited for the Reds stupidly to walk by the same spot and they attacked them as they walked. It was a maze; a gazebo of mud; a jigsaw puzzle of lank, wet, putrid, evil-smelling grass; a sewage farm of decaying matter and gases.

Lu Chien walked on and suddenly she sank to her knees, not used to the extra weight. Her body let out an involuntary cry of fear.

She halted, frozen in fear. Kate could see her, just see her, although the rain was coming again in a torrent. But Lu Chien was not sinking any farther. It was all right. Gently Kate coaxed her out. She coaxed her up to take another step—to the right and slightly upwards, making her brain register the terrain as she went.

Then she softly coaxed her to take another step upwardly towards the right. She did so—and Kate saw her reach slightly more solid ground.

Then Lu Chien stopped again. Having gotten her right foot to safer-feeling ground, she was frightened to move her left, for she felt that perhaps she had overstepped herself with her right and would lose her balance if she moved. She was not used to this sort of pack on her back. It was a very different kind of weight from the medical supplies she carried. The baby also now seemed considerably heavier than Lu Chien remembered her being. She had put on weight, the little one. Should she tell Kate Doctor it was too much? Would this weight make her topple? Could she swing her left foot over to the right enough? She bent slightly, feeling the weight on her back slide slightly upwards. *Ai-ee*. This was impossible. But she must think. She must concentrate. She must learn to do it or she and the baby would surely perish.

With great concentration—so great she could feel herself sweating profusely, despite the rain running down her face—could feel herself sweating on her brow and under her clothes, the fresh sweat mixing with the stale, for they all had that half sheen of dried perspiration all the time on this march, with great concentration she lent her weight just slightly to the right, the way one does when turning right on a bicycle, and let her left foot glide lightly towards her right. It was risky, but it worked. It was balancing herself and the baby on one foot, but it worked. Kate breathed a sigh of relief and they all moved on.

After an hour or so Lu Chien got a rhythm of sorts. Kate, when she could, watched and encouraged her. Lu Chien was secretly very proud. She had such tiny feet—bound feet—and yet for once she felt them to be an advantage. She was used to taking careful, tiny steps. She was doing well.

Then the White cavalry charged once more. This time it was a particularly vicious attack. Kate would never forget the anguish and hate she felt as, in the midst of the fighting and trying to tend the wounded and dying, she saw Yang Ho in the thick of it, hacking with his general's sword like some madman. At one stage he must have been less than fifty yards from her. Had he seen her?

Hwang was now down on all fours again, like a dog sniffing at grass, feeling with his hands deep in the mud, feeling for a safe spot to mark with his stick so he could call the others on.

He looked forward for a moment, as he knelt there, hoping to see a fresh horizon, hoping to know they'd made good time, hoping that they might arrive in eight days instead of ten. But there was nothing. Nothing except mud and rain—coming in heavier now than ever before, like a dark curtain over the land.

The Whites began to harry them even more. The Reds had no alternative but to increase their pace. Groups in the Long March were being cut in two, losing contact with each other. There was confusion. For once, the cohesion of the Long March—the thing which had been its very strength—was broken.

There were no options. No way out. They just had to hurry on. To run again for their lives. This line of Chinese Diaspora, this Chinese Exodus, this group of believers persecuted for their beliefs, this people intent on founding a new nation in a new land to the north.

And so they went on, fast now, fast in the green slime and fast in the black mud; fast in the rain and fast in the wind; fast in the desolate wilderness of no trees and no animals and no people save themselves and a few scrawny bushes which had declined to leave.

They wished for the rocks that had cut their feet on the Great Snow Mountain, for at least these gave something to feel, something to see and avoid as one went on. But these marshes were like taking every step into darkness on the edge of a cliff—not knowing how near the precipice was and if the next step would be your last. Even in their haste they heard the cries and saw the heads of those near them disappearing in the mud. The Whites were killing many now. But the mud was killing more.

Yet perhaps none of this would have seemed as bad if they could have relied on a steady surface of the ground—a flat terrain under the sliding black-green surface of the mud. But what land there was in this unlit swamp, this dark-by-day place, undulated. It was like mountains and valleys all at once—flat, up, down, sideways, who-knows-where. And sometimes, quite suddenly, out of the depths, a piece of land showed above the water, like an ark in the flood.

Yet such a bluff, above the swamp, could be the most dangerous of all. For there could be a treachery of innocence here, an appearance of safety that was attractive and beguiling.

Towards midday they came upon such a place. It was like a river bank. And it ran for some distance.

Its great advantage was that once on top, one could travel for perhaps a quarter of a mile, perhaps more, in relative security and speed. Once on top one could see where one was going.

When Hwang saw it this day he made for it. He saw its outline in the rain like a house with a beckoning light in the middle of winter.

Because of his agility, he traversed the bank quite readily. Placing himself on top, he made signals for the others to follow.

They moved with speed and anticipation of a rest. To be able to walk normally, once on top of this small cliff, even for a few yards, would be a rest indeed.

The cliff of mud, the river bank type of outcrop which Hwang now stood on and which the others now approached, to his shouts and beckoning, looked for all the world just like a large piece of normal, above-the-ground, slippery mud.

Lu Chien was soon next in line. She began to approach the incline. But this incline, while not visible from a distance, was nevertheless visible from a few yards, and other groups, cut off and disoriented and in similar straits themselves, now descended on it. Indeed Kate herself was hurrying towards it, behind the groups of wounded she had been attending to. Because it was a broad slope, the only problem to negotiate was its slipperiness; and because the Whites might cut into them at any minute, rushing with their swords and hacking as well as firing, it was a natural thing that all these groups moved at once, like an assault wave on the beach. Kate, looking from a distance, suddenly saw Lu Chien swallowed up in a crowd of bobbing heads and weaving bodies, intent on getting out of danger. Lu Chien was so tiny. Where was she? Kate became apprehensive and ran towards her, shouting orders for the people on the banks to slow down.

"Be careful comrades—watch out for the little ones."

The long marchers were, in fact, very careful of each other, even in such a movement, and there was little jostling or pushing. It was just that Kate couldn't see Lu Chien or the baby, and she was worried the sudden onrush of noise and bodies from behind might have frightened her.

Then she saw her! She had slipped—whether from fright or just by accident she knew not. But she was all right. She was on her hands and holding. Kate suddenly realized that the bank was steeper than she had thought. And longer. It was several yards long and a few yards high. What if she fell back? There was a swamp at the foot of the slope. One could drown there. There could be quicksand there. This slope was less of a blessing than they thought.

The others from different groups were clambering past Lu Chien now. Yu-Ma, despite his stolen strength, was at the foot of the slope, like a baseball catcher. And Kate was sure Lu Chien would be all right, that she had simply decided to stay on her hands and knees for a moment because it was the most stable position; that she was giving the others time to pass until she had a chance to stand up properly again and move more easily. But even as the wave of other groups thinned, Lu Chien made no effort to move and Kate realized she must have frozen again. Someone must move to help her up, but who? Kate was the only one available.

"Hold on, Lu Chien, I'm coming!" she shouted.

She began to edge towards her, a perilous task in the slippery mud. If she were not careful, she might slide down herself into the swamp.

Little by little Kate inched towards her. Kate thought of Shanghai. It seemed so long ago. The rain was coming in waves now, on gusts of the wind, cutting Lu from view. But in a moment she would be with her. In a moment she would be able to take Angelique from her. She reached Lu Chien and breathed a sigh of relief.

Slowly, carefully, she comforted Lu Chien and the crying baby, and transferred the pack, with its precious burden, from Lu Chien's shoulders to her own. She would have to carry Angelique herself. It was only when this operation had been completed that Lu Chien stood up. But as she did so, she turned, swayed perilously, and reached out to grab Kate's hands and safety.

As Kate saw this happening she lunged for Lu Chien. But she

was too late and she would never forget that look on Lu Chien's face as she stood up and went half around towards her in the involuntary reflex action towards safety, only to have her two tiny reaching-out hands hit empty air. She saw her fall and begin to slide—scrambling for a foothold and failing to find it—towards the swamp. Kate reached towards her again, but suddenly slipped herself and felt the pack on her back skew down and to the side.

The look of horror on Lu Chien's face as she grasped and missed was nothing compared with the look of terror on Kate's face as the baby came out of the pack and slid down the hill.

Instinctively, Kate went into a tumble roll towards the mud at the bottom. Yu-Ma also dived in. But they were not quick enough. None of them were—and the baby slid into the swamp just as Kate and Yu-Ma reached it and a few seconds before Lu Chien came splashing down.

Frantically, they started thrashing around in the water on their hands and knees. She must be there! She must! But how long could a baby survive under water? How long could anyone? And this was no ordinary clear water made for swimming. As the precious seconds passed Kate's medical experience took over. She motioned quickly with her arms, apportioning a third of the area to be searched by each of them and indicating with a dampening down motion of her flat palms towards the earth to go a little more thoroughly and slowly.

Lu Chien began to scream as the mud took hold of her and started to suck her in. Kate jumped towards her—perhaps the baby was in the quicksand too! In all their terror-filled days of avoiding quicksands, now they were looking for one—and Lu Chien had found it!

Kate shouted for the rope. Hwang pulled the loose end of the cloth rope from under his shoulder and threw it to Yu-Ma.

Yu-Ma jumped in, wrenched at Lu Chien's arm, and in an instant had his hands under both her armpits and was lifting her bodily clear of the mud. Hwang grabbed hold of her and with some effort was able to pull her clear. Yu-Ma was sinking fast himself, but no matter. Kate knew Hwang would know what to do. She took the offered rope from Yu-Ma, tied it quickly about herself, and dived head-first into the mud.

She could see nothing but searched desperately with her hands now. She knew she had only seconds—if that.

Then she struck something hard. Good! It was a rock ledge of some sort. It meant the pool had a boundary. She worked in from it, pushing the heavy mud aside. But it ran in towards her hands and body the moment she did so.

She was swallowing mud herself now, but she forced herself deeper. She must find the bottom. She must find her child or die here in the mud with her. She would not come up without her. She was moving in mid-step—like a swimmer treading water— when her foot hit something. My God, had she kicked her child?

But whatever it was, it was soft. It was moving! It had to be the baby!

She swung around and grasped at it with her hands. She felt something like a large rubber ball and as she grasped she yanked the rope against her body with all her force, putting a tension on it to indicate to Hwang to pull her up. Suddenly the rope jerked so taut—so taut against her that she nearly dropped the baby. Hwang, pulling her weight against the huge pool of mud, was nevertheless pulling so strongly it was as if Kate were swimming across the water.

Suddenly she was clear. She was coughing and spluttering, but she was conscious enough to start splashing the baby's face with swamp water, dunking it once quickly to try to clear the mud, tipping it upside down and holding it by its feet to let the mud run clear, spanking it to try to get it to cry, to take in air, though she feared for its silence. She quickly undid the rope around her and threw it to Yu-Ma who had been quietly treading mud to slow his own sinking, although both he and Kate knew she had risked his life to try to save the baby.

Crying herself now, and close to hysteria, Kate laid the infant flat and began to blow into its mouth forcing her own breath inside its tiny body.

She continued this for several minutes.

Then Hwang touched her shoulder and quietly drew her to her feet.

"The main column has moved on, Kate Doctor," he said softly, "and the Whites will be here any minute."

Kate nodded. She had known it was hopeless but she had kept trying. Slowly she took the muddied baby up and pressed tightly on its lips with her own.

"It is better this way, little one," she whispered, "Better than being killed by the Whites.'' But even so, she still held on to it, and it was Hwang in the end, who, with tears in his eyes, had to undo her fingers and let the baby slide back into the mud—into the only grave the world allowed her to use.

It was almost impossible for those traveling behind to catch up to those at the front of the column in such treacherous conditions.

Kate marched on, sobbing, barely hearing as Hwang told those in front of him to pass the news on from person to person until it reached Shen.

Even so, the going was so hard, it took some hours for Shen to reach her. Just as they were stopping for the evening she saw him approaching in the descending dusk. As he came closer she could see that he had been crying.

He took her in his arms and they stood silently sobbing together for some time, standing in the pouring rain.

"I should have been there," he said, attacking himself in his anger. "I should have been with you and the baby."

"I *was* there . . . and I should have been carrying her all the time myself . . . Then it may not have happened."

"Sssh. Don't blame yourself. You did all you could."

They kept hugging each other tightly. "We mustn't blame ourselves," Shen continued. "Our child died because some men would make slaves of others and we are fighting a war to be free. Blame the war. Blame Yang Ho . . . there's one more death on his conscience. Let us hate Yang Ho because of it—not ourselves. Let us determine not to let him kill any more of those who are close to us . . ."

Kate nodded slowly, still stunned and in shock herself. "Yes, Yang Ho," she said quietly, "he is to blame."

The terrible irony was that the next day they reached the end of the marshes. The Long March was over. But Lu Chien was like a zombie. More than half a dozen times, as they had hurried on to rejoin the main column, Kate or Yu-Ma had had to break off to run after her as she wandered off in a daze, wandered off, none of them had any doubt, to be with the baby. She blamed herself. She had lost her will to survive. Something had snapped and the messages were not getting through from her brain to her body. They had to tend her like a little girl, cossetting and protecting her and, in the end, leading her by the hand, for it was the only safe way. They all spoke lovingly and consolingly to her. But she did not talk at all and appeared not to hear them, or, indeed, even to know them.

And yet they had been victorious. But at what cost! They would never be the same again, any of them. On any day, at any hour, without warning, their minds would go back *there*—to the marshes, to the Tatu, to the Yangtze. To the extermination campaigns from which they had fled. To the hunger; to the tears; to the smell of fresh blood upon the earth; to a baby dying in the mud.

This was their Long March. They had traveled nearly 7,000 miles. They had had only straw sandals or bare feet. Of those who had started, less than a third remained. But by the end of 1935 they had reached the goal of a secure base in northwest China.

# BOOK VI
# Destination
# Shanghai

*1936-1939*

## 55

*Even after their arrival in North Shensi, and their ultimate goal* of linking up with other remnants of the Red Army so that now there would be the real beginning of a communist nation, it took them a long time to get over their ordeal. They seemed idle and disinterested and locked within themselves.

Lu Chien had still not spoken a word.

They had caves to live in now, caves in the great yellow turreted loess hills which formed a ring around them and seemed to cocoon them from danger. The Japanese were not far away—across the Yellow River—but that enemy would have to wait.

In the meantime, it was luxury to live in the deep, spacious caverns which so honeycombed the hills that there was room for all to sleep and to be sheltered from bad weather. And some of the caves were large enough for vast numbers of them to sit together and discuss and plan for the future. It would not be enough to declare freedom from tyranny and an end to corruption. Education needed to be totally reformed, to be made available to all, even to the poorest. It was essential to teach everyone the principles of communism so that each new generation would grow up to understand its responsibilities—and the need to stamp out anything which might damage the new health of China.

They would begin making their laws straight away. This was to be a communist village from now on, and the peasants who had welcomed them would be the first members of the expanding new communist society. Every vestige of landlord and warlord control must be wiped out. Then the Red Army would fan out from there to control the land—and people's thinking—in surrounding areas.

Reforms began immediately. Divorce was declared available

on demand and free of cost. All buying and selling of wives, children as house slaves, concubines, and prostitutes, was outlawed. All rights of parents and relatives to arrange marriages and interfere in marital arrangements were abolished, including dowries and the concept of not coming empty-handed to a marriage. Marriage ceremonies were free, but couples living together had the same rights, and all children of any relationship were legal.

Within a few short months all opium trade in the area—and its supplies—were wiped out. Foot-binding was prohibited.

The pain of the death of Angelique had dulled to a throbbing ache in Kate's heart. She busied herself for a time with her professional duties. Under her ever-watchful eye, her comrades all rested and ate, and put on weight. They also went for walks incessantly, as if unable to comprehend that one could now take a walk for pleasure, after supper, in the last light of evening. They would walk out and see the incredible beauty of the sun coming down over the deep yellow rings of the loess hills— standing in the gray light like giant beehives in the distance. One could walk out and stand in reverie and not fear White Army ambushes or overhead planes. Those walks were in fact the only things they could persuade Lu Chien to do. And even then, she walked holding desperately on to Kate's hand. She had done this before, of course, but the desperation had not been there. She was consumed with guilt, blaming herself for what had happened to Angelique. For if she had not been so weak, if she had not stumbled and fallen, the baby would not have slipped from the pack on Kate's back.

Now there was this desperation as if she could not trust herself, as if she needed the constant reassurance of others.

Yet from the loess hills, from those rings of drifting eternity, she seemed to take some strength. So they would walk out before dusk, these two, Kate and Lu Chien, and stand for hours, stand on the highest hill looking out over the valley until the sun went down. They would stand and gaze into the distance, and Lu Chien's hand would be pushed tightly into Kate's, held there tightly, and she would not let go until they got back to the safety of their own cave in which they lived.

They were a family now, and they all lived together as on the march, as if each were brother and sister to the other. For more than a year they waited for Lu Chien to speak. Kate had other doctors examine her, though they could do nothing. But they expected her to get better and one day start talking again quite naturally. Yet as one year passed into two, they all began to realize that Lu Chien—for whatever deep reasons of pain lost within her, and for the blame she laid upon herself—had decided to join the silent world of Yu-Ma.

After a time she even stopped holding Kate's hand. She seemed hardly to know her and followed Yu-Ma everywhere he went, followed him like a little shadow trotting behind. It was as if she felt that in his world of beauty and peace and silence, pain would not touch her.

Then, after a time again, she started to eat less and less. No one could understand why until one day they found her on all fours, eating grass. Then for a period she would eat only cold rice. And then she ate a little hot rice one night, one night only, and Kate began to know, and to fear, that somehow in her mind Lu Chien had never left the Long March, or had returned to it now, and was eating only what they had had to eat during that time; and Kate feared that Lu Chien had now reached the stage of reliving the night they had the last of the rice.

Kate counted out the days mentally and believed she was right. Then one night, when Lu Chien would eat nothing, Kate got up and went out and searched for hours until she found some green rice and brought it back and measured out a small quantity such as they had eaten in the mountains just before the marshes and placed it into her hand and she ate it.

But with her will sapped and so little food, Lu Chien was back to skin and bone again. And then one morning no one could find her. They searched everywhere. She had never wandered off before. They had not thought it necessary to guard her. Everyone in the village knew her anyway. They searched feverishly. They searched until they eventually found her, away from the village, at the foot of one of the loess hills. Her neck was broken. They all blamed themselves for not watching her; Kate more than anyone. But they were not to know that she had made a commitment to herself before the baby was born; before the march began; that when she thought she could not go any farther she would cease to be a burden to them.

There was a note among her things written in black ink in her classical poetic style. It told them of her vow. She had gone, she said, though she knew it was contrary to communist belief, to be with her beloved Wu.

One day, not long after Lu Chien's death, Hwang came and told Kate a peasant messenger had arrived with a message for her from a friend.

On the messenger's insistence, she followed him to a deserted Tibetan monastery on the edge of town. But before she reached the monastery Kate had seen a lone, long figure of a man, standing just outside the gate. She started to run towards him, shouting:

"Daddy, oh Daddy!"

They stood hugging each other tightly a long time, tears streaming down both their faces. "Oh Katie," the old man said, and Kate realized suddenly that her father was much older, "oh Katie, I do miss your mother so. Since the day they told me in prison of her death I have prayed that one day I would see you alive . . . I didn't even know if you'd escaped safely when you tried to rescue me . . ."

"Ssh," she said, stroking his white hair gently with her hand. "Ssh. It's all right now. We have each other again."

When they did come apart, Clem Richmond quietly knelt on the ground in silent prayer. Kate knew that he was praying silently to respect her beliefs in case she might not wish to offer thanks herself. It was typical of him, this loving respect for others who might believe differently. It was what the Chinese loved about him.

So Kate knelt beside him, taking his hand. "Dear Lord," she said, "I thank you for returning my father to me, and I pray that you will bless the soul of my dear mother."

Her father smiled at her in thanks as they stood up. Kate could see he knew she had prayed only out of love for him, but he was grateful nevertheless. They walked and walked for some time after that, holding hands and hugging. Then they returned to the caves to eat, and sat by the campfire long into the night, Kate telling her father everything that had happened to her, including, eventually, the tragic news of the death of his granddaughter. Shen came and joined them for a time, telling how he had had his people searching for more than a year until they found out where Yang Ho had hidden Kate's father after he had been moved from the walled city. Then they had staged another rescue attempt—not wanting to mention it until they were sure it was successful. Wang Lee himself had taken charge and made sure nothing went wrong this time. But the old man had been very frail and close to death. So Shen had ordered him brought to the monastery and nursed back to health before Kate saw him.

A few days later Kate and her father held a simple Christian ceremony for Bette and Angelique in the grounds of the deserted monastery. They found a plot and made two wooden white-washed crosses—one large and one small—which they put on the empty graves along with the first wildflowers of spring.

"Tell me something, Daddy . . ." Kate said as she took his hand and they walked back to the town after the ceremony.

"What, darling?"

"How can you be a Christian and Communist both?"

"You can believe something is good for the people and country without losing your fundamental Christian beliefs. But I'm not even sure I am a Communist, Katie. I started helping them because they asked me. It was Shen, you know, who first came to me. After you left to study he came to the clinic sometimes—usually to bring someone poor who needed treatment. Then the day came when he told me who he was and that they needed a place to meet. Only later did he enlist my aid in medical training—"

"Yes, he always was good at enlisting people . . . look how he got me involved . . ."

"You love him—?"

"Yes, Daddy, I do—in a way."

"Will you stay with him, darlin'?"

"I don't know, Daddy."

"And are you a Communist, Katie—?"

"Me—? No." She paused, thinking. "I don't know. I suppose I am in some ways. But not formally—I'm not a member of the party. I've come close to it at times. So much of what they believe is attractive. Basic egalitarianism. Putting an end to the injustices of the old regime. It's like Christianity in some respects—

everyone with an equal chance of heaven, everyone loving his or
her neighbor—but of course they don't believe in God. They see
religion only as an evil weakness. That is one of the things that
stops me. And then they do believe in the use of force to achieve
their ends, not only in ruthless bloodshed but in compelling
everyone to accept their way of life. I often think their freedom
has more chains around it than they can see. Their communism
is turning—maybe has already turned—into totalitarianism.''

''And yet you lost your baby and nearly died yourself for
them. Why did you sacrifice so much if you had such doubts?
Was it just Shen?''

''Partly. But when I first joined with them, I had no choice. I
was a fugitive, with a price on my head. I still am. But I stayed
with them simply because they needed me so much. They're
ordinary men and women, and they fall sick and they get wounded,
and they depended on me to be their surgeon and their doctor
and their friend. They were so brave too. I couldn't not help
them, and all else followed from there.''

''That's what we're here for darlin'.''

''I know. But you sometimes wonder when the pain stops—''

# 56

*W*hether Shen read Kate's mind she never knew. She was
barely conscious of having the thought herself. Any sort of
deliberate, planned thinking was still an effort. Shen's reflex
action of fighting and burying himself in his work was a better
cure.

But one day Shen came to her, after a day of heavy meetings,
and suggested they go for one of their walks. It seemed some of
the best and bitterest moments of her life had been spent walking.

''Wang Lee is going back to Shanghai,'' Shen said casually as they began to walk away from the town. Perhaps Shen had hoped, by the very matter-of-fact tone of his conversation, to elicit some sort of casual, non-involved response from Kate—to make her part of the conversation almost unawares. But when she did not reply he went on.

"It is important for a doctor to go with him and the Politburo has chosen you."

She looked at Shen with her faraway look.

"My darling Shen," she said softly, "That is a lovely thought but I cannot go . . ."

"You are the most qualified to go," he said. "You are a battle doctor and we need advice on supplies. Besides . . . there would be an opportunity to see Jane . . . and Ling Ling . . . You could give her a kiss for me . . ."

"I cannot go . . . It is impossible."

"Nothing is impossible."

"That is true. But I am still so tired. And would it be safe? There is still a price on my head and the Japanese are coming aren't they . . . ?"

"Yes. There will be a war with our old enemy, Japan. There will be a world war. As for the price on your head, I can guarantee nothing. But I would send you with Wang Lee, who is the safest. Although he and Ling Ling are not married, he is really like family. And although his description is well known now, he still seems to manage to elude them."

Kate's voice was very quiet and level as she spoke. She had been thinking all the time Shen had been speaking.

"If I went . . . I couldn't guarantee that I would return immediately."

"I know . . ."

". . . Or even that I wouldn't leave China for Hong Kong . . ."

"I know that too."

"You are giving me an opportunity to leave you. To leave you forever . . ."

"Yes."

"To leave and never come back . . . ?"

"Yes."

"Why?"

"So you will know what you really want . . . You have seen so much pain . . ."

"So have you . . ."

"Yes. But I was born to it . . . and I have a belief to keep me going."

"I'm frightened to go," she suddenly blurted out. "I don't want to leave you."

"I know. But it may be only for a time. A few months—six at the most."

"Oh Shen," she said, "Oh, Shen," and the tears came tumbling down, the tears she could not cry before. She cried herself out and afterwards she wondered if the road back for her had started then.

They walked on for a time in silence until eventually Kate spoke.

"It seems strange . . ." she said slowly.

"What?"

"That for one so committed to healing, the two men in my life have been men of arms."

"Yes," said Shen. "You believe in war yet?"

"I did for a time. I did back there for a time. I believed in war, and revenge, and the smell of smoke after battle. I wanted to kill every White in sight. Now I am not so sure. I certainly can't hate all the enemy—just the ones who hurt me personally. Does that make sense?"

"Of course. Not all Whites are bad. I would be a poor soldier if I liked killing their brave young men. And they have many good generals who are not like Yang Ho. The Yang Hos are the bad uncles of the world who must be opposed at all costs—even if it means killing their soldiers. Fail to kill their soldiers and lose the war and the result is that the men like Yang Ho take over."

"The evil men theory? It seems too simple."

"All explanations seem simple afterwards."

"We will talk of it another time—when I return."

"Will you return?" he said.

"Of course . . . in a few months . . . six at the most."

"Of course."

"Shall we walk back?"

"Yes."

They began to walk.

"You have enriched my life, Kate Doctor."

"And you mine, General Shen."

# 57

*The Generalissimo, Chiang Kai-shek, would still not believe the* Reds had won. He had been regrouping for a big drive into the Far North towards the Pao An camp in Shensi, where Shen was.

But as Japan became more and more militaristic towards her old enemy China, and it was evident there would be a Second World War, even some of Chiang's generals advised in favor of a united front of Kuomintang and Communist against the Japanese. The Reds had already proposed this as the only possible means of avoiding full-scale invasion by Japan. Many of the Generalissimo's commanders agreed. It would be a massive stupidity to lose the country to Japan while fighting the Communists: to lose China while Chinese fought Chinese.

Perhaps neither side expected a truce to last. Yet it was also true that in the Northwest some unexpected goodwill was already being evidenced by the Whites towards the Reds. The Japanese already had Manchuria. And to show with what disdain they treated the Chinese, when there was an anti-Japanese strike in Tsingtao, Japanese marines marched in and took over the city. The fragmentation of China itself was again seen as China's main weakness. There were enormous pieces of Japanese property in China, including factories and warehouses and businesses. The Japanese were not, had never been, a counterpart Asian nation for China. With America and Russia and Great Britain and France they ranked as equal colonial powers—imperial powers with their footholds in commerce mapped out all over China and their own special area in Shanghai as the other concession powers had. A promise from the Kuomintang government that the strikes would not be repeated caused the withdrawal of the Japanese armed force from Tsingtao. Yet the incident showed that fragmented China, in the throes of civil war, was so weak internally that a foreign power could land troops on its doorstep at will.

This incident combined with another military incident to begin to force Chiang Kai-shek's hand.

His White Army in the Northwest, whose commanders were almost to a man in favor of an alliance with the Reds, had nevertheless been forced to follow orders to pursue the Reds. But the Reds, knowing the White commanders' attitude towards a united front, had been unwilling to attack the Whites. When Chiang Kai-shek still did not soften his approach and still was not prepared to discuss an alliance despite the Tsingtao incident, the Reds struck at the Whites again with another of their brilliant maneuvers. In a surprise attack, Shen captured and disarmed a large slice of the White forces in the area.

Chiang was furious and went north himself to investigate, flying into Sian on December 7, 1936. But his local general's inherited warlord army, formerly loyal to the Whites, had signed an unofficial truce with the Reds.

Then there was an anti-Japanese march and student demonstration. Pro-Chiang police opened fire on the students. One of the students shot was the son of a local White officer. A series of military conferences followed at which Chiang Kai-shek made it quite clear that he intended to mount a Sixth Extermination campaign against the Reds. His senior officers were dumbfounded. They saw this as an invitation to full Japanese occupation of China.

While the Chinese Kuomintang armies were busy fighting the Reds—yet again—the Japanese would be free to march in and take what they would. And they were already invading a nearby province. More than this, some of the officers heard through their own intelligence corps that Chiang's personal gestapo, the Blue Shirts, had compiled a blacklist. Many of these top commanders, who had spoken in favor of an alliance with the Reds, had little doubt that their names would be on it.

Over the period of the Long March, many Kuomintang troops had defected. But now, in one move, the Kuomintang was to provide more than two White soldiers for every Red soldier killed on the march. The rebel commanders decided, on December 11, that they would arrest the Generalissimo and take their combined forces of nearly 200,000 over to the Reds.

The next day the coup took place. The rebel Whites captured police, Blue Shirts, the airfield, and the whole of the general staff. Chiang was captured fleeing in his nightshirt.

Negotiations for his release went on for weeks. At first the government in Nanking haggled, threatened, and then marched towards the North. The Reds took the opportunity to move their base to Yenan, and from there, as negotiations continued and the White Army marched on from Nanking, they quietly annexed most of Shensi not already theirs.

There were many proposals and counter-proposals between the now warring factions of the Whites to try to secure Chiang Kai-shek's release and reinstatement in Nanking.

Eventually he was released and a number of face-saving solutions were found so that soon the Reds' original suggestion of a combined front against Japan became a reality.

The Sian incident in which Chiang Kai-shek had been captured was followed on July 18, 1937, by the Liukochiao incident, in which the Japanese troops claimed that Chinese railway workers had shot at them. In retribution the Japanese surrounded Peking with several thousand troops.

This was tantamount to a declaration of war. There would now be seven long years of fighting—for Reds as well as Whites.

Their differences would be forgotten for a time as they faced the common enemy, Japan.

With a massive army now including 200,000 Whites, Shen crossed the Yellow River and drove straight at the heart of the Japanese army.

# 58

*By early 1939, Kate and Wang Lee were on the outskirts of Shanghai.*

Once out of the hinterland, passed first from muleteer to muleteer, and then from railway stop to railway stop, the tempo of life began to pick up for Kate. But she was still skin and bone and only time would cure that. Even so, she did not expect the reaction she got when, on her first night back in the city, she prepared to approach Janey.

Wang Lee had excused himself. He had urgent business with Ling Ling. So it had been agreed that from a certain point they would travel separately.

They parted around the corner from the teahouse they knew so well, which was close to where Kate believed she might see Janey.

In fact the arrangements to procure medical supplies on the black market would be made through Ling. Kate had given Wang Lee a list. Later Kate would check it to see the supplies were genuine and had not been watered down. Her presence was also necessary to order the best substitutes if some of the items could not be found.

For the big thrust southward they were determined to have the best medical supplies available.

With Wang Lee gone, Kate now looked about her. There were troops in uniform everywhere. She was glad she had brought a scalpel with her from the North Country which she had kept hidden under her padded peasant's tunic. It was easy to forget how times had changed. It was easy to forget that it had been more than six years since she had been in Shanghai.

Her thoughts turned to Janey. She and Wang had arrived in the city just before dusk. It had been Janey's pattern in the old days to visit her hairdresser late every afternoon. Kate hoped she had not changed this habit—or her hairdresser.

Kate made her way quickly through the backstreets to the Street of Barbers. Finding the shop, she prepared to walk past its window.

She felt suddenly nervous—uncertain what to do or say. For a moment she was unable to move. Then slowly, deliberately, she forced herself to shuffle forward; to peer in. She stared in hard for a moment but could see nothing. Then, there in the shop, a long way back near the rear, was Janey. She was sitting under the newest of metal hair dryers and was reading a glossy magazine, her face just visible. Kate wanted to run and hug her and let the tears flow down. But she became frightened again, worried that someone might see her. Or even worse—worried that Janey might!

So there she waited, near the shop and in the lee of the brick wall, until, thankfully, dusk descended.

Even then, as it was almost dark, and the lights went on in the shop, Kate was not sure she would ever be able to speak to her. She realized she was anything but over the ordeal of the march and her lost child. It would be many months, more perhaps, even years, before she was better again.

The lights in the shop went out. She could hear Janey's laughter coming near to her. She hoped a car was not calling for her. She used to like to walk and window-shop, taking a rickshaw or limousine from one of the ranks nearby. It was Kate's plan to follow her and talk to her on one of the streets when she was sure no one was around.

She waited in the shadows and saw Janey come out and move off. Slowly, painstakingly, little by little, Kate followed. When they were well along the sidewalk she called out in a whisper, *"Yang Kwei, Yang Kwei,"* and then immediately darted back into the shadows as Janey turned around.

"What is it, Elder Born, what is it you wish?" Janey said slowly in Cantonese.

So Janey had learned some Chinese! Kate shrank back even farther. But Jane was coming towards her now, opening her purse. It seemed impossible she had not recognized her. But she had not.

Just as Janey was about to draw level with her, Kate said softly and simply, in as much of her old voice as she could muster, "Jane, oh Jane."

# BOOK VII
# Karma

*1939-1940*

# 59

*Janey took Kate home and put her to bed and found her oldest* and most trusted *amah*, who had brought her up, to look after her.

"You must get out of Shanghai," Kate said to Janey the night after she had brought Kate home, as Janey sat on the foot of the bed, feeding her chicken broth. "You must get out soon. Very soon. We are coming back. Promise me you and the baby will not be here when we come. Promise me. Promise me."

"There, there. We'll see. Drink some more broth."

"I shouldn't really. There is so little food left."

"There, there. Drink just a little."

"Give it to the children. Keep it for the children."

"Drink just a little. Please."

"Just a little then. But promise me you'll save the rest for the children."

"I promise."

"My baby is nearly two now. How old is yours?"

Janey knew that Kate was hallucinating, uncertain whether she was living in the past or the present. But she would say nothing to distress her.

"Isn't that nice? Both our children are the same age."

"Yes. Drink just a little more. Please."

After Kate had gone to sleep, Janey poured herself a stiff whiskey and tried to think what to do about Blake. He had been in Hong Kong on business but was due back that night. One thing was patently obvious—Kate was in shock and could not see him tonight or for several days at the very least. That would give Janey time to think about what to do. Janey was not far from a state of shock herself. Kate had been the last person she had expected to see. And she was very worried about the way Kate's mind kept wandering.

But in the meantime Janey had to find Blake before he came home unannounced. He had kept his suite at the hotel, and often slept there—particularly when he worked late at the office. Janey did not mind. It always had been a marriage of convenience, really. They got on well as friends. They loved each other in a way.

Janey rang for the amah to give her further instructions about Kate and then ordered her limousine sent around. If she were lucky, she might just catch Tom at the station. His train would arrive shortly, if it was on time.

Fifteen minutes later, Janey was waiting outside the station. Blake came out accompanied by a porter, with his luggage, and a stunningly attractive Chinese girl dressed entirely in Western clothes. Blake appeared to say goodbye to her. In any case she moved off. Had he seen Janey's car waiting there from inside the station? Had the girl been traveling with him? Well, at least he was discreet.

Janey told her driver to stand out. He did so and Blake immediately came over.

"Darling what a pleasant surprise," he said, tipping the porter as the porter deposited Blake's bags in the trunk which the driver had opened. "How nice of you to come and meet me. Nothing wrong, I hope . . . ?"

"Well, in a way . . . Kate's back . . ,"

Blake looked at her but said nothing. Had there been the hint of a frown? Janey could never tell. She envied his cool control of his emotions.

He got in beside her and offered her a cigarette from his gold case. She took one and he lit it. Then he took a cigar from his black leather cigar case, cut and lit it, and sat back as he held its smoke and then exhaled.

"So . . . Janey . . . Katie's back . . . How's she feeling? She's well, I hope?"

It was a typical Blake smoke-screen. You never did know what he was thinking.

"Darling . . . ?"

"Yes . . . ?"

"I've got a favor to ask. . . . She's not very well . . . in fact she's very unwell . . . she's . . . a little funny in the head. . . . Her mind keeps wandering. I think it's only shock . . . but . . ."

"You'd prefer I didn't see her?"

"Exactly."

"Of course, darling, if that's what you want."

Was he serious? Or was it another smoke-screen? Janey knew that if he tried to see Kate he would probably keep it from her. Still, she had to try.

"She's at home, Tom. I'm looking after her . . . Would you mind awfully staying away for a little while . . . at least until we get her on her feet? Then, if she wants to, you and she can meet."

"Of course, that's fine with me, darling. I'll stay at the hotel. Want to drop me off there now?"

Janey nodded. "Thanks, Tom."


Kate was in bed for two weeks. Only Janey, Wang Lee, Blake and the *amah* knew she was there.

It would be three weeks at least before all the medical supplies Kate needed could be assembled. When Janey told Kate that Blake had been in Hong Kong on business but was now back, although he was working late at the office a great deal and might not be coming home, Kate wondered if the marriage was not all it might have been. Or perhaps they were doing this for her sake, to avoid a confrontation. Perhaps Blake didn't want to see her. But she was still too worn out to worry. And the part about him working late was true. It had always been his habit, if he did not have to go to a specific social function, to spend long hours working late at the office down by the waterfront.


Under Janey's tender care Kate was becoming herself again. She was starting to think clearly once more. Or was she? At the time she would have said she'd never thought more clearly in her life.

One night, while Janey was entertaining friends and Kate was supposed to be resting, Kate got up, dressed, and slipped quietly down the stairs and out of the house.

It was a long walk to the city from the house overlooking the harbor. But that was all right. She wasn't exactly unused to walking; wasn't exactly new to it. And she had time, plenty of time. She had all the time in the world. She didn't want to be too early. She believed one shouldn't be too early for this sort of thing.

But what if he wasn't there? Then she would hide in the city until the next night or the next or the next until he was.

But what if there were others with him? As long as she could get close enough to speak to him it wouldn't matter. And he'd want to speak to her. She was sure.

It had been a long time but she had not forgotten one single street or alley or lane or sign. She loved this part of town, down by the wharves. It was still her city and she missed it so. Her parents' clinic was just around the corner. It was closed now. She turned right. Then left. Then right again and left. Up, down, and over the stone bridge.

She reached the street and turned down. It was not the most salubrious of neighborhoods. The wet pavements had the luminous glow that the reflection of lights bring. She began to hurry. It had taken her longer than she had thought it would. She hoped she might not be too late. She hoped to God he would be there for she did not believe, now that she had started on this errand, that her courage would last another twenty-four hours. In the haze before her eyes she saw only her parents and her child.

She walked around to the back of the building.

She was convinced now that she was too early. It was just midnight. What time did it start? She had no idea. Then suddenly, Ling Ling's face was at the window, peering out.

Kate halted, wanting her to know she was there. Wishing to show herself. Wishing to shout out, "It is the *yang kwei*, the *yang kwei* . . . it is the *yang kwei* foreign devil white doctor."

Had Ling Ling seen her? It was impossible. But nevertheless she shrank back farther into the shadows just to be sure.

Then the door was opening and Ling Ling stood in the shaft of yellow light. "Who's there?" she whispered. "Who is it?"

Kate sat crouched in the bushes, breathlessly silent. Ling Ling closed the door.

Just then Kate heard a car stop on the sanded drive. It was at the front of the house. There was the sound of laughter and merriment, the voices of carousing. Then goodbyes. It was the wrong car. This one was picking up guests leaving at the front.

Another hour passed and it was cold now. But that was all right. She was used to that too. Used to everything, really. There wasn't much they could do to her they hadn't done already. She had been forced most bitterly to give herself to Yang Ho. She had starved and tired unto death. She had lost home and friends and family and child and walked halfway around the world in a cause they said would never last. She drew her clothes tighter around her.

Then there was the sound of another car. This one sounded closer. There was a light-beam cutting the darkness. Then the car stopped. Someone was getting out. One person? Yes, she was right. There was only one person—crushing the sand with each step in the silence of the night. Whoever it was was coming alone. Pray to God it was the one she wanted. A few footsteps more and she would know. A few footsteps more and the light would be on him. She would be able to see him in the glow of the light from the back windows.

The car was reversing out now. She could hear the higher-pitched whine. A few more footsteps and she would know.

She was crouched in the clump of bushes right at the foot of the stairs. He must pass by her! He must! There would be no need to talk now. No need to draw him away from others. He was coming alone if he was coming at all. But what made her so sure it was he? Did she believe in Chinese Fate after all? In Chinese Destiny? Was she some old, toothless Chinese fortune-teller reincarnated from another age? Was this her personal karma that she had an appointment with this night?

He was around the corner now and there was no feeling of relief that it was he, only a feeling of resignation, of being part of something else that was only dimly happening to her.

As he put his foot on the first step, she stood forward from behind the bush, her right hand inside her tunic.

"Yang Ho," she said quietly, and saw the look of amazement, of surprise, on his face.

"The much-traveled Dr. Richmond," he said sarcastically. "A pleasure to see you again."

"And you," she said, with a sarcasm mixed with anger. "I have thought of you so often, remembering every moment of our last meeting. You might say it helped keep me alive." She was smiling.

Yang Ho smiled too. His men would be here soon. He had only to whistle. Soon the United Front might mean a pardon for more such as Kate Richmond. But she would die before that came through . . . die in his prisons that night. He went to reach for the pocket in which he kept the whistle.

But her hand—her surgeon's hand—was faster. She saw his look turn sour as he saw her hand emerge from her tunic and the dull yellow light flash on the blade it held. He went as if to step back but she was too swift. At this game she was better than he. She was the best in the world: the best damn cutter in the land. She had had enough experience, thanks to him: plenty of people to practice on, maimed and dead and dying thanks to him; some thousands; some hundreds of thousands. And her hands were strong; so very strong. There was strength in her thrust as the scalpel went in and out. A good cut! Just below the heart, but nevertheless a good cut.

He was crying out now, from the pool of blood into which he had fallen. But she was gone—gone running—running for her life for the back fence and the anonymity of the dark alleys and backstreets beyond. She could feel her adrenalin pumping, forcing her on. Effortlessly she cleared the back fence.

Two streets and three alleyways later, she emerged into the Saturday night crowd on the Bund.

They would never find her now. They did not even know she was in the city. Only Janey knew that—and one old trusted servant. But she would not return. It would not be safe to be seen. She would have liked to have seen Blake—for old times' sake—just once more. But it was better this way. Better for Janey, too. Kate would find Wang Lee and they would leave the moment the supplies were ready. She suddenly realized she still held the scalpel. She was gripping it as if it were set in concrete. With great difficulty, for she was starting to tremble now, she took it from her right hand and, moving unobserved by those passing by, walked quickly to the parapet surrounding the Bund and cast it into the water.

\*     \*     \*

In that euphoric state which accompanies the confrontation of danger, wrapped in that psychological cocoon of near-trance which nature provides, she walked defiantly and carelessly down the Bund in the broad light of night. Though her face was on wanted posters, this strange *yang kwei* face with black Chinese characters above it which appeared not to belong to her, she did not care. She almost challenged them to see her and arrest her; to put her in the witness box at her own public trial so she might tell the world what she knew: what she had learned in the past three-quarters of a decade; in the past half-century! Tell them of the innocence of a missionary daughter returning home from America by ship. Of her confrontation with evil—at first little by little and then in huge blasts so icy they took your breath away and left you gasping—gasping and bereft; stunned; stunned that life could be like that; stunned that life would never be the same again. You had met the Abominable Snowman and stared him in the eye.

Well, she had done that. She had not only stared the unforeseen circumstance in the eye—the Yeti that comes out of the mist of life when you least expect it. She had also stared evil in the eye. And she had killed it—or at least part of it. How long should a man such as Yang Ho be allowed to go on? How many thousands more should he be allowed to murder in battle? How many thousands more should he be allowed to abuse sexually? How many more mothers should he be allowed to kill? Well, he would do no more killing now!

It was a farce, really, this war business. They should put doctors in the front line more often to do the killing. With one scalpel blow she had accomplished more than the entire communist army in several battles—saved more lives, anyway. She smiled to herself. It verged on an evil smile, she knew. That was another thing she had faced—the evil in herself. She had faced that on the many sleepless nights she had planned her revenge. But she had discovered, too, like so many before her, that sometimes someone has to have the moral courage to choose the lesser of two evils. She had saved more lives with her one sharp scalpel thrust that night than all the years bending over makeshift operating tables on the march. And that, ultimately, was what

her business was about—saving lives. That was how she had
justified—rationalized—it to herself on many nights. But now it
was done. And she was glad. She dared them to come now.
Come for her if they would. But she would not retract or back
down. She had walked her narrow straight line of destiny.


When Janey discovered Kate had gone she kept phoning around
town until she found Blake.

It was not until late in the evening that she finally reached him
at his hotel.

"Tom."

"Yes."

"Kate's disappeared."

"My God."

"Just walked out. I'm worried about her. She's still not right.
Still unwell. Can you look for her—discreetly? There aren't too
many people she would go to . . . Only the Communists or Ling
Ling or perhaps Carpenter if he's back in town."

"I'll check. Don't worry. We'll find her."

"Thanks awfully, darling."

"You bet. You try to get some rest and I'll phone the moment
I hear anything."


Kate reached the Cathay Hotel and slipped quietly around to
the back entrance. She knew the entrance well. It was the one
they had used, she and Shen, to get Blake back to his hotel. How
many years ago? Three, four? Five, six, seven? Oh well, it
didn't matter.

She knew she wouldn't get in the front lobby. Not the way she
was dressed. Not in her Chinese peasant clothes. But there was a
phone in the back corridor. Or used to be. Yes, there it was. She
picked up the receiver and waited for the switchboard to answer.
In her best American voice she asked for John Carpenter's room.
When, a few moments later, she heard his voice come on, she
breathed a sigh of relief.

"John?"

"Yes. My God—is that you . . . ?"

"Don't say anything."

"All right."

"I'm downstairs. May I come up . . . ?"

"Of course."

"I'm reading something in your voice. Would you prefer to meet somewhere else . . . ?"

"No. I'm not worried about myself. I can take anything this military dictatorship can dish out. I'm just concerned about you. The hotel is swarming with Kuomintang . . . officers . . . most of whom would recognize you on sight . . ."

"We shouldn't talk anymore . . . I'll be careful . . ."

"Room 207 then. I'll leave the door unlocked . . ."

He heard the phone click off.

Hurriedly Kate turned, took her bearings, and headed for the elevator. There was a terrible, overwhelming feeling of deja vu as she rode up again after all these years.

When the elevator reached the second floor she slipped quickly out and along the passage. Carpenter's room was near the main elevators. She wondered if this were a professional thing. She knew some people preferred to be close to elevators.

She took a deep breath, grasped the doorhandle, and felt it turn in her hand.

She entered and closed it quickly behind her.

Carpenter was standing across the room, his big thin-bear presence pervading everything as always. She felt the warmth of his feeling across the room. Saw his kindly smile. And the next instant she was running to him, hugging him, as he began to stroke her peasant scarf over her hair. Then she quite suddenly burst into tears.

"Oh John," she said, "oh John, you don't know how much I needed you to be here tonight. I've just killed Yang Ho."

After he had held her a little while, Carpenter took her into the bathroom and ran the tub. There was blood all down her faded gray quilted coat and dried blood on her hands. It was an irony of Chinese life that no one had noticed or cared.

He was sure she was in shock. She stood there, unable to undress herself or move. He poured her a whiskey. He made her drink it straight down and gave her another to hold and sip while he gently undressed her and sat her in the bath and sponged the blood off.

"It'll take more than that," she said cynically, as he scrubbed her fingernails with a nailbrush. "It'll take more than that. How long's it been? Half a lifetime of killing? But it's personalized now. It'll take more than that . . ."

Carpenter had seen enough of wars and killing himself. He had been in France and had been covering wars of one sort or another ever since. He knew shock and battle fatigue when he saw it. Kate had them both. Actually, he was less concerned about the shock than the battle fatigue. She would come out of the shock in a day or two. But after what she'd been through with the Reds . . . ? The battle fatigue . . . ? That was another thing. That was longer term. And it wasn't just disillusionment with all the killing. It was disillusionment with the Communists, too. Any sensitive soul sooner or later became disillusioned with the killing. It was surprising Kate had lasted so long, really. As for communism . . . ? Well, totalitarianism was totalitarianism.

He left her in the bath while he ordered some food. Then he made sure he closed the bathroom door when the food arrived. She should be safe with him for a day or two. Ordering a little extra food wouldn't matter. They expected gentlemen to have ladies coming and going. After that he'd get her out with the communist underground. It was strong again now. Much stronger than the Whites realized. He would go looking for Wang Lee at the teahouse.

Then he thought of something else and moved quickly to the phone.

It rang at the house of Ma Yen the Mandarin. Even though the old man had never become a Communist he had been forced to live in an old house in the poor part of the city. But he had actively connived with Hsing-tao against the Kuomintang. The old man, as a mandarin, had many high-level contacts. Any information he gleaned he passed on to Hsing-tao. He also acted as a contact point for foreign scholars and press people such as Carpenter. Gradually, as he became more trusted, old Ma Yen had introduced Carpenter to Hsing-tao, who had eventually been replaced at Yang Ho's by soldiers. Hsing-tao now lived with the old man and looked after him.

The phone rang a few times and Hsing-tao answered.

"You know the voice—?" Carpenter said in Chinese.

"Yes."

"Something has happened at your former mistress's house. It may be necessary to get her away from there quickly. It is very serious indeed. Send someone closer to the area than yourself. Time is of the essence. It is very urgent. Do you understand?"

"Yes sir, I do. Thank you for caring . . ."

They hung up and Carpenter turned his attention back to Kate.

He led her from the bath and dried her, and then put her in the clean white hotel robe and sat her down and made her eat the steak and salad and french fries he had ordered with some wine. Just before the last of the wine he gave her some liquid A.P.C.

The crushed aspirin potion was all he had but with the alcohol it would help. As soon as she'd had it he took her in and put her to bed.

Carpenter locked the door of his room and rode down to the lobby. He'd have to check the story of Yang Ho's death before he filed, of course. He'd just go around to Army headquarters and see what he could find out.

But as he reached the lobby he was not in any doubt that what Kate had told him was true. The hotel was like the unofficial Kuomintang Officers' club and the place was abuzz with excitement. Carpenter spoke to a young officer he knew.

"What's the excitement?"

"Haven't you heard? Yang Ho has been murdered. Murdered on the steps of his mistress's house. How do you like that . . . ?"

"Come on, tell me another."

"It's true, I tell you, true. An official announcement will be made shortly."

"Well, I'd better get down to army headquarters . . . any idea who did it . . . ?"

"Some communist spy, I suppose . . ."

"Well, thanks for the tip."

The young officer nodded and moved off. Carpenter was about to go himself when he felt a hand on his shoulder. He turned around to see Blake. They had met once or twice at cocktail parties. It was inevitable in a city the size of Shanghai where both were important men. Besides, Carpenter knew of Janey from Kate and had gone to see her when he had first arrived. There was no love lost between the two men. Each knew of the other's background with Kate. But they managed to be civil to each other.

"Evening John," Blake said. "Sorry to stop you but I couldn't help overhearing . . ."

"Oh that? Could be just a rumor, of course. Still I'd better get down to military headquarters to check . . ."

"A word before you go . . . ?" Blake's voice was unusually quiet.

"Sure, go ahead," Carpenter said.

"You haven't seen anyone we know, have you . . . ?"

"I don't know what you mean."

"A particular friend of ours . . . yours and mine and Janey's . . ."

Blake looked at Carpenter. Carpenter did not miss a beat. He was too old a hand to be caught off-guard.

"If you mean who I think you mean, not since I was last in the countryside," Carpenter said.

"If you run into her, tell her I'd desperately like to speak with her, will you . . . ?"

"I'll certainly pass on the message next time I see her—which could be another year or more."

"Sure. I understand. Thanks, John."

"You're welcome."

Each went his separate way. But Carpenter did not leave the hotel without wondering if Blake knew anything and feeling ill at ease about Kate being in the room on her own. But it was preposterous. There was no way Blake could know. It was just a coincidence. Yet he determined to hurry back.

# 60

*Shen had known that in forcing Kate to go he might never see* her again. But she had worn herself out—on their behalf—and he owed her the chance to be with her own people again. If she decided to stay in China, he wanted it to be a decision she made after rest. She had given so much! The Politburo had voted unanimously that, when the time came, she would be offered a place in the Cemetery of the Martyrs in Peking.

It was three weeks since she had left and he had heard nothing until today when Wang Lee had sent word of what she had done.

Kate Richmond kill Yang Ho? It hardly seemed possible, they said in the camp. Hwang went so far as to query the intelligence report, although it had come through Wang Lee's network. But Shen knew it was correct. He had seen the light of hatred in her eyes many times. It had been in his own eyes the night their daughter had died. He had even said to Kate, "One more death to blame Yang Ho for . . ." Had he been wrong to say that? Had he planted the thought?

The confirmation Hwang had sought of Yang Ho's death and Kate's part in it had arrived and celebrations began in the camp.

Shen took only a quick glass of mao tai as a formality with the troops and then walked away a distance to be alone. He felt to blame. And in a real sense he knew he was—he and the ideology which had driven him since childhood; since the day his dear aunt had given him the crumpled piece of red New Year's paper. Red for communism. Red because the word for red in Russian meant precious and well-loved and the Chinese had adopted it. Red like a blood red rose, the symbol of love. Beautiful to look at but thorny to grasp. Had it all been worth it? Had it even been fair?

From the time he had asked her to help Blake when he had been wounded, there had been no turning back and this was where it had led: to the events of this day.

Shen could not avoid feeling responsible. Kate would not have been part of the Communist Revolution, if it had not been for him; and if she had not been part of it, she would not have been so changed by all the killing that, in the end, she could only find peace in retribution.

He could hear the troops still celebrating, but he continued to walk, still locked in his reverie about Kate and his own plans for the future.

Shen's crossing of the Yellow River to fight the Japanese was, in a sense, symbolic—for Shen as well as China.

The Yellow River had always been a natural frontier between China and the outside world. So often in the past it had been Mongol hordes and old hated enemies such as the Japanese sweeping down across the river.

Now the new China, the China led by Shen and others, was crossing the river to the outside world, taking the battle to it.

But Shen knew that the very war which had enabled him to do this would enable another crossing of the Yellow River. Kate had symbolically crossed her Yellow River many times. She had crossed it when she had been born in China. She had crossed back over for a time when she had gone home to America to study. But then she had returned to cross it again and be more a part of China's turbulent history than any non-Chinese would ever expect to be. And now? Another crossing was open for her again.

For a time she would have the opportunity to cross once more.

Peking and Tientsin had fallen. Greater Shanghai would soon come under the Imperial Japanese sword as well. But inner Shanghai—the International Settlement where Kate was going—would be safe for a time. Perhaps even for a year or two. It would give Kate time to heal and think. But when the Japanese finally moved against the International Settlement (of which they were one of the co-powers) as Shen was sure they would, it would be time for Kate to make a decision.

But for the time being there was a truce between Red and White and Kate would be free to cross over again to her own people if she wished.

She was no longer on the wanted list.

\*　　　\*　　　\*

Sitting in his tent by candlelight, the Japanese campfires visible in the next valley, Shen put his calligrapher's brush down, waited for the ink to dry, and then folded the parchment into an envelope and addressed it to Kate. Before he sealed the envelope with wax he dropped in a small gold star. Kate was right, of course. She knew the balanced ones like Shen would never be able to control the fanatics like Mao. Not for a long time, anyway. She'd been right about Yang Ho, too. By killing him she had opened the Whites' jugular vein. She had cut off Chiang Kai-shek's right hand so their opposition would never be quite as strong again. And she had made way for the rise of the more moderate White generals who had forced Chiang into a united front against the Japanese. Yes, China had a lot to thank its precious *yang kwei* for.

He called his orderly and handed him the envelope.

"By special messenger. All the way to Shanghai. And hurry. Into her hands alone . . . or by safe courier across the border if she has left the country. Understand . . . ?"

"Yes Comrade general . . ."

"Good."

He was tired. So very tired. And it was only four hours before dawn when he must be up to prepare for the battle.

Well, he would have Kate with him always, to keep him safe in battle and keep him fighting for the day they could return. Was that uncommunistic to believe in the eternal presence of one's family? Probably. That one day he and Kate would be together in the Celestial Heaven with his dear old father Shen Fu and his mother Lin Tan and his baby sister and Ling Ling? He still believed that. This made him a very bad Communist indeed. Not a fanatic like Mao.

# 61

A *week later Kate answered the door to Carpenter's hotel* suite in Shanghai.

The lad outside looked strangely familiar.

"Doctor Richmond?"

"Yes. Don't I know you . . . ? Haven't I seen you with Mr. Carpenter . . . ?"

"Yes, Madam. I act as courier for his film across the border."

"Of course. The madam is not necessary. Please come in. I will get him for you."

"It is you I wish to see, Madam . . . and I wish someone more worthy than myself might be here to do this. But I am instructed to inform you, on behalf of the People's Republic of China, that for your service to our people, for conspicuous bravery under fire, and for an action of individual heroism in Shanghai, you have been named a Hero of the Revolution, awarded our Nation's highest honor, the Gold Star, and that, when we reach Peking, a place will be made available for you in the Cemetery of the Martyrs should you ever require it . . ."

The young man handed her the envelope, stood back, and saluted.

Tears were streaming down Kate's face.

The young man turned to go.

"Wait. Please wait . . . I don't even know your name . . . and there is so much I wish to ask you . . ."

But he was already gone.

She closed the door and walked back into the apartment. Carpenter was at his desk in the study off the main room.

He got up as he saw her coming towards him.

"Why Katie," he said, "you're crying . . ."

"Yes," she said, with gentle irony, "aren't I though . . ."

# BOOK VIII
# Across the
# Yellow River

1940–1949

# 62

*H*ad Kate always intended to return to Shen? Was the time with Carpenter an escape—or a testing of her affinity again for things Western?

Perhaps she had even wanted to see whether she could respond to John Carpenter's obvious deep affection for her. She was fond of him, but as a friend, that was all. They had not slept together in all the years she had known him, although he had often wanted to, particularly on this last visit, as her health improved.

She was grateful for his friendship but there really had only ever been two men in her life—Blake and Shen. Even Shen she had learned to love out of deep friendship and she had never fooled herself that the chemistry was quite the same as with Blake.

If there'd been any doubt about that, it had been taken away by being in Blake's house. Kate did not think she could have trusted herself to see Blake. But he was married to her best friend—and that was the end of it. Kate was not at all certain about her return to Shen. But she knew that if she did not return it would always haunt her. And there was nothing for her in Shanghai. Communist or not, she had signed on for the duration. Now that her baby was gone, what else was there for her to do but to tend to her Young Celestials—her boys who had become men—those who were left of that elite corps of fresh-faced Young China who had first formed the nucleus of Shen's army?

They had promised to walk in a liberated Shanghai together, she and Shen, and the others. That war was not over yet. There were medical supplies to get back. It had taken Wang Lee several weeks under her supervision to get the necessary things together on the black market.

Now the Japanese were at their doorstep. They had not yet moved against the International Settlement. She could delay no longer.

So, in the late spring of 1940, despite Carpenter's protestations about the danger, Kate slipped quietly out of Shanghai in peasant garb once more. She was in the company of the ubiquitous and ever-smiling Wang Lee, who drove at the head of a convoy of Japanese lorries. Kate was past asking him how he did these things anymore, although she did look at him long enough to let him register his proudest mischievous grin when she saw that all the accompanying guards and drivers were not only in Japanese uniforms—but were undoubtedly of Japanese nationality as well!

It was summer and the morning after Kate's first day back. Kate stirred beside Shen as the first light came through the windows. It had been a hot night and both lay naked under a gently stirring fan, the big four-poster bed covered with mosquito netting.

He would be awake soon. She slipped quietly from the bed and, without bothering to put on a robe, made green tea for them from the giant thermos flask which stood beside the enamel washbasin. They had quarters in an aging "guest-house," as it was called under the new regime, although it was really an old colonial hotel.

Everything seemed to have a new name and status under the new regime.

When the head comrades told them the day before that they had been allocated one of their finest rooms, she and Shen said they would have preferred their quarters in the caves with Hwang and Yu-Ma and the others. But the political commissar would not hear of it. A senior general like Shen, and Madame Doctor, a Hero of the Revolution, it was unthinkable. Such people must have their best quarters. Were not the caves safer from the Japanese, Kate had ventured? The political commissar had looked at her as if this were a direct reflection on Shen's military ability. Shen had just laughed and shrugged his shoulders.

And the truth was, it had been nice for them to be alone on her first night back. She knew he had missed her. Knew he had given up so very much to be with her and was often the subject of much criticism because of her, despite her status within the People's Republic. She had often wished he might have married a good honest comrade who would have tended to his needs like a faithful Chinese wife.

So this morning she made the tea and had it ready when he awoke.

"Good morning, my husband," she said in a quiet and loving tone.

She saw the look in his eyes and watched him swallow hard.

"We are not married," he said with difficulty.

"No," she said, "we are better than that. We are free to love or not to love." She handed him the tea through where the mosquito net drapes came together and then put her tea down while she threw one net back to make room to sit beside him on the edge of the bed.

They sat there drinking in silence for a time.

"You know what I was thinking?" she said, a lump in her own throat now.

"No?"

"How much you have missed because of your loyalty to me and how I wish I might make that up to you."

"A man is rich who has even the small use of a treasure."

"That is very old-fashioned Chinese," she said.

"And none the less true for that."

"That is so. But I see so much already that is very new Chinese. Everything has a new name and everything is much more regimented than when I left."

"The bureaucrats. We are a nation of bureaucrats back to Imperial times and I think this is one thing the revolution will not change and will always be our Achilles' heel."

"I heard new songs and operettas."

"To socialize the young . . ." he said sarcastically.

"You do not approve . . . ?"

"Do you?"

"No. But I am a Westerner."

"Perhaps it is the only way. Thank goodness I am a soldier. Such things are not my concern."

"One day they might have to be."

"Yes. But not until after I have beaten the Japanese. I have only two days' leave, you know."

He saw her face cloud over.

"I should have told you last night," he said, "but I didn't want to spoil it."

"That's all right . . . I expected it," she said slowly. "I wasn't even sure you'd be able to get away from the Front."

"That's the other side of our relationship . . ." he said.

"What?"

"The things you put up with and how you always understand."

# 63

*For the remainder of 1940 and a large part of the next year,* Shen was away at the Front and Kate hardly saw him.

They had decided against marriage for the time.

That way it was less official. The general was not actually married to the round-eye non-Communist. This was certainly better for Shen, and Kate understood.

But there was also a subtle desire in her, too, to remain free. Unmarried she could return to Shanghai—or Hong Kong or America—any time she chose.

The extremists in the party still worried Kate, as they did Shen. But whenever they discussed it, Shen simply shrugged and said, "What can I do? They are political commissars. I am just a soldier. What can I do?"

"Watch your back, that's what you can do," Kate had said. "They know just how powerful you are. And getting more powerful with every battle."

"I don't look at it that way, Kate Doctor."

"I know. That's what worries me."

The events of late 1941 changed dramatically the lives of

those in China—as well as the rest of the Western world. With Japanese attacks on Hong Kong, Singapore, and finally Pearl Harbor in December of that year, Japanese Imperial intentions were no longer in any doubt. In Shanghai, where Japanese forces had ringed the greater part of the city but not the International Settlement, of which they were one of the co-powers, Kate's father finally agreed to leave. Kate and Shen had been doing everything possible to try to convince him and Janey and Ling Ling to get out before the Japanese annexed the International Settlement. But the infamy of Pearl Harbor and America's subsequent declaration of war left Clem Richmond in little doubt about staying. Through Wang Lee's network he was smuggled out to Hong Kong only hours before the Japanese moved against the International Settlement and interned all foreigners in it, including Blake, Janey, and Ling Ling. Kate was glad for her father, but worried about Janey and her son Anthony and Ling Ling. And even Blake, if she were honest.

But she was used to war by this stage. It had been more a part of her adult life than anything else.

She kept busy—with the children, mostly. More and more she was turning to pediatrics and limb reconstruction.

She also aided the Politburo with its educational reforms. This was one area in which she could help. She did not agree wih the propaganda in the teaching, so she mostly ignored it. But as long as the young ones were encouraged to learn, that was the important thing. That was the path out of the feudal system.

By 1942 General Stilwell was installed in Chungking under the command of Chiang Kai-shek with a United States loan of over $500 million to help the war effort.

# 64

*Early in 1943* Kate got a letter from her father. He had accepted a post as medical officer at the orphan settlement of Rennies Mill in Hong Kong. He was installed with one of Janey's old *amahs* to look after him in a palatial home Blake and Janey owned overlooking Repulse Bay.

The other significant news of 1943, so far as Kate was concerned, might have seemed almost inconsequential to anyone who did not know the background of foreign domination of China.

The Western powers finally agreed to drop all claims to Chinese territory. This meant that the International Settlement of Shanghai, so long a thorn in the Chinese side, ceased to exist. Once the Japanese were routed, Shanghai would become a free city. This was crucial. The Communists claimed the International Settlement had sided with the Nationalists the night of the Shanghai Massacre.

When the Communists mached on Shanghai, there would be no Western powers to help the Nationalists this time.

But first, the war got bloodier and Kate had to return to the front full time. Shen's army was being supplied by the Americans with precious life-renewing drugs flown ''Over the Hump'' of the Himalayas from India into China by the famous ''Flying Tigers.''

As the war in the Pacific gathered momentum in 1944, President Roosevelt made General Patrick J. Hurley American representative in China.

Then in 1945, Churchill, Roosevelt, and Stalin signed the Yalta Agreement. On May 8 it was VE Day—Victory in Europe—

and by August 14, after the bombing of Nagasaki, Japan had surrendered.

Mao immediately flew to Chungking to confer with Chiang Kai-shek. The war against Japan had produced a united front in China.

Despite the bitterness of Red against White, and White against Red because they dared to rise against them, both had fought side by side until the common enemy was defeated.

Some, among them the Western allies, hoped for a more durable peace. President Truman even sent General George C. Marshall as a special envoy to try to keep the peace between the Communists and Nationalists.

But barely had the last Japanese foot been removed from sacred Chinese soil than it was as if the war had never happened; as if White had never joined with Red; as if the Extermination Campaigns had never ended. In 1946 full-scale war exploded once more.

Yet one thing had changed. The Reds were now quite clearly the aggressors. They had not trusted their old enemies, the Whites, to come to the conference table.

In 1947 it was obvious there would be no negotiated peace and General George C. Marshall was recalled to America to become Secretary of State.

In a series of brilliant maneuvers, Mao and Shen struck out.

Even so, it would be another two years before their goals would be finally in sight.

Kate was strangely tired. Tired of all the war. And she could not confide it to Shen. He had too much on his mind. But she would see it out until Shanghai. That was what she had signed on for, really. She had never told anyone else. Only she and Shen knew. But it was that which had brought her back. What he had written at the bottom of the note in which he'd enclosed the Gold Star. All through the Long March, in the darkest hours and their deepest depression, they had comforted each other with one thought whispered into the ear of any of those faltering who had lived through the massacre of Shanghai:

"Next stop Shanghai . . . next stop Shanghai."

At the foot of his note, in his fine calligrapher's hand, Shen had known how to reach her. "Next stop Shanghai," the beautifully formed characters had said, "Next stop Shanghai."

## 65

*The Red Army was 300 miles from Shanghai. In a massive* thrust Shen had pushed southward as he had always said he would. It was no longer a matter of "if," but "when."

Ling Ling did not know why she had chosen this moment to go through Yang Ho's things. Perhaps it was because she knew she would be moving as soon as her brother arrived. She opened the old wooden trunk hooped with common metal. Shen would want her to keep that. She rummaged through and came across a letter addressed to Kate. She had forgotten all about it. It was the one Blake had asked her to send. She had tossed it in the trunk but when Wang Lee had refused to deliver it she had forgotten about it.

On an impulse she opened and read it. She couldn't believe her eyes. Blake protesting his innocence. Well, he *had* been very much in love with Kate. Ling Ling could understand that. She had come to accept Blake as a friend again. He had been very good to her with money and she had never been able to work as well after her beating.

She rummaged in the trunk some more and came across Yang Ho's things. She did not know why she had kept them, really. His orderly had brought them over in a small parcel the day after Yang Ho had been killed. "A few personal belongings," he had said. "I did not know where else to send them." Ling Ling had nodded and thanked the boy, not wishing to upset him. They had both fared badly at his master's hands and that had made for a common bond of understanding. She had looked at the things briefly. There was a notebook or two which seemed mainly about military matters, and his medals. She had tossed them, too, into her trunk.

She picked up the notebooks one by one, and glanced at them again. She had thought there were only two notebooks. But then she saw there was a third at the bottom of the trunk. She took it out and opened it and began to read, astounded to find it was a diary. My God, and what a diary! It was typical of Yang Ho in a sense. Everything was written from his point of view to demonstrate how clever he was.

Ling Ling winced when she came to the part about Kate Richmond. The poor girl! Then a few pages on something else caught her eyes and she could not believe it. Her heart sank and an awful feeling of guilt swept over her as she retraced the words to make sure she had read them correctly:

Thomas Blake is a fool who thought to trap me and betray me. He had promised the armored cars to the Red Bandits and never intended to return them to me. But my intelligence service was more than equal to his feeble attempts. After paying out the money to Shan Li who was acting as middleman, I recovered the armored cars myself before Blake had time to transfer them to the communist command of the infamous Shen. Thus I helped avert a communist takeover of Shanghai and caused them to flee in terror . . .

There were other entries about how effective the armored cars were in cutting escaping Communists down in the streets. But she had read enough. Tears were streaming down her face. That poor man! That poor misjudged man!

There was no question of Yang Ho having made it up. Ling Ling knew him too well. He would never write that if it were not true. And she was sure the less distorted version would favor Blake even more.

What was she to do? Tell Shen? Certainly, when she saw him. But that would not be until Shanghai fell now. She could not even see Wang Lee in the meantime. No one was crossing lines at the moment. It would be foolish to try to get through. It was too dangerous with the Communists so close. But there was something she could do in the meantime. Something to begin to right the wrong she had done.

She called her head girl. "Mei Lai . . . Mei Lai . . . lay out my best things, quickly, and order my car."

She told them both—Blake and Janey—as they all sat stone-faced in the palatial living room.

"I'm so sorry, Thomas, so terribly, terribly, sorry . . . if only I'd read your letter then . . . or urged Wang Lee to take it . . ."

"You were not to know. I probably would have done the same thing . . . after all, as far as you and your friends in the communist army were concerned, I had turned the tide against them and been indirectly responsible for the murder of thousands. And in any case, the only two people in the world who could possibly corroborate my side of the story were Yang Ho and Shan Li. Shan Li would not have exactly been seen as a reliable witness, and there was no way he was going to tell anyway because it would have been against his own best interests. In any case, all that was long ago and in another country . . . and besides, that war is over . . ."

"Not quite," said Janey.

Ling Ling rose to go. "I will of course tell my brother the moment he arrives in Shanghai . . . I will make sure the record is corrected . . ."

"That would be nice," Blake said, rising with her. "At least I won't go down in history as an enemy of the Revolution. But I doubt I'll ever be a friend. Too much water has gone under the bridge. There will be those who will not believe; who will see it as a fabrication; who will still want someone to blame for the night of the massacre. And I am the city's leading capitalist."

Ling Ling nodded. She placed Yang's diary quietly on the seat next to Blake.

After she had been shown out, Blake and Janey sat together drinking their whiskeys in silence.

"It must be an enormous weight off your shoulders," she said eventually. "I just don't know what to say."

"It's all right," he said. "I'd sort of gotten used to it. I'm a realist. There was nothing I could do. Even if Ling Ling had sent the letter or arranged the last meeting I asked for. I doubt anyone would have believed me without proof . . ."

"I'm sorry I didn't," Janey said, starting to sob.

Blake walked over and sat down beside her and put his arm around her.

"It doesn't change anything between us," he said gently. "That was all a long time ago. Besides, you did something much more important than believing me. You married me not minding if I had. . . . And we've had some good years together, you and I. We've got a son nearly 12 . . . Some would say we've got a good marriage . . . We even love each other a little. . . ."

Janey hugged him tightly as the tears came tumbling down. But she knew it wouldn't do. It wouldn't do at all. He had been all the things she might ever have wanted in a husband . . . kind, generous, thoughtful. But she knew he had never stopped loving Kate and now Kate had to be told . . . immediately . . . Her oldest friend had a right to know now. . . . There was no guarantee Kate would ever reach Shanghai, and no guarantee Blake and Janey would be there if she did. Kate had lived a charmed life so far but there would be some bloody fighting before the Reds reached the capital. No, she must be told now. In a sense Janey knew it would be a relief to have it out in the open. She would ask Ling Ling's help in the morning. Somehow she had to reach Kate, wherever she was, as soon as possible.

When Janey slipped out of the house early the next morning without telling Blake, she went straight to Ling Ling. She clutched the diary, which she had taken from among Blake's things, close to her.

At first Ling Ling refused to help her.

"Please," Janey said. "Please. I have an awful premonition that if I don't tell Kate as soon as possible, something awful will happen and she will never know. We owe it to her, you and I, to tell her . . ."

"It is unthinkable," Ling Ling said. "Do you not think I thought of going straight to the *yang kwei* doctor myself? But it is unthinkable. It is not possible to cross the lines at the moment. Even the most expert are not trying . . . all the approaches to the city are mined . . ."

"If you do not help me I will go to the fat old teashop proprietor . . . he will help me . . ."

Janey saw Ling Ling's eyebrows rise. "I did not know you knew him . . ." she said, frightened for a moment.

"Can he help me?" Janey said, desperation rising in her voice now.

Ling Ling looked at her and understood. So that was what it was about. Kate and Blake! Janey wanted Kate to know so Blake would be free to choose. Then if Blake chose Janey it would be with everyone having full knowledge of all the facts.

"If anyone can help you, the man in the teashop can," Ling Ling said quietly. "He can give you a pass to the Red Army. You will be passed through to Shen if you are lucky enough to reach them. But no one can help you with the White Army. You must cross their lines first . . . and the minefields . . . They are vicious dogs and are torturing anyone found with a communist pass."

"Please tell the old one in the teashop I have your blessing . . ."

"No. I will not do that. But I will take you to him and explain the circumstances. Then he must decide."


By dusk that night Janey was on her way. She had wanted to dress as a peasant but they had advised against it. She was to pose as a Western correspondent covering the front lines. There had not been time to steal a press pass for her, but a rough one had been forged that afternoon. The old teashop proprietor was hopeful it would pass scrutiny, particularly close to the battle zone where the guards would be preoccupied. Ling Ling had lent her her car and insisted that Hsing-tao, her former gateman and now guardian of old Ma Yen, go with her as driver. "He is strong and resourceful in Chinese ways, *Yang kwei*," she had said, "and for all your time in China, you are a Westerner who has lived in a Westernized Chinese city. Things are very different in the countryside. You may have need of one such as Hsing-tao . . ."

"He is your oldest most loyal servant," Janey said. "I cannot take him."

"That is why you must. If you are intent on going, you must allow me to try to make some retribution for the pain I have caused . . ."

They had kissed each other like sisters then, and a short time later Janey had left with Hsing-tao.

Janey rode in the front seat beside Hsing-tao. She had a typewriter and camera to make herself look as authentic as possible. The trunk and much of the back seat was loaded with extra gasoline. They could not rely on supplies being readily available at the front line. Each had a small amount of luggage and some food. Janey had stolen back home at lunchtime while Blake was at work and had taken his pistol and some ammunition.

They drove all that night and into the next morning. Because of Jane's urbanity and charm they were having little trouble with checkpoints. In any case many of the White soldiers seemed to take the view that if some Western correspondent was stupid enough to want to see the front line, that was her business.

But both Janey and Hsing-tao knew the problem would not really arise until they reached the final White checkpoint this side of the front line. No opposing side in a war voluntarily passed correspondents over from one side to the other. They would have to stop at the last White point, pretend to be covering the front line from the White's side, and then find a way to slip across to the Reds.

They had discussed this. Hsing-tao said it would be too far to try on foot. If there was a road or a track nearby, they should try to make it by car in the middle of the night, or when the Whites' attention was diverted.

They reached the White checkpoint late that next afternoon. The White commander insisted on entertaining Janey at dinner and telling her how the Reds would never get past him. He had them pinned down—less than two kilometers down the road. Janey talked politely for a time and then excused herself. The White officers were passing the port bottle around. The Reds were on the doorstep of Shanghai and the Whites were still passing around the port.

Many Westerners in Shanghai still did not believe the Reds would ever get there. Janey had made a fortune taking a percentage getting money out for those who were slightly less optimistic.

Gradually she and Blake had liquidated all their holdings. The family house was all that remained in Shanghai. Everything else had been transferred into Hong Kong property or to American banks in Hong Kong.

Janey saw Hsing-tao dozing in the car. He roused himself quickly as he heard someone approaching. Janey told him about the White officers. Just as they were talking there was the sound of gunfire out to the left of the field in which the army was encamped.

Janey looked at him questioningly.

"Reds," said Hsing-tao authoritatively. "Shen loves night attacks . . ."

He looked steadily across at Janey. "There will never be a better time, Mrs. Blake," he said with deadly seriousness, "but before you decide my mistress asked me to caution you one more time . . ."

"I must go, I must," she said, "but I am happy to go alone. I am a good driver. Just point me in the right direction . . ."

"We are already in the right direction . . . the Red Army headquarters is one and a half kilometers directly north of us . . ."

Janey looked astounded. "You knew all the time. You knew exactly where the Red Army was . . . or would be?"

He nodded.

"Give me the keys."

He shook his head. "If you go, I am to go with you . . ."

Janey got into the front seat beside him.

"Now?" she said.

"Now," he said, nodding, and roared the engine to life as the next round of Red gunfire sounded.

Some soldiers shouted as they skewed around and headed for the road. The camp was suddenly coming alive with the realization of the closeness of the Red Army attack.

They made the road and sped on towards Shen and safety. Nothing could stop her now. She felt exhilarated! She put her hand on Yang Ho's diary in her pocket to check it was still there. She had put it there the night before in a plain manila envelope addressed simply to "Doctor K. Richmond."

The White artillery opened up behind them and soon shells were whistling overhead. A few yards more and they would have made it. Hsing-tao was ducking and weaving behind the wheel of the car to avoid the shells landing perilously close to them.

Then a shell landed dead in front of them and everything went black.

When Janey awoke she was in a field litter under a tree. It was nearly morning. Kate was standing beside her.

"Hsing-tao . . . ?" Janey whispered urgently.

Kate shook her head.

"Oh dear," Janey said.

"Don't worry now," Kate said, surprised at how lucid Janey was and trying to keep her own tears back. She had taken three large fragments out of her chest. Thank God for morphine.

"My coat . . ." Janey whispered again. "My coat . . . there's something in my coat for you . . ."

"I found it and read it last night," Kate said. "They brought you in just before midnight."

"The part about Tom . . . have you read the part about Tom?"

"Yes, darling, I have," Kate said, bending down and kissing her on the cheek. "But why did you come . . . why . . . ?"

Janey did not answer. Kate heaved a deep sigh, bent down and kissed her friend of over thirty years one last time on the forehead, closed her eyelids, and then walked off to be alone with her memories and her tears.

# 66

*In March 1949 General Shen Sun Lung swept deep south into the heart of Kuomintang territory for one final battle. The last of the White Army blocked his way to China's stronghold of European capitalism. For several days there had been fierce* fighting in the countryside. It continued for nearly another Chinese moon.

Then, on April 21, near midnight, more than 1 million communist troops, supported by some 2 million peasant volunteers, swept across the Yangtze River on a 400-mile front.

They waded with their American-made automatic weapons held over their heads and supported by 75 mm and 105 mm artillery fire.

In the water, at the head of the army, with her old unit of the Young Celestials—some of whom were not so young anymore—was Doctor Kate Richmond.

The battle for Shanghai had begun.

The Whites resisted bravely. Knowing themselves to be so hugely outnumbered they determined to expend every last bullet before they were overwhelmed. But although there were many communist casualties, they could not be stopped and the conquest of the city was comparatively easy. By morning Shanghai was in communist hands.

But there was one heavy price they had paid, which tarnished the victory for Shen and Kate and the many others who had been together from the beginning.

It was Hwang who brought the news, tears streaming down his face. "Wang Lee—he's dead."

They couldn't believe it. Wang Lee had seemed invulnerable. He had risked his life time and time again, and had never come to harm, as though protected by some supernatural power.

"How did it happen?" Shen asked.

"We thought it was all over," Hwang said. "The firing had stopped. And then this son of a dog came out of a house. He had his hands in the air, and he walked towards us. Then when he was quite close, he suddenly dropped his right, snatched the pistol in his belt, and fired one shot. It was point-blank range. He died too. I broke his neck."

Kate wept, burying her face on Shen's shoulder.

Later she went to see Ling Ling. She was still living in her luxurious, expensively furnished apartment. She looked little older, but there was an additional sophistication about her, a studied poise, which was not merely assumed but had become part of her. The news of Wang Lee's death had reached her soon after the Communists entered Shanghai. Perhaps, Kate thought, she had already shed her tears for him. At any rate, she seemed entirely self-possessed.

"I had always believed that you and Lee would marry," Kate said.

"Perhaps we would have. But I have my career to think of, of course. After Yang Ho died, I went into the theater, you know. I am what you Westerners call a star, here in the city."

She was not boasting—merely stating a fact. "Now that Shanghai is liberated, I can become the most successful actress in all China. They say that Mao likes actresses . . ."

Had war also changed Ling Ling, Kate wondered, or was it just that she was denying her grief?

"You will come to Wang Lee's funeral, though," she said as she was leaving. "He is to be buried in the Cemetery of the Martyrs."

"Yes. Yes, I shall come to that."


There were many such burials, and then the new rulers of Shanghai sought their revenge. A list of enemies of the people was drawn up, and one by one, hour by hour, they were rounded up.

Blake was still high on the list. Shen had been unable to change that—and Kate feared for Blake if they found him. She had no way of knowing whether he had fled the city or not.

The trials began and Kate was dumbfounded. She had had no idea it would be this bad. Many who had stayed were her friends who had thought the Communists would be lenient—only to discover they were given the mockery of trials, and then . . .

They should have left the city weeks before, but they had been born there and had their businesses and their goods and money there. Now perhaps it would be better to put bullets through their brains and escape the vengeance that way. The Communists came for them day after day, ignored all they said, and took them away, to be put on trial immediately, in public.

Kate remonstrated with Shen, who said he was powerless to stop it.

Then there was the trial of an insignificant school teacher. He had taught Kate and Janey as children.

Kate pleaded with Shen before the execution. But Shen insisted again he could do nothing. His voice was but one of many on the Politburo, which decided these things. They stood together, she and Shen, as the shots rang out.

Kate stood silently, remembering, and it seemed a long time before she moved on. Shen let her go. He knew she wanted to be alone.

Kate walked on and kicked at the dust on the road as the heat came up to meet her. What had the school teacher done? Taught the wrong history?

She couldn't help feeling that something she had already seen and lived through was starting all over again.

That evening Kate and Shen dined alone in a room in the Cathay Hotel. It had been renamed the "Peace" Hotel.

After the meal Shen turned to Kate. He was very serious.

"I am going to tell you something because of how dear you are to me," he said. "But you must never divulge where it came from."

Kate nodded.

"Your friend Blake is in Hong Kong," Shen said slowly. "He escaped with his son the day after news of Janey's death reached him."

"I don't understand," Kate said. "Why are you telling me this?"

Shen smiled. "Let us say it is for Wang Lee's sake. He spoke to me of you more than once, saying something about a debt of honor created on a ship many, many years ago. Some day he would repay you, he said. Perhaps this is a way of honoring Wang Lee's debt, of honoring my debts to you . . . of honoring all our debts to you . . ."

"Once again you are giving me the opportunity to leave you . . . ?"

"Yes."

"To join Blake . . . ?"

"Perhaps."

"But it is more than that—you don't want me here . . . ?"

"My dear Kate Doctor, I wish with all my heart that you would stay—that you could stay—but you see how things are . . ."

He stopped short of being disloyal to the communism he loved so. She knew he meant that even she might not be safe the way the tide of anti-European feeling was running. She also knew that if she stayed she would hold him back. A white *yang kwei* wife or mistress was not exactly an advantage for a rising star in the communist firmament. And there was Blake! Things would be different now that she knew he had not betrayed them—not betrayed them or her!

"Perhaps I should go . . ." she said, barely sure that it was the right thing to do.

"Perhaps it might be best . . ." Shen said quietly.

He put his arm around her shoulders and walked her to the couch and poured them each a drink.

"Hwang is coming to see you safely across," he said. "I told him this afternoon, after the trial, that I thought there would be an important mission for him tonight."

# 67

On October 1, 1949, Mao Tse-tung officially proclaimed The People's Republic of China from the balcony atop Tiananmen Gate overlooking Tiananmen Square. Shen stood close to Mao, both dressed in steel blue Sun Yat-sen suits.

In Hong Kong, it was lunch time. Kate smiled at Janey's son, Anthony. She put the tea down in front of him and her father. Just before the Japanese occupation of Shanghai, when Kate's father had been leaving for Hong Kong, Blake and Janey had suggested Clem live in their Hong Kong house. Later, when Blake escaped to Hong Kong, he had asked if Clem would mind if Anthony lived in the house with an old *amah* who had escaped with them until he got settled. Blake himself had taken a suite at the Peninsula.

The same night Shen had suggested that Kate escape to Hong Kong, she had used the escape route from Shanghai.

It would be a long time before she ever saw her beloved China—or Shen—again.

Looking back on their conversation that night, she realized how hard it must have been for him to give her the opportunity to break their long association. He knew her better than she did herself. With the long struggle over, Shen had also recognized Kate's distress at the purges and the chains that the new regime was forging for itself. He had known that she would never feel quite fulfilled if she did not have a chance to pick up that special relationship where it had been left off all those years ago. He had seen her longing for things Western, and her desperate desire to see her father again—to return to ordinary, everyday medicine. As for Shen himself, he would always be in her heart, but they had both changed, and their destinies were drifting apart. She no longer belonged in his world.

"Where did you say you were going?" her father said, as he began to pour the tea.

"Down to 'the Mill.' I want to read some of my notes on the boy with that wound that does not heal. There must be some treatment I've missed."

She had been helping her father at the settlement for orphans at Rennie's Mill, where he had been working since coming to Hong Kong.

"Good," her father said. "Good. Children are great medicine . . ."

His words trailed off, as he realized what he had said. "I am sorry," he said hurriedly, "I just didn't think."

"It's all right," she said, smiling gently at him. "We can't not talk about it sometimes. She did exist. She was real."

"I know . . . it's just that you've been through so much . . ."

She heard his voice falter.

She walked back and put her arm around him and hugged him. "And so have you. But we're healing, aren't we? We're healing slowly . . ."

Kate moved towards the door, stopping for a moment at the hall mirror to check her makeup. Was that why she had not seen

Blake? Did she want to be better healed? She knew now that it would take time. But she was frightened of seeing Tom. She had so misjudged him. It had already been ten days since her arrival in Hong Kong, but he had not been to see her. They were living in his house, but he had stayed at the Peninsula. On the weekend, when Anthony went to see his father at the hotel, Blake had not come for him as he usually did. He had sent a hotel limousine—one of the Peninsula's ubiquitous emerald green Rolls Royces. And that was another thing that worried her—all that money! After her many years living with the Communists did they still have anything in common? Had the money changed him? But she knew that as soon as Blake had heard the Communists were buying medical supplies on the Shanghai black market, he had used the money from Yang Ho to subsidize their supplies without them knowing. That had been in Janey's letter also. He had been one of Kate's main providers of medicine all these years. That and the money he had given to Ling Ling had completely wiped out the Yang Ho money.

And now Kate must face him again. She knew it was time. She had known since she had gotten out of bed that morning. She knew Blake would not come of his own volition. And not because of any stupid sense of pride. He would want her to come when she was ready, and not before. He was giving her time to heal. For all his worldly ways, he understood people almost as well as her father.

Would Blake realize that Kate knew he was innocent? Of course he would know. Ling Ling would have told him after what happened to Janey—if Blake himself had not guessed.

Kate was dressed in a simple pale blue cotton frock with a black patent leather belt and black patent shoes.

She looked in the hall mirror one more time. "Don't wait supper, Daddy," she called back over her shoulder as she opened the front door, "I may be a little late . . ."

She closed the door and began to walk. She would go to the Mill first to do her work and then hail a cab.


Two hours later Kate stood in the lobby of the Peninsula Hotel. She knew it was going to be awkward. She picked up the house phone with more trepidation than she had ever felt in her life. She had been applying skin creams continuously from her first day in Hong Kong. She had sent the *amah* out to the night apothecary almost as soon as she had arrived.

She heard the phone buzz at the other end.

"Hullo?" There was no mistaking that voice. For a moment she thought she was going to be unable to answer. She felt weak at the knees.

"Tom . . . it's me . . ." she said simply. "There's something I need to say to you. . . . Something important . . ."

"It's so very good to hear your voice . . ." he said warmly. "Would you like to come up or shall I come down . . . ?"

"Would you mind awfully . . . ? Coming down I mean . . . ? I think I'd prefer a drink in the bar if you wouldn't mind?"

"Of course. I'll be right there. Wait for me in the bar."

They hung up and Kate walked in and found a good leather seat by a table in the corner. She lit a cigarette nervously and then stubbed it out just as Blake came through the door. His black hair was gray around the temples and he was limping. But he had not lost his cynical smile and when she saw it she could have cried.

He came over and kissed her on the cheek—rather, she thought, like a friend of the family. Rather like he would have done if Kate had come to visit the house as a friend of Janey's. Well, when all was said and done, that's what she really was.

"I'm awfully sorry about Janey," Kate said as he eased himself into a chair, "awfully sorry the way it happened. Her feeling she had to tell me . . ."

Kate heard her voice begin to go. Blake leaned across and put his hand over hers on the table. "It's all right," he said, "it's all right. It was the war. No one was to blame . . . except perhaps those who started it . . . Janey understood. Besides, she felt she owed it to you to level the score. She understood . . . in the end at least."

"And I should have known about you . . ." Kate went on . . . "should have known you wouldn't do that . . ."

Blake half-laughed. "It was probably a reasonable assumption given my track record at the time, wouldn't you say? Let's be honest, I did very nearly do what Yang Ho wanted. Until I found out what he'd done to you. . . . Then I wanted blood. . . . Not exactly the purest of motives . . ."

"Well, I understand about that . . ." Kate said with feeling. "I understand about wanting blood and revenge . . ."

Blake said nothing but smiled gently, signaling to the waiter to bring two whiskies of four fingers each. "Scotch still OK—?" he asked.

Kate nodded. "You know, don't you?" Kate said.

"What—about you killing Yang Ho? Yes, I know."

"Ling Ling—?"

Blake nodded. "She told me the night before I escaped with Anthony. Wang Lee had told her just before he died."

"What lives we have lived," Kate said with a sigh as the drinks came. . . . "Is your leg all right?"

He nodded, raising his glass. "I always seem to get myself shot while escaping. This time I didn't have my personal surgeon close by. . . . But it's healing. We were lucky. Wang Lee provided an excellent young man as a way of saying thanks for me helping Ling Ling. Someone he'd known in his Star Ferry days. A gentleman who is already specializing in escape routes out of China for dissidents like myself. A gunboat fired on us and a stray bullet hit me but we got away in the end."

Kate nodded and suddenly grasped his hand firmly. "Oh Tom," she said, "it's been so bloody. What happened to us all?"

"The most tumultuous event of the twentieth century—that's what happened . . ."

"But life goes on . . ."

"Something like that . . . It's worth drinking to . . . champagne?" he said softly.

"To drink away the past and remind us that all any of us ever have is the future . . . ?"

He nodded, smiling. "The future together . . . Katie . . . The future to make up for the past . . ."

"I don't think I've ever wanted anything more than to be with you, and have a family. . . . All I've ever really wanted from life is to practice my medicine and spend the rest of my life with you."

"Let's get the champagne and go tell your father. The best champagne in the house is, needless to say, in my suite."

Kate laughed and they stood up and walked towards the door with their arms around each other.

## About the Author

Australian-born novelist Maxwell Grant is a former newspaper and television journalist whose first story was published when he was fifteen. He has worked for the Associated Press of America and United Press International, and traveled extensively in the Middle East, Europe, America, and Asia—including China, where he interviewed the late premier, Chou-En-lai. His last bestselling novel was INHERIT THE SUN.

Mr. Grant currently lives in Australia where he is at work on another novel about China.

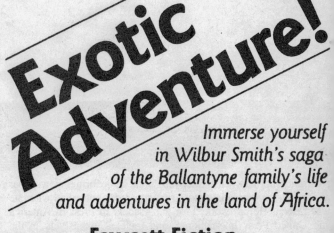